# THE LIONESS
## AND THE
# RAT QUEEN

### THE SLICKDUST TRILOGY
### BOOK II
### BY
### NOAH LEMELSON

A Tiny Fox Press Book

ISBN: 978-1-946501-66-0

Library of Congress Control Number: 2023938644

Tiny Fox Press LLC
**North Port, FL**

*To Bessy,*
*You make all my tomorrows happy ones.*

# The United Provinces of The Æthmach Republic

## (As Well as Some of the Lesser Regions of the World)

### 1603 AD (After Methren)

# PROLOGUE

"Well, here it is."

The minister got out of the armored autocar and blinked out the sun and dust. "It" did not look like much, a cave in the side of a hill, surrounded by chaparral and rusted scrap. Nothing in the ruins that surrounded the cave suggested human habitation, besides a couple of lines of hanging laundry and a firepit. The minister glanced back at his wastefolk guide, who sat lazy, or perhaps nervous, next to his driver. Was this truly the place the woman had said to meet? The guide gestured up the hillside and the minister made out a lone figure, a man with metal arms leaning next to the cave's entrance.

"Are you one of the bounty hunters?" the minister shouted, as he trudged up to the man.

The man lowered his sunglasses and nodded. Holes in his trousers revealed that his legs, too, were mechanical prosthetics. The minister glanced around and noticed that resting in the nearby shrubs was a metal horse, some sort of animal-shaped golem, and two motorcycles that looked of similar craft.

The minister pulled out the files from his satchel. "I was told I could meet here... a woman who calls herself 'The Queen of Rats.'"

The bounty hunter snickered. "That's what they're calling her?"

"That's... what my superiors told me," the minister said.

"So, we'd be her little ratlings..." With great difficulty, the bounty hunter managed to stifle his laughter. "And these superiors? Who'd they be?"

"General Levair," the minister said. "I'm stationed in Ordone. Well, usually I am. I'm actually currently filling the position of one Minister of Justice Mr. Lambert Henra, due to some difficulties in Huile. I'm a Minister of Justice as well, uh, name's Alain Sauveterre. I should have begun with that."

"From the UCCR." The bounty hunter nodded his head. "I suppose that explains the uniform. You Resurgence guys always pay well. You're still interested in Gracchus Gut-Cutter?"

"Huh?" the minister asked. "Oh, yes, the raider. Um, I believe the bounty for him is still active."

Shouts suddenly echoed from inside the cave. Violent, angry, confused. Then gunshots, the clatter of furniture knocked aside, a scream, more gunshots.

"What is going on—?" the minister began.

"Did you want Gracchus alive or dead?"

"Alive or... either," the minister said, stunned by the violent ruckus. He supposed he should run for cover, but the bounty hunter's insouciance was infectious. "Though uh, alive I believe is more. 5,000 frascs."

The bounty hunter put two fingers to his lips, and released a sharp, vibrato whistle, like some shrill birdsong. "5,000 frascs for Gracchus alive!" he shouted.

The gunshots silenced, and for a moment all commotion ceased. Then suddenly there was a roar, feet against stone, body against body. A short struggle ensued, with only grunts and shouts making it out of the cave. After a long quiet, a figure emerged. Gray and tall, with etched horns further decorated by a mess of trinkets and charms. A salvi, carrying on his hulking shoulders a limp raider, hogtied and bruised. The minister recognized the grimace of Gracchus Cut-Cutter from his wanted poster.

"So do you have the frascs on hand or are you writing a check?" the bounty hunter asked.

"I don't have... I suppose a check could..." The minister shook his head out of its daze. Did they really double-book him with an active hunt? "I'm here to offer your leader a job," he said, finally.

"A job?" A woman in a vest and military pants stepped out from the cave and skidded down the scree. She was wearing a similar pair of shades as the metal-armed man and the salvi. Her sun-faded hair was cut short, and her face was covered in the usual web of scars, nicks, and subtle discolorations that came with a life in the Wastes. The man offered her a clope, which she lit and took a long drag.

"I take it you're the captain of this squad?" the minister asked.

The woman nodded. "A job, you said?"

"Right." The minister pulled out the headshot from his binder. The figure looked innocuous enough, a young man, mid-twenties, with a wood-toned complexion and lazy stubble. "I'm sure you've heard of the chaos down in Huile. We're looking for a man we think may be responsible. Goes by the name Marcel Talwar."

The woman took the photograph and stared.

"Current charge is terrorism and treason, though there's still a lot we don't know, so we need him for questioning," the minister explained. When the woman didn't respond he continued: "Supposedly he's ex-military, though he didn't serve long. Not sure how he got caught up in a violent insurrection, but there we go. Do you know him?"

"Name's familiar," the woman said, handing back the photograph. "How much you offering?"

"70,000, alive," the minister said.

The woman whistled. "Talwar, Talwar, what trouble you have gotten yourself into."

"So, are you interested?"

She stared off into the horizon and nodded. "Yeah, I'll find the man."

"Excellent," the minister said. "We don't know his current location, but we believe he may have headed westward, deeper into the Wa—"

The woman raised her hand to silence the minister. The afternoon wind sent her smoke of her clope swirling out alongside her gaze into empty nothingness that stretched out for kiloms beyond.

"I said, I'll find him."

*I have heard many claim that the past is a buried thing, abstracted to the atheist, spectral to the superstitious, but there seems to be a rare agreement that the past is somehow 'less real' than the present. And yet it is written that the Demiurge surveys the past with as much clarity as the present, as if the whole of time were the sketched schematics of an engineer. Ancient creation is time's base, upon which is built the shafts and gears of history, our own present modernity one clicking mechanism among uncountable, no more notable than any other.*

*When viewed in this way, it is clear the past has never left us, that it is no lesser than this very moment I speak. It is obvious that the present is part of, and can only function because of, what was built beneath. These thoughts should give us gratitude, to our ancestors, to the Ascended, and of course, to the Demiurge. But they should also give us pause. For any break in the past, our past, for there is only one shared past, any crack, or rusted screw, or out of place shaft will alter the proper motion of our present day. Regrets, mistakes, sins, these are corrosions upon the machine of time, and they cannot be disregarded, cannot be ignored.*

*For if these things are not mended, or if they are too far gone be mended, then the past will make itself known. Just as a machine will smoke and burst if the wrong piece is damaged, so too can something long thought forgotten wrought havoc and destroy any chance at a future.*

> — *Excerpt from the final public sermon of Hierarch Antonious Vespillo, given three days before the outbreak of The Severing War.*

# Chapter 1

The wind came from a land called, in happier times, Vastium. Now that name lived only in history books, replaced with *The Wastes*, and the wind borne from this broken and blasted land bore the mark of its mother. Hot and acrid it was, bitter and quick. The wind flew over the landscape, past cities turned lost necropolises and verdant fields now dusty basins. It witnessed with equal disdain scrapshacks with chimneys smoking, abandoned manors buried under blankets of dust, and factory complexes that had in gilded times been modern and grand, but now lay crumbled and utterly forgotten. It flew past the pits of mudlions and the dens of wastehounds, though the camps of mutants and the unruly taur herds of desperate ranchers. As it flew kilometre past kilometre, the hate that pressed it on wavered, along with its strength, its fury bursting over shattered bunkers and buried shrines to fetid things. It grew weaker and weaker, as the land around it began to resemble something not exactly civilized, but vaguely adjacent to an analogy of civilization. Half-paved roads and rusty bridges, towns made of scrapmetal and refurbished ruins. It descended into one of these towns, down its narrow dirt streets, taking the dust of the place with it, on this last leg of its journey. It flew and faded, from gale to wind to breeze, until, with its last strength, it sputtered through the opened door of the Troll's Heart Bar and Tavern, and into the face of one Marcel Talwar.

* * *

*Achoo!*

The bald man with the beard looked up over his cards to stare at Marcel. The sneeze had been far too dainty for a hardened raider, which, despite his rough clothes and put-on accent, Marcel wasn't. Marcel was a vigilante, self-declared, and before that a private detective, once a soldier, *war hero really,* and way back when, a mediocre medical student with a wanderlust born from an upper-middle-class ennui. But it was very, very, important that Marcel maintain his lie, pretend to be the Martin Bonecrack that he introduced himself as, so he transitioned his dainty sneeze into a deep, baritone bout of coughing.

"Damn wastelung," he growled, picking up his cracked glass of whiskey and sipping. He glanced at his hand of cards. A two, a five, and duke of swords, a two of petals, and a jester of gears. Not great, but not horrible. "I'll raise an aurem," he said, tossing the coin onto the table.

"Match," said the bald man with an eyepatch. This was a different bald man than the one with the beard, who was a different man than the bald man with the tattoo of a naked woman fighting a needlecat on his face. Three bald men at one table. This would not be a problem in it of itself, Marcel bore no antipathy for hair-deprived folk, the only issue was that the man he was hunting, one Felik Rector, had been described by a well-bribed local as "that bald bloke who's been hanging 'round The Troll's Heart."

The other two bald men matched the bet, and Beard revealed the next card. A mistress of swords. As Tattoo scrunched his forehead and the needlecat on it in thought, Marcel took the moment to glance around the room. The bar was a shabby thing, well in line with a wastetown such as this, all scarwood and scrapmetal sheets. A steel-armed barwoman stood beside a broken mirror and wall of bottles, all too sun-worn and dust-covered for their labels to be read. A man played a jaunty tune on the keyboard of a calliope, steam bursting out from pipes in the instrument's back. These pipes interwove with others that cut in from the floor in a sort of messy trellis up the wall and into the rooms upstairs.

Their table was not the only one occupied, though it was far from a busy afternoon. A table over a principate soldier was napping, face in a puddle of his own beer, blue cap soaked. The man sat as a reminder to Marcel that he was in the den of his enemy, though so far the Principate soldiers that occupied this nowhere town had not made themselves a problem. In the back corner sat the final customer, Marcel's co-vigilante,

Kayip. The large monk, also bald, hid his features under a heavy hood, the glint of his featureless half-mask barely visible in the dim.

"I fold," Tattoo said, as Beard stared at Kayip with some suspicion. Marcel had to admit, in retrospect, that a heavy hooded cloak was actually a fairly conspicuous look on a hot summer's day.

"I raise five aurem," Marcel said, to turn attention back. It's not like it mattered much if he won this hand. Eyepatch turned to stare at him, and then studied his cards.

"So," Marcel said. "What business you folks in?"

"Trade," Beard said simply.

"Murder," Eyepatch said, with a tone that made it unclear if the man was joking.

Tattoo merely grunted and waved over the barkeep for another drink.

Marcel scratched at the cogleg beneath his trouser, phantom pain bothering him as it was wont to. Eyepatch matched the bet.

"I've been looking for new work," Marcel said. "Heard there's some bigwig stiffland businessman making noise out here."

Tattoo snorted and shrugged. The calliope-man started a new, off-tempo ditty.

"Name is..." Marcel said. "Well, Demiurge-be-damned, name slips from my tongue like a brasshare off a mucktoad's back. Lazamis or something?"

"Oh Lazarus Roache?" said Eyepatch. Marcel tried not to react strongly to the name but nodded as if, *yeah, that could be it.* "Supposed to be on a mad buying spree, grabbing what he can from every slaver, and even buying manmeat off palewhat plantations, if they have any spare. Haven't seen anything like it in my years."

"Can we... not discuss the slaver's trade now," Beard said, shooting his eyes towards the drunk Principate soldier.

"Oh, those imperials won't bother us none," Eyepatch said. "Was a slaver myself, back when I was young and reckless. Heck, used to hire Domitus here," and he pointed to the tattooed man, who grunted, "as muscle."

"But not anymore?" Marcel asked. "'Cause I've been meaning to make some inroads, a little *networking*, if you will."

Eyepatch shook his head. "It's a damn political trade now, you work with the Crimson Eyes, suddenly you piss off the Iron Strixes, sell to the Fist-Biters, and then you have Trog-Skinners on your back."

"What about you?" Marcel said, throwing in another aurem coin to the growing pile in the center. "You said you're a trader."

"Mechanical equipment," Beard said, a bit too quick. "Ya know, engineer stuff."

"Hmm... I happen to know a few exiled Icarian gearheads," Marcel said, which, exempting the plurality, wasn't actually a lie. In fact, the engineer was just a floor beneath them, waiting for the signal to strike. He thought on some of her esoteric ramblings. "Do you sell ætheric inverters, by chance?"

The man nodded, matching the bet. "Sure, sure, mate. Not on me at the moment."

"How about..." Marcel threw some random technical sounds together in his head. "Sangleum reoxidating prelighters?"

"Have in the past," Beard said. "But caravan's empty."

That settled it for Marcel. Between Beard's twitchiness at the slaver talk and the holes in the man's knowledge, he was certain enough that Mr. Beard was, in fact, Felik Rector. He faked a stretch and kicked his boot out, just far enough to knock a well-placed coin into a hole between the floorboards.

* * *

Down below in the steam-filled basement of the bar Sylvaine Pelletier was struggling to get the moisture out of her fur. *Hair, damn it, hair!* For over twenty years the young woman had been trying to purge from herself all the bestial slurs and insults her childhood bullies had drilled into her. Unfortunately, those children hadn't been alone; it seemed all of society had been bent on reminding her of her fur, and her ears, and her claws, and her razor-sharp teeth. Even the oh-so-enlightened United Confederacy of the Citizens' Resurgence had treated her with little more than bemused and begrudging tolerance, keen to subtly remind her, in too many ways to count, that no matter what she did, who she tried to become, she'd always be a Ferral, a beastwoman.

She shook her head, droplets of steam and sweat flying, and stared down at her glove. An ætherglove it was, the tool of an engineer, and she, the first Ferral engineer in recorded history. She'd almost be happy about that, if the cost of this position hadn't been binding her will to the machinations of one Lazarus Roache.

With a sigh, she did her best to banish these thoughts and continued to grope around in the disorganized guts of the small turbine room. The bar, it seemed, had been built on a pre-Calamity powerplant, and was still providing æthericity to half the town. Poorly, by Sylvaine's estimate, whoever had done the repairs had done a hack job, rusted pipes jutting in random directions, steam leaking from every coupling. It was a fetid steam too. She didn't want to guess where they were getting the water, but it smelled tainted with sangleum and sewage. *Gear's-grits* she was desperate to get out of here.

A clink and a clang. A coin bounced off pipes and metal casings and landed in a puddle near Sylvaine's boots. She bent down and squinted in the dim. It was a frasc, a UCCR coin, Marcel's signal that he was ready above.

Sylvaine closed her eyes and raised her glove. The task was simple. Overload the turbine and send a burst of steam upwards. It should provide just enough a distraction for Marcel and Kayip to apprehend Felik. With Kayip's autotruck parked in the back of the bar, it would be an easy escape out of this troglyn's armpit of a town. But that all depended on Sylvaine being able to precisely overload the turbine.

She sucked in her breath. It had been days since she had last tried some æthermantics, tried to manipulate the mechanical æthers to alter machines from a distance. It was the signature skill of engineers, a skill denied to Ferrals, but given to her by Roache's miracle drug/mind-enslaving narcotic, slickdust.

*Come on, this is easy. You're in control.* Sylvaine told herself. She let the power flow through her, first a trickle, then more. It moved through her blood, down veins and up arteries, round and round, energy pooling at the edge of her glove. It came surprisingly easy, intense but tame, and she focused it onto the machine, envisioning the required results, trying to manipulate the metal and machinery into her desired permutation. It was working, *it was actually working!* Stable and in control, she was the engineer she pretended to be, not just some failed bestial experiment by Lazarus—

The power erupted suddenly, violent and molten through her blood. The fine spark of æthericity became a thunderclap, and the machine she was manipulating burst in a sudden fury. She opened her eyes to see a wall of steam rushing towards her.

* * *

"Just a pair of dukes," Marcel said, tossing his cards down right as the floor burst. He fell from his chair as men shouted and screamed, the calliope exploding on a high note, knocking the musician down as the entire room stormed with steam.

"Kayip now!" Marcel shouted, too stunned to stop himself from using the monk's name.

He heard a scream through the sudden fog, as the monk charged somewhere. Sounds of fighting, grunts and punches. A man in blue rushed into view.

"Attacsh, attacsh!" the drunk principate soldier shouted. "Resurrrgence bomb, terrororists, getss the police!"

As the drunk stumbled out towards the door, a bottle was swung at Marcel's head. He dodged the blow and responded with a gut punch. The assailant groaned and fell to the ground, staring up dazed at Marcel with one eye, the other lost behind an eyepatch.

"I have him!" Kayip shouted, as Marcel staggered forward. There was indeed a bald man in the monk's hands, his face half-obscured by Kayip's azure bracelet, and on that very confused face Marcel could see a bloodied tattoo of a naked woman and a needlecat.

"Not our guy!" Marcel yelled, as Felik's footsteps rang out from the top of the stairwell. Rushing up the other direction, Sylvaine stumbled, panting, fur covered in wet soot, canine-like nose sopping.

"I'm sorry," the Ferral engineer said. "I just, I was almost, I didn't mean—"

"Upstairs!" Marcel shouted, running past her. Kayip dropped the tattooed man and followed.

A gunshot brought Marcel to a halt at the top of the stairs. He hid behind the bend as Felik fired off two more rounds.

"Are you hit?" Sylvaine asked as she caught up.

"I'm good," Marcel said, pulling out a hand mirror from his pocket to glance round the corner. A trick he had learned during his time as a

Resurgence scout. "Listen, Rector, we know you've been in contact with Lazarus Roache, just come with us and we can talk this all out peacefully."

Four more gunshots was the man's response. The fifth clinked empty. Felik cursed and dashed into a side room.

The trio rushed out, only for Felik to slam the door shut and locked it tight behind him. Marcel kicked the wood in fruitless frustration. Felik was the first and only good lead to that tycoon bastard who had brought ruin to Huile. Without him, they might be forced to wander the Wastes for another month blind, all the while Roache plotted whatever horrific revenge he had in store for Marcel's home. They couldn't afford to let the man slip.

Kayip began to mutter a prayer in his strange Church-tongue, rubbing his bracelet, but Sylvaine stepped forward.

"No, I can do this."

The Ferral woman closed her eyes and put out her glove. Marcel thought he could hear her whisper something to herself. A flash, barely visible, and the door clicked open.

Kayip did not wait but burst through. Felik was on the other end of the bedroom, struggling to get the window open. He aimed his empty pistol and clinked off two impotent nothings. The monk screamed and charged forward, into Felik and then beyond, past glass and rotting wood, out the side of the inn.

"Gear's-grits, Kayip!" Sylvaine said, as she rushed forward, Marcel running after her. She made the jump with ease, down to the alley below, landing beside the trash heap where Kayip and Felik had fallen. Felik had stumbled away and was grabbing for any piece of metal he could use as a weapon.

As for Marcel, the drop looked rather precarious for someone with a brass limb. He reached over to a gutter-pipe half-a-metre away, and started to straddle down, centimetre by centimetre. It was slow going, his cogleg strong, but not quite a lithe as one made of flesh. Using windowpanes and jutting bits of wood he managed to ease himself down the side of the building, just as Sylvaine and Kayip had corned Rector, who was waving about a rusted shower curtain as a desperate spear.

Marcel pulled out his Frasco six-shooter, a relic from his soldiering days, and aimed languidly in Felik's direction.

"Okay, give it up Rector. It's over," he said.

Felik nodded, a grim look on his face. "'Suppose it is. For the four of us."

"Freeze in the name of the Imperator!" came the shout from behind. Marcel turned to find half a squad of Principate military police, rifles aimed, bayonets glinted in the evening sun.

Just a minute more, and they would have been driving out of here.

"Well, shit," Marcel said, dropping his pistol to the dusty road.

# CHAPTER 2

It had been a miserable day for Justice Officer Belona Agrippus, which is to say, it had been a normal day for Justice Officer Belona Agrippus. Every day she woke up in this trash heap of a town was just another shameful reminder of how far she had fallen. When she had first came here to Holtag, three years ago, she had done so as a conqueror, the indomitable General Agrippus, the Terror of Bastillia, the Lioness of Vastium.

And now? Now she was filling out paperwork in a cramped office in the ass-end of nowhere. A rusted fan creaked ungracefully above, next to a punching bag covered in patches from overuse. The room was filled with stacks of filing cabinets, themselves full of faded documents written on wastepaper that no one would ever read. Yet was Belona's duty to make sure each form was signed, stamped, organized, and filed without error. Yes, the bureaucrats back in Drevstad loved their red tape.

*Charles Millefleur, taur thief, twenty-five-years hard labor.* Guilty! Signed, stamped. She tossed the paper into the pile. *Lina Caron, prostitute, twenty-years hard labor.* Guilty! Signed, stamped. *Magnus Scar-Nose, slaver, execution by hanging.* Guilty! Signed, stamped.

That last one almost gave her satisfaction. When she first led her army across these lands, she did so as a bringer of law and order, slavers and raiders and Resurgence rebels captured by the hundred and pressed up the wall. A single order, a single round of gunfire, and the world was purged of their filth and treachery. Things worked slower now, more dully inefficient, more blatantly corrupt. While she was filing papers, raiders walked free in her town, made deals behind closed doors, paid off Principate guards who were little more than arrogant provincials given rifles and uniforms. This was the cruelest bit—even in her degradation, even in her low position, she could not even be allowed to do her job right. Why was it the business of bureaucrats back in Kaimark if pickpockets here were given a day of imprisonment, a year, or were just shot? But no, it would be too gratifying to allow the shamed general to even have the power to bring Principate order to this shithole. Best to let her rot, among her failures and memories.

She glanced out the browning window, to the browning town beyond. Pre-war ruins and rusting scrap-shacks, its streets filled with listless merchants, taur herdsfolk, working girls, and bored soldiers. A nowhere outpost, the last remaining vestige of her conquests, left untouched by the Resurgence's revanchism largely due to its remoteness and utter uselessness. Take away the occasional banner of the Principate, and it would be indistinguishable from any other wastetown. And in the middle of the road, marching about with unearned pride, was the living embodiment of her disgust. Thin form in too large a uniform, chin pressed out in a sneer, oily black hair tucked underneath an officer's cap, strutted the insufferable Commandant Lechslov. Why the man was making his rounds out here, Belona couldn't guess, normally he wasted the day's hours at his excuse for a manor he requisitioned in the middle of town. *Oh, Imperator help her,* the man was coming through her door.

"Evening, Justice Officer," he said with an unnaturally chipper grin.

Belona just grunted and sighed another form.

"Have I offended you?" the man asked. "Oh right, my apologies." He made a grandiose bow. "I forgot I was in the presence of the Lioness of Vastium! My dear conqueror, have any glories to report? Any new triumphs? Perhaps over a swarm of gnats, or an errant scraprat?"

"You humiliate yourself with your false deference," Belona said.

"I admit it is unnecessary," Lechslov said, "considering we are, technically, of the same rank. But I was just thinking how difficult it must be for you, used to battalions of soldiers saluting your every stride, singing songs written in your honor. I just wanted to give you a reminder of the good old days. The days before you lost our dear Principate an entire army and brought shame upon our beloved Imperator's name."

"What do you want Lechslov?" Belona asked. "Your time may be worthless, but it surely can't be this worthless."

"Indeed, it is not," Lechslov said, squeezing past Belona's desk and the towers of file cabinets that surrounded it. "I was just coming to inform you that several hours ago we apprehended four out-of-towners involved in a bar fight which took out æthericity for the northern half of town."

"How did a bar fight take out..." Belona began, "Wait, why am I just hearing about this now? This is a criminal matter; this is the purview of the Justice Officer!"

Lechslov shrugged. "Military is my command, and until I could determine that this wasn't a military matter, I took it upon myself."

"And what was the cause of the fight?"

"Not something military-related. I'll leave it to your austere wit to figure out the rest of the details." With that he tossed a dense file onto Belona's desk, sending flying dust and paper.

The woman sighed. Of course, as soon as paperwork got involved, it was suddenly her duty again. She opened the file and started to study the limited notes.

"And what do you know about the perpetrators?" she asked.

"One's a slaver, goes by the name Felik Rector."

Belona was almost going to ask how a slaver was drinking free in the town, but she was pretty confident the answer began with *b-* and ended with *-ribes*.

"The other three," the man continued, "didn't give their names, or rather gave very poorly thought-out fake names. One's a southerner, maybe of Utarran or El'Helmaudi stock, but with a Bastillian accent. Wears a cogleg and claims to be a politically disinclined bounty hunter or something, but his pistol is of Resurgence design. Thought you might be pleased to take your vengeance on the terrorist, considering how they whipped your behind at Huile."

"Lechslov, my patience is wavering," Belona growled.

"The next is a beastwoman, a what-you-call-it, *ferral*. Had an engineer's glove on, must have stolen it, horrid thing."

Belona scribbled down some notes. "And the last?"

"A tall bald man with an odd accent, or maybe a speech impediment. Has a mask of unmarked metal over his left eye. Also has some strange paraphernalia, probably stolen, one of the Church's Cracked Disc, and a strange azure bracelet.

"Yes, well, we get all sort of crazy—" Belona paused, as memory struck her. *Metal mask, priestly Disc, azure bracelet.*

"Are you alright?" Lechslov asked. "If you have some… womanly issues afflicting you this day, I'm sure we can get Colonel Goss to—"

"My only ailment is an idiot wasting my time," Belona snapped. "Unless you have something useful you like to add.

Lechslov sighed, overly loud. "The gratitude I get for my service. Well, it has been a pleasure, my dear Lioness. May the rest of your day be bathed in glory!"

The Commandant strode to the door, and then paused. "Oh yes, there was something else. One of the frightened occupants of The Troll's Heart said that someone had mentioned a name. Lassa-something. Rope, Roak, not sure. Ring a bell?"

Belona shrugged. "Probably some raider or waste merchant, I couldn't guess."

With that the man took his leave. Belona waited until he was well and gone, before pulling open her drawer and rifling through the pens and papers, the rusted staples and out-of-date stamps and others such useless bits and bobs. *Lazarus Roache.* That's the name Lechslov butchered, and she knew it very intimately indeed. Any doubts she had about the bald man with a mask were now gone. She had only met one who fit that description, a mad monk who years ago had given her a warning. A warning she had failed to heed fully, and for that mistake, had lost Huile, lost her generalship, and lost her honor. But if the monk was back looking for Roache, then there was a chance, wasn't there? For justice. For revenge.

At the very bottom of her drawer, she found it. The little maroon box, with its clasp stuck with disuse. She opened it, and inside its velvet touch was an emblem, metal pressed into oakwood block. Its shape, a glit-bronze lion, with wreath and sword, and beneath its rising claws the once-noble name: *Agrippus.*

She held the emblem and watched the light glint against it for the first time in nearly three years. A smile snuck across her face, for it had suddenly become a *very* good day for Justice Officer Belona Agrippus.

* * *

"They took my glove."

Sylvaine was lying down on the splintery wooden bed in the small holding cell. It was a dank burrow they had been thrown into, a cell in the basement of some military building, with light provided only a single flickering lightbulb and a toolbox-sized window where the last beams of the sun faded. By her feet Kayip sat in meditation, while Marcel paced back and forth around the stained metal bars. How weak the bars looked; how easy it would be to turn them to slag with æthermantics. But of course...

"Those bastards took my glove."

"Yeah," Marcel replied. "They took my pistol too."

As if *that* was a comparison. What was his pistol, just some generic six-shooter anyone with some extra frascs could buy from a military surplus store? An ætherglove was not just the most important tool in the engineer's kit, it was what made someone an engineer. Not the pin of the Engineer's Guild (though they had confiscated that too), it was the glove, and the Knack to use it, that made an engineer out of your generic corner-store mechanic. Any Ferral with time to study could become a mechanic. She was an engineer. Had been an engineer. Now she just felt naked, and empty in a manner she couldn't even describe.

Even when she hadn't had the Knack, had been just a desperate woman playing pretend up at the Guild Academy, the glove had comforted her, had made silent promises. There was something special about that combination of leather and brass, that interweaving of tubes and wires. There was something so undeniably civilized, so undeniably human. Beasts didn't create, beasts didn't infuse machines with life, didn't tear through the fabric of reality to harness pure æther. Beasts destroyed, beasts went wild and mucked everything up. Beasts stared at their furry hands and felt sorry for themselves.

Sylvaine let her hand fall and stared at the ceiling.

"It's a shame they confiscated your bracelet," Marcel said to Kayip, as he pushed on the bars. "Your sword would make short work of these."

"I do not believe they know what they stole," Kayip said, eye still closed. "It seems their curiosity and greed have protected them."

"Is that one of the Demiurge's creeds?" Sylvaine asked deadpan. *"Trust thy wandering hand and thy greedy eyes."*

Kayip blinked. "No, I do not believe that is in any scripture."

"Well, I'm no religious man, but if you know any prayer to get us out of this, I'd be glad for it," Marcel said.

Kayip shook his head. "If you mean miracles... I am no miracle caster, and certainly not without my Disc. But the Demiurge can offer peace, of the mind, of the spirit, in even the darkest times."

"Yes, let's read from the Chronicles of the Ascended," Sylvaine mocked. *"And the Demiurge said to them: befriend not the beasts and brutes of the wild, for they have forsaken my creation. Thrust them out and show them no mercy."*

"I... did not know you have read the Chronicles," Kayip said.

"I haven't," Sylvaine said. "But I've had that line shouted at me quite a few times on the street."

"That's not..." Kayip stumbled over his words. "There is much debate over the meaning of those words. Many in the Synod have debated that these do not apply to ferrals at all."

"Oh, a debate!" Sylvaine said. "Merciful Demiurge, how blessed I am to have my existence be *debated* over. There are some interpretations that even allow me to exist. *How considerate!"*

There was silence for a moment.

"I mean," Marcel mumbled. "They say the Demiurge loves all his creations."

Sylvaine stared at the man. "Marcel, you aren't even religious."

"Yeah, sure, but I've been to church," he said. "A few churches. They had potlucks sometimes."

"Sylvaine..." Kayip said. "Your anger is... reasonable. The Church of the Ascended may be inspired by the Demiurge, but it is a construction of man, and like any construction of this world, it is flawed."

Sylvaine sighed. "I'm surprised you of all people would admit that flaw."

"It is because I know it the best. Because I have seen what horrors, when twisted by the ego of its parishioners, the Church can do, what it can make someone into," Kayip said. There was something in his voice, a halting softness, that made Sylvaine think he was actually telling the truth. She wondered not for the first time what the man had seen on his wanderings, how had becoming a lonesome, itinerant monk in the first place, instead of the more traditional, settled kind.

"Really though," Marcel said, tapping the bars, "this isn't the important thing at the moment. What we have to do is figure out a way to get out of here."

"There is no way out of here," Sylvaine said, sitting up. "This is it. We've spent the last month running this way and that chasing Lazarus's tail, and once we get just a centimetre closer, just a possible lead to a possible lead to a possible clue as to where he went, we get shoved in a Principate prison, to be judged at the mercy of the Imperator."

"Not known for being merciful," Marcel mused.

Sylvaine let out a hollow laugh. "At least you're human. The Principate policy with regards to ferrals isn't that far off from the old Church's, only with more artillery fire." She leaned on the wall and shook her head. "Sorry. Sorry, I'm being so... If I just didn't muck up on the turbine, we might have actually nabbed Felik, and be resting in some cave ten kilometres from here."

"Well, it was a joint fuck-up, to be fair," Marcel said, sitting down next to her.

"I just... wish we actually got to bloody Roache's nose," Sylvaine said. "Imagine if this were some pulp. The heroes wander around the Wastes for a few weeks, then get arrested and executed in some podunk nowhere town. A bit of an anticlimax."

"I read a literary novel like that, in university." Marcel scratched his chin. "Some symbolism about the death of romanticism and mysticism in the modern age. Though I always suspected the author was just kind of depressed."

"This does not seem the end to me," Kayip said. "Many times, I have been close to death. Yet the Demiurge is not done with me, with us, I think. There is still a plan, even if we cannot see the full extent—"

Footsteps echoed down the stairwell at the end of the basement. The three went silent, as a stocky guard wearing Principate blue strode over. He glanced at Kayip.

"Him. Interrogation. Now."

<h1 style="text-align:center">Chapter 3</h1>

The interrogation room looked less like a Principate Regulation Intel-Extraction Center, and more like an unused storage room attached to an ailing autocar repair shop. This was because the interrogation room was indeed an unused storage room attached to an ailing autocar repair shop. It was the best Lechslov would allow Belona Agrippus, as intelligence gathering was apparently not considered a high-priority objective for a Principate outpost at the edge of enemy territory. As far as Belona could tell, the strategy Lechslov employed was to promote the growth of brothels, black markets, and general corruption, to allow the town and its accompanying military base to best integrate with the sleaze and lawlessness of the Wastes.

Belona did what she could, shuttering the windows, setting up harsh lamplights, hiding the stacks of tires to the side and setting up the ominous rack of thumbscrews, scalpels, æthermantic shock cables, and other more subtle instruments. She had not actually been forced to resort to *enhanced intel-extraction* in a good many years, the sight alone was usually enough to convince interrogees to plead guilty to whatever they had been accused of.

Still, as Belona set up the table, she wished she could at least have gotten rid of the suffocating smell of oil and figured out where those scraprats kept sneaking in from.

"You really think it's him?" Colonel Goss asked, pushing forward a metal chair. The rotund and balding man was doing his best to help set up, his decorated uniform damp with sweat. "I mean, after escaping custody, he simply wanders into our town?"

"The description matches," Belona said, "And I have heard reports of chaos among the Resurgence occupation of Huile. Perhaps the monk is on the hunt again."

"If I may, I would be wary of him," Colonel Goss said, wiping wet from his brow. "I mean, he is a criminal. Untrustworthy, a *terrorist* even. He may try to attack you, or break free from—"

"If I had trusted him, I might not have lost Huile," Belona interrupted. "Just because he escaped your custody doesn't mean he's a threat."

"I, well, I mean," Goss mumbled, red in the face. "I don't even know... we had him in handcuffs and everything."

Belona shook her head. "My apologies, my dear Goss, I did not mean to besmirch your loyalty or competence." That first bit was true. Goss was one of the few in the town who still held loyalty to his ex-general, despite currently outranking her. The second part was a lie. The man had maintained his position due to luck, not skill or intelligence.

"This may be our chance here, Colonel," she continued. "Our only chance. To right the wrongs of Huile. To undo our defeat."

Goss released a deep and anxious sigh. "If that is your recommendation, Ge—Justice Officer."

A knock on the door. With a salute, awkward but genuine, Goss took his leave. Belona sat down and dimmed the lights to as near a proper level of intimidation as could be managed under the circumstances. Protocol was to leave her face partially obscured, so that the interrogee was never certain who was at the other side of the table. With the poorly tarped-over hole in the roof, this would be impossible.

A guard, some local ruffian, led the subject in, potato bag over his head. With a wave of her hand, the guard left. The prisoner was as tall and muscular as Belona remembered. He would have made a good soldier.

With a tug, she removed the bag. If doubts still lingered, there were none now. Bald, tanned, with the same dented half-mask covering the upper-left side of his face. Kayip blinked his one good eye in the stark light, and as he stared at Belona, a small smile grew upon his face.

"It is good to see you are well, General," Kayip said.

"Not 'General' anymore," Belona said.

"Ah, that is a shame. While I do not hold the same values as your Principate, I admire your skill and leadership. It is unfortunate that your leaders failed to recognize those qualities, and pinned to you a defeat that was not yours."

"Perhaps they recognized those qualities too well," Belona said. "And were looking for an error to capitalize on."

"Politics." Kayip nodded.

"We're not here to discuss the past," Belona said, leaning forward.

"I was under the impression that Principate interrogators did not care for discussion much in the first place," Kayip said, glancing towards the instruments of torture.

"Are you afraid?"

"Of the judgement of the Demiurge, but little else," Kayip said.

Belona shifted back into her seat, her arms crossed. "You seem to have maintained your suicidal foolhardiness. Yet you are right not to fear, for this is not a normal interrogation. I simply wish to talk."

"About what?"

"About what you are doing here. About the last time we met. About Lazarus Roache."

"You wish to dig into memories." Kayip nodded again. "Memories are cruel things, are they not?"

* * *

Memories were indeed cruel things. In their joys and in their sorrows. No, in the contrast between their joys and their sorrows. For it was from the greatest height that one is most at risk to fall.

Belona remembered both well. It had been a mere three years before, the late summer of 1746. A year that she knew would be stamped into history books, the first year in over two decades that a Principate army marched over the Atsols into Bastillia, home of the UCCR, with a plan of total conquest. Border States cities had laid down in submission one after another, *Katshar, Adaldorf, Vatil,* even *Holtag,* as minor a prize that was. Raiders had fled into the Wastes, and long-neutral parties found a sudden love for their Imperator.

Then came Huile. The usually neutral mayor had turned hard on the Principate, sending thugs out to murder loyal subjects of the Imperator, or so reports had claimed. Belona at first decided against intervening, the city was far out of position in Resurgence territory, but a sudden and unexpected pro-Principate revolt led by some sangleum tycoon brought it into her hands. Were a Resurgence countercoup to succeed it would bring dishonor and break the image of Principate invulnerability, her action was forced.

She took control of the city, and its valuable æther-oil refineries, only to find the victory short-lived. For this was where the Resurgence would make their counterattack, deprive Belona of the initiative, surround her army, force her back behind the walls. Her expertise was assault, quick strikes, constant aggression, not buckling down for a siege, not spending weeks upon weeks digging trenches, reinforcing defenses, executing spies, and rationing out dwindling supplies. Resurgence artillery pounded day and night; her safety only secured by her decision to place her camp in the city's sangleum refineries. The UCCR would have gladly blasted the city proper, flattened the apartment tenements and the shops, turned the town to rubble and the civilians to corpses. But they would never risk destroying the æther-oil fields. So, she waited, and waited, and waited, as her army grew anxious, as the enemy mocked her on massive dictaphones.

The misery taught her patience, but she knew no victory would come by playing the UCCR's game. She waited. Waited until they got bored, waited until they got cocky and arrogant, until the walls crumbled, and her trenches collapsed to dust and mud. Waited until they attacked.

* * *

As the Resurgence gathered to strike at the southern wall, Belona mobilized at the north gate. Her army was with her, in warwalkers and rushtanks, in motorcycles and dathkreis. They had taken every vehicle they could requisition, even civilian autotrucks on whose back they had welded heavy motorguns. She rode with this column, the Lioness at the head of her pride, shouting out commands on a voxbox from the passenger's side of a landship. The metal behemoth smashed through the ruins that dotted the city, arced around the walls, and flanked the Resurgence army mid-assault.

"All troops forward!" she had shouted over voxbox, as the first of the UCCR soldiers turned towards the oncoming fury in panic.

They smashed into the side of the enemy column. The landship thumped over Resurgence bodies, then wove, like a great serpent, her men firing out of the flanks at those soldiers who managed to avoid the initial crushing. A glorious slaughter surrounded her, motorbike gunners decimating Resurgence skirmishers, dathkreis carving enemy limbs from bodies. Warwalkers strode above it all, lanky legs clanking over the battlefield, as their roaring guns turned fleeing troops into red mist. The ground, once rocky and ruin-covered, had been blasted flat by the Resurgence bombardment, leaving the enemy without cover. As shrapnel tore glass from the front of the landship, Belona could even smell the battlefield, gunpowder and dust, blood and the acrid stench of the æther-oil refineries. Wind whipped past her, as did flying pebbles. The driver swore and swerved, Belona laughed and shouted commands.

Then came the whistle of artillery. The enemy fired desperately, indiscriminately barraging her army and their own.

"Keep up the assault!" Belona shouted into her voxbox. "Do not fear, do not relent, the will of the Imperator demands—"

A blast. Dust and smoke and tumbling. For the briefest of moments, the world went black.

Then Belona staggered to her feet. The world roiled and turned, but she steadied herself. Her body was bloodless, aside from a gash on her chin. Nearby lay the landship, like a great metal pill bug turned on its side, smoldering. She had been lucky, thrown free when the artillery shell went off. Around her was chaos, glorious, wondrous chaos, shouts and screams and the echo of gunfire.

A wartruck skidded to a halt beside her, a young feminine face framed by black hair peering out with shock from the side window.

"General Agrippus!" the soldier shouted.

"Ah, Private Seidel," Belona said. "How goes the battle?"

"General!" Seidel said. "Are you injured? We need to get you back to the camp!"

"Nonsense," Belona said, spitting out a tooth. "The battle is yet to be finished." She glanced up at the back of the 'truck, where a multi-barreled motorgun lay, unmanned and unused. "Where is your gunner, private?"

"Dead, general."

"Then I will take their position."

With that she hauled herself up onto the back of the wartruck. The armor that surrounded the gun was half blasted away, but the motorgun itself seemed in working condition, with ammo to spare.

Seidel stepped out of the 'truck, fear on her face.

"General..."

"Give me your voxbox," Belona commanded. "And get moving!"

The woman did as she was commanded, handing her general the bulbous machine, which she strapped to the side of the turret, transmitter in her hand. As the 'truck started moving, Belona began to speak.

"Soldiers! Fear not, your general is alive and well!

She rotated the gun and fired into an approaching platoon of Resurgence soldiers. Bullets whizzed by, one nicking her shoulder, but she did not falter, letting her lead fly into the enemy. Artillery roared, pillars of dirt and stone bursting up all around. The wartruck skidded round a collapsed bunker and past a de-treaded rushtank, where a Principate driver had resorted to firing off pistol rounds from its smoking top.

"Victory is at hand! Leave none alive!" Belona shouted into the voxbox. As the 'truck rendezvoused with the main imperial column, she led them on sweep round the side of the city, turning to strike at the retreating foe. This was the vital moment, if she could break the assault into pieces, it would shatter the resolve of the Resurgence. This city would cease to be her cage. It would become a new forward operating base from which she would punish the traitorous UCCR for a century of disloyalty and hatred. She sucked in her breath and clinked on the voxbox. The orders were clear, there was nothing more to say. So instead, she softened her voice, and let flow not her harsh commands, but the dulcet anthem of her homeland.

*"From the bright shores of Kaimark,*
*To the eastern mount peak,*
*No land stands untouched,*
*By the light of our glory..."*

* * *

Hours later, Belona returned to camp. Private Seidel had been drenched in sweat and pale-faced, but her general was invigorated. She stepped out of the wartruck and walked over to a break in the walls of Huile. There she stared out over the battlefield, where her reserves of infantry were fanning out to rescue the injured and finish off the enemy. Behind her, in the refinery came a rousing cheer. Soldiers, some fresh from the battlefield, other in the medical crews or working as military police, gathered round in the alleys of the refinery complex, crowds of men and women standing between the hulks of iron and smokestacks. They cheered and cried her name. *General Agrippus! The Conqueror! The Lioness of Vastium!*

31

She firmly bid them return to their duties. Belona would speak in time, of course, but only when the last Resurgence scoundrel had been driven from the sight of the city, when her victory had been made total and complete. What a glorious oration she would deliver then!

For now, Belona walked towards the camp, a town of blue tents set up in between the blocks of bricks and iron scaffolds that were the Lazacorp refineries. There she found one of her Majors, by the name of Hans Krimme. His short-cut red hair sat stiff under his cap; his uniform dirtied by battle. She noticed a cut on his leg, oozing slightly.

"General!" He saluted.

"Are you well, Major?" Belona asked.

"Ah, it is not a thing." Krimme smiled. "Some lucky Resurgence idiot managed to get past the wall and lunged at me with a bayonet. Do not worry, few made it as far as he."

"It is good to hear it, Major," Belona said. "You handled yourself admirably. Perhaps there may even be a promotion in honor of your heroism."

"Not heroism, just my duty, and even if it were, it would be a lesser heroism than your own," Krimme said. Belona could see the blush on his face, the barely contained smile. "Anyway, there are no open positions."

"Arrangements can be made," Belona said. "There's a certain gadfly by the name of Lechslov that may need his ego checked."

"I... would not dare suggest," Krimme began.

"It is not your place to," Belona cut in. "But let's not waste time, what updates do you have?"

As they walked through the streets of the refineries, past medical tents and æther-oil tanks covered in the emblem of the Imperator, Krimme gave his reports. Causalities were low, *their* causalities at least, and Huile itself was calm. Since the coup, and the systematic executions of Resurgence loyalists, the pitiful excuse for a city had been sufficiently cowed into submission. It was not an impressive settlement, small for a city, most of the building pre-Calamity and abandoned. It existed only as an extension of the refinery, a place for Lazacorp workers to eat and sleep. Of course, even that was barely necessary, as it seemed the refineries were run off slave labor, mutant slaves. It was a despicable sight, inhuman and horrific. Once order was restored, she would euthanize what mutants remained, and replace them with loyal Principate workers.

"And general," Krimme said, "we finally found that last terrorist. The madman who killed the old mayor."

"Ah yes," Belona said. This assassination and the power vacuum it created had spurred the Principate coup, led by loyalists and organized by one Lazarus Roache.

*Lazarus Roache...* She should like the man; he had delivered a city to her. Of course, it had been a city in the middle of enemy territory, one that brought her invasion to the brink of collapse. His company, Lazacorp could provide untold amounts of æther-oil to fuel her campaign. Æther-oil harvested by mutant slaves. The man always wore a smile and had kind words to share, and yet there was a hollowness to his every action, a subtle twitch in the man's eye that suggested to her a vague duplicity even when she couldn't find its specificities. Each word that slipped from his lips felt just a bit too cloying, a bit too planned.

And speaking of the man, there he was! Striding through the streets straight towards her, flanked by his weary-looking butler. His hair a short-cut gold, his teeth statue-perfect, his bespoke striped suit pristine, with a matching, short-brimmed hat that seemed far too antiquated a style for a man who appeared younger than she.

"My great General Agrippus! Infinite congratulations!" Lazarus Roache said with a clap. "What a magnificent victory, it reminds me of the tales of the Imperators of old!"

"I did not know they told such tales in the UCCR," Belona said.

"Those who wish to hear them can find them whispered," Lazarus said. "Why, I still remember being a young boy, sitting in my backyard reading old Principate pamphlets my dear father sneaked to me, dreaming of the day I could throw off the lies of the Citizens' Confederacy and return my home to good, old-fashioned Principate steel and order."

"Do you have a point? I am fatigued, as you can imagine."

"Yes, indeed I do General. I know your time is valuable." The man glanced back and forth, as if looking for unwanted ears. It was all a show, Belona could tell, a way to give his words undeserved weight. There was always some show or trick with Lazarus Roache, Belona had met his kind before. Inferno, her father had been a man not unlike this Roache, and it was by the grace of the Imperator that she escaped from that doddery drunkard's magniloquent pontifications.

"This is about the..." Roache began, "...tactical suggestion I made to you at the start of this siege."

"Yes, the sangleum gas, I recall," Belona said.

"Indeed!" Lazarus said as they turned a corner, past mutants workers slaving over steaming machinery, Lazacorp guards corralling the crimson-skinned abominations with truncheons and bayonets. "We have more than an excess of raw æther-oil, easily weaponized, and the artillery to use them. It would be the simplest thing to surprise the enemy with a barrage of our own, after all the cruelty they have launched our way."

"You proposed this shameful stratagem before our assault, and the cowardice proved utterly unneeded," Belona said. "Look at the dust that is your lack of faith. I have vanquished the foe, without resorting to chemical warfare or other perfidies. Such tactics are beneath me and my army."

"I understand your well-deserved pride. I had lofty expectations of you, and yet you shot even these out of the water. I reckon that there has not been a leader like you, nay, a *hero* like you since the days of Franz Diedrev himself! Yet, I must insist. You have broken the Resurgence, but they are vermin. And we know what vermin do, they scuttle away, they breed, they return. You do not shoot vermin; you tent your house and gas them out! If you were to prepare the artillery tonight, you could wipe the last vestige of the United Confederacy of the Citizens' Resurgence from the outskirts of this city for good! Listen..." The man stopped in such a way that for Belona to continue walking she would need to barrel straight into him. She decided, reluctantly, against that course of action.

"I am bound by duty and honor to supply your army with sangleum, a service I am more than thrilled to provide," Roache said, smile so close to genuine that its artificiality was all the more unnerving. "But we need to make sure Lazacorp's holdings here are secure, so that we are safe from Principate aggression once you leave."

"Once I leave?" Belona shook her head and chuckled. "Mr. Roache you have woefully misunderstood the situation. All this," she waved her hand around, at the squalid mutant tenements, at the leaking pipes and rusted equipment, "is unacceptable. Beneath the standards of the Imperator. And that's to say nothing of the rumors that you have been cavorting around with raiders. Such actions stain our rightful legitimacy. No, this will not be allowed to continue. We will be taking full control of these refineries. Your so-called Lazacorp shall be dissolved within a fortnight."

"I... General... Miss Belona..." The man stumbled over his syllables. It was the only time she had seen the tycoon truly taken aback, unable to get a sensible word in. "That… is unnecessary. I am a loyal servant of the Imperator. I gave you this city, I handed you this damned city on a silver platter with a cup of fresh sangleum to wash it down!"

"Indeed, you did," Belona replied. "And if you manage to make yourself less irksome, I may even reward your loyalty with a mid-level management position within our refineries."

Lazarus Roache glanced at his butler, who made no comment, then sucked in his breath and managed to collect himself. "General Agrippus," he said, with his manufactured smile. "Perhaps we can discuss this matter over a cup of tea?"

"No need, it has been decided," Belona said, marching forward, knocking the shoulder of the tycoon when he didn't move in time. Krimme had to jog to catch up. "Now Major, I believe you had a prisoner for me to interrogate?"

* * *

When she had reached the Intel-Extraction Center the prisoner was already in his chair, chained and bound. He was not what she had expected, larger for one, a giant of a man, tanned and scarred, and with a mask over his left eye. She wondered how a man so bulky and conspicuous had managed to hide out in occupied Huile for so many weeks. He did look quite worse for the wear. Bruised and filthy, his clothing torn, blood leaking from under his mask. The man smelled awful, some horrid combination of sewage and body odor. The only thing aesthetically pleasing about him was his bracelet, of a strange azure metal, that hung from his shackled arms.

The center itself was up to par. Darkened to the point of disorientation, a single light blaring, guards just out of sight. Belona let herself linger, studying the man from the shadows. Though his posture was one of dejection, one good eye glanced around with a frenetic focus. Was even now the man looking for an escape?

She stepped into the light and sat down, opening the file. The man had already been interrogated, but to little effect. The file was all but empty.

"Name," Belona said.

"Are you General Agrippus?" the man asked.

"*Name,*" Belona insisted.

"Kayip," the man said. "You know this."

"Surname."

"Just Kayip. It has only been just Kayip."

"A wastefolk tradition?"

"A Church one," Kayip said.

"Yes," Belona tapped her notes. "It does say here that you have disguised yourself as an itinerant priest, or monk, or some other nonsense."

"You must stop him," Kayip said.

"I have not asked you a ques—"

Kayip lunged forward, the chains catching him, the entire chair moving forward a quarter-metre. "Lazarus Roache, you must stop him."

"This is not about Lazarus Roache, this is about you."

"All of this is about Lazarus Roache," Kayip said.

Belona paused. Then went off-script. "What do you mean?"

"You are the General? Yes, I can feel your confidence," Kayip said. "All of this, the coup, your victory, it is for his designs."

"Coup?" Belona scoffed. "It was you, you and your gang of terrorists that started this whole thing. Murdered loyal Principate citizens in the name of your old mayor, whatshisname..." She had to glance through her notes. "LuGouffe. Who you were quick to kill off to hide your identity."

"Never killed citizens," Kayip said. "Never touched LuGouffe. I only told him the truth. That is why Roache had him killed."

"So, this is your excuse, your defense?" Belona shut the notes. "Claim complete innocence? Blame it all on Lazarus Roache. Excuses did nothing to help your co-conspirators."

"Dead," Kayip said. "All of them. Before you even got here. Also, him. Also, Roache. Couldn't let you know."

"Know what?"

Kayip sucked in his breath. "The man has plans for this city. I do not know all the details, but I know the outline. He requires blood. On an industrial scale. Needs to corrupt thousands."

Belona shook her head. For a second, she had been genuinely curious, but it was clear now that she was dealing with a lunatic.

"If you don't have anything valuable to add—"

"You do not believe me," Kayip said. "But you must. Have you drunk the man's tea? He poisons it with a drug. It influences minds. It's demonic."

"I have not drunk any poisoned tea, what I want is some actual intel—"

"The mutant slaves!" Kayip said, desperation in his voice. "Where do you think he gets them from?"

"Waste slavers?" Belona shrugged.

"Many, yes, but not as mutants, as normal humans first," Kayip said. "He does this to them, corrupts, them, mutates them. It is how he controls them. And when he is done, he will harvest them."

"This is... idiotic," Belona said. "I have listened to many defenses, many excuses, but this is, somehow, the worst I have suffered to hear."

"Not a defense, not an excuse," Kayip said. "I have failed to make you believe, to make you understand. I do not care what you do to me, my death is a given, and I do not hide from it. But Lazarus Roache cannot be trusted. He will give you gifts, favors, do all that he can, but in the end, he will betray you. He always does."

"And now you care for the cause of the Principate?" Belona asked.

"I have no love for that Imperator you worship as if he were the Demiurge himself," Kayip said. "But what Roache will do once he betrays you, it is too great a sin, a blight on mankind. Death and madness beyond our ability to imagine."

There was silence for a moment. In a darkened corner a guard coughed.

"Well," Belona said. "You will be happy to know I do not trust this man, for my own reasons. I will be removing him from his position."

"You have arrested Roache? He is in chains?" There was a sudden hope in the strange man's voice.

"No need," Belona said. "He is under my control and has been informed he has no future except submission."

"There is all the need!" Kayip said, shaking against his restraints, voice nearly hoarse. "If he is desperate, then you are in the most danger. He will never submit, he will never obey, if you do not end his life now, it will be too late! Please general, you can end this. You can end this now!"

# CHAPTER 4

"But I didn't end it," Belona muttered, far from the glories of her forgotten victories, far from Huile, in a hovel's excuse for an imperial town, the dregs of her ambition. "I thought him safe in my control, dallied, distracted by other matters. Despite your warnings, I underestimated the depths of Roache's treachery."

She stared at the monk, at the same prisoner now in a very different place. It had not even been three full years, and yet she could see the age in the man, felt it in herself. Despite the conditions of his now second capture, the strange monk smiled.

"You tried," he said.

Belona almost laughed, leaning forward in a manner against regulations, allowing her darkly bemused features to be clearly read in the light. "And tell me Kayip, how would you know that?"

"You told me as much then, and you are an honest woman," he said. "You did what you could, you did your duty."

"If I had done my duty right, we wouldn't be sitting here now. I'd be out leading my army, Phenia in my sights."

"And I'd be locked away in some work camp, correct?" The question was tossed soft but still hit sharp.

Belona leaned back, the shadows again taking her. "I thought you a selfless crusader. Would you not accept such a fate in exchange for Roache's head?"

"Perhaps. Would you General?"

*"General..."* How mockingly sweet the word. "I'd give anything for that to be true, to have my army again with me. But not even your Demiurge can bring back the dead, the past is buried."

"It is a bitter truth to accept that what is lost, is lost," Kayip nodded. "But there are still things that can be done. If not glory, then revenge, justice. You are an Officer of Justice now."

This did prompt Belona to laugh, despite herself. "Yes, and I take my duty seriously. Regardless of the sage advice you offered, you are here before me a criminal, and I must do as I must do." She realized as she spoke how hollow the words must sound. It would not be fitting to offer a trade, and yet the man had knowledge that she desired far greater than any inclination to enact pointless punishments.

The monk turned in his seat, studying her even in the dark. "We both know the value of duty, Justice Officer, but what if justice could only be done beyond the bounds of your duty. Which would you choose to serve?"

"So, are you saying you know where Roache is?" Belona's voice betrayed more eagerness than she meant to reveal.

"Only how to find him, only possibly," Kayip admitted. "Only a chance. Like the one that slipped away from us."

"A chance with a price tag, I assume."

"No bribes, no drevs or aurems or sangleum," the monk now leaned forward himself, manacles glistening in the lamplight. "I only wish for you to ask yourself, General, Officer, what you would you be willing to give, what you'd be willing to do, for justice?"

Belona broke protocol again, to stare up at the darkness of the ceiling, where her memories swirled. The monk had returned after all this time, not for her, and yet in a way perhaps for her after all. To present her a second chance. So rarely were those given, and the price inevitably steep. What would she give up for it? Only that equal to what was taken. And for Belona Agrippus, that was everything.

* * *

Looking back on that night in Huile, it was odd for Belona to recall what little affect the strange prisoner's words had had on her in the moment. They were just the ramblings of a desperate lunatic, which were a drev a dozen in the Wastes. She had been more bothered by the lack of workable intel she had gathered from the interrogation. No reports of other UCCR

39

cells inside Huile, no names of other collaborators. As far as she could tell the monk and the small posse he had gathered had really been all the armed resistance there was.

Yet she had not signed the terrorist's execution warrant. Instead, she had ordered him transported north. There may yet be some information of value hidden in that man's head, she reasoned. The unspoken truth of it was that she almost respected the supposed monk. His will was far greater than the standard cravenness she had seen from Resurgence rats. He never tried to defend himself, was happy to die in the service of his goal. Even if his goal was the result of delusion-driven vendetta, the devotion was admirable.

Yet as the night wore on, after the victory speeches, and the meetings with her advisors, after her quick, efficient bath and the flurry of letter-writing that kept her up hour after hour, Kayip's warning had lingered with Belona. Even as she lay in her cot in her tent, she had started to wonder. What if the man was not entirely delusional? His story was strange, and certainly false in places, but Lazarus was involved in the slave trade. It was not beyond impossible that he was mutating some of his workers, perhaps to isolate them or... well, she wasn't sure. She had seen strange things in the Wastes, twisted beasts and restless spirits, abominations of pre-Calamity experimental engineering and rogue æthermancers, even those horrid aberrations that some called demons. And Kayip, odd as he was, seemed to be one of the few to see past Roache's charms, to see clear the hollow sack of pretension and venality that she recognized in the tycoon.

So, far past midnight, Belona found herself taking a walk around the Huile refineries. Most of her soldiers were asleep, besides a few guards, who saluted quickly when they noticed her coming. She found herself wandering deeper into the Lazacorp section, neat blue tents replaced by squalor and mutant shanties. Finally, she strode past the darkened windows of the Lazacorp central office. There she was surprised to find Major Krimme, in the midst of a squad of soldiers.

"General!" the man said, as surprised as her. He threw up a salute.

"At ease," she said. "What's going on here?"

"The guards we had overseeing the Lazacorp central office never returned from their shift," Krimme said. "And I got reports that the door to the office was sealed tight."

A soldier kicked the door to confirm that it was, indeed, locked.

"Get an engineer on this immediately!" Belona ordered, an ambiguous fear starting to roost in her thumping chest.

As if on that command, a man ran from the dark, a large ætherglove over his right hand.

"Major Krimme, I'm here as—" The man noticed Belona and saluted.

"Quickly, soldier," Krimme said, gesturing to the door. The engineer bent down.

"Why was I not informed?" Belona asked.

"My apologies General, this came to my attention just fifteen minutes ago," Krimme said. "I did not wish to wake you with something so minor."

A spark flash from the bronze doorknob. "Done!" the engineer said, as the heavy wooden door creaked open. Soldiers pushed through, handtorch beams cutting through the dark. Belona stepped forward and flicked on the light. Ætherlamps buzzed into life, revealing pristine brick walls, brass filigree fixtures, a luxurious El'Helmaudi rug covered in flowers and caniform chamroshes, and at the end, by the far doorway, the body of a Principate soldier, splayed and bloodstained.

The squad fanned out, as Belona rushed forward to check the body. Dead and cold, face white, chest a mass of minced viscera that not even a point-blank scattergun shot could produce.

"What in the Imperator's name...?" Krimme said.

Belona glanced down the hallway. Empty, the far rusted door hanging open. She had toured this building before, there was a stairwell there down into the depths of the refineries, down into the underway, that dismal maze of basements, sewers, pipeworks, and pathways.

She pulled out a pistol. "Major! Take your squad underground and figure out where the man has fled to. You two, follow me."

With not a moment's hesitation Krimme led his soldiers into the dark, down the hallway, and then into the depths below. With two soldiers serving as backup, Private Ivanov and Private Rimkus, Belona took it upon herself to search the upper floors.

The main stairway was an overly grand thing, all imported Vidish wood, with gilded lamplights and faded portraits of ancient who-knows-who on the walls, (probably provincial notables, an oxymoron). Up a floor she found more corpses, the remains of the guards she had stationed to keep an eye on Lazarus. Their bodies were a nauseating sight with limbs turned to liquids and skulls collapsed in on themselves. Æthermantics was her guess, of the befouled flesh-focused variety. Their weapons were holstered, so it must have been a sudden ambush.

Yet it was clear enough that Lazarus and his cronies had fled in full, so she had her soldiers fan out and inspect room by room. Most were just narrow offices. Belona was somewhat surprised that no filing cabinets had been opened, no documents taken or destroyed. Perhaps they hadn't the time.

Finally, she made it to Lazarus's office. This ornate and garish room was a mess. False walls and secret lockers had been opened and left in that state, racks that no doubt held rifles and other weapons now empty. So, the man had always had an escape plan.

Her eye found its focus on one of the far racks. There a gas mask now hung. It was the only one left, but there had clearly been many of its kin hanging beside it. Belona inspected the mask, rough leather, speckled glass, it reminded her of a blackened skull. What in Inferno did Lazarus Roache need gas masks for?

The world suddenly shook. Windows shattered, doors swung, as an explosion roared somewhere below. Suddenly everything clicked in Belona's head.

"Gas attack!" she shouted, as she frantically threw on the mask and began to wrap cloth around every centimetre of open skin.

"General!" Ivanov stumbled into the room, arm over mouth. Belona glanced around for another mask or any sort of protection for the man. Coughs echoed from down the hall, Rimkus's, followed by hacking and a gurgling scream. Ivanov turned round; wisps of a crimson smoke glittered in his 'torchlight. Sangleum gas.

It pounced on him like a wolf. He staggered under the assault, coughing and fruitlessly tossing his fist out to clear the air. The gas pushed into the room, overwhelming him, digging into his lungs as he sought desperate breaths. His coughs turned to wheezing, turned to drowning cries of agony, his skin bubbling crimson. With a wretched wail, the man fell to the floor and started to vomit red gunk. As he tried to move his head, his lips sagged and sloughed off. The gas was doing its work, transforming his insides into mush, and with shaking gasps he expelled his liquified organs onto the rug.

"Heeeeeelllp..." he moaned, the elongated syllables stuttering with agony.

Outside were screams and gunshots. Belona rushed to the window. The world had gone dark, the power dead. She shouted a warning, but her words were impotent. In the flashes of gunfire and the glare of handtorches, she could see the smoke ascending from the depths of the refineries, like great hands clawing up from the abyss of Inferno itself. It rose up, then billowed down, into the streets, into the tents. Even from up here she could hear their pain, the horror, and shock as thousands upon thousands awoke from their cots to a sudden grasping, suffocating death. The army, her army, was torn from their peace, from their slumber after a hard-won victory. They screamed as one. It was an unearthly wailing, unlike anything she had ever heard, on the battlefield or off. It was a horrid sound, agony made manifest on an inhuman scale. A dirge of the damned, improvised in a shared torment by those condemned by her own inaction. It was a song of pure suffering that would never escape Belona's memory.

The sound stuck with her as she rushed down the stairs into the underway. It haunted her every moment of every minute of every hour that she spent hiding amongst the sewers, every second she spent fleeing through unknown and forgotten passageways. The sound hung to her as she stumbled into sunlight, days later, and it followed her as she made contact with the remnants of Lechslov's northern forces. It lay in her ears as she was court-martialed, the moans of the dead excoriating her as she was stripped of her command and sent off to a nowhere town. Even now, as she sat across the table from Kayip, three years later, even now as she sat listening to the man's story, she could still hear the wailing.

# CHAPTER 5

Wailing in the dark. Shouts and screams and gunshots echoing from every direction as the world shook. A labyrinth of dark and death. The flash of muzzles, the glare of handtorches. A bayonet sliding into a body, bullets falling into flesh, their flesh, his flesh. Marcel felt a burst of pain in his leg. Stumbling, crying.

"Get up Talwar."

Alba. His captain. His lover. Head a blackened skull. A gas mask. Pulling. Pain and shouts and screams and distant wailing. A man's features melting, the crimson smoke billowing, reaching, grabbing. A face among the smoke, flayed and bleeding. Then skin started to wrap round it, layer by layer, hair the color of gold's glint, teeth too perfect, smile too knowing. A hat and a jacket and a condescending wink.

"Excellent work!" Lazarus Roache commended. "Couldn't have done it without you."

* * *

Marcel jolted awake, panting, covered in sweat. A dream. Just a dream, just the same old, Demiurge-damned dream. Marcel's relief was short lived. He was still in the jail cell, at the edge of that Principate slumtown Holtag, awaiting... well something horrible.

He lay back down on the floor. The cell only had one bed, which is to say it only had one raised board of splintering wood. He wondered if he should try and get back to sleep but didn't want to risk falling back into those warped memories that made up his nightmares. To that night under Huile, when he had lost his squadmates, his friends. The night he had saved the city from oppression, the night when he had lost his leg, the night he had been made a war hero, the night he had done nothing more than forward the machinations of Lazarus Roache.

*Lazarus Roache.* A man who took a noble victory and turned it into an eternal shame, a man who took a free city and transformed it into a prison. Marcel wondered what was happening in Huile. He had promised Desct, the last of his squadmates, the current very tenuous ruler of Huile, that he would bring Lazarus to justice. What could he say to Desct now? He didn't even know where the murderous tycoon was hiding! Somewhere in the Wastes, he knew exactly as much as when he left Huile. Lazarus was somewhere in the Wastes, surrounded by cronies and hired brutes and who knew what else.

In the moonlight he noticed the gleam of Sylvaine's eyes. An unnerving sight, like the reflection of a cat's stare. It wasn't hard to imagine being some prey animal when looking back at that stare, he had read plenty of adventure pulps with the hero besieged by barbaric ferrals, glimpsed only by the glow of their eyes between the leaves. Of course, most ferrals he had met in real life seemed to just be trying to get by, like anyone else.

"Can't sleep either?" Sylvaine asked.

Marcel shook his head.

"Understandable," she said. "And Alba, she's your ex, right?"

"What?" Marcel asked.

"You were muttering her name in your sleep," Sylvaine said. "She's your ex, right? Led your squad."

"Yeah, the Huile Sewer Rats," Marcel said. "With Desct, and Danel, Rada, Henri, and Lambe— well, he doesn't count."

"Dating your superior office, that has to be a violation of some military code or something?"

"Maybe," Marcel admitted. "Things were pretty loose in that army, to be honest."

"Hmm..." Sylvaine laid her head back and stared at the ceiling. The two were silent a few minutes, the only sounds were from outside, the howls of wild strixes and the muffled moans from some brothel across the street. Marcel's mind started to float back to Alba. Her touch, callous but warm. Her voice, dulcet when wanted, stern when needed. Her body, muscular and lithe. Her eyes, sapphires. Her insults, bitter and cruel. Her judgements, distant and unfair. The way she walked out of his office, out of his life, as if nothing they had built ever meant anything. What would she think now? Would she credit Marcel for taking down Blackwood Row or view the carnage Roache unleashed as one big 'I-told-you-so.'"

"I can imagine you must be nervous," Sylvaine said. "I mean, what your squad did, must be considered a war crime."

"Unleashing sangleum gas onto an army?" Marcel said, stretching. "Yeah, probably. But the Principate's done far nastier, far more often. Inferno they were planning to release the same gas on the citizens of Huile, just as some petty punishment. Can you imagine? A cloud of choking death, civilians falling one after another, their blood clogging the gutters."

"As opposed to the way we left the city," Sylvaine said. Flashes of that night's violence cut through Marcel in a moment, bodies on the street, mobs lifting corpses as trophies.

"We did the right thing," Marcel said quickly. "Best we could." He wondered how Desct was handling the situation. Mayor Desct, General Desct, whatever title he came up for himself. Not that he envied the man, Marcel knew his friend was trying as best he could to clean up after that bloodbath, to bring some measure of justice and peace to the city, just as Marcel was, in his own way. He just hoped Desct would be able to keep Huile safe from Lazarus's plotting, now that they had mucked up their ramshackle quest.

"I'm not saying we didn't do... the best we could," Sylvaine said. "Just... It wasn't what I expected when I joined this whole hunt-down-Lazarus-Roache thing."

"Well," Marcel mused. "At least you might get out of this without facing the gallows. Besides the attempted kidnapping, you haven't committed any crimes against the Principate."

Sylvaine laughed hoarsely. "Marcel, I'm a Ferral. My existence is a crime."

Another awkward silence filled the room.

"Actually," Sylvaine said, "I don't think they still use gallows. I mean maybe out here they do, but when I talked with an Imperial Engineer in Icaria, she said the big thing in Drevstad were *mortiferous-level ætheric dischargement units*. Basically, a chair attached to an æther engine, shoots a bolt of energy straight into victim's spinal cords for an instant execution."

"That doesn't exactly make me feel much better."

"Hmm..." Sylvaine muttered. "Well, I think it's interesting, at least. Takes a lot of power and precision to focus an æther bolt like that. I wonder how they keep it from overheating. I should have looked up the technical diagrams when I was in Icaria."

Silence returned. It always seemed to insist on returning. An oppressive hush hiding just below the conversation, waiting for words to fail. Marcel couldn't stand the silence out here. He had been a city boy, born and raised on the hum and buzz of the sleepless Phenia. Out here the silence left you with nothing but your thoughts, and those hadn't been particularly pleasant.

"You know," Marcel said, sitting up. "I think I read a pulp where something like this happened. The hero locked up in a dungeon, for a crime he didn't commit, awaiting a cruel execution. But in the end, he escaped."

"Yeah?" Sylvaine asked. "How did he do that?"

"Uh," Marcel said, "I think dragons were involved."

"Oh, was this *Realm of the Dragonlords?*"

"Yeah!" Marcel said. "You've read it? I loved that book growing up!"

"It's..." Sylvaine strummed her finger. "Sure, it was decently okay."

Footsteps clanked from the metal stairway. Marcel turned, his heart frozen, as two figures descended from the far end of the hall. The front one strode forward, a massive brute of a man, moonlight from empty cells reflecting off the silver buttons of his blue principate uniform. Behind him Marcel could hear the shake of shackles, held by his smaller partner.

Then was this it? Marcel wondered. Not even a show trial, not even the formal mockery of justice that was the supposed norm for the Principate? Were they just to be taken outside, chained up, so that they wouldn't squirm as the Principate officers put a bullet into their brainstems? Why the secrecy? They hadn't even been interrogated yet, had they discovered what they needed from Kayip, learned what Marcel had done and now some vengeful officer had taken it upon himself to exact his revenge secretly, to finish off the despised war hero before someone swooped in to take his prize? Marcel had long wondered how he would face his death if it came to that. Would he be the man he always desired to be, face his murder with a stoic countenance, let his last words be a cry for freedom as this monster in his blue uniform—

"Kayip!" Sylvaine whispered.

Marcel blinked and squinted. As the man approached, he realized that it was indeed the monk. How in the Demiurge's name had the man purloined a Principate uniform?

"I am glad to see you are well," Kayip said. He glanced at Marcel. "You are covered in sweat."

"Oh," Marcel said, wiping off his panic-perspiration. "It's a muggy night."

"I am here to break you out," Kayip said, with a calm tone as if it were the simplest task in the world. He tossed through the bars another uniform. Marcel picked it up, it was roughly his size.

"Who is she?" Sylvaine asked.

Marcel could now make out the second person. A woman, not old, though she seemed to wear what age she had in her stride, in her bent lip and sharp gaze. Despite this, she was not quite bad-looking. She had pale skin and taut features, eyes sharp and nose aquiline. On her chin was a misshapen scar, and her black hair was pulled up in a bun behind her decorated cap. Compared to Kayip she was not too tall, yet walked as if she were. Marcel could make out the shine of a pistol hanging from her right hip, her left-hand holding chains.

"Do not worry," Kayip said. "She is a friend."

"That is not the term I would use," the woman said. "But you want Lazarus Roache dead, and I want Lazarus Roache, bled, gutted, and left as a miserable corpse on the side of the road. So, we're working together." She said it not as a suggestion, but an order.

Marcel shared a quick glance with Sylvaine. This was not exactly what he was expecting, but he hadn't a surfeit of other escape plans.

"You're a Principate officer?" Marcel asked.

"Yes, an Officer of Justice, and you are criminal scum," the woman said. "Yet the injustice of letting you three free is far outweighed by the justice of killing Roache, so shut up and put on your disguise. Quietly."

"What about me?" Sylvaine asked.

The woman slipped the chains through the bars. Handcuffs and footcuffs, attached in the middle with links that were almost comically large.

"There are no... beastwomen in the Principate army," she said. "You'll be playing a prisoner."

* * *

The chains were utterly, horrendously humiliating. Sylvaine shuffled forward, legs locked in three sets of bindings, arms wrapped around herself and chained behind her. Her head was covered in a massive and bulky muzzle, whose hinges dug into her neck.

"That doesn't look comfortable," Marcel said, as he guided her, dressed like a soldier. Sylvaine said nothing. It wasn't comfort that was the issue. Sylvaine was well used to discomfort. These bindings were not for some normal prisoner, handcuffs would be enough for your standard drunkard, taur rustler, or serial killer. These chains, this collar, was for something wild and dangerous, something thoroughly inhuman.

"Pick up the pace," the Principate officer hissed. There was a viciousness to this woman, the way she strode, the way she glanced back at her. Even in her smell there was a meanness, some bitter pheromonic something that humans never seemed to pick up on but was as strong as her unwashed body odor. Sylvaine wondered if her own humiliation had been intentional on the woman's part. Kayip stepped up close and put his hand briefly on Sylvaine's shoulder.

"I am sorry. It will be only for a short while," the man whispered.

She owed the monk a lot. Her life for instance, now several times over, but she felt this humiliating charade put them pretty close to even.

They reached the end of the small jail, really more a long sheet metal shack with a basement and a good deal of pretension, and found the lone guard, a short, hefty middle-aged man, fast asleep behind his desk.

They were all silent as they walked past, the guard snoring loudly. A lucky break, it seemed Holtag security was impressively lax. The woman reached her hand carefully for the door handle, then paused. After a moment of, presumably thought, the woman turned, and to Sylvaine's horror, marched over, and slammed her first three times on the guard's desk.

"Wha?" the guard said.

"Stiller!" the woman said.

"Officer!" he said, panicked.

"I was not aware you were paid to slumber," the woman scolded. "Do you even have the papers on the prisoner?"

"Prisoner?" the man said. He blinked around and stared at Sylvaine. She supposed she should bare her teeth, or growl, or something to add to the act but decided she would prefer to be sent back to the cell for execution than play pantomime Ferral.

"I thought there were supposed to be three of them?" Stiller said, shifting through his papers.

The woman paused. "Stiller, are you telling me you slept through the transfer of two prisoners already?" She spoke with believable, enraged incredulity.

"No, Justice Officer! Of course not, I just, I'll get the paperwork sorted right away."

"This is a court-marshalable offence," the woman sneered, with what struck Sylvaine as unnecessary belligerence. Were they not trying to silently escape?

"Officer, this is all, it's a misunderstanding," the man stammered and blubbered. "Please I'll, I'll get it all in order, I'll make sure—"

The woman sighed, unnaturally loud. "I have no time for this. Stiller, if I didn't have you canned for the wastehound incident, I won't for this. A trial enough to get guards whose sins are limited to sloth alone. Listen, I have orders to transfer this one to a work camp up north. Just write up some preliminary transfer papers and keep your damned mouth shut. When I return, I'll settle the details and backdate them."

"Thank you, thank you! The Imperator's mercy guides you, Justice Officer!" the man bowed his head swiftly and repeatedly with utterly shameless sycophancy.

With that settled, the woman led the three out the back and to a large, canvas-covered transport 'truck. Kayip and Marcel lifted Sylvaine up into the back, then stepped in after her.

She was surprised to find her stuff set neatly on the floor of the truck. There was her bag, a rumpled backsack filled with her few possessions, mostly clothes and some æther circuits and gearworks. On the top of it, tucked in neatly to its front pocket, was her ætherglove, unharmed and beautiful. Sitting beside all this was Marcel's bags, and Kayip's, as well as weaponry, lots and lots of weaponry. Repeater-rifles and bayonet heads, scatterguns and grenades, all of Principate make. Even a full on motorgun sat in the corner, blackened steel oiled and shined. Sylvaine couldn't help but admire the machine, with its half-dozen rotating barrels, and its bulky but efficient æther-motor. So drawn was her focus to the machine, that she nearly missed the tied-up man who sat next to it, who only grabbed her attention by shaking violently and mumbling through his stained-rag gag.

It was the bald man, the one with the beard. Felik Rector. Tied and bruised and looking something between terrified and utterly furious. Sylvaine shared a glance with Marcel as the truck started to move.

The Justice Officer drove them through the narrow dirt streets of Holtag. The city was asleep, or close to it, tenements and scraphouses bearing dark windows, most covered in a layer or two of iron bars. There were no public ætherlamps lining the roads, the only lights beside the stars above were those of their truck, and the occasional torchlights of drunk soldiers wandering back from some petty debauchery or another.

As the truck bumped over potholes, which made up the majority of the streets, Marcel leaned forward, gesturing with his head for Sylvaine and Kayip to listen.

"Who is this woman?" he whispered.

"An… ally," Kayip said. "I have met her before, tried to convince her to help me remove Lazarus Roache. She was not in a place to heed me then, but she is glad to listen now."

"I didn't know you fraternized with the Principate," Marcel said, a hint of anger hiding beneath his voice.

"I am apolitical," Kayip said. "But it is not my standard procedure. I was arrested, to tell things short. Escaped, but the woman forgave her grudge on this account."

"I'm with Marcel," Sylvaine said, shaking her manacles. "Friends don't exactly lock friends up."

Felik mumbled something inaudible.

"Ally, not friend," Kayip said. "And I think this act alone should demonstrate her usefulness, if not anything else."

The 'truck rumbled to a stop. Sylvaine glanced out a tear in the soft-top to see that they were at the edge of town, just a few metres from the chest-high, slapdash excuse for a wall. The Wastes loomed tantalizingly beyond it, but closer still was a military checkpoint, where a caravan-truck was idling. An old, weary-looking merchant stood by the truck, as soldiers inspect his papers.

"All right," the closer soldier said. "Seems in order. Exempting, of course, the exit-tax."

"Exit-tax?" the old man said. "I already paid an entrance-tax. I wasn't told about an exit-tax."

"Wasn't told about an exit-tax?" the second soldier said. "Heard that, mate? This guy didn't hear about the exit-tax?"

"Well, if you don't have an exit tax-form filled out," said the first, "then we're going to need to charge an additional exit... uh, exit-tax-form-not-filled-out fee.

"Fifty drevs," said the second.

"Fifty!" the man said. "That's absurd, I can't possibly—"

"Now it's seventy," said the second. "For wasting our time."

"Or..." said the first, stepping up close to the merchant and pressing his finger into his chest. "We can redo our cargo inspection. You'd be surprised what re-inspections turn up. Lots of time we find hidden drugs, or weapons, or Resurgence paraphilia, during these second searches, things the person... *forgot* were there. You know what the punishment is for smuggling, don't you?"

With a slam, the Justice Officer got out of her truck and marched forward. Sylvaine held her breath.

"Belona!" the first soldier said, with some shock.

"Private Vasquez," the woman apparently named Belona said. "You will use proper titles."

"Apologies, Justice Officer," he said, as the second soldier saluted, nudging Vasquez to do the same. Sylvaine was surprised to see their deference. To her it was clear the woman's rage was false. From the subtle tremors in her voice, the slight twitchiness to her movements. Perhaps the darkness assisted her, humans seemed terrible at managing anything at night.

"What is the meaning of this delay?" Belona asked.

"Me and Private Tezel were just... I mean," Vasquez mumbled.

"No delay, none at all," Tezel said. He gestured threateningly towards the merchant. "Go on, we said you were clear. Move it!"

The merchant did not hesitate. He jumped back into his caravan-truck and drove down the winding road and into the shadows beyond.

"You're... traveling?" Vasquez asked.

"Transporting a prisoner," Belona said.

"Ah," Tezel said. "Then we'll get your papers sorted quick and—"

"Truly?!" Belona said, with false but loud fury.

"Well, it's policy," Tezel explained in a confused tone. "We have to double-check all paperwork to make sure there's been no errors. Regulations straight from Drevstad, you co-signed them, no exceptions."

The woman was silent for a long moment. What would she do if she couldn't bluff her way through, Sylvaine wondered. Would they be back in their cells, or would the guards opt for a nighttime execution?

"Shit," Marcel mumbled to himself, hand on the door's handle. Sylvaine could hear it shake, but where did he think he would run to if things went south? And how in Inferno could she run in shackles?

"You have already wasted my time trying to threaten a bribe from that innocent man," Belona snarled with a burning rage that nearly convinced Sylvaine. "And now I am to understand that I will be kept even longer? I will be sure to discuss these matters with Commandant Lechslov when I return. Everything I saw tonight, detail by detail."

"But... I didn't mean... the policy clearly states that..."

"I'm sure your paperwork is clear, Justice Officer," Vasquez said hastily, pushing his guardsmate back. "My friend, he's just a stickler. An idiot really. Go on through! By the Imperator's grace, we will await your return with eagerness!"

Belona grunted and stomped back into the truck. They drove off without ceremony, silent, out of Holtag. Down the slight hill the truck puttered, into the wilds of the Wastes. Darkened scarwood trees and fields of brambles passed behind the truck. A soot-sparrow whistled out its birdsong, unusually early, and a clutter of needlecats scampered into tin-leaved bushes. Sylvaine glanced out the tear in the canvas to see a moon-brightened landscape of dusted ruins and clustered palewheet farms which looked three bad hours away from complete destitution. She twisted her ears for the sounds of autocars or motorbikes, the sounds of alarm, but no, they were not being followed. As the distance grew Holtag started to seem little more than a pile of rubbish on a hill, and the disorganized Principate military base that sat beside it looked no better.

As the two middens finally disappeared behind a hillside bend, Marcel started to chuckle. Then laugh.

"Demiurge-be-damned," he said. "That actually worked."

Belona was not quite so cheerful.

"Disgraceful... Shaking that man down for a bribe...." Sylvaine heard her whisper. Belona suddenly punched the dashboard of the truck. "And it is their duty to make sure everyone, *everyone!* Presents their papers! No! Exceptions!"

*To say that the true nature of the Imperial line is a divisive subject, is to say a spidertank could damage a drawing room rug. It's accurate but undersells the severity of the matter immensely. The shattered world we live in now is a direct result of these disagreements, and having the improper opinion is liable to have one ostracized, if not summarily executed. Luckily, as a member of the Engineer's Guild, I am sufficiently nonpartisan to give an objective recounting on the facts of this matter.*

*The line of the Imperator stands alone amongst rulers of men for many reasons, such as its ties to the Church of the Ascended and the massive breadth of the Imperium it once ruled. But of greatest importance is its longevity. The last universally agreed Imperator, Beghart Diedrev, was a direct descendant of Anselm Diedrev born a thousand years prior. Such unbroken lines are completely unknown by, say, the Kings of El'Helmaud, who rarely last more than a generation or two before some palace intrigue switches up bloodlines. Of course, this means the authority to rule Æthmach is tied intrinsically to the lineage of the Diedrevs. Even the Regency Republic, though fundamentally democratic in nature, was forced to ground its authority as an interregnum body between the last Diedrev and some hypothetical future Imperator. This was, at the time, merely a fiction created to earn the support of Kaimark and other lost provinces in the wake of the fall of the Imperium. Everyone knew that the last of the imperial bloodline died on the Torish battlefields of the Malva Wars.*

*This strategic mythmaking would end up being a central ingredient to the fall of the Regency Republic, after the ascendancy of General Franz Voigt, or has he started calling himself, Franz Diedrev. The founding of the Principate itself was based on this claim, that Voigt was in fact Diedrev. He had the look of the Diedrev and their imperious nature, as well as success in battle and the support of a growing discontent among conservative branches of the Republic, all vital pillars of his coup. His claim lies in documents supposedly kept by the Malva Thalassocracy, following the lineage of a lost son of Beghart, who indeed did disappear around his father's death, and was presumed to have followed his lineage into the grave. Of course, such documents can be faked, and therein lies the debate that has torn up our world, and even divided the priesthood of the Ascended, not that they ever needed more excuses to bicker about. The Principate claims the linage pure, the UCCR claims it false, (though some Resurgence scholars have argued it does not matter either way.) Many in the Resurgence have even speculated on the parentage of post-Franz Imperators, claiming that the man was a homosexual (possible, but this had not prevented many of his similarly-oriented Imperators from siring offspring) and that the current Imperator of the Principate is a mere puppet.*

*As for the truth of the matter, I cannot say for certain. But it is a reminder of the intellectual freedom of the Guild that this city of Icaria is one of the few places in the world where such debates can happen with words and pen, and not blade and bullet. Though, I would advise some of my more impish colleagues not to torment visiting partisan engineers, as tempers may burn brighter than one realizes, and none of us wish to bring the fires of war to our fair streets.*

*—"Fictions of Power" By Batar Axelrod.*

# Chapter 6

They drove throughout the night and into the morning, putting as many kiloms between themselves and Holtag as possible. It was slow going—it was always slow going in the Wastes. Roads were often more theory than reality, paths cut through brush and bramble, or merely a series of rutted tracks over long, empty plains. The dark didn't help, they could only be sure of the road if it was within the limited gaze of the 'truck's headlamps. Despite this, the imperial woman drove with a determined alacrity, stopping only after dawn rose over the near hills, to pick up water from a well and allow the others time to stretch and empty their bladders.

Marcel took the opportunity to shed the horrid mazarine cotton and replace it with something less miserably imperial. His simple get up of a weather-beaten coat, a simple brass-buttoned undervest, and denim pants suited him better than any uppity uniform. That was the nice thing about the Resurgence, aside from the occasional military parade, one's clothes didn't much matter for the average soldier. It was a sign of his Confederacy's humility. It also didn't hurt that inconspicuous civilian garb allowed one to slip back amongst the common folk should some ambush or assassination attempt fall through, as Alba had been keen to teach him.

"Grhrhrhrhr!" shouted Felik through his bindings.

"Perhaps he must relieve himself," Kayip said, sitting down in the middle of the truck for meditation. His hand was gripped tight upon his Cracked Disc, an azure rune-marked piece of ancient metal. Marcel had seen plenty such artifacts like it in museums or churches, but it was rare to see someone handle the old trinket with such genuine devotion. He had a sudden urge to read up on some recent textbook to figure out what the scholarly consensus was on where such objects came from, though he suspected the answers would be some academic jargon-veiled version of *who fucking knows?* He could ask Kayip, but the man would probably just say it was left over from the mythical Ascended, before they had re-joined with the Demiurge in some *blahblahblah* celestial rapture *yatata.*

"Hey Sylvaine, want to help me with the prisoner?" Marcel asked. The woman was long unchained, they had barely made it throwing distance from Holtag before she vehemently demanded to be released. Currently she was wearing her ætherglove. Normally one wore clothing and did other things as well, but Sylvaine was doing nothing but very actively wearing the glove, holding it, touching it, inspecting every minute pipe and mechanism.

"Sylvaine?"

"Hmm?" the woman said. "Did you say something?"

"Never mind," Marcel muttered, walking over and grabbing Felik by the scruff.

He led the raider punk over to a weepwood tree, its branches bent, sap leaking from cankers in its bark that resembled elongated eyes. Everything in the Wastes seemed strange and vaguely diseased. Something to do with the Calamity, or the oozing sangleum deposits it left behind.

Marcel helped Felik pull down his zipper and loosened his chains just enough for the man to be able to work his own worm out. As the raider whizzed, Marcel glanced around. It was strange to think that the blasted landscape around him had, a century ago, been the very beating heart of civilization, dense cities connected by networks of railtracks and paved asphalt. Remnants of the past sat around, rusted trains overgrown with shardvines, hills covered in empty brick husks, and massive upways, great roads build on sprawling bridges of concrete, now stood cracked and half-collapsed. Their naked supports seemed to him like windowless spires, or featureless giants, standing side by side along the width of the valley. The nearer years after the Calamity were visible as well, both in ruin and growth. In the chaparral and shrubs, of odd browns and bright reds, in the newly born streams, which trickled down cracks torn in the earth. In the caws of the mutated skragger birds that flew above, or the bellows of taur herds corralled at a wary distance some kiloms off. Nearby sat the remains of some motorgun nest, the weapon itself torn to pieces by time and eager scrappers, graffiti written on a nearby bunker wall, itself so aged that its snarky message had faded into illegibility.

All the while the raider kept peeing. Marcel half-wished he'd re-taken up his smoking habit back from his university days, just so he would have something to do.

"Grhmmhrhr..." Felik said.

"Okay, okay," Marcel said, helping the man zip himself up.

'Ghhrrmrhrhrhr!" Felik said, louder.

"Pardon?"

"GHRHRHMMRHR!" Felik gestured as best and violently as he could towards his gag.

"Fine," Marcel said, untying the tight, stained rag. "But if you shout too loud, I'll put a bullet through your head."

"Rusted pus and troglyn's scrotum," Felik said, spitting. "That was foul. What was that taur-fucking, shitbrained, stiffland bitch-hog using this rag for?"

"Ah yes," Marcel said, "the exact urbane witticisms I was expecting from you."

"You sit with that scumrag in your mouth for eight hours and see what ya spit out!"

"Here," Marcel offered his canteen. The raider grabbed it clumsily and greedily, drinking down what he could. Beyond him was the target of his curses, that Principate officer. She had barely spoken a word on their drive so far and was currently using some jury-rigged pump and filter device to suck up what potable water she could from an old, cracked well.

Felik finished his drink and caught Marcel's gaze.

"You don't know that bitch, do ya?" he asked.

"Recently introduced," Marcel said.

"She's crazy," Felik said. "Absolute bat-shit insane. Wants to find people to blame for her bitch-rage. Ya know, I'm just a scrap merchant, caught up in all of this, but I'm sure she's spat some crazy stories—"

"Felik," Marcel interrupted. "I know you're a raider and slaver. From the Taur Maw gang. Met with representatives of Lazacorp eight, no nine days ago. We've been tracking you for the better part of a week."

The man was silent, thinking. He smiled. "Worth a shot, eh?"

Marcel shrugged.

"Listen, you're a Resurgence guy, right?"

Marcel shook his head. "What makes you say that?"

"Your pistol." The raider gestured. "A Frasco six-shooter. Issued by the U-double-CR."

"Maybe I stole it off a corpse," Marcel said. "Or bought it."

Felik Rector shook his head. "No mate, because you would have tossed it by now. Things a piece of skragger shit, not worth the iron ya could scrap from it."

"It's not!" Marcel said with indignance. "It's a simple, effective weapon representing the utilitarian and egalitarian values of—"

Felik burst into laughter, a guttural and hacking sound. "Yeah, you're a Resurgence boy all right."

Marcel bit his lip, disappointed by how easily he had been goaded. "All right, so what if I am?"

"It ain't a bad thing, mate," Felik said, leaning back on the weepwood tree. "But I know Principate shiteaters hate Resurgence men, and Resurgence men, by the Demiurge's ballsack, they fucking hate the Principate. What do ya think that woman's going to do when she figures this out?"

Marcel shrugged. "If the pistol gave it away to you, I'm sure she's figured it out."

"Then you have to strike first," Felik said. "Listen, we're on the same side here. Raiders and the Resurgence, we both hate the Principate."

"We are not... remotely on the same side," Marcel said.

"We both oppose tyranny; we both want to keep the Imperator off our back. We just want to live our lives in peace, self-sufficient and free."

"Free? Peace?" Marcel stammered. "You raid towns and rob traders and deal in slaves! You're scum."

"Stifflander words," Felik said, leaning forwards and gesturing vaguely to the horizon. "Ya don't know what it's like out here, in the Wastes. It harsh, mate, brutal. Ain't enough taur meat, ain't enough water, and certainly ain't enough damned æther-oil. Yet we live by our own rules, we live free. Of course, freedom costs something, don't it? So, we take some of the weak, some of those who suckle off the Principate, or, let's face it, would die on their own out here, give 'em housing, have them tend our herds, or farm our crops. It's the only way."

Marcel gave a hollow laugh. "Honestly, a pitiful argument. You know how I know there's other ways? Because I lived them for twenty-plus years. You're scoundrels and petty tyrant brutes. And if you weren't the only one on hand who knew where Lazarus Roache was, I'd place my 'skragger shit pistol' on your forehead and pull this trigger." That last part was mostly a lie. As much as he hated the raider's guts, Marcel was not all that keen on killing. Excepting the thousands killed by the sangleum gas he had released during the Battle Under Huile, Marcel had only ever killed one man by his own hand, and even now the memory made him nauseous.

Felik sneered. "Oh, you think you're all proper and noble, don't you? I know the UCCR, seen the cities that fly their banner, either direct or by alliance. Inferno, I've done plenty of business in those Border States who claim to love the Phoenix, and never once been bothered none. Everywhere's the same, everywhere the weak work and the strong profit. It's how mankind is, mate. Maybe where you come from, ya don't call them slaves. Maybe ya give them nice titles, call them workers, comrades even, sing nice things about them in your anthems. Oh, they ain't *slaves*, they can choose, they got freedom, the freedom to work or the freedom to starve. It's all the same, boy, just out here we ain't got no stiffland pretensions."

Marcel clenched his fist, willing himself not to punch out the idiot. The raider didn't know what he was talking about, just a bunch of excuses to make the world seem as vile as his own heart. Bitter memories of Huile tried to sneak into Marcel's mind. How the city allowed slaughter and slavery of its mutant workers. But that had been an aberration, a corruption, made by one Lazarus Roache. He had poisoned the minds of Resurgence officials using slickdust, had hired raider muscle to keep his secrets from the populace. It was a horror to be avenged, an indignity on the name of the United Confederacy, one that would be purged once Lazarus was brought to justice.

A sound in the brush made them both near jump. Marcel pulled out his pistol and aimed. After a long moment, a bulky tortoise stepped out from the chapparal. Its shell shined like tin, and its neck was long and pustuled. It stopped to stare at the two a moment, chewing something crunchy, before turning and continuing on its way.

Marcel shook his head and holstered his gun. Idiot raider had him on edge.

"Listen," Felik said. "I think we got a bit off-track, what with our philosophizing and all that. My point being, ya ain't got reasons to trust this imperial bitch. You and me, we can make ourselves a deal, something mutual benefitting."

The bitterest thing about the man's words was the grain of truth. Marcel *had* been wondering if they should get rid of the imperial woman, one way or another. It seemed an insult to the memory of his late squadmates to work with someone who served the wretched boots of the Principate. But hearing it from this thimble of taur piss, it reminded him how childish such thoughts were. She was just some petty officer of a nowhere town, not the Imperator themself. He had a mission here; he couldn't let his own pride and anger get in the way.

"It's not about trust," Marcel finally said. "The woman helped us out of Holtag, and as long as she keeps being useful, we won't dishonor ourselves with treachery. Don't get me wrong, she tries anything, she's gone, but I'm not overly worried. Anyways, there's one of her, one of *you*, but three of us, and we're united in cause and thought."

Sylvaine finally wandered over from the truck.

"So," she said gesturing over to the distant Belona. "What, uh what are we going to do about her?"

"How do you mean?" Marcel asked.

"She's Principate, right?" Sylvaine said. "I know what you've done with Principate soldiers."

"Sylvaine," Marcel hissed. "We're not going to just kill her!"

"You should," Felik interjected.

"I didn't say kill," Sylvaine said. "Just... I don't know, leave her somewhere. She can take care of herself."

Kayip appeared suddenly. Marcel almost swore, it was always surprising how silently the large man could move.

"We will be peaceful with this Belona," Kayip said. "I make no claims that she is pleasant, or even a good person, but she is aligned with our aims, has assisted us, and will continue to assist us. In this manner, I believe she can be trusted."

"Okay, but you two weren't tossed in an excessive jumble of chains and bindings and thrown in the back of her truck."

"I think the beastwoman has a point," Felik cut in.

"I wasn't talking to you."

"Your rage is understandable," said Kayip. "But the Chronicles of the Ascended tell us to withhold true judgement until the day the skeins of our mortal understanding are untangled by the graceful finger of the Demiurge."

"Well, I don't see any celestial fingers descending from the clouds." Sylvaine gestured dramatically to the sky. "So, I think I might start making my own earthly decisions…"

The two bickered softly, Felik attempting and failing to interject. Marcel turned to study the distant Principate woman, apparently named Belona. That name seemed oddly familiar, but he couldn't place it. As her filter did its work, Belona stared out at the roads they had come down from, with a wary but steel-hardened gaze. Then suddenly she pulled a knife out, from some hidden place. She undid her bun, her long curly hair flowing down to her shoulders. He could see, in the early morning's light, that her hair was not oil black, as he had thought, but in fact a very deep brown, like that of a tree which had weathered more than its share of sun and smoke.

With a sudden movement, Belona lifted the knife and started to hack at her hair, curls falling like dead leaves. It took a solid minute, but when she was finished her hair reached only to the back of her neck, jagged and uneven. She bent down to pick up the dust-covered clipping, then lifted them above her head. The wind took the hair, sending them flying up and off, away into the Wastes.

A smile, long and strangely genuine, stretched itself over the woman's face.

# CHAPTER 7

They spent the rest of the day on the road, as much as there was one. Belona and Kayip seemed to know where they were heading, and took shifts, as did Marcel. Sylvaine had never learned to drive so she stayed in the back, sitting and thinking and watching the Wastes roll past. Trees, and ruins, and taur herds and general nothing. Once she thought she saw a troll in the distance, a great figure of misshapen stone stumbling slow on the horizon, but that might have just been a trick of the sun. They made better speed than they had the night before, but not by much. The truck was designed for off-road travel, but the cracked Waste landscape presented a hearty challenge. Every twenty minutes or so they had to stop, get out, climb a rock or ruin, and scout out the next kilom, lest their truck disappear into a hidden ravine or mud pit.

There wasn't much talk, the imperial hadn't shared even a word with them besides the occasional rudely barked direction. Not that the rest of them were chatty. They were all too tired for one, had shared a couple hours of sleep between them the night before. Marcel dozed on the floor of the truck for a good part of the afternoon, and Belona took a nap at some point after, sitting up perfectly straight in her seat. Sylvaine wouldn't have believed the woman was sleeping if not for her soft snores. Sylvaine walked past to grab a ration bar. The imperial's eyes opened suddenly, the rest of her silently still as she stared at Sylvaine. She hated that stare, so full of distrust and contempt. Sylvaine grabbed her food and stepped away. The imperial shut her eyes, and within moments was snoring again.

Sylvaine chewed the bar slowly, there wasn't much else to do to kill time. She'd be happy with a pulp, Marcel had brought one or two, but she knew if she tried to read on these winding paths her meal would soon end up as vomit on the floor. Instead, she pulled out some scrap from her bag.

With her gloved hand on the pieces of metal, she closed her eyes and sucked in her breath. It was an easy task, just turn this junk into... a piston, or a cog, or something even simpler, like a smooth bar of metal. Basic introductory æthermantics. She had done such dozens of times, hundreds. And yet, now she was afraid to try. Her powers had become more erratic and wilder since coming out to the Wastes. Perhaps it had to do with the Wastes themselves, the oozing sangleum and the broken ætherlines that sat underneath the soil. But she suspected it was not just that alone. She had gotten her powers from Lazarus Roache, from his horrible wonderdrug, his Slickdust. This drug had been a chain, a way for him to control her, quite literally, but without it... how long would her powers stay, how long would she remain an engineer? Supposedly the tycoon's final injection of the drug had ignited her Knack permanently, but to believe that would be to take the words of a serial fraudster as honest truth. She hoped she was no longer *that* foolish.

Sylvaine sighed and put away the scrap. It would be nice to talk to Kayip. The man was not always great with words, but he was one of the few people she had met who would actually listen to her, no matter how long her rants and ramblings became. But the man was asleep, and it was best to let sleeping monks lie.

"Ya know he's a liar, right?" Felik said, noticing her gaze.

"Hmm," Sylvaine said.

"Not a monk, or a priest, or..."

"An iterant hieromonk, I think he called himself" Sylvaine said. "Like some sort of priest who lived in a monastery, but now wanders around. I don't know, I don't really care."

"It's a lie," Felik said. "Oh Kayip, we know Kayip out in the wastes. Ya think that imperial bitch is crazy? He's absolutely taur-fucking insane. Ya have no idea what he's done, Inferno, I don't even know all of it. A violent murderer he is, just puts that whole pious monk act. I mean, what sort of war monk, or waste priest or whatever can't even cast miracles? That's the whole point of the Church, ain't it? To use them old artifacts, like that disc and such, to do magic."

"Æthermantics," Sylvaine corrected, "just of a different sort than engineers do."

"Right, whatever. Point is, he can't do it. So, let's put some logic there, it must be that he's lying. Lying to ya, and your friend there, the whole time."

"Is this your plan, to try turn us against one another?" Sylvaine asked.

"Listen, I can tell you're a stifflander."

"Because I'm a ferral?" Sylvaine asked.

Felik shook his head. "No, I've seen ferrals who have taken to the Wastes. Nah, it's the way you talk, and hold yourself. A little haughty, a little naïve. I'm saying you miss things that people out here don't miss."

"So, you're saying that Kayip doesn't even believe in the Demiurge," Sylvaine said. "That his whole rambling on about the Chronicles of the Ascended and the Decalogues and all that are an act?"

"Precisely!"

"Hmm..." she stared at the sleeping man. Everyone had their secrets, a Kayip had more than a few. And yet had any of them mattered? Clearly the man had seen things he'd rather not speak, hard not to out here in the Wastes. Yet despite whatever past he had had, he had always been kind to her. She might not know every line of the schematics of his mind, but she understood perfectly how the monk ticked. That seemed more than enough to say she knew that man.

"A secret duplicitous atheist?" she mused. "Well, I wish you were right, Felik. I like the man, but his inane piety is one of his most fatuous qualities."

* * *

A little after sundown they finally made camp. They had driven up a hill, past the remains of crumbling opulence to stop in front of a pre-Calamity manor. A *dusthome*, a friend of Sylvaine had once called them, and the name was apt for there was little else in its crumbling walls but dust. The only decoration was a torn portrait of a corpulent child which had fallen to the floor. Anything of value had been stolen, and not just the jewels and rugs and finery. The pipes had been torn from walls, decorative faux-marble columns smashed, and the ornate furniture burned in haphazard firepits dug into the ground. Still, the remaining walls and half of a roof provided some shelter, and a good defensive position were it to come to that.

Kayip put up the tents while Sylvaine set up the ætheric heater the imperial had brought. She took a moment to study the monk as he worked. What stories had he not told her, of his travels in the wastes. Despite their time together, she really did know little of his past. He caught her gaze, and she glanced away, annoyed that the raider's words had gotten to her. Kayip was Kayip, that's all that mattered.

Marcel, for his part, was on make-sure-Felik-doesn't-try-anything duty. Belona took up the job of going room to room with a scattergun, to confirm that they were, in fact, alone.

"Clear," she said as she returned. Then the woman just stood there a minute, gun in hand. Sylvaine found it rather unnerving, her calculating stare, finger near trigger, as if she were still deciding whether she's made the right decision joining them, or if she should try and get the jump.

Finally, she put the weapon onto the ground.

"I think it's time we formally introduce ourselves," she said. "I know the aliases you gave, but this this is the sort of mission where we'd need to dispense with such obvious lies. I'll be first. I am Justice Officer Belona—"

"First names only!" Kayip interjected. "That is the rule out here. There is a lot of bad blood in these Wastes. I do not know all our pasts. It may be better that we keep things impersonal, so that we do not bicker amongst ourselves when trying to hunt our real enemy."

Sylvaine glanced sideways at Marcel. This was certainly for his safety. If the imperial discovered his past, there was no predicting what sort of mad vengeance she might unleash.

Marcel nodded. "Yeah, first names, that's all we've gone by so far," he lied.

Belona stared at the man, and then the monk. After a few tense moments, she nodded as well.

"Very well. Just Belona," she said. "Justice Officer. I'm here to bring Lazarus Roache to his overly delayed execution. I am under the impression you share my aim."

"Marcel, bounty hunter," Marcel said, a title Sylvaine had never heard the man claim. He leaned back on a fallen column with an exaggerate ease. "In the past I fought as a... mercenary. Also did a stint as a private investigator. Seen quite a few things, is what I'm saying."

"Mercenary... that's a nice way of saying you're a past Resurgence rat, right? I'll assume you know how to sharpshoot and plant bombs. I know it must be unusual to be hunting after a fellow wretch instead of gnawing at the ankles of civilization, but I'm sure you can be useful."

"Better to be a rat than the Imperator's personal bootlicker!" Marcel snarled, standing suddenly.

"Good, you have fight in you." Belona turned to Sylvaine. "You are?"

"Sylvaine."

"A cultured name," Belona said, as if it were a great surprise. "Well, if need be, I know your kind can rip a man's face off with one claw swing."

"I will do no such thing!" Sylvaine shouted. "I am an engineer! Trained in Guild's Academy in Icaria. Maybe you've heard of it?"

Belona stared at her ætherglove with some amusement, it was clear she did not believe a word. "What madness has grabbed the Guild in these last few years. Soon they will have troglyns and palebears applying."

"We must remain civil," Kayip said, letting a hint of irritation into his words. "We have just met, and there is a long journey ahead of us."

"Agreed," said Belona, finally sitting down.

"I'm Felik," Felik said. "And—"

"We know who you are," Marcel said. "We don't need your life story, Rector, just tell us where Roache is."

"I have already extracted that intel," Belona said, pulling out a map from her bag. She placed it on the ground between them and pointed to a faded symbol circled in fresh ink. "Narida Heights, several days drive northwest. We have long suspected it was a haven for slavers and raider gangs, but unfortunately Holtag's military leader took a quite lax attitude towards such evils. According to our good friend here..." Felik had been sneering but cast his gaze down when Belona turned. "...This is where Roache had holed up."

"Is it well-defended?" Marcel asked, sitting down.

"I would not call it a fortress," Belona said with a wave of her wrist, "but for a squad of four, yes it would be impossible to take. We could reasonably expect to face several dozen raiders and armed Lazacorp guards, maybe more. I very much doubt we are the only ones who have ever tried to kill Roache, security will be heavy. Now it may be possible to infiltrate it through an underway passage, this whole region is perforated with old underrail tunnels, forgotten sewerways, and smugglers' passages.

We would have to strike at night, go in, kill the man, and get out. Even then there is a high probably of fatalities or complete failure. I trust you are comfortable with this."

The heater buzzed and grumbled, as Marcel mused. In a distant hall Sylvaine heard the flap of some scavenger's wings.

"Seems... a rather foolhardy plan," Marcel said, leaning back, arms crossed.

"If you do not have the guts for it, we can make do with three," Belona said.

"I've done foolhardier," Marcel said, sitting back up straight. "If that's where he is, that's what we must do."

"Let's make sure we don't get ourselves killed," Sylvaine said. "We're not all soldiers, we didn't all make oaths to die for some abstract cause."

"Oaths, what oaths?" Marcel asked.

"Don't soldiers have to take an oath?" Sylvaine said. "Or that might have just been in a pulp I read, my point is—"

"*We* took an oath." Belona said, with a pat of her fist to her heart. "To fight for the Imperator to our last breath, and to water the fields of the Principate with our blood. Perhaps cowards need no oaths."

"Hey, I didn't say there were no oaths," Marcel cut it. "I mean, we just didn't take ridiculous suicidal oaths declaring that our spirits as eternal lickspittle to his imperial highness. No, we took oaths of liberty! To fight for the United Confederacy, to fight for our fellow citizens, until all men and woman could join together and celebrate a free—"

"Forget! About! The oaths!" Sylvaine said. "My point is, we can be smart about this. If this raiders' den, or whatever it is, is out in the middle of nowhere, it must have its own æthericity generator. If that's in the basement, we might be able to overload it, or even blow it up. Maybe we can wait 'till Roache leaves, ambush him then. Let's just not rush things and get ourselves killed."

"Ya know," Felik said, scratching his beard. "You guys are driving an awfully long way to simply kill a man. Ya could have this all done in two nights."

The four of them stared at the raider, who was wearing a wry smile.

"What is your meaning?" Kayip asked.

"I mean, ya have a chance to kill this Roache guy much quicker and easier." Felik gestured for the map. Marcel pulled it over and the raider pointed to a canyon at its edge.

"Here." Felik pointed. "The tycoon is hosting a meeting the night after next. Some trade deal, slaves I think, with a couple of raider gangs, Trog-Skinners, Crimson Eyes, Steel Claws. It's in an open gulch, lots of high places to put up a sniper. You get a good shot; it could be in and out before they even know you're there."

Marcel turned to Belona. "I thought you said you extracted all the intel."

The Imperial glowered. "You made no mention of this."

"What, when ya had a knife to my throat? Yeah, forgive me for forgetting details. All ya asked was where the man was, and I told you."

"Then why are you telling us now?" Sylvaine asked.

"A deal." Felik grinned. "Ya want to kill Roache. I help you get to that man, ya let me free."

"It would be an abdication of my duties as a Justice Officer to let you free."

"You've already did plenty of abdicating today," said Felik. "Inferno, are ya going to rearrest these three as well? Who's more important, me or Roache?"

Belona paused and thought. In the corner of the room, a small rodent started rustling through its nest. "If you can get us Roache," she nodded, "then I will consider giving you a head start."

"That's all I ask," Felik said.

"There is an issue I see," Kayip cut in. He tapped a line drawn in dark ink over the faded map. "The Great Ravine here. The only crossing is in Bridgetown. That is all the way over here, there is no chance we could make it in time."

"Ah, not the only passing," Felik said, pointing down to where the apparently recently-form ravine met with some hills. "Here. Scrap-Thief's Crossing. An old railway turned bridge."

Belona laughed. "I see your game. That bridge and the hills around it are raider territory. You seek to lead us into ambush."

"No," Felik said. "That's not... listen, I ain't saying its safe, only that its safer than trying to assault Narida Heights with two retired soldiers, a ferral, and a madman. Trust me, I know it can be a treacherous pass, but that's only when its actually crawling with raiders. I know the schedules; they'll already be off heading towards Roache's meeting. And if worse comes to worse, they're my pals, I can sweet talk us past, no issue."

"It could work," Marcel said, scratching his metal leg.

"Do not place your life in a raider's hand," Belona scolded. "I know these folk, they deserve no trust. And he has lied again, that is not the only path that will work." She slammed her finger towards a valley right at the bottom edge of the scribbled-in ravine. *Opus's Glory* was written on it.

"That charnel-field..." Felik said, suddenly pale in the face. "Are you mad?"

"Who's Opus?" Sylvaine asked.

"A great Imperator from ages past who..." Belona shook her head. "It's an ancient name. Point is, there was a great battle there, during the Severing War. A battle that never ended."

Marcel leaned on his elbow. "How does... what?"

"A necromantic aura hangs dark and dreary upon that accursed vale," Kayip said.

"So... skeletons?" Marcel said. "You're saying that we can't go through this pass because there's a bunch of skeletons with guns?"

"Yes! Exactly!" Felik gestured.

"No," Belona scoffed. "I've sent scouts there. Their ammo is long used up. We're talking about skeletons with bayonets."

"That's... not a thing." Marcel stared at the imperial, as if trying to scry out the punchline of some poorly translated joke. "I mean I've read about some spilled æther causing weird post-mortem effects on corpses, but a whole haunted battlefield?"

"Well, not haunted." Sylvaine explained. "There has to be a source of ætheric pollution, like sangleum if we were talking about unstable æther. This would have to have been caused by Morbis æther, which is not all too common, but considering what the Calamity dug up, it's certainly not impossible for some mass of it to coincide with a battlefield."

"It's insane is what it is!" Felik said. "You guys really do have a death wish."

"I would give us above fifty-out-of-a-hundred at surviving the crossing," Belona said. "Better than I'd give any other option. Unless you are so taken by fear."

"I'm in." Marcel nodded.

A clanging suddenly echoed from down the hall. Kayip jumped up. He grabbed his bracelet and whispered a prayer. The bracelet suddenly moved, shifting, transforming through arcane and forgotten mechanisms.

It elongated in his hand and sharpened quick, into a thin, single-bladed azure sword.

Sylvaine caught Belona's gaze, which was full of shock. Kayip had mentioned he had been her prisoner before, no doubt she now finally understood how the man had escaped.

The monk snuck forward, towards the sounds.

"I thought you scouted this place out," Marcel said to Belona, as he took out his pistol. She shushed him, scattergun at the ready. Sylvaine listened closed, and when Belona wasn't looking, sniffed the air. Old carrion cut through the musk of the dusthome, but little else was distinct.

A cry from the far room. Kayip's. Sylvaine dashed forward. A skragger flew out past her. She found Kayip in what had probably been a kitchen at some point, the monk swinging his blade wildly at another of the bent, reptilian birds. Beneath them was a long-desiccated corpse of a mutant man. His horns were cracked, his face ripped apart by scavengers, his crimson torso was torn round the stomach, to reveal dried viscera spread across his body.

"Is he... from Huile?" Marcel whispered to Sylvaine, as Kayip chased the skragger out of the ruins.

Sylvaine shook her head. "No, Desct and all of them were all human at one point, flesh mutants. This is a womb mutant, born a mutant. Look, his horns are symmetrical, his skin is, or was, consistent, not patchy. No strange growths or tumors, no mechanical-like aberrations," She felt like she was reading off a textbook, and realized she was, from some near-forgotten class in the corner of her memory. It was easier to disassociate, just a bit, to intellectualize, in situations like this.

"Right," Marcel said. "Yeah, obviously. I just... yeah."

Kayip approached the desiccated body and kneeled. He seemed to be praying.

"A heck of a thing to miss," Marcel said to Belona.

"I didn't miss the corpse," Belona said. "Corpses are everywhere in the Wastes, if we stop to gawk at each deformed..." she paused, squinting, then stepped forward. "No, I did miss this."

She pointed to a small wooden figurine placed behind the head of the mutant. It was of a man, tall, and muscled, and flayed. Great ribbons of skin rolled down from the figures back, rolling round to form the statuette's base. It wore a grimace of pain, but also something else, arrogance, perhaps, and contempt. It was only a twenty or so centimetres tall, and yet there was something immensely threatening about the figure, as if it could, at any moment, step off its stand, dragging its wood-carved skin, eager to inflict its excoriation upon others. It was so unnerving that Sylvaine almost missed the rune behind it, a symbol of an eye, drawn in blood. She knew the blood must have been from the victim, but unlike the withered corpse, this blood looked vibrant and wet.

"Damn raiders," Belona said. "They worship all sorts of foul things."

Kayip was mumbling something. Sylvaine bent down. She could smell his tears before she saw them, dripping down from both his good eye and from his mask.

"I'm sorry," he whispered. "I'm sorry."

"Did you know him?" Sylvaine asked, but knew it was a ridiculous question. The corpse was too torn to be possibly recognizable.

Kayip shook his head. "It does not matter. It is the same either way. I am sorry."

Sylvaine looked towards Marcel and Belona, who seemed equally baffled. Sylvaine had no sense what brought on this grief, Kayip had already seen much death, what was another body? Of a stranger, no less? There truly were things she did not understand about the man, perhaps deeper things than she had before realized. What questions had he never answered, what questions had she not even known to ask?

Felik glanced at her with a smug nod, but she would not give him the dignity of acknowledgement.

"He needs to be buried," Kayip said, his words pained. "An honorable burial. To be re-united with the Demiurge."

"Okay, Kayip I'll..." Sylvaine stumbled for her words. "I'll find a shovel."

# Chapter 8

Dreams and memories. They were the teachers, the first teachers, when man was wild and untamed, blighting a land that wasn't theirs. They were the preceptors, the guides, when man first found that holy red liquid, seeping up from lesions in the earth. Oathblood. The remains of the Gods. The Gods who once were, the Gods who would be again. In its consumption, with its pain, through its rituals, Oathblood gifted those who sought them dreams and memories. Of the splendor that was, of the treachery that destroyed it, of the righteous devastation that must come.

Other men burned it. Defiled it in order to stabilize it, remove its righteous hate, then used the resulting æther-oil as fuel for their machines, mockeries of the divine mechanisms of the Truegods. And in doing so led themselves to a predictable end. To a chastisement in fire, to Calamity.

But dreams and memories, these were still pure. These were still the messages of the Gods. And in these Hieronymus Lealtad Namter wandered. *Dreams*, of a city of celestial beauty, crystal spires and cloud-bound angels. *Memories*, of a one-eyed prophet, Verus, whispering forgotten truths over sangleum fumes. *Dreams*, of a city of fire and rot, cherubs with dripping sinews and abattoirs that walked on legs of scabbed rust. *Memories*, of Verus stripping him, whipping him, cutting skin from flesh, revelations through pain. *Dreams*, of a figure both horrible and beautiful, flayed skin worn round like robes, floating in a void beyond life, beyond death, promising everything. *Memories*, of a betrayal impossible, of master turning against student, turning against Gods, of daggers and sabotage, of a refinery burning, of pacts broken. Madness, insanity. Namter's eye burned.

*Now.* A jolt of pain. Namter's hand flung up to his face, though he struggled to hold it down. Pain was good, pain was punishment, and punishment the only path. His eye was burning in glorious pain. No, not his eye, his socket, the space where his eye had been, where it had been carved out. There burned agony, true agony, but as his fingers reached his eyepatch, he stopped himself. He let the pain overtake him, blessed the pain, gave thanks for the hurt. He deserved it, all men deserved it, that is what he was taught, through visions and through Verus.

*Verus.* It had been a month, but the sorrow was still fresh. The man, the Prophet of the Wastes, the Awakener, Namter's mentor and teacher, had betrayed him, betrayed him and Roache and the whole of their Enterprise. He had destroyed the means for which they would have transformed the city of Huile into Tribute, vivifying sacrifices for a slumbering god. Verus had once gifted Namter purpose, a purpose beyond all the petty bickering of man, beyond the empty ambitions of the Principate and the Resurgence, beyond the Church and the Guild and all those fancy lies called civilization. But Verus had betrayed that purpose and had died for its betrayal. Namter could make no sense of it. Had the man's hatred of Lazarus Roache grown so great that he would throw everything away for a petty vendetta? Namter couldn't believe that, and yet could find no other explanation.

Even more mad, Verus had made common cause with that monk. Had allied with that incessant thorn in their boot, and the mutant slaves as well. Breaking the divine commandments that condemned the skinsick to use them as weapons was blasphemy enough, but to willingly work with a member of that church of lies? Verus had always despised the monk, hated him with a righteous anger, unless that too was an act. Such was Lazarus's theory, anyhow, that the monk had only survived so long because of Verus's secret interventions. Namter was not so sure, but if Lazarus was correct, then perhaps Kayip would no longer possess the ability to vex them. This was little comfort, there were larger issues than a mad warmonk. Issues so pressing that Namter had no choice but ignore the ache that pounded in his chest. It was his duty to hide his doubts, to bury the sorrow, to carry on with his divine mission, and all the drudgery and danger that came with it.

A groaning skid, momentum pushing Namter off balance. He opened his one original eye, his human eye. He was in the back of a transport 'truck, worn walls of bolted iron surrounding him, with only a single weak ætherlamp for light. There were nicer 'trucks in the caravan, but mortals deserved no comfort, and so Namter sat with the cargo. The cargo in this case were human, or rather, had once been human. Pumped so full of slickdust they had mutated into bulbus sacks of crimson flesh, immobile, twitching, oozing, incapable of anything more than pained moaning. These mutants were being transported to serve as Tribute. Yet, for reasons yet unknown, the 'truck had stopped. Had they reached their destination? It seemed hours too early, though Namter did sometimes lose time when enraptured by meditation and prayer.

There was shouting outside and a knock on the cargo door. Namter stepped over and lifted it up, the hot, dust-infected winds of the Wastes blowing in to greet him.

"Awakener," said Brother Valere. His hood was down, markings of eyes sitting in a ring around his short-cut brown hair, like a crown. Namter opened his mouth to correct his brother that he was a mere Watcher, but no, the man was correct. With Verus dead, Namter was both Watcher and Awakener, even as the second title felt unearned.

"Brother Valere, what is the matter?" Namter asked, stepping out and glancing around. They had stopped in a pass between two sharp hills, rocks and ruins dotting the ridges. An unnerving place to halt, even if all nearby raider gangs had long since pledged allegiance or obeisance to Lazacorp. The caravan itself was made up of eight large autotrucks, each filled with tribute and marked with the faded sunset logo of Narida Heights. Around the caravan were raiders, Skragbark Scoundrels, Fist-Biters, and Crimson Eyes, mostly, in their war-buggies and motorcycles. They were milling about uneasily.

"The bridge is down," Brother Valere said, playing idly with the orb of Oathblood that hung from a long chain upon his neck.

"Show me, Brother," Namter said.

* * *

He was led to the front of the caravan where there sat, in the declination between three hillocks, a massive gaping pit. An excavation site, from the time before mankind had been chastised. On the near side was a great crane, now rusted and bent, steel rope hanging down towards nothing, frayed. The road, or what remained of it, went over a massive bascule bridge, with the near side leaning unhelpfully skywards. Presumably the bridge had been built this way to allow the crane to move from one side of the pit to the other, a wasteful design from a decadent age. Unfortunately, that didn't explain why the bridge had been raised. It most certainly hadn't been when they had come over in the opposite direction.

There were three men there already. Two were raiders, of the Crimson Eye gang, a simple brute by the name of Gracus, lazily aiming his repeater-rifle at nothing, and an even simpler engineer named Har, who was currently wrist deep in a mess of machinery by the bridge's control booth. Brother Tacticus was the third man, half his blonde hair shaved off to reveal lines of carved runes, in the manner of the Truegods' tongue. He nodded as Namter and Valere approached, but did not greet them, did not call them Brother. Namter could see the suspicion in the man's gaze, a low-burning anger. He was not alone, there were many in the Brotherhood shaken by Verus's betrayal. More than a few had even whispered that perhaps Namter was keeping some truth hidden from them. These accusations pained Namter, and not in a holy way. It was not his ego, or even his honor that he mourned, but the sense of Brotherhood, of a united community bound by convictions. It was to be his duty to repair the damage Verus had wrought, but he was not sure he was up to the task.

"Looks to have been ripped apart by some scavenger," Brother Tacticus said, gesturing vaguely behind him. "Someone came in and stole the æther-circuits from the control box."

"Such theft is easy, why go to the bother of lifting up the bridge first?" Valere asked. "That reeks of sabotage."

"Indeed," Namter said, turning to Gracus. "Make sure everyone is armed and ready. Send some men out to scout the ridges."

"If they come, we can take 'em," Gracus said, despite having no knowledge of who 'they' might be.

Namter walked over to the engineer. Har rustled through wires and scratched his ass with his ætherglove. He noticed Namter and stood, knocking his head on the way up and cursing.

"Yeah, shit's as fucked as a ghulshrew in a stymph dove's nest," he grunted.

"What?"

"It's broken." Har's face was a shade of crimson, his skin hardened around his eyes and nose, resembling scales, almost. The effects of slickdust use, a lot of slickdust use. Inferno, even the man's Knack, his engineering ability, was thanks to the drug. Such untrained, slickdust-powered engineers were not as skilled as Guild-trained, nor as intelligent, nor as diligent or creative or useful. But they were cheap, and there was a certain loyalty fostered by complete addiction.

"I can see that its broken," Namter said. "I need you to fix it."

"Well, without the æther-circuits, this control box ain't doing nothing."

"What about the bridge?" Namter said. "Can't you just break the mechanism and force it down?"

"Oh," Har picked at a sore on his cheek. "Yeah, I can maybe do that. But then we won't be able to life it up again."

"Why would we ever need to..." Namter shook his head. "Just do it, now."

"Of course, Mr. Namter, but uh, you see, uh, my powers, they haven't been real good lately, and I was thinking."

"Here, just take it," Namter said, pulling a vial of slickdust from his pocket. It was a strong dose, able to satisfy an addict for a week if they had the self-control to ration out their usage. Of course, Har pulled off the topper and snorted it up within seconds, coughing and hacking in his gluttony.

"Go, go!" Namter waved the man off.

As he waited for the engineer to do his work, Namter stepped over to inspect the pit. It was a truly prodigious hole. If he had to guess, it started life as a mine of some sort. Down below he could see why the mine had been expanded to such a prodigious size. Bits of azure ruins stuck out from the carved walls or sat on artificial ledges. Elegant arches and gleaming walls of white, somehow untouched by the dust of the Wastes. Ruins from a forgotten age, worshipped by the Church idiots as the lost homes of the Ascended. The rapacious Guild, on the other hand, eagerly looted those same ruins, desperate to uncover the technological secrets of past civilization. None of these fools truly understood what these strange ruins even were. They were a warning, a reminder of the fate of humanity, and the devastating rage of neglected Gods.

A scream echoed out from the top of the ridge. Namter turned to see a raider stumble and fall, a spear in his chest, a horned figure standing triumphant above him. The mutant wore a leather jacket, opened in the middle to reveal a massive scar that was visible even from the bottom of the hill. Another raider charged with bayonet to avenge his comrade, and the mutant pulled out a pistol, putting three bullets in the man's stomach. He shouted, and from the top of the hill charged more mutants, dozens of them, screaming with rage.

"Ambush! Ambush!" came the cries from the caravan, as the raiders began to fire.

"Clan Vapulus," Valere shouted. And indeed, it was, Namter recognized the bastards from their ostentatious chief alone. Bladescar, the dramatic bastard had taken to calling himself, a rat that'd been gnawing at the ankle of Lazacorp for the better part of seven years.

"Brother Tacticus, defend the engineer," Namter commanded, as he pulled out his pistol. The Brother grasped his orb of Oathblood, and then smashed it between his hands, glass slicing his palms, mixing the blood of man with the blood of Gods. Namter rushed forward with Valere, who crushed his own orb as he ran.

A line of raiders charged up the hill to meet the mutants' descent. An idiotic move likely brought on by either slickdust euphoria or withdrawal. They were cut down by the scrap-blades, spears, and bayonets of the mutants, but at least the attack slowed the mutants' assault long enough to allow the more level-headed raiders to take cover behind the 'trucks and motorcycles.

Screams and shrieks cut through the air. Namter fired off a few rounds, hitting one mutant in the head and another in the chest. Their garb was not unlike the raiders, taurhide stitched in the vague mockery of pre-Calamity fashions, though many seemed to wear their shirts open, man and woman alike, mimicking the style of their chieftain.

As for Bladescar, the young mutant lugged a great axe seemingly made from the sharpened door of an autocar. He rushed down to the one part of the line where the raiders had broken through, hewing a man in twain with a wild swing. Namter aimed his pistol and fired off at the chief's direction but hit only dirt.

A cry, a squad of mutants had noticed the assassination attempt and were charging down from the ruined husk of a shack towards Namter. Brother Valere stepped forward, whispering words of an ancient and blessed language. The nearest mutants shuddered at the sound, clutching tight their ears, as did nearby raiders. The mix of man-blood and Oathblood on Valere's hand began to sizzle. Then it burst forward, like a crimson snake. The burning blood arced and flew, cutting through three mutants, leaving behind charred flesh and splintered bones. This gift of the Truegods brought terror as much as death to the enemy. They retreated, as did the rest of the mutant frontline, the melee transforming into gunfight, each side huddling behind cover and taking what potshots they could.

"If it continues like this, we could be snared up here all day," Namter said, crouching down, and scanning the hillside.

"Is their goal to free the Tribute?" Valere asked. As he did, a mutant near the top of the hill pulled out what looked to be a ramshackle grenade launcher and fired. One of the near transport 'trucks burst into a storm of metal shards, burning flesh, and horrid shrieks.

"They want petty revenge, nothing more," Namter said, scanning the hillside for the chief. If they could take out Bladescar, not only would it break the enemy's will to fight, but it might unravel Clan Vapulus once and for all. But the chief was absent, and all Namter could see were mutant rifleman and sharpshooters, one near aiming her rifle straight at—

"Awakener!" Brother Valere shouted, as he jumped forward and knocked Namter down. A gunshot went off, blood bursting from Valere's neck.

"Brother!" Namter cried, as Valere fell to the dirt. He gurgled, sputtering, unable to speak, his breath desperate and wet. Namter turned, and with holy rage ripped off his eyepatch. Suddenly, he could See. See both what the world was and what it should be. A glorious future, or gleaming past, or some alternative present, Namter could not say, but with his Eye that was not an eye, he could see a world unlike the one before him, perfect and beautiful, and yet ephemeral and indescribable, hints of ivory spires and floating gardens, gilded light and incomprehensible grace, a paradise that slipped from his vision the moment he focused.

No, he must let it slip, must not be distracted by its glory. As he stepped forward, he could not help but notice how hideous the world was that he walked through, how rancid and rotten and ruined and ugly, all the more now that he had true beauty to compare it to. The sight disgusted him, and he nearly gagged.

The hideous mutant sharpshooter loaded her rifle and took aim. Namter stared at her, straight in her eyes, with the Eye that wasn't, with the void that lived in the space where his right eye had once been. He could see the mutant hesitate, horrified and mesmerized, even from this distance, at a glimpse of the Truth that lived in his empty eye socket. Words came to his mouth, in a tongue not of man's. He pointed, and from his fingers came a ball of black fire, spinning upwards, and bursting over the mutant, transforming her and her crumbling excuse for a sniper's nest into swirling ash.

More mutants charged. Namter turned his baleful gaze, trapping one in his sight. He muttered more incantations, the mutant shaking, seizing, bloating out. Then with a blast he exploded into blood and viscera, knocking comrades to the ground. The mutant's blood pooled around his remains, blessed by Namter's words, and started to congeal. A figure formed from the blood, bent and grotesque. It was something alike a woman, but with no skin showing, completely wrapped in bloody linens like some horrid medical patient. On its back sprouted two protrusions, but these were cracked and bound as well, leaking blood and pus onto the funerary shrouds wrapped around it. On both the linen and shroud were massive, rusted spikes that dug into the twitching figure. As it staggered forward, it tore these spikes from its bodies. With a scream, it swung its spike-adorned ribbons of linen out, skewering the terrified mutants. The creature was an awful, disgusting sight.

*No,* Namter chided himself. It seemed disgusting only since he was looking at it wrong, seeing it through human eyes tainted by the material world. With the Eye gifted to him, he saw the figure as it was: a winged angel, her skin pure and pale, hair golden and glittering, body naked and perfect. She swung her whip, an instrument of divine punishment, at the mutants, who tried in vain to flee. Upon her great white wings she flew up, gliding volant a moment, before descending upon the enemy, striking them down, one after another, as they howled and ran back up the hill.

The mutants' shouts were matched by the screams of the raiders, who cried out in horror. Weak and blind as they were, they were unable to see the angel as she was and were terrified by the lies their false eyes told them. They could not See her as he did, they could not understand her beauty.

Her overwhelming, numinous, divine beauty.

# CHAPTER 9

Hours later, after making it back to camp and sending off the Tribute for storage, Namter washed himself. Water buffeted him, flowing through pipes he had ordered, from a well whose digging he had organized, with a filtration system he had bought wholesale during a trip up to Icaria. The water smashed over him, each droplet taking with it some dust, or blood, or other filth. And yet it couldn't clean the man underneath, as humanity was forever soiled.

Namter got out of the shower, which took up a third of his modest tent, and stared at the naked body in the mirror. A middle-aged man stared back, with thin greasy hair and a slight bent to his posture built up over decades. Only his eyepatch reminded him that there was something greater, something hidden within him that was not him, that was superior to him, higher than this pitiful sack of misery and weakness. Part of him understood now why his master, Lazarus Roache, had been so desperate for a reprieve, so willing to take a deal whose breadth he had not fully comprehended. Namter could not as easily understand why the man had coveted youth, when a young human body was no less pathetic than an old one.

With a deep sigh, Namter got dressed, not into the robes of his Brotherhood, but the simple vest and black coat of a butler. Though he had just returned, he had much work to do, and no time to dally.

First, there was payment for the caravan, forms assigning slickdust pay for most, aurem pay for the wiser. Next, he had to set æther-oil rations—with the refineries in Huile lost they could not burn the fuel so prodigally. Then he resolved a quick dispute between the Fist-Biters and the Trog-Skinners, some slaves traded, a few idiots sent to death in the fighting pens. He had to add an item to his itinerary, organizing a hunting party to punish Clan Vapulus, but this took little time. What took more was a contract dispute regarding some Lazacorp guards who had begun to use their days off to do some slave-raiding, stealing valuable cargo from other raiders under the protections of Lazacorp. This was not technically forbidden under their contracts, but Namter was eventually able to get them in line by reminding the wayward guards that they were 'at-will employees' and if their employment was terminated, they would find themselves alone in the middle of the Wastes between several angry gangs eager for violent and humiliating retribution. Finally, he went to pay his respect to Brother Valere, his catafalque hidden away in the Brotherhood's quarter.

Namter stood before the corpse, barely older than a child, disfigured by the bullet meant for him. He grasped Valere's cold hand and whispered a prayer, promising the Brother that his death would not be in vain, that their righteous cause would see its end, a new age of glorious humbling. He noticed Brothers whispering among themselves as he did so, but he had not the energy to wonder what lies were being passed round.

As he left the tent, Brother Tacticus followed him. Namter kept his hand near his hidden pistol; he had been ambushed once by a traitorous Brother and would not make the same mistake twice. Tacticus did not attack him, though his face was red enough with fury to justify Namter's fear.

"Watcher," Brother Tacticus said, "How can you honor our fallen Brother while at the same time besmirching our righteous cause?"

"Brother Tacticus," Namter said. "I have only ever served our Master, what nonsense do you spit?"

"The Tribute!" Brother Tacticus said. "Meant for our Master. The Tribute that should feed his rebirth! The Tribute Brother Valere died protecting!" The man had to silence himself a moment to gather coherent words. "I saw it taken. I saw it being sent over for slickdust production! 'On Lazarus Roache's orders, apparently."

"Lazarus..." Namter shook his head, he couldn't believe it. No, that was not true, his distress was not disbelief. He *wished* not to believe it, and yet found the accusation so believable. Some Tribute had always been diverted towards slickdust production, a necessary evil. But at this late point, when all resources should be given over to the Reification? He could understand Tacticus's rage, he felt it himself.

"I hadn't heard," he said. "I will figure out what's going on, my Brother. The Tribute *will be* going to our Master. I promise you that."

* * *

Namter stomped his way to Lazarus Roache's tent, a big purple gaudy thing the size of an immodest townhouse. He stopped by the door to calm himself. His duties were still split, and regardless of his emotions now (or for the past forty years) the Law of Obedience meant he must perform his role. And his role was that of a butler, of a lowly assistant. So, taking a breath and patting the dust from his jacket, Namter entered with the proper meekness.

Lazarus Roache's tent fit the man, warm and garish, comfortable and expensive. There were imported Vidish oak floorboards, a griffon-fur rug, a gilded bedframe with silken sheets, a mahogany desk with matching chairs, a hat tree covered in identical short-brimmed hats, and several vitrines filled with clockwork knick-knacks and pre-war antiques. Portraits hung on a wall whose sole structural purpose was to hold portraits, and in the corner stood a small marble statue of some ancient hero or chieftain, not chosen for whatever his historical significance had been, but for his uncanny likeness to the tycoon. It was the glitzy veneer of civilization manifest and could lull one to forget that the cruelty of the Wastes sat mere metres away. Though it might be hard to forget that at this particular moment, considering that in the very center of the tent a vivisection table had been wheeled in, complete with the grotesque, still-breathing body of a mutant, limbs lost in a tumorous growth of flesh, cut down the middle and perforated with medical tubes. Standing above the body was the man himself, Lazarus Roache, in his signature striped suit, casually perusing the scene of carnage.

"Ah, Namter," Lazarus said. "Get the kettle going, will you? We have company."

"Company, sir?" Namter asked.

From behind the mess of pumps and machinery emerged a woman. Her grey hair was wild and curly, her eyes sharp and mean, her wrinkled skin tanned by uncountable sunburns and other burns as well. On her right arm sat a bulky ætherglove of a bespoke and ramshackle design, on her head was wrapped a headband augmented with adjustable lenses, and upon her torso hung loose a leather smock decorated with oil and viscera. Namter barely kept from shuddering. He knew this woman well, thought her long gone.

"Good... evening, Miss Veneficus," Namter said, with a tongue full of venom.

"Ah, you tired scraprat, it's Miga to you," Miga Veneficus said. "Come on now, what's with the face? Thought we were old friends."

"I must remind the madame," Namter said, walking over to set the kettle. "That last we saw each other was as our Awakener was violently exiling you from camp for your foul witchcraft."

Miga stretched a smile. "Right, right, Verus. Can still see the slaghead, running out half-naked with that machete, drunk out of his mind, inventing all sorts of creative curses. That man was crazy, but clever as a strix, can see why you kept on kissing his arse. Good arse it was, I'll admit, at least for how it goes out here. Good *cock* too." She put an inordinate amount of emphasis on the word *cock*, a lot of volume too.

"I'm afraid the madame may be mistaken," Namter said. "For Verus did not touch alcohol, it was against the True Faith. And he most certainly did not lay down with waste-whores!"

"Namter!" Lazarus said. "Let us be civil. Miga here is a guest."

"She is an exile! A prostitute! A witch! ...Sir."

"Haven't been a prostitute since my youth days," Miga said, plunging her hands deep in the dying mutant. "And though I like the whole witch title, truth be told, I'm just a humble, genius inventor. *Exile*, sure, but it seems to be the man who did that whole exiling thing turned out to be a murderous traitor, nice cock or no. Isn't that right?"

Namter opened his mouth, but managed to shut it before he could unleash the violent stream of insults that he desperately wished to unload. He picked up the tea tray and brought it over to Lazarus's desk. "Yes, unfortunately, some madness overtook him."

"Eh, don't sound so sour, Hieronymus," Miga said, as she removed some organ, bloated beyond recognition, and examined it under a lens. "Worked out for you, got the old man's job."

"Yes," Lazarus Roache cut in. "Let's let bygone be bygones. Miga here was showing me how we might double slickdust yields from these mutants at very little additional cost, with no loss in potency."

"You've made no improvements to the formula while I've been gone," Miga said, tossing the organ into a bin. "But I've been doing plenty of thinking and experimenting on my own. Hard to do without Lazarus's blood, but I can see my theories are paying off."

"Sir," Namter said, pouring two cups of tea. "That is a matter I'd like to discuss. These bodies, they are Tribute. For our shared Master. I thought we had decided to cease production of slickdust."

Lazarus leaned back on his desk. He picked up the cup of tea Namter had poured for Miga and handed it to his butler. Namter hesitated, Lazarus had never offered him tea. He took its warily, and Lazarus bade him sit next to him with a casual pat. After a moment, he did. Miga, for her part, kept up her work on the mutant, taking blood samples and monitoring heart rate and injection flow.

"Namter," Lazarus said. "It is true that at this point in our contract we were meant to be providing our benefactor with Tribute, but, as you know, there have been unforeseen circumstances."

"Contract..." Namter shook his head. "Sir, this is no petty pact, it is a holy duty assigned to us."

"Everything is a contract," Lazarus Roache said. "No matter what you call it, no matter be it with an employee, a company, or sure, a God. It is a contract, and it has rules, and we, my dear Namter, broke none of them. Verus has been the proverbial wrench in the works. For whatever bitterness drove him, he destroyed our ability to provide the requisite number of Tribute by the assigned date."

"So, your solution is to waste even more?" Namter said. "To make slickdust to pay off raiders while starving our Master?"

Lazarus sighed. He pulled out a vial of slickdust and poured it into his tea. He mixed it with a spoon and sipped. Namter noticed, round the man's eyes, wrinkles, hints of age that he had not seen for almost seven years now.

"Namter you are the best of us," Lazarus said. "Always my number one, through thick and thin. You have your ideals, good ones at that, and, despite the world always disappointing you, you have stuck by your ideals."

"Sir..." Namter said, unsure of what to make of the words. Lazarus always had a compliment ready, but it was for someone else, for a business associate, or a loyal worker, or a puppet, or a politician. Never for his butler.

"Yet ideals played too straight can betray themselves," Lazarus said, sipping. "We can get the required Tribute, but not now, not in a month's time. It is all because of Verus, because of him that we are in this situation, but the solution is not to underperform, it is to set a sensible delay."

"A delay?" Namter said. "Our Master made no mention of delays."

"And he made no mentions of betrayal by his own Awakener," Lazarus said. "Imagine the day of the Reification, The Flayed Prince awakens but there is not enough blood to sustain his physical form! After millennia of slumber, of patience and planning, everything is ruined! This would be a tragedy beyond tragedies, a betrayal, not by Verus, but by us, his still loyal servants. All that we have built would be gone to waste! Listen." Lazarus locked his gaze with Namter's. "Just listen. If we delay, just a bit, just a few years, we could be back to where we were before the whole mishap, in a better place even. With the allies we have in Stinktown we could take back Huile, get the refineries going again. Why, with the connections we have in Icaria we could restart our Enterprise, not in some piss-edge Border State nowhere, but in the crashed city itself! Imagine the power, imagine the profit. Imagine the Tribute! And a ready-made kingdom built for The Flayed Prince to awaken to."

"It is..." Namter shook his head. "No, we must play our roles. You are the agent of the Gift, and I am a mere Watcher, meant only to be sure that you and the Awakener—"

"You are the Awakener!" Lazarus laughed. "Or have you forgotten? It is your duty to see that the Tribute is fulfilled, and I am telling you how to do it. Together."

Namter thought on this, as Lazarus sat and Miga worked on the mutant's writhing body. Truth be told, what the man said made sense. They had lost Huile, their plans to industrialize Tribute production had failed. And it was not their fault, it was Verus's doing. Yet Namter now had to make decisions he was not prepared for, and so he must bear responsibility for its consequences, regardless of the reason. But a path of delay had never been suggested, it was arrogance to think that they knew better than a god. Unless Namter's own resistance was due to his hatred of his current position. He desired more than anything for the Reification; could such yearning be blinding him to an obvious truth? The Flayed Prince had waited thousands of years, a few more would not be a great burden. Surely a delayed Reification was better than an insufficient one. If only he could speak to his slumbering God, all might be made clear. Namter was stuck with this painful ambiguity. He thought he had left such moral morasses behind when he had joined the Unblind.

"Very well, I will… consider the possibility of delay," Namter said. "But it is too big a decision to be made lightly. We must be honest with each other, and frank about all our dealings."

"Of course, of course." Lazarus placed down his teacup. "You are right, wise counsel as always. I did not wish to overload you with more burdens… but no, no, secrecy was the path that Verus chose, and look where that led! We are partners, you and I, an honest partnership."

*Partners.* What a strange word, he had never heard Lazarus refer to him with such equitable language. He almost smiled at the thought, but instead simply nodded. "It will be difficult explaining all this to the Brotherhood."

"I'm sure you'll do well," Lazarus said, patting his butler on the shoulder. "You always do Namter. That's why you've always been my favorite."

The mutant gurgled and moaned, spurts of red shooting from his torso, as its twitching limbs fell still.

"Taur's shit on a troglyn's prick!" Miga swore, half-painted in blood. "Hieronymus be a dear and wheel another in. This one's too dead."

*So, what exactly is æther? Chances are you know a bit. Æther is what makes your lights in your house glow and your autocar move. Maybe you've read horror pulps about spooky ætheric aberrations haunting old ruins, and you probably have a pretty good sense that æther is important to engineers somehow. But maybe you haven't thought much more about æther, and I don't blame you, with all fast-paced progress of modernity, all the gizmos and gadgets distracting you, who has time for technical foofay?*

*Well, let me run you through basics of æther, in so simple manner simple a manner even a fool could understand! (Not that you are one, of course!)*

*Æther is a sort of force, or energy, that ignores many laws of common non–ætheric physics. This is useful for imbuing machinery with properties that would not otherwise be possible, for manipulating machines and other artificial objects with an ætherglove, or simply powering home appliances. How convenient! Yet there is a dark side of æther as well. Untreated æther-oil, or sangleum, works quite differently than the Stable Æther you pump into your autotruck. It's erratic and highly mutagenic, so if you see any crimson spurting from the ground on your evening walk, maybe take another street. And contact your local engineer! Just because sangleum's dangerous doesn't mean its worthless, we need to get stable æther from somewhere!*

*Of course, all that I've described is the result of common, Mechanical Æther, which is merely one form of four. Yes, four! There are four main classes of æther, how about that? It's just that most don't have useful functions in industry or home life, so chances are you ain't used to them.*

*First off there are the Natural Æthers, whose two subforms interact with plant-life and growth, or predation and beasts, retrospectively. If you've ever seen a cinegraph show with ferrals wearing animal skulls and muttering nonsense incantations while trees grow violent and animals go into a frenzy, well you're seeing the natural æthers at work. It's also theorized that the natural æthers are what allow the Vilkolak to transform into wolf-things! Ain't that wild? Natural æther is, of course, utterly worthless for human use.*

*Then there are the Elemental Æthers. Bal, which is associated with heat, fire, lightning, storms, and general destruction, and Svel, which is associated with frost, earth, water, and lengthy geological processes. The* giant Vulkers of the far north are wielders of elemental æthers, which flow wilder in their lands, as are the fire-haired Ifriti of Muhit. Alas, though some engineers have attempted to utilized elemental æthers, the results have been mixed. And highly explosive!

Finally, we have Anima and Morbis, the Æthers of Life and Death. One must always be sensitive when talking about Anima, due to its religious importance. It is said by priests of the Ascended that this æther is the tool of the Demiurge himself, gifted to his followers for their most sacred of rites. Indeed, many old artifacts, be they truly built by the Ascended, or by pre-homid autochthons, utilize life æther to achieve feats that even the greatest of engineers can't match. So pretty impressive stuff!

The less said about Morbis the better. It is the foulest of æthers, its destructive capabilities rivaled only by sangleum. The æther of death perverts all that it touches, corrupting the natural life cycle, and haunting humanity with twisted agonized specters of those we once loved. Even the insatiably curious Engineer's Guild forbids all direct experimentation with such a horrid æther. So, my advice? Stay well enough away...

—"A Friendly Guide To Æthermantics So Simple Even a Fool Could Understand" By Astrida Lund.

CHAPTER 10

Marcel was used to destruction and ruination, but Opus's Glory was a real step up. Most ruins in the Wastes resembled something vaguely recognizable, old rotting cubes with window holes, blocks of concrete and brick, rusting metal pipes and gears whose exact purpose he could not quite determine, but that he could at least guess at. Yet these unending hills of scrap and rot that rolled over the wide gulch did not clearly resemble anything. Not an old mining town, not a forgotten city, not some destroyed agri-factories, not even the railway nexus that they had once supposedly been. Just piles of poorly heaped desolation, without even the decency to disappear under the dust of the Wastes, brazen with its utterly vast, devastating, useless nothing.

*Nothing.* He scratched his cheek as he mused. Had he been told the day before that there was nothing between him and Lazarus Roache, he might have assumed it great news. Yet it seemed some nothings were a lot harder to navigate than others. The Wastes quickly transformed one into a taxonomer of *nothings.*

Somewhere, on the other side of all that nothing, was Lazarus Roache.

"There are routes cut in between the mounds," Belona explained. "Used by smugglers and such years back." The four of them kneeled at the crest of a hill, staring down at the once-battlefield beneath them.

"Paths used by criminals... How do you know them, then?" Marcel asked.

"I sent scouts, back when I had such command—"

91

"We should move soon," Kayip cut in suddenly. "It is best not to linger. The dead get restless at night, and there is still daylight left."

"I'm not sure that's a good idea, look," Sylvaine said, pointing down. Marcel squinted but could make out nothing, until Kayip offered him a pair of binoculars. There, cresting what might have, at some distant time, been a bulky piece of artillery, came six large skuttling legs. And then another set of legs, and a third. The evening sun shined off the metal-sheened carapaces of the creatures, halfway between exoskeletons and autocar frames. The monster's mandibles were not unlike those of a mantid's, with rows of grinding blades as teeth that dripped with oil. On their heads were antennas, like those of voxboxes, but twitching with insect anxiety. Their eyes were lenses of a sort but seemed bulbous and imperfect in a strangely biological manner.

"Rust locusts," Sylvaine said, and indeed they were. Marcel could count a dozen or more crawling around the battlefield, each somewhere between the size of a large dog and small horse.

"For every locust you see there's at least a hundred that you don't," Belona said. "Frightened away the scrappers and scavengers about a year ago. In their numbers they're far more dangerous than any ghul or geist. But the dead unnerve them, so they scatter before nightfall."

"Then we best make what progress we can," Kayip said, standing up, "in the brief interval when the two sleep."

* * *

They idled in the 'truck as the sun started to set. Sylvaine and Kayip stood on the looted corpse of a warwalker, watching the rust locusts languidly scuttle away. Right as the last rays of sunlight disappeared the two ran back to the 'truck, and without a word they descended down the road and into the depths of the battlefield.

It was quiet in the gulch, unnaturally so. In the Wastes there was usually some sound, be it the stomp of distant taur hoofs, the cries of skraggers and troglyn packs, or just the busy wind. But here there was nothing, no footsteps, no beasts howling, no chirping of crickets. All Marcel could hear was the crunch of the wheels, the groan of the engine, and the moanings of Felik Rector.

"Idiots. Stiffland stuck-up suicidal taur-fucking rusted pus idiots," the man babbled softly from the back of the autotruck.

Belona kept her hand tight on the wheel, unblinking gaze dashing from the empty edges of the road. Or what could be called a road, more of a winding section of rubble that had been crushed almost nearly somewhat a bit flat. Unseen things creaked and cracked as the 'truck lumbered forward, Marcel breathlessly fearing that something would puncture the thick tires. Still, he saw nothing that he might consider a threat among the shadows. Only a persistent cloud of dust that hung around the broken war machines and concrete pillars, giving an impression of moonlit mist.

There was muttering. Marcel turned back to see Kayip grasping his Disc and praying, quick nonsense words in Oradea, the Church-tongue. Even Sylvaine was tense, ears flickering, turning her head to sniff about, stopping when she noticed Marcel's stare, red in the face.

Marcel was starting to wonder if they were all sharing some sort of paranoid delirium. It was well known that ætheric specters occasionally lingered after death, or that certain unnatural disasters might temporarily reanimate some recently deceased flesh, but a whole army of the dead struck Marcel as a bit, well, ridiculous. He had only heard of anything like that happening right after the Calamity, and truth be told, most tales about the post-Calamity period were fabricated hyperbole anyhow, stories best left for pulps. Perhaps they were being a tad silly, spooked by too many nights in the Wastes, where every strangeness seemed believable. And yet, when he stared out the side window, he could not stop himself from being startled by every shadow.

"Shit, shit!" Belona said, as the 'truck lurched to a stop. "No, no, Demiurge damn it all!"

In front of them, between two peaks of rubble, stood a sloped wall of stone, too orderly to be simple ruins.

"How did you get lost?" Sylvaine hissed.

"I didn't! This *is* the way!" Belona protested.

"You needed to use the past tense there," Marcel said. "Because no 'truck's getting through now."

Belona open the door and stomped out. Sylvaine and Kayip shared a glance, then stepped out the back. Marcel held his fist on the cold handle a moment, staring out into the blasted landscape, seeing ghastly figures in shards of rust or cracked tank barrels. He sucked in his breath, swallowed an embarrassing amount of dread, and stumbled outside.

They had stopped in a dead end, hills of rubble and exhumed earth blocking every direction except the one they came in, and a narrow path beyond the opposing wall. He walked over towards it, handtorch beam sweeping. Not all that impressive of a wall, little more than two metres high. But it was all stone, not a piece of the rusted scrap or broken gearwork that decorated the hillsides.

"You claim to be an engineer," Belona said to Sylvaine, "can you clear it?"

Sylvaine shook her head. "Nothing metal, nothing constructed."

"Yes, I am sure that is the reason," Belona said, with unsubtle sarcasm.

"First rule of engineering is that you can only alter mechanical—" Sylvaine began.

"I do not care," Belona said as she started up the tallest hill. "Just defend the 'truck while I am gone. You there!" she pointed to Marcel. "Come on, going to see if we can scout out an alternative route."

"Alright, but don't slow me down," Marcel said, jogging up after her.

He found it quite difficult to catch up to the woman's arrogant strides, the hill crumbling as he stepped. As he climbed, he swept his handtorch down to make sure he didn't skewer his foot on some forgotten bayonet. A glare of white shone bright under his light.

A skull, picked clean and cracked. Below it, a red-brown uniform, torn and ripped to only be recognizable by the dirt-encrusted badge still hanging on its chest. As Marcel squatted, he could make out the symbol of a Phoenix volant engraved onto silver. It was intricately detailed, with rolling feathers that morphed seamlessly into flames, a curved beak crying out for freedom, as specks of ash fell below to reform the pyre from which it was born. The symbol was so familiar, and yet slightly alien, of a more elegant and antique design than Marcel was familiar, the maximalism of the late Interregnum Republic which bled into the aesthetics of the Phoenix Rebellion. It was unlike the streamlined, abstracted Phoenix that graced the banners of the UCCR war camps, or that once flew in the atrium of Huile's city hall. He was surprised the medal hadn't been looted in the past century. Then again, the Wastes were large, things got lost. Whole battlefields had been forgotten, he wondered if the soldier's next of kin ever found out where they fell. Actually, that presupposed his kin survived the Calamity itself, a heck of an assumption. Marcel pocketed the badge, better it end up in the hands of a good Resurgence soldier who could honor the sacrifices of his ideological ancestors.

"Come on, quickly now!" Belona shouted.

"Here, here," Marcel hissed, as he reached the top. "I know you're new to the whole reconnaissance thing, but generally you don't shout if you're trying to sneak."

"The issue is time, not stealth," Belona said, as she flicked a switch on her oversized handtorch, sending forth a blinding beam which swept the floor of the war-torn gulch, reflecting off tank chassis and fallen motorguns, and too many glints of white bone to count. She raised her finger and began to trace routes across the flatter depressions and wider trenches, as if she were some child wandering a printed maze in a coloring book.

Marcel did his best to follow along, spending a few minutes searching out the path that extended from the other side of the wall, and working back to see if met up with a route behind them. They had to work quickly, if they lost the night wandering this labyrinth, they'd miss their one good shot at catching Roache unaware. Yet it was no simple puzzle. Marcel cursed himself for trusting that the imperial had known the path.

"So why exactly did you have to send scouts out here?" Marcel said. "You know, before?"

Belona was silent for a moment. "I was tracking some runaways. Criminals."

"I didn't know your jurisdiction went beyond the walls of Holtag," Marcel said.

"Yes well…" she said. "I suppose my leash was loosened in this instance. Let me guess, you're curious if they were Resurgence terrorists?"

"I was just wondering what they had done to agitate the long, clawed fist of the Imperator."

"Don't recall," Belona said. "Don't even remember if they were Resurgence or just raiders, or whatever. When you've executed as many as I have, they tend to all blur together."

There was something forced in the way she spoke. Marcel was starting to become convinced that there were details she was leaving out, or perhaps that the whole story was fabricated. For one, Belona did not strike him as a woman who would forget anyone who had tried to escape, who had wronged her. She'd seemed the type to let these things fester in her mind, to obsess over losses, gloat over victories. He was trying to figure out the best way to pry when something caught his eye on a far hill.

Movement.

Figures began to stand up from the dust and ruin. They were wearing blues, or reds and browns, or sometimes nothing, a stained white in the moonlight. Marcel tried to convince himself it was some pack of scavengers who had hidden themselves in the day, but he knew that would be a comforting delusion. Bones rose from ragged piles, forming thin desiccated outlines. The dead were moving. Some reached down to help their comrades, or else picked up rifles and blades. Then, as one, they began to march.

"Uh, Belona—" Marcel began, as the woman grabbed his shoulder. He turned round to see skeletal figures rising mere metres away, limp creaking into place, weapons raised. They wore the dust-faded blue of the Principate.

Marcel and Belona began to back up, hands on their pistols. Then suddenly, something grabbed Marcel's leg. A faded voice, like recording played on a warped vocaphone, arose from below.

*"Capt'n, I got the scouts!"*

* * *

"I just don't see how one arrogant... woman, is going to make the difference in our hunt for Roache," Sylvaine said, standing back to the 'truck.

Kayip nodded, idly touching his bracelet as he scanned the clearing around them. "She is rough, and her ideology is cruel, but she is a good soldier, and will not betray us. I know what traitors are, I have seen too many."

"It's not all about betrayal Kayip," Sylvaine said. "You don't feel, I mean, when she makes remarks about... You don't get it, do you?" She slammed the back of her head against the 'truck, which made a satisfying thonk. Felik grumbled some nonsense. One of the few benefits of driving through this unnerving place was that it had finally spooked the raider into silence.

"She is rude to you because you are a ferral," Kayip said. "I understand that this is upsetting."

"Upsetting..." Sylvaine shook her head. "Not sure that's exactly the right word for it. Getting mud on your new lapel is upsetting, having a brand-new auto engine sputter to death is upsetting." She raised her ætherglove and felt the cold of its copper with her other hand. "She won't even entertain the idea that I'm an engineer. And how can I blame her? I mean, I will because she is... awful. But if I wanted to prove her wrong, I could just do some ætheric engineering, fuse some metal together, fix some broken something with a snap of my fingers. Only... I'm not sure what will happen if I try. It might just as well explode, and prove that... *her*, right."

"It is no fault of yours, the æthers run wild here in the Wastes," Kayip said, gesturing around the battlefield.

"If I were a normal engineer, then maybe I could use that excuse. But I'm... I don't know what I am," Sylvaine said, kicking a white stone.

Kayip scratched his chin, thinking. "You know, when I was in the Vatsehir orphanage—"

"You're an orphan?" Sylvaine asked.

"Oh, yes," Kayip said. "With the Vatsehir Cathedral as my guardian. It was a good place. Not a pleasant place, or an easy place, or a friendly place, but it was better than being tossed to the Wastes, which some children were. While I was there, I discovered that I was different."

"Different?" Sylvaine said.

"Yes different," Kayip said. "I did not find women to be as fascinating as many of my fellows did, I saw no need to pursue them. At first the Church looked kindly upon this, but soon I began to have other urges, in the opposite direction, which the priests did not approve of. I did not know what to make of this, why it was that I was different? I grew angry and violent. It was not until what would become my Order came through, not until they saw me, and saw my promise, that I understood. For to them my difference was no sin, but proof that I had been chosen by the Demiurge, chosen to join their Order. And in this way, I did not feel my difference was a curse, but a blessing."

"Huh," Sylvaine said. She was pretty sure the monk had shared something important about himself, albeit wrapped in layers of Church weirdness. His sexual orientation was never something she had cared much about, but opening up was a vulnerability that the man had not before been willing to show. An attempt at understanding.

"I'm glad you told me that, Kayip," she said. "But it's not quite the same, right? I mean urges are one thing, you can hide those. Not that you *should*, I mean, I'm just saying... Well, just look at me!" Sylvaine gestured at her body. "There's no hiding, no mask, even my glove doesn't seem to do it. It's like... like back home. In Taliers. My father, he's an accountant. Used to organize the finances for this trading firm, really a conglomerate of firms. All behind the scenes stuff, even in the good old Citizens' Confederacy no one wanted a Ferral as the face of anything. He loved his work, always came home with a big smile."

Sylvaine sighed, long and deep, it almost hurt. "I hated that smile. Hated it more than anything. How could he be so happy? Every day was filled with insults and mockery. 'Grab that,' 'calculate that,' 'fetch those files, won't you, beastman?' *Beastman*, as if it were nickname, not a slur. 'Wow, I didn't know Ferrals could be good at math.' Not good, great! Gear's-grits, the man was a centimetre away from a mathematical genius. And yet his skills were always a novelty, not proof that people's assumptions were taurshit, just an amusing abnormality that could be safely ignored. And though the company ignored him most days, the days they didn't, dear Demiurge, how they showed him off, like he was a trophy! Why, they have a *ferral* working for them. How generous, how openminded, how wonderfully fucking inclusive! They would have sunk years ago if my father wasn't working double-shift to make the numbers work, yet they always talked about his job as if it were a charity case, as if the piss-poor pay was a benevolent favor. And, of course, my father would never complain, he would always smile, always tell me how lucky our family was. I could never make sense of it. Never make sense of that smile."

Silence. Above on the hill, Marcel and Belona were sweeping their handtorches about, no doubt trying to find an exit route. Kayip raised his hand, uncertain, and then placed it softly upon her shoulder.

"I am sorry, Sylvaine," he said.

"Yeah," she said, surprised by how comforting his grip felt. "Thanks."

Suddenly something moved. An instinct deep in Sylvaine flared to life, her fur suddenly sticking on end. Kayip noticed her fear, and with a quick prayer unrolled his sword. The ground creaked and cracked, from every direction it seemed. Sylvaine tuned her ears and noticed strange winds that almost began to sound like words. As she struggled to make out the spectral voices, bones began to clink nearby, then started to rise.

# Chapter 11

A squad of Principate soldiers, once-Principate soldiers really, encircled Marcel and Belona. They menaced with rusted bayonets and scatterguns that lacked functional pump-actions. Their faces of wind-worn bone moved with uneven jitters; their eyeless gaze was distressingly piercing. Some had bits of mummified skin sticking stubborn to arms or faces, others stumbled forward with missing limbs, moving without pain or concern. Every unnatural thing about them sent Marcel's instincts into a frenzy. He was glad his bladder was empty.

The soldier by his feet still gripped tight, but had been unable to stand, lacking, as he did, anything beneath his torso. He clanked onto Marcel's legs a set of shackles, but they had long since rusted-away, and simply slipped off. The soldier didn't seem to notice, indeed none of the dead appeared aware that their weapons were beyond disrepair. Marcel was not sure how much that mattered though, there were two dozen of them, with plenty of sharp bits that could still cut into flesh and tear open stomachs. And it wasn't like Marcel's pistol was going to do all that much to people who have already suffered far worse than a few bullet holes.

One of the skeletons, wearing a field captain's cap, walked forward. A ghastly ethereal voice leaked out from their throatless neck. *"You thought you could sneak past the barricade, didn't you?"*

"We were, uh," Marcel stammered. It was a challenge to improvise when surrounded by deathless abominations. "Just, uh... passing through?"

*"Scouts they are,"* came the voice from below. *"Phoenix rebels! Trying to sabotage our defenses, capt'n."*

"I am no rebel!" Belona said, with indignancy.

*"Hear that?"* said the dead captain. *"This girl ain't no rebel."*

"We're travelers, that's all," Marcel said, gathering himself somehow. He glanced over his shoulder to see that on the hills below two groups of skeletons had begun to fight each other, miming gunshots, throwing dead grenades, and jabbing with bayonets. Were he not terrified, it might have seemed almost comic theatre.

*"Travelers?"* the captain made a motion as if spitting. *"What travelers decide to wander through a live battlefield?"*

*"Scouts, spies, they are!"* the half-soldier said. *"That's what they said. 'Scouting things,' 'sneaking.' I heard them, they admitted it already!"*

"I am a soldier of the Principate," Belona said, pushing forward so she was mere centimetres from the captain's blade. She talked with a causal indignance, as if speaking to insubordinate guards as opposed to the living dead. "I served my Imperator with ferocity in the Battle of Tesakovgrad."

*"Tesakovgrad!"* The captain made a ghastly hissing sound. Marcel surmised it must have been laughter. *"There is no such battle. Tesakovgrad is a loyalist city, rebels forces have never stepped foot in it."*

"Then your intel is far out of date," Belona said.

Sounds of battle started to wash over the hills. The stomps of rotting boots, the crunch of steel against bone, but more as well, faint gunshots, the groan of engines as if a great distance away, the roar of artillery that didn't exist. Was Marcel going mad under the pressure or was the spirit of the battle itself coming alive?

"Come on, let's not argue minutiae," Marcel interjected, attempting a very strained chuckle. "The point is, we're friendly."

*"Aha!"* cried the half soldier, reaching suddenly in Marcel's pocket to retrieve the Phoenix-engraved medal. *"Not only a rebel, but a rebel commander! Captain, this could turn the battle!"*

"Not mine," Marcel said quickly. "I looted it off one of those... disgusting, evil, traitorous rebels. Demiurge damn those freedom-worshiping bastards!"

*"And that Frasco pistol of yours,"* the captain said. *"That looted as well?"*

"...Yes," Marcel said.

"Ignore my idiot subordinate," Belona said. "We were sent in from a military base in Holtag to assist in your assault, to scout out the enemy lines undercover."

"*Holtag,*" the captain said. *"Didn't that town get bombed by rebel æroships?"*

"Your general," Belona said. "Pyotry Sovanov, I know his kin. I fought under his great-grandson, General Nikolai Sovanov."

The name seemed to ring true, as the dead glanced at each other. Marcel gave a side-eye to Belona. How in Inferno did she know that bit of trivia? Were Principate soldiers so obsessed that they memorized each and every general, and where and when they were put into the ground? On second thought, that did seem plausible.

*"Great-Grandson?"* the captain unleased his horrid laughter. *"Our general is still a young man. Come, I shall take you to see him before you are executed."*

Marcel got a glimpse of something down the hill. Soldiers of bone, wearing browns and reds, creeping up the hill, towards them. The Principate dead seemed unaware of the approaching rebel attack.

"Um..." Marcel stumbled, trying to kill time. "Your young general. I mean, it seems that, well, he could still have a grandson. You know, kids grow up fast, and a lot of time has passed. It's been decades, right?"

*"What nonsense are you babbling?"*

"I mean, what... What year do you think it is?"

The captain stared at him, managing to show contempt despite his lack of skin and muscles. *"1656. You idiot."*

*1656.* That was almost a century ago, the year of the Calamity. These poor souls had been blasted by that ætheric disaster so hard it knocked the memory of their death clear out of their skulls.

*"Yeah,"* said the half-soldier still gripping tight Marcel's leg. *"And it'll be a glorious year! A year of victory. After night after night defending this station, tonight will be the night when we drive you traitors in rout!"*

"How long have you been fighting?" Belona asked.

The dead murmured amongst themselves. The captain stood tall. *"We've defended the Opus Glory railway from Phoenix aggression for well over thirty-thousand consecutive nights!"*

"Thirty-thousand!" Marcel said, fear temporarily replaced by disbelief. "How many days do you think are in a year?"

*"Enough with your tricksy words, traitor,"* the captain said. *"I've suffered enough from your kinds' deceits. I've been blasted by clockbombs and shot through by snipers. I've been cut to pieces in ambushes and peppered by motorguns. I am a proud Principate soldier, and we never shall give in to the lies of the Phoenix Rebellion. A Principate soldier never gives up, not when shot, or flayed, or crushed by a tank. We keep fighting! Now shut up and come with me. The enemy could be on us at any minute."*

The captain turned around and found that the enemy was indeed on them.

* * *

Sylvaine held up her ætherglove, back-to-back with Kayip as the dead rose around them.

"Okay, okay," she said, trying to think if any of her classes in Icaria covered how to deal with the undead. No specific lessons came to mind. "Why don't you... cut through a few of them, then we can run back to the 'truck and drive out of here. Meanwhile, I'll uh, throw a rock or something." Æthermantics would do little against bone, and she certainly wouldn't debase herself by clawing them like some rabid animal.

"What about Marcel and Belona?" Kayip whispered back.

"Gear's-grits, they're soldiers, they should be the ones rescuing us," Sylvaine said, though she knew from experience that, at least in Marcel's case, this was an unreasonable expectation.

One of the dead soldiers stepped forward, aiming a rifle it didn't seem to realize had no barrel. *"Are you the reinforcements we requested?"*

"Uh," Sylvaine stammered.

*"Of course, they are!"* said another soldier. *"Can't be Principate, those tyrants would never recruit a beastwoman!"*

"Ferral!" Sylvaine corrected, thrusting up her glove. "And I'm an engineer."

The dead hesitated a moment, bones clinking as they wavered in their uneasy animation. Then, as one, they cheered.

*"An engineer! An engineer!"* one cried. *"Command has heard our request! An engineer! The battle shall be won!"*

Immediately the skeletal soldiers rushed them, weapons down. They crowded round, cheering in their strange distant voices, sounding more like a sudden squall than human celebrations. While some started to sing an anthem, some old Regency Republic song Sylvaine had heard in a historical-adventure cinegraph, others stared warily at Kayip's sword. The monk let his blade wrap around back into a bracelet.

"Maybe we can find a peaceful resolution," he whispered.

*"Come quickly, engineer!"* One of the soldiers grabbed her arm and started to pull. The rest followed alongside, Kayip among them, as the squad brought her to a pile of rusted gears near where the wall met the hill that Marcel and Belona had crested.

*"I'm sure you've already been given instructions,"* said the soldier. *"We brought this machine in at the beginning of the battle, hand-crafted in cloud-touched Icaria, but the damn thing broke down on us."*

"What?" Sylvaine asked, before she realized that this massive misshapen lump of metal was indeed a war machine of some sort, a very strange sort. Giant treads and spider legs, many-jointed limbs covered in blades, a dozen cockpits set on rotating bearings, a cannon the width of a wine-barrel bent in one direction, a motorgun the size of an adult taur-bull pointed in the other. The design was ambitious beyond a fault, a work of insane genius, or some form of insanity at least. This was, no doubt, a Guild creation, a weapon that could have wrought immense devastation if nothing went wrong. Unfortunately, with a design this complicated a million things could go wrong, and by the look of it, half of them already had.

"I'm not sure this is in a repairable condition," Sylvaine said.

The skeletal soldier made an ethereal hissing noise that sounded angry. *"We've been risking our lives here! You must fix it! For the glory of the Phoenix, for the freedom of all mankind, we must fight! We must take the station and save the Republic!"*

Sylvaine wondered if it would be worth pointing out that they were several lifetimes late on the whole saving-the-Republic thing. Kayip pushed through the crowd.

"If she says it cannot be fixed, then it cannot be fixed!" he said. "Leave us be, in the Demiurge's peace."

This did nothing to mollify the crowd. If anything, their hissing and grumbling grew louder. Beyond the hills of scrap, Sylvaine could hear thousands of soldiers marching, charging, and screaming commands. The battlefield was coming alive, in a manner of speaking. She grabbed Kayip's shoulder and shouted. "It's okay, let me take a look at it, I may be able to get it running again with some spit, elbow grease, and some good old Resurg— uh, Phoenix Rebellion can-do spirit!"

The crowd cheered, as she pressed Kayip down and whispered into his ear. "Stay back."

Sylvaine peeled off a piece of rust-choked metal and crawled into the war machine. The insides were in about the state she expected, decayed to shards of nothing, be it by the elements or the work of eager waste-born critters. She pushed past the disgusting remains of an oozefly nest towards the main æther-engine, which looked large enough to house a cheap bachelor. She followed a fuel tube to the back of the machine, where she could smell a fuel-tank of æther-oil, still half-full.

She waited a few minutes, then hit inside of the body a few times, meaning only to make a sound but actually smashing through the rust. "It's in better shape than I thought!" she shouted. "Get close and in position, I'm about to get it moving!"

As the soldiers cheered and mounted the dead machine, Sylvaine inched back to the opening. She stepped outside the machine and placed her hand on the metal, pulsing æther-waves through it until she zeroed back in on the tankard. She wondered if giving the time, parts, and control over her powers, if she could have rebuilt it. It was a moot question, of course, she had none of those things, and the wisdom of giving a bunch of insane, undead soldiers such an implement of destruction was questionable at best anyhow.

"*Is it ready?*" one of the soldiers asked, sitting just above the æther-oil tank, broken pistol in his eager hand.

"Yeah," Sylvaine said, focusing her energy towards the tank. "Just about."

* * *

The dead rebels charged. Blade against blade, bayonet into bones, fists and kicks and thrown scrap. Marcel froze for a moment. Then he kicked himself free of the soldier who grasped his legs and started shooting at the skeletons wearing blue. Three bullets flew through the ribcage, doing nothing, the fourth smashed through the jaw of the Principate officer, who stumbled, then collapsed completely, skull rolling down the hill.

"Marcel!" shouted Belona. He turned to see a dead soldier thrust forward with its bayonet. Marcel jumped to the side, the blade cutting his jacket. The soldier turned and made to attack again. With a panicked fury, Marcel kicked with his cogleg, managing to knock the gun from the dead man's hand and fling himself to the ground.

Belona elbowed one skeleton, then dashed forward and shoved her pistol at Marcel's assailant as it staggered for its weapon. With a blast, its skull burst into shards. The woman turned round quick to block the punch of another disheveled soldier. She kneed it in the spine, sending it down, before pistol-whipping a third skeleton, with a satisfying crunch.

Marcel could not help but stare impressed. Belona fought like a street-brawler, quick, dirty, and effective, yet moved with the grace of a dancer. There was something mesmerizing about her elegant brutality, an unfettered focus on the kinesiology of combat. A punch thrown with the arc of a flying stone, her kicks snapping like lighting. The woman's perfect coordinated harmony between will and body was somehow as beautiful as any portrait or artistic cinegraph.

A soldier rushed her from behind, swinging a rusty spade. "Belona!" Marcel shouted, shaking off his trance. He fired off two rounds from the ground, chipping the skeleton's femur, causing it to momentarily stumble. Just enough time for Belona to pivot and catch its ribcage with the handle of her pistol. Using that as leverage, she pressed up her free palm and popped the soldier's skull clean off.

Belona pulled her weapon free and swung round for a new target. There wasn't any, the Principate squad had been routed. The dead rebels cheered their victory, one of them helping get Marcel to his feet. A banner was hosted, of old pipes taped together, with hanging scraps of fabric that presumably once held a Phoenix. The soldiers saluted the remnants of dirtied linen with a lively vigor.

*"May the Phoenix rise!"* they shouted. *"Remember the Regency Republic! Remember the Senators of the InterRegno! Let no sacrifice be in vain! Death to the tyrant! Death to Franz Diedrev!"*

Marcel did not bother to inform them that the first pretender-Imperator had been dead for as long as they had. He picked up his looted medal and presented it to the skeleton with the most prestigious looking cap. "Name is Marcus Talbert. I'm a reconnaissance agent up from Phenia, was stationed in a little city called Huile."

The rebel captain nodded. *"Yes, I have some cousins in Huile. Grand old city! I loved the parks."*

"Yes, lovely parks, best in Bastillia by my reckoning," Marcel said. He hadn't a clue the city ever had any greenery, must have been part of the devastation that once lay outside its scarred walls.

*"What are you doing so far from your post, Mr. Talbert?"*

"Almost dying, if you and your men hadn't come," Marcel laughed. "In truth, me and my partner are doing an emergency trip, to deliver a message coordinating the assistance of reinforcing units to this position."

The soldiers murmured, suspicious but eager. The captain glanced over at Belona, who could barely hide her scowl.

*"Your partner has an... imperious air to her."*

Marcel forced another laugh. "Indeed, good eye. She's ex-Principate, served under the usurper himself down in the El'Helmaud Wars. Learned the error of her ways and repented, in her manner, but yes some of her nasty imperial habits have yet to slip."

He heard her mutter something vaguely offensive to the skeletal soldier inspecting her weapon.

"Anyways, captain, we need to get moving real quick. I was wondering if your boys could form an escort of some sort, so that unpleasantries like this do not repeat, and we can get you some well-needed reinforcements."

The captain stared out, thinking. Marcel wished the man had some skin or muscles, not just to avoid the unsettling strangeness of talking with the dead, but so he could see more clearly what emotions were moving through the deceased captain's noggin. Finally, the skeleton shook his head.

*"Not sure that'll be possible,"* he said. *"An Inferno-and-a-half it was just to take this hill. Look what I'd have to bring you through!"* He gestured out to the wide gulch, where a hundred small battles were taking place, Rebels charging Principate positions, Imperials assaulting Phoenix defenses. A loop that had played itself out uncountable times.

*"Sometimes I think this war will never end,"* the captain said with a deep, ethereal sigh. *"But we have our duties, you understand that. We were told to take that station, and by the Spirit of Liberty, we shall."* He pointed out towards a mass of trashed rubble that looked just as much a midden as the rest of the battlefield. Marcel nodded knowingly.

"Listen, you see, though, us two can turn the tides of this battle," Marcel said. "Got a message for..." He thought hard on old history textbooks but came up with nothing. Instead, he searched his mind for historical-fiction pulps, and one popped to mind. "Aceline Avion, of The A.S. Roiland's Justice."

*"Don't know the name, but I know the ship,"* the captain said. *"Didn't they capture it just a few weeks ago?"*

"Sure," Marcel said. "Repairs go fast. And an æroship could turn this stalemate into a decisive victory.

*"That may be the case,"* the captain said. *"But you'll need another way to get your message through. The battlefield ain't crossable."*

Marcel was about to protest, to find a way to explain to the tragically deluded dead that all the ammunition had been gone, and that if they could just get directions they easily could plough through any opposition, when the first explosion went off. A vibrant green blast, a few hills down, sending bones and metal flying, lighting up the gulch with a horrible iridescence. Then there was another blast, then a third, sending thunderclaps across the battlefields.

"What in Inferno?" Marcel asked, sharing a stunned glance with Belona.

It was time for the captain to chuckle. He lifted something from the inside of its coat. It looked like something in-between a butcher-shop's choice liver and an industrial vacuum pump. "Glands from rust locusts," the captain said. "Ammo's going to run dry sooner or later, but with a little ingenuity, these can be made into pretty effective landmines. And we have been quite busy."

More explosions, rust and rubble falling from the hills of junk. Marcel stumbled over towards Belona, who was staring in horror at the green blasts.

"I don't think we can drive through this!" Marcel shouted.

"Impressive deduction there," Belona spat.

Another explosion, much closer. Marcel glanced back down the hill, towards their 'truck. At the base there was some mess of machinery, inflamed. Skeletons lay burned and scattered around it, and Marcel could see, in its flickering light, Sylvaine running as fast as she could.

*"Principate attack!"* the captain shouted in confusion. *"Sabotage, sabotage!"*

The machine groaned and crackled, and then erupted. A great burst of fire and the smell of sangleum. The hill shook, then started to tilt.

"Shit! Shit!" Marcel said, which was of little help.

Slowly, the hill began to slough off waves of rust and dirt, junk falling in tiny avalanches, then small ones, then larger and larger trashfalls.

Marcel started to dash down the hill, moving with the momentum. It took all his focus not to trip and join the tumble. Soldiers did the same, or else collapsed in the waves of junk and stone. Below, Kayip had cut his way through a squad of skeletons and leapt into the 'truck.

"Kayip, Kayip!" Marcel shouted, barely able to keep his footing, weapons and autocar parts and concrete chunks and bones and unearthed fossilized who-knows-what flying past him. He stumbled, and ducked, his hands flailing.

"Marcel!" Belona shouted, as a chuck of metal whizzed at him. The woman jumped forward, into Marcel, sending them both rolling down the hill. Marcel hit the bottom with a groan. The wind was knocked out of him, but all limbs seemed to be in place, even his cogleg.

"Up! Quickly!" Belona shouted already at her feet. Marcel staggered up as Kayip's autotruck turned round. The dead were chasing, shouting angry somethings. In the distance, he could hear explosions, the blasts of the rebel's improvised mines. The 'truck veered close, Sylvaine already in the back. Belona jumped on beside her, as the ferral helped Marcel on.

"Move! Move!" Belona shouted, and Kayip complied. They drove on, fast as the wheels could manage to turn, out the way they came, past skeletons charging and bombs blasting. Few paid them attention, focused as they were on their own struggles.

Marcel turned to see the soldiers still fighting, with broken rifles and rusted bayonets, up on the ridges above. They fought the same battle that they had fought every night for more than a lifetime. A persistent echo of the Severing War, an animosity that near alone had survived the Calamity. How long they'd continue this pointless fight he could not guess. After bones wore to dust, would their spirits fight, unseen but for the faint cries of their rage, mistaken by travelers for an uncanny wind? Above, the sky of the battlefield was lit green, as the gulch shook with a century's worth of hatred.

# CHAPTER 12

"Well, that was a bust."

Sylvaine opened her eyes to see Marcel staring at the dwindling remnants of a campfire, muttering to himself.

"A Demiurge-damned bust-and-a-half," he said, under his breath.

Sylvaine pushed herself up, she hadn't really been able to sleep anyways. They were camped in a hilltop grove. Well, grove was perhaps giving it too much credit, most of the trees were black and stonelike. Fossilized by the æther-roar of the Calamity, now just standing shadows, branches splintered and sharp as knives. Not that the hillside was lifeless. Unfortunately, the opposite was the case. Weeds and brush had taken up residence in the intervening years, some even sprouting from the dead boughs. Rustgrass encircled the clearing, and in the red-tinted leaves of kilnbushes rustled small creatures, ghulshrews by their smell, with hungry, metal-winged stymph doves making nervous crackling coos above, hopping along branches, searching for a meal. Down the hill Sylvaine could hear the crunch of churned dirt as waste-born hogs, corpse-tuskers they were called, grunted and dug through roots and topsoil. Somewhere more distant she could hear the shrill whistle of a soot-sparrow, and in the dim basin of a nearby valley wandered wilds herds of taurs and paledeer. Despite the destruction and corruption of the Calamity, wilderness had returned in force to these lands. She wished nature could take the hint, and just kindly sod off for once.

Marcel finally noticed that Sylvaine was awake. He gave a weak smile and shook his head. "I suppose it was a pretty bone-headed plan, wasn't it?"

Sylvaine nodded noncommittally. Honestly, if the dead hadn't mined the battlefield, they might have been able to make it through. But, as it were, it had been just another opportunity to catch Lazarus Roache that had slipped through their collective fingers. Soon he'd be safely ensconced in Narida Heights, and no one had a theory yet on how they might de-ensconce him. She stared up at the sky. It would be dawn in a couple of hours, she could see the first hints of light, the slight dimming of the stars around the horizon.

"I told ya it was crazy," Felik said. The man had not even pretended to sleep, eyes bleary and bloodshot. "Could have just gone my way. Would have been easy, we would have been free."

"Maybe so," Marcel said. "Or maybe we'd each get a bullet in the neck courtesy of your raider friends."

Felik coughed. "Where's the trust in this world anymore?"

A skragger flew by in awkward arcs, landing with surprising precision on one of the fossilized trees near where Kayip was in silent meditation. In its toothed beak was an arm, human by the looks of it, sleeve torn, skin withered and mummified by sun and dust. Sylvaine didn't even bother wondering who it came from. Out here such grotesquery just seemed the norm. Marcel watched with a sort of disgusted fascination as the reptilian bird began tearing skin from bone.

"Liberty's bloody heart," he muttered.

"Yeah," Sylvaine said. "I can't begin to understand why anyone would want to live out here."

"Maybe it's their home," said Belona. Sylvaine glanced over, she had been quite sure the recumbent woman had been asleep. Indeed, she still looked asleep, head on her bag, eyes closed, breath deep and slow.

"Well, the whole world's not as fucked as the Wastes," Marcel said. "So, unless they're chained in place, which I'll give that some are, they could take the first autobus, horse, good pair of boots, *whatever*, and just leave."

"You really don't understand what home means, do you, little rat scout?" Belona said, begrudgingly sitting up. "One does not simply abandon their home, even if it is scarred and ruined. Look out," and she gestured towards the darkness, to the overgrown ruins and arid gullies lit only by moonlight and the occasional flash of lampflies. "This was all once Vastium, the greatest land ever tilled by human hands. The birthplace of the old Imperium, the heart of civilization, of culture. Can you imagine it at its height, the grand boulevards, the whirring factories, the gilded citadels, the rolling, verdant farmland? The Demiurge himself could not craft anything to rival its splendor! How can you ask that people forget what their home once was? Is not even a memory of an age so grand superior to our current petty squalor?"

"Well, you can't exactly eat memory," Sylvaine said. "You can't live in memory, can't build a hydroætheric contra-rotating turbine out of memory."

"And what memories could you possibly cherish?" Belona asked. "I trace my lineage back to the noble families of this land, those who first ruled in the name of the Imperator, those who helped raise humanity up from an age of barbarism. It is in their memory that I fight, it is their legacy I see buried here. It is only by returning to their greatness can the enemies of the Principate be felled, only by their example can the world be rebuilt upon these ashes and Vastium made whole again."

"You know, my family's from Vastium too," Felik said.

Belona stared at the raider with abject disgust.

"Believe it or not, I do know home," Marcel said with a smirk. "I'm fighting for mine. To return home knowing it's safe and sound, with Lazarus Roache deep in the ground."

Sylvaine glanced at the man, unsure what to make of his rhyming aside. Did he truly believe Huile would be all good and dandy once Roache was out of the picture? It had been in pretty rough shape when they left, lots of fires and corpses. She had never seen a machine repaired by the application of bloodshed. For herself, the problem was quite the opposite. Her once-homes were quite safe, Icaria and Taliers both, but there was no way she could ever return to either.

"Safe and sound," Belona chuckled. "Ah, I pity you Resurgence worms. How can there ever be true security without the guarding arm of the Imperator?"

"I can't believe you're still parroting that imperial propaganda," Marcel spat. "Especially after what we saw in Opus's whatever! Cadavers still praising their dead imperator. Fighting an empty battle, totally forgotten, lost in their zeal and pointless rage."

"That is the moral you took?" Belona gave a vicious grin, lips curled like a snarling hound. "Figures, the ignorance and improbity of your Confederacy has made you blind. Did you miss the dead rebels extolling the empty vices of their dead rebellion? Even with their blood drained, they set their undying wills towards sabotage and trickery. There is indeed no rest for the wicked. While my noble principate soldiers kept fighting for honor and glory. They did not idle after they had died but continued their task beyond even what their duties demanded."

Sylvaine wondered if the woman somehow did not notice her own hypocrisy, praising her side for the exact same actions she took as condemnatory for her enemy. Probably not, so enraptured as she was in her own righteous anger. To be fair, it wasn't as if Marcel was particularly more self-aware.

"The cause of the Phoenix Rebellion isn't dead!" Marcel said, standing up, which looked a bit awkward as everyone else was sitting. "Liberty and freedom live on in the heart of the Resurgence."

"An echo of an echo of past treachery," Belona said, meeting Marcel's height. "The UCCR exists only as a stubborn child made country, desperate to avoid punishment for the Calamity its forebearers inflicted on us all."

"Are you seriously, actually blaming the Calamity on the rebellion?" Marcel was nearly shouting. Felik jostled himself out of the way of the two, while Kayip kept meditating. "It was that damned facility, the what's-it-called, that weapon on the æthergrid that your Principate built which destroyed all of this, Vastium, your home. It is your Calamity!"

"Our Calamity!" Belona sneered, chin-scar bending. "The Omphalos Facility's purpose was one of peaceful energy production, it was the rebel terrorist attack on it that caused it to detonate."

At this point, the argument descended into chaos, accusations shouted at each other, with hand gestures flung wildly and bits of spittle flying. Sylvaine sighed and rested her head onto the fossilized tree. The story she had been taught about the Calamity was closer to Marcel's telling. Whatever Belona's excuses, the Omphalos most definitely *was* a weapon. A machine built upon the central nexus of the æthergrid, it could have powered all the cities of Æthmach, or just as easily destroy them. It had done the latter, vitrifying a metropolis of millions in the time between a clock's tick. This had only been slightly unexpected. Sylvaine had read old Icarian textbooks pre-dating the Calamity that openly theorized the possibility of ætheric weapons like the one that would later be used to sever the world. She had also learned in Icaria, from Guild sources which were no doubt more objective than any partisan propaganda, that there were some specks of truth to the Principate's claims. There had been an attack by a Phoenix Rebellion army in the hours leading up to the Calamity, and from voxbox messages from engineers inside the facility, it seemed like the rebellion was in full and complete control of the facility at the time of final, cataclysmic activation. But trying to dissect the disaster and attribute the proper proportions of blame struck Sylvaine as futile sophistry. The Calamity happened, she could see the evidence by just glancing down the hill, why bother reigniting the war that had spawned it?

She turned her head to see that Kayip had opened his one good eye. With a weary sigh, he uncrossed his legs and stood.

"...And if you think the Imperator wouldn't be happy to wear your cured skin as an evening gown," Marcel ranted, jabbing his finger forward, "then you're an even more stupendous idiot than—"

"Enough!" said Kayip. "We were to rest here and plan our next move, not broadcast our position to every raider, slaver, and scrapper within ten kiloms."

"Yes, please quiet your rat-tongue, before it gets us all killed," Belona said.

"You are acting no better," Kayip said. "Is winning some argument more important than bringing Roache to justice?"

Belona bit her lip. "I merely sought to educate."

"She's spreading her lies as thick as a glutton knifes butter on his morning-fucking-toast!" Marcel shouted. Kayip glared. "Fine. Civil!" Marcel said, hands up in resignation.

After a few seconds of exchanged scowls, the two combatants sat back down. Kayip nodded and descended to his cross-legged position, though he kept his eye open. For a moment, something akin to tranquility returned to the campsite.

"Gear's-grits, you two," Sylvaine said. "This war's been burning for more than a century, split the world in two, do you really need to fight it out here as well?"

"The Resurgence has only ever been defending freedom," Marcel protested. "Inferno, it's your Guild who were profiteering off the war and helped the Imperator build his damn death machine anyhow."

"How can you even... how dare you!" Sylvaine sputtered in fury. "You're throwing this on the Guild? Why, why, we are, they are, the uplifters of humanity! We never started any wars; we just build what's needed for... I mean, it's not a craftsperson's duty to monitor what someone does with their creation, the Guild only ever—I mean how dare you! Without the Engineers' work people would still be living in caves and hitting each other with sticks, are we, are we supposed to stop our innovation just because some idiots decided to use it improperly and, I mean, listen, what I'm saying is, I mean, we only ever... Are you insane? Do you hear yourself? Blaming the Engineer's Guild! What nonsense! We only ever built what was ordered, that's not profiteering that just, really, if the guild didn't make the weapons someone else would have. And it would have been worse, and inferior quality, and how *dare* you!"

Kayip let his head fall and rubbed his temple with exasperation.

"Oh, Imperator's mercy," Belona said rolling her eyes. "Can you stop with this little engineer's schtick. I don't care what lies you tell yourself; Ferrals cannot be engineers. Their blood is wrong. I know of campaigns in Videk against the tribes, and not a single time has any hirsute bastard picked up an ætherglove and started melting tanks. So please spare us your insanity."

From one insult to another. Sylvaine opened her mouth but found no words. Just the shame that she didn't dare prove the woman wrong right here right now.

"Belona!" Kayip snapped.

"It's true, she is an engineer," Felik cut in, unexpectedly. "I saw her, in that battlefield. She put her glove to that war machine and turned it into slag with a single bolt of æther." He turned to Sylvaine and flashed her a smile. She didn't know what quite to make of that.

"True as the morning dew," said Marcel, finger jabbing. "Seen her do a heck of a lot more, too. Sorry if that bursts your shoddily crafted Principate prejudices."

Sylvaine considered pointing out that Marcel hadn't really believed her either at first but decided against it. Belona glanced around, and seeing a united front, leaned back and shrugged.

"It is a strange world," she said.

"Indeed, it is," said Kayip. "Perhaps after what we saw in the gulch, it may be good to discuss what we might be up against when we make it to Narida Heights."

"A bunch of raiders?" Belona offered.

"More than that," Kayip said. "Lazarus Roache has aligned himself with a sect of waste-born cultists, who worship the foul children of the Calamity, demons."

"*Ætheric aberrations,*" Sylvaine and Marcel corrected in sync. Sylvaine continued: "And there's nothing supernatural about them. Just the reflections of the darker side of humanity's collective psyche made physically manifest in the medium of raw æther."

Belona shook her head. "I'm with the priest. *Demons* is the preferable term, no sense hiding the nightmares behind technical lingo."

"There was a time when I would tell everyone I met this truth," Kayip said. "Most folk outside the Wastes simply labeled me mad, so I've been more reticent in recent years."

"I wouldn't have believed it myself," Marcel said, "If I hadn't seen the strange powers Roache's old foreman had."

"Oh, I believe it fully," Belona said. "I've campaigned in these Wastes; I've seen what can come out of them."

"And he has this drug, slickdust," Marcel explained. "Gives him the power to control others' minds."

"Yes, I know that mutagenic poison," Belona said. "Bastards have been smuggling it around Holtag for years. It doesn't control minds, it's just like any drug, it's addictive, it preys upon peoples' weak wills."

"No," Sylvaine said. "I've—*we've,* seen it in action. It messes with internal æthers, gives Lazarus Roache, only Lazarus Roache I think, suggestive powers. At high doses, he could command someone to stab their sister, and they'd do it."

Belona glanced incredulously over to Kayip, who seemed to have become her barometer for rationality. The monk nodded.

"Well demon-powers or slickdust or whatever makes little difference," Belona said. "They're just another weapon at our enemy's disposal. Stealth is our only chance to get the bastard. If we get caught out in a pitched fight, it won't matter if Roache's men are bringing rifles, or magic, or sharpened sticks. It's a numbers game that we'd lose. The key is to be prepared and vigilant, to wait for the exact right moment to..." Belona trailed off. "Someone's approaching."

"What?" Sylvaine asked, before focusing her ears. The rustle of brush. Someone *was* approaching. Two people by the sound of it, sneaking up the hill. How had Belona heard them before she did?

With a series of silent gestures and head movements, not all in agreement, Marcel pulled Felik back towards the 'truck, while Sylvaine, Belona, and Kayip moved forward, down into the brush, slowly, searching for the intruders. Belona had her rifle at the ready, while Kayip had unfurled his azure blade from his wrist. Sylvaine awkwardly carried a pistol, but had no intention of using it, better leave that to the soldier and war monk. Instead, she squinted through the dark, and caught the gleam of a weak handtorch. Two figures were down below, in the middle of a patch of needleshrubs. She bent her ears and listened in.

"...Shit. Shit. Shit. Ouch. Shit," muttered the first, in a deep voice, trying to move his leg.

"Quiet Erwin!" hissed the second, in a nervous tenor.

"Demiurge-damned Wastes, caught my damned pants— Shit!"

"The deserter's camp's right there, get your stiffland arse loose and come on!"

"Shut it, Jurgis, I'm coming. Imperator's shit, it just digs into you, doesn't it?"

"What kind of scout are you?"

"One trained in a civilized land, where the plants don't have thorns made of fucking metal and—shit!"

"Well, just stay here and don't make more noise. I'll try to get visual on the deserter. Get yourself loose, and we'll head back to camp. Maybe I can even get a good shot off and we can head back to Holtag tonight."

A shot did go off, from Belona's rifle. It burst into a wall of burnt brick not far behind the two scouts. They both yelped in different pitches. They dashed back down the hill in an immediate rout, the one called Erwin able to free himself from the brush surprisingly quick when his life was on the line. Belona fired off two more shots, neither hitting their targets. The two jumped onto motorcycles left beneath a skragtree and drove off as fast as their wheels could spin.

Sylvaine trudged back up the hill, the rest already back at the top.

"They're scouts from Holtag," Sylvaine said.

"I'm aware," Belona said. "I know their vehicles, recognized their incompetence."

"Speaking of incompetence, great aim you got there," Marcel said with a sneer. "Were you even trying to hit them?"

"Killing them would have made no difference," Belona said. "Those aren't long-distance trackers or bounty hunters, they must have a base camp nearby, with more soldiers. We have to get moving, now." She kicked a rock with impotent fury. "Demiurge damn it Goss!"

# CHAPTER 13

*"Demiurge damn it Goss, what have you gotten yourself into?"* Colonel
Goss muttered to himself; coat wrapped tight to protect himself from the
waste-night's chill. He stood by the edge of the military camp, the first such
he had been in in over two years. It was meant to be a reconnaissance
mission, that's what Goss had signed the papers for, just a simple search
that would, like most Holtag forays into the Wastes, fizzle out in a few days
due to extenuating circumstances such as 'dangerous raiders,' 'issues with
supply lines,' or 'a crippling lack of morale and general poor work ethic.'
Instead, the expedition seemed to involve half of the armed forces of
Holtag. Behind him was an actual army, one a fraction of the size Belona
Agrippus had once sent to Huile, but still, a real true army that was, at least
in theory, his command, his responsibility.

"You say something Colonel?" asked Commandant Lechslov, sitting
on a foldable chair, idly carving a figure into wastewood. He swore, and
squinted at his creation, some misshapen soldier's face, now noseless, and
tossed the half-carved stick into a pile of similar failures, before picking up
a new piece of wood, offered by a nearby soldier.

"No, Commandant," Colonel Goss said, trying to hide his slight anger
and overwhelming anxiety. It was Lechslov's fault this whole thing got out
of hand. The man had come to him, the morning after Belona had left,
asking what had happened to the Justice Officer and her prisoners. Goss
had given him the answer he had rehearsed with his once-general, that the
woman had been given transfer orders to bring the prisoners up to the
Darbas Work Camp. And that should have been that. The lie was good

enough, a middle of nowhere labor camp that would excuse the woman's absence long enough for her to get her proper vengeance, and it's not like Lechslov had ever before shown interest in actually checking up on these things. But then the man had started ranting about some Resurgence terrorist. Turned out a soldier who had been in the Troll's Heart Bar had recognized one of the prisoners from a wanted poster. A *UCCR* wanted poster, of all things. Just recently posted across Resurgence and neutral towns, for the capture of one Marcel Talwar, who had supposedly conspired to aid in some insurrection down in Huile. It must have been the Huile thing that triggered Lechslov's obsession, because he made the unprecedented move of actually calling up the Darbas Work Camp on the voxbox, and when he found out there was no transport order the man had gone ballistic. And then Goss...

*Demiurge damn it, Goss!* All he'd been trying to do was to deflate the whole thing, show how ridiculous Lechslov's questions were. Why, there had just been some mistake. Maybe the order was to a different work camp. Belona would set things straight when she returned. Why, Lechslov didn't honestly think the woman had committed treason or something? *Treason.* Why did he have to say *treason,* why did he have to use that word? For once that djinn had left its lamp, there was no way to push it back in. Suddenly *treason* was a possibility, then not just a possibility, but a probability, then not just a probability, but an almost certainty, only requiring the last piece of evidence. Lechslov had always hated Belona, for jumping up the imperial command while he languished, but this paranoia was on a whole new level. Of course, Goss couldn't deny the man's request for a small expedition, that would be too suspicious even if Goss technically had the power to veto it. But somehow that simple reconnoiter had ballooned into whatever this was, with Lechslov at the head, and Goss certainly couldn't stay behind and let the man commit whatever madness he would try to against their old general.

So, he was here. Freezing his buttocks in the frigid wind. Waiting all night for a pair of scouts who, by his guess, had probably gotten themselves killed somehow.

"There they are!" came the shout of one soldier. Around the bend of a hillock came two Beghart-7 model motorcycles. They drove down the unpaved, hole-ridden excuse for a road, and after a few minutes puttered to a stop nearby. Two frazzled soldiers, Private Jurgis Kalnin and Private Erwin Edhart, stepped off their motorbikes and saluted.

"At ease soldie—" started Goss.

"Your report?" interrupted Lechslov.

Erwin stepped forward. "We approached the enemy position, but were, uh, spotted and had to retreat."

"That's it?" Lechslov asked. "I trust you two with this vital mission and you come back with nothing? Nothing at all!"

"Of course, not nothing!" Jurgis said. "We got a good look at the enemy position, and some great intel."

There was silence for a moment. A strix screeched somewhere distant.

"Such as?" Lechslov asked.

"Well, right," Jurgis said. "The Justice Officer, she was, uh, not alone. Making camp with the prisoners."

"Out of their chains?" Lechslov asked.

The two scouts glanced at each other.

"...Yes?" said Erwin. His voice was far from sure, and Goss was starting to suspect their reporting might not be entirely truthful.

"Damnations, I knew it," Lechslov scowled. "She's planning something with them. Something antithetical to the goals of our noble Principate."

"Well," Goss said. "I don't think we should be hasty in our conclusions. There's a lot of reasons they could be temporarily unchained. I mean you didn't overhear anything, so you don't even know what they are up to."

"You didn't get close enough to listen in?" Lechslov asked with irritation.

"Oh no, we did, sure we did," Erwin said. Goss silently cursed himself for giving them the idea.

"Yes, Commandant, they were saying..." Jurgis began. "That they... were going to make contact... with..."

"Raiders," Erwin finished. "Some raiders connected to that Felik guy."

"Fascinating," Lechslov said. "I always knew that woman was perfidious. Perhaps she is trying to trade the prisoners, or worse, using them as leverage to make some political connections. Is this new behavior, or has she been plotting and scheming for years, right underneath our noses?"

Goss was starting to sweat despite the chill. Prisoner trading, rendezvous with raiders? None of this made sense, none of it was part of his ex-general's plans. No doubt assumptions were being made, but if he pressed too hard, he might reveal his own biases, reveal that he himself had had a hand in the Agrippus's completely justifiable and honorable deceits. It was up to him to cool the situation down.

"Gentlemen," he began. "I have been in the service many years, served in many campaigns and battles, and I've found the most common mistake made is to be too hasty with limited intel. Justice Officer Agrippus has been a loyal servant of the Imperator for years, though her behavior is suspicious there may indeed be an innocuous explanation, one that does not warrant wasteful military action."

"If she's so innocuous," Erwin said, "why did she shoot at us when we were spotted?"

"She did?" asked Goss.

"She did!" shouted Lechslov. "Then that settles all doubts. The woman had attempted to enact violence upon the servants of the Imperator. Colonel," he turned to Goss. "With your permission, I would like to reorient the goals of this expedition from simply tracking Justice Officer Belona Agrippus and her co-conspirators, to capturing them for the purpose of formal interrogation."

"Well, I mean," Goss began. "That might, uh, seem reasonable given the circumstances, but—"

"Excellent!" Commandant Lechslov said. "I'll begin preparations now. Good work gentlemen, I think we shall have our answers very shortly."

With that the man strode back to camp, the soldiers following. Goss's mouth opened and closed, as he desperately searched for the words that could turn this all around, that would protect his ex-general and then get all back to Holtag. The only whispered words that came were: *"Demiurge damn it, Goss."*

# Chapter 14

"...So why do you fight so hard to crush the will of the people?" Marcel asked, holding tight to his seat as the 'truck bounced rambunctiously across the churned landscape of the Wastes. Perhaps it was a mistake to have the one-eyed Kayip drive, but Sylvaine seemed to be guiding him decently enough from the front seat. Across the 'truck Belona sat beside a half-sleeping Felik, a supercilious smirk stretched across her face.

"I fight for order," Belona said. "So that the people's will gets manifested not by the greatest charlatan, but the greatest man."

"You mean that petty, spoiled, tyrant Imperator, born into a lineage of distant, isolated luxury?" Marcel chuckled bitterly, staring out at the endless ruin they were passing.

"His lineage built the first imperium; built the civilization you squander." Belona stamped her boot on the floorboard. "Inferno, Franz Diedrev lived a mere century ago, and he reformed your sick republic—"

"—*Destroyed* it, and then started the Severing War which blew up your own fucking homeland!" Marcel interjected, bouncing a centimeter off his chair as the 'truck crunched over an ill-placed rock. "And I've lived in this 'chaos' you describe. Honestly, not so bad."

"Yes, perhaps for you comfortable upper-middle class types, it does not seem awful."

"How—?" Marcel began.

"It is written on your face, on your hands," Belona sneered. "You had an easy childhood. You did not live in poverty or squalor, did not work for piss wages in dense factories buildings until your bones ached."

"The Citizen's Confederacy has been the best thing to ever happen to the labor class!" Marcel shouted. "My family would always vote for the Worker's Union Party—"

"Oh, you voted!" Belona laughed. "How brave and noble! You stamped a piece of paper and patted yourself on the back so that someone who lied about caring for workers might win over someone who lied about caring for merchants."

"If someone tries to pervert the will of the people, we exercise our right to protest and force them out!"

"And are you one of these protesters? Fighting for the UCCR on one day, and protesting against it on another?" Belona asked, studying him as the 'truck crunched through a bramble patch. "No, I don't believe so. Maybe you marched around with some drinking friends, singing empty slogans, but you are no unionist firestoker. No scars on your face, I bet you stayed at home reading philosophy books in your parents' fancy townhouse."

"I have been to protests!" Marcel said. It was the truth! Sure, he had never gone to those rare riots that sometimes broke out in the Phenian industrial districts. One can criticize or reform, but it was foolish to try and burn anything down. He was sure this nuance was lost on the imperial. As was the fact that private learnings of any sort, philosophy, history, even *fiction* could be a praxis. And his parents never owned a townhouse! Just a sensible midsized apartment.

"And if our Confederacy is so pathetic to you, why do you wage endless war to try and crush it?" Marcel continued, glancing out at the desolation that passed them, which seemed proof enough of the Principate's evil.

Belona shook her head. "Do you think I like war, Mr. Mercenary, Mr. Bounty Hunter? War is duty, the duty is to unite all humanity under one peaceful banner. I have seen what war does, and I have seen the slime that comes with it, the parasites who make their fortunes off the suffering of others. I wish only to end that suffering. If some die in the process, it is a lesser evil."

Marcel squeezed his eyes tight at the pure stupidity of this all. Belona seemed like she had some intelligence to her, but in truth she was just a living vessel of propaganda. Maybe the only way to get the Imperator's lies out of the head of someone like her was to use bullets, that's what Alba would do. Inferno, that's what they had to do in Huile. There was a common theme in Resurgence literature, or pulps at least, of the redeemed imperial, the servant of the Imperator who recognizes the lies they fight under and switches sides, often dying heroically in a final act of atonement. But perhaps that was just a fairy tale. There was no saving people this caught up in delusions. Killing them was almost a kindness then, even with something as unpleasant as sangleum gas.

He stared out the back of the 'truck, but all he found was a shrinking taur-heifer staring back.

"It's just baffling…" Marcel said. "All the Citizens' Confederacy wants is freedom, autonomy, and equality."

"Yes, just freedom." Belona gave a dry chuckle. "Freedom is why the Resurgence keeps planting bombs in Principate cities, why they fund terrorist movements in our lands."

"Liberation movements!"

"And this equality you love to harp on?" Belona said, scratching the scar on her chin. "Let me teach you a secret. People aren't equal. Never have been. The vagrant bumming change is not the equal of a soldier defending her homeland. A petty thief or scammer is not the equal of a loyal worker. People make themselves unequal, Marcel, and all the Principate does is acknowledge that."

"Strix-fucking-guts!" Felik said suddenly. "Do ya two ever shut up?"

"Your opinion wasn't asked, raider scum," Belona snapped.

"Raiders, want to know why there are raiders?" Felik asked. He tried to get up but was unable to work his chains right in the jostling 'truck. "Because of the bickering of two giants, the UCCR and the Principate. In the middle, is everyone fucking else. And you know what? We're happier that way."

"Happier in your butchery and barbarism?" Marcel asked.

"Happier and freer. You know why? No taur-fucking ideology. You two are so glad to kill and die for some nonsense ideas some politician or academy fool made up in his head."

"Freedom isn't some abstract philosophical ideal," Marcel said with a stomp. "It's real and present, in the heart of every man, woman, and child of the Resurgence."

"Ya want to know freedom?" Felik shook his chains. "Let me loose, and I'll show you. We raiders are the freest people of all, free to do what we want, go where we want."

"That's not freedom, that's chaos," Marcel said.

Felik gestured. "Now you're sounding like that imperial bitch."

Belona causally knocked the raider to the floor. "See, he proves the emptiness of this nonsense idea of 'freedom.' Life is about duty, about serving something. He serves nothing."

"Nothing?" Felik wiggled back up. "No, the only difference is the people I help out, I rely on, are my mates. No abstract notions, no nation states or prime ministers or Imperators. Person to person, how it should be."

"And the slaves?" Marcel asked.

"Oh yeah, me and my mates trade slaves as well."

Belona stared at Felik. "It's like I'm looking into the future of the UCCR."

* * *

Sylvaine glanced back from the front seat to watch Marcel and Belona shout at each other. *Gear's-grits*, at this rate one of them was going to kill the other. She hoped it was Marcel taking out Belona, but honestly, if it came to fists and knives, she had to give the advantage to the imperial.

The raider, for his part, turned to catch Sylvaine's eye through the glassless window. He smiled and nodded knowingly. As she wondered what in Inferno that was about, a wave of static suddenly burst from her glove. A yelp escaped from her mouth, her fur on edge.

"Are you all right?" Kayip asked, glancing over.

"Fine," Sylvaine mumbled, not quite confident. She examined her glove, which was shaking slightly. Tiny sparks of æthericity flew on arcs between her fingers, reacting to the slightest focus, the slightest alteration of mood or mind. She raised her gloved hand up and out the open window, afraid that a spurt of irritation or flash of surprise might cause her to unwittingly slag the dashboard of the 'truck. More crackling and sparks, air sizzling as flashes of æthericity bounced off from her glove's sparkpoints.

What was going on? Sylvaine tried not to panic, had her brief stint of engineering broken something inside her, unleashed the shattered remnants of her Knack, set wild her powers? Or was this now a symptom of her æthermantics leaving her, a final frizzing dissipation as the last remnants of slickdust cleared her system? Yet despite the familiar fears, these theories seemed lacking. There was no heat inside of her, no crawling echoes of Roache's words. This idle aimless energy didn't feel like it was coming from her, but from somewhere else. From the wind, or the earth, or *something*.

"Ah," Kayip said, with another glance. "I believe there is an explanation coming. Do not worry, you are not the first engineer to have trouble here. You will see."

Kayip pulled the 'truck over and got out. The rest followed suit, Belona mumbling something about scouting the area, and Marcel taking the prisoner off to a tree to do his business. Kayip gestured to a pile of stones that was probably once a building, or a town.

"I have a fuel cache hidden here. It has not been my first time crossing the ravine, and I suspected it would not be my last."

The desolation that surrounded them seemed the usual for the Wastes. Wild plains covered with dots of taur herds, hilltops host to ruins or sickly copes of scarwood trees, great pillars of concrete that had once been raised upway roads but were now simple obelisks that commemorated nothing. The only oddity was a long row of raised earth, devoid of even the scrappiest weeds. She dimly remembered looking at an old map, and seeing written, in recent ink, *The Great Ravine*.

Sylvaine raised her hand in the direction of the supposed ravine, and found that her glove reacted, vibrating and fizzing. With caution, she walked up to its edge. Indeed, it was "great," a massive gash in the earth that stretched far in both directions. Sylvaine could not see the end of it, and, if the map was correct, would have to make half a week's detour if she wanted to. Its width was significant, but not as impressive. A fast motorcycle with significant buildup and a good ramp could plausibly make the jump, though any idiot who might try it would no doubt be turned to red mush as they landed on the rock-strewn landscape beyond. Yet 'great' as this long hole was, it was not a ravine. Ravines were natural structures, the results of millennia of work by busy streams or rivers. This wound in the ground was not natural, Sylvaine was certain of that. Heat emanated from its depths, and nothing grew in its shadows nor for metres around its edge. As Sylvaine stared down, she could see no bottom, just darkness, down and down and down, the far wall of the faux ravine never seeming to meet up with the near, no matter how deep.

Wait... no, not just darkness. Sylvaine could see something, a faint hint of glowing red, so far down she could not be sure it wasn't her imagination. A distant aura of crimson that ran down the length of the ravine, moving, flickering, glowing almost bright for an instant, before cooling down to near indiscernibility.

Her investigations were interrupted by a sudden moan.

"Oh, there we go! Freedom at last!"

Felik was pissing into the massive chasm. Marcel stood beside him, looking away down the slope with some embarrassment.

"Taur's balls, ya guys really don't believe in regular bathroom breaks, do you?" the raider said, continuing to drain himself.

Sylvaine snorted in disgust and turned to see Kayip walking in from the other direction, holding a large browning can that bore the off-sweet aroma of æther-oil. He gestured down the supposed ravine, to a distant assemblage of sheet-metal shacks and listless windmills that crowned both cliffsides.

"Bridgetown, we should be able to get there in an hour, and there's a campsite not too many kiloms past. It should put us within striking distance of Narida Heights, but far enough to avoid scouts."

"I hope so," Sylvaine said. She still didn't know how they would crack that egg, how they would get Roache. The best option seemed to be to take it slow and set up an ambush for when the tycoon left to... make diplomatic calls? Take a tour of local ruins? Pick up milk? She wasn't sure what Lazarus Roache exactly did out here, but he'd have to leave sometime and then they could strike, probably. Of course, the imperial would be far more hasty, desperate to attack quick, regardless of the dangers. Between her death wish and the monk's martyr complex, Sylvaine was starting to wonder if she was the only one who would very much like to live through all this, *thank you very much!* Even Marcel seemed to get a distance in his eyes when discussing heroic sacrifices.

Well, it was go forward or... nothing really. She had jumped on this revenge train for the full ride, and there weren't any stops out here. Sylvaine glanced back at the nothingness of the Wastes they had just driven through. It was hard to imagine anyone making a life in these barrens. Just ruins and grasping plant growth, the only sign of habitation the occasional plume of smoke from a chimney of a scrap-built shack, or the embers of a burning one. She did notice, not too far out, what looked like a man on a horse. As she squinted, it seemed to her as if the equine mount was reflecting glitters of the midday sun, but before she could get a better look, the figure disappeared behind a copse of twisting skragtrees. Somewhere a soot-sparrow trilled.

"Bloatbeast's arse," said Felik, stepping over. "Am I the only one that needs to unleash a river here? You two really need to drink more, dehydration is a killer out here in the Wastes."

"Yeah, whatever," Marcel said, pulling the prisoner's chain with a loose grip. He stared down the hill, in the direction of Belona. "Hey Sylvaine, can you watch this idiot for a bit? Need to make sure that… woman hasn't decided to flee, or vox' up Holtag, or something."

"Sure," Sylvaine said, as Marcel stomped off to investigate his paranoias.

Felik approached the edge of the cliff and whistled as he stared into its depth.

"You're pretty smart, right?" he asked.

"I went to the Guild Academy in Icaria."

"Nice," the man said, though she very much suspected he had never heard of it. "So, do you know what the deal is with this ravine? The story I've been told is that a long time ago, before the Calamity, all of this was… well not a big hole. Flat I guess, maybe with a few more trees. Then the Calamity happened and *crack!* Big tear in the ground. I don't think anyone's got to the bottom, maybe you could ride an ærocopter down, but I wouldn't want to try the climb."

"Would be a terrible idea either way," Sylvaine said. "Look." She put her glove over the rising hot air and sparks started to fly. A sudden bolt of æthericity shot from her glove, arcing over the ravine, and turning some buried something into a burning pile of melted metal.

"Dang," Felik said. "Yeah, I've heard of engineers complaining about this thing."

"It's a broken ætherline," Sylvaine said. "I'm sure of it."

"What, like some power lines?" Felik asked.

"Not quite. These lines are massive, and ancient, they go under the earth, all around. All civilization, be it in Æthmach or Muhit, is built on these ætherlines. It's what lets ætheric engineering work, the oil I burn in my glove just gets the reaction going, it's these ætherlines where I'm actually drawing power."

"Really?" the man seemed genuinely marveled. "I had no idea. Seems important."

"I mean, yeah," Sylvaine said. "Why do you think nobody's circumnavigated the globe? You go too far off the grid, and the æthermantics just fizzle. Æroships fall from the sky, boat engines stop working."

"Why don't you build more grid?" Felik asked.

"Can't," Sylvaine said. "No idea how. I know the Malva built up some pseudo-replicas for their own ships, but they refuse to share their notes. Even so, at the best those would be weak and primitive compared to the real ones."

"Wait," Felik said. "Then who built these then?"

"Well," Sylvaine stretched her neck and pondered the best answer. "If you ask the monk, he'll say it was the Demiurge, or his 'Ascended,' or whatever."

"But you're not some superstitious fool."

"I mean, I believe in facts, evidence. All those stories, the Church, why did they come about? Because some dead Imperator had some delirious visions? People are just desperate for answers and the world isn't keen on giving them easy."

"But the Guild knows the truth." Felik nodded.

"No, not really," Sylvaine said. "I mean there's an explanation, of course. These lines, the ruins with their advanced technology, all the result of 'pre-homid autochthons.' But what does that mean? It means we have no idea who built them. Just that they're old and gone."

"Ya seem pretty dang smart," Felik said. "Wiser than anyone I know out here, that's for certain."

"Not a high bar."

"Oh, you'd be surprised," Felik said. "But you're definitely smarter than any of those three you've been putting around with. So, what do you think about the ætherlines? What's your theory?"

The man was asking a lot of questions, but to be honest Sylvaine didn't mind answering them. It was nice for someone to pay attention to her, for the right reasons, to learn, not just to gawk or mock.

"I think the Church's Ascended theory isn't entirely off," Sylvaine said. "Someone human or human-like built these things. But I don't think they ascended off to Paradise, they just did what we're doing now. They blew themselves up for some stupid reason, and now we have to piece together the wreckage."

"Maybe it was Ferrals," Felik suggested.

Sylvaine gave a hollow laugh. "Yes, us Ferrals. Built civilization then fucked off to live in the trees."

"I'm serious! Maybe they realized they didn't need such things and left it for us humans."

"I wish I could even imagine that," Sylvaine said. "No, Ferrals have lived in the wilds cause that's all they can do. Humanity built all this, I mean they blew it up too, but they did first build it, while Ferrals spent centuries making huts out of twigs."

"Obviously not because of lack of talent!" Felik said. "I mean you went up to Icaria, and that's supposed to be the greatest stifflander city. And you're an engineer."

Sylvaine stared at her sparking glove. "Not out of my own ability."

"Slickdust?" Felik asked.

Sylvaine just nodded. It had seemed too good to be true, Roache's drug, a miracle substance that would unlock her Knack, make her the engineer she always dreamed of. Well, it was true, but that truth came with a lot of asterisks, hidden clauses in a deal she hadn't realized she was making.

"So, ya took the drug, got the power, and aren't under Roache's control?" Felik said. "Sounds to me like ya made out well."

"Sounds like you're a damned idiot!" Sylvaine snapped.

"Hey now," Felik said. "Nobody likes being under that man's yoke, but you escaped. And once he's dead in the ground you'll be totally free, and a powerful engineer. I respect that. Out here in the Wastes, you got to make your own way, take what you want, and crush the consequences. Either you're a raider, or a slave, and from where I'm standing you don't look like a slave."

"I hope I don't look like a raider either."

"Nah, too clean." The man smirked as if he just told a great joke. "But really, listen, you're not like those three. That wild monk, that imperial bitch, and uh, Marcel. You've got good sense, and honestly, you're better than this, better than some band of aimless vigilantes."

"You're trying to divide us again," Sylvaine said.

"No, no" the man raised his cuffed arms. "I mean, I won't pretend I like them, but I get what they're doing. Listen, they might think I'm just some waste-born bandit bastard, and maybe I'm not far off, but that doesn't mean I'm the enemy, or want to stop you."

"What do you mean?"

"Lazarus Roache, you're not the only one who hates him," Felik said. "Oh, he's powerful out here, alright, throwing around slickdust and cheap æther-oil. But plenty o' folks know what kind of worm he is. I, for one, wouldn't mind the man's head on stick."

Sylvaine folded her arms. The man could be taurshitting her, but it was plausible taurshit "So what? You want to be promoted from prisoner to active participant in our 'band of aimless vigilantes?'"

"I'm just saying you're smart enough to know when to put practicality over ideology," Felik said with grin. "And a little trust can go a long way. Just think about that, okay?"

Sylvaine avoided his gaze and glanced down towards the 'truck, where Kayip was finishing up checking the tire pressure. He waved towards Sylvaine.

"Yeah," she said. "I'll keep that in mind."

# Chapter 15

About an hour later they reached the corroded gates of Bridgetown. Two jumbles of scrapshacks and refurbished ruins sat on opposite ends of the ravine, each protected by walls of sheet metal and welded machine chassis, covered in rings of razor-wire. The town was well-inhabited, each domicile shoved wall to wall with the next, with only one main road through the middle, spitting out the occasional tiny side street that could generously be called an alleyway. It was a sleepy hamlet, but not asleep, as people watched from windows and doorways with a trained wariness. Sylvaine did not much like the eyes on her and was glad that this was just a through-trip. Unfortunately, it was not quite as quick a one as she would have hoped, as they found that the bridge, from which the town was named and presumably built for, was down.

"No one's going through today," said the bridgeman in his stall-shack. He had introduced himself as Mr. Bridgemin. Sylvaine could only wonder if that was a name he granted to himself, or if it was a strange coincidence, or if he were from a short but illustrious lineage of bridge-keepers, from when the town was founded some half-century or whenever before.

"Why?" she asked.

Mr. Bridgemin gestured over to the ramshackle platform that was the bridge. It had been lowered by a chain to hang down vertically against the ravine slope. On the other side, the second half of the bridge was still up and steady, though that did them very little good.

"Can you bring the bridge back up?" Sylvaine asked.

"Can," the man said. "But I don't much see why I should."

"So, it's a bribe you want," Belona scowled. She was standing next to Kayip and Marcel, the latter of whom kept glancing back at the 'truck and flashing his pistol at several rough looking men who were eyeing the vehicle. Sylvaine suspected that if one of the ruffians started removing tires no one in the town would shout to stop them.

"Bribe's a harsh enough word for it," Bridgemin said. "Listen here, stifflanders, every town's got their trade. We ain't got an agri-factory, and we're not lucky enough to be sitting on a reserve of sangleum. Heck, if we were, no doubt raiders would have united to knock down our walls. No, our trade is the bridge, we got one of the only ones and it's what keeps us fed. So, unless you're townsfolk who need emergency crossing, or some raider lord who wants to play diplomacy, then the rule is that to cross the bridge, you pay a toll."

"What do you want?" Marcel asked. "Drevs or frascs?"

Bridgemin laughed. "No stiffland paper money. Aurem maybe," he spun one of the faded coins in his fingers, the face on it worn from centuries of use. "But better to see what you have in that 'truck of yours might be worth a trade."

Sylvaine shared a glance with the three. She wasn't sure how the bridgeman would react to the armory hidden in the back of the 'truck. He might panic, though considering how valuable the guns were he'd more likely try and make it part of the trade, perhaps by force.

"Please," Kayip said, "we wish your town no ill will, we are hunting a criminal—"

"Yes, yes, Lazarus Roache," Bridgemin said. "I remember you monk. What posse is this, your third, fourth?" He laughed as Kayip looked aside. The monk had mentioned he had worked with others before, but Sylvaine had not quite realized the extent. She wondered what had happened to the previous groups, but suspected she might not want to know the details. Then again, it was the Wastes they wandered, she supposed they had a cardsharp's luck not to have lost anyone so far.

"Well, that tycoon is still alive and rich last I heard, so you'll need a better excuse," the man continued. "Speaking of, didn't that tall friend of yours from a few years back promise payment when she returned from Huile? I'm guessing she's in no place to pay any debts now. Well, I think this crossing might cost double payment, be lucky I'm not adding interest."

Belona stepped forward and fished something from her coat. She waved what appeared to be an emblem, though too quick for Sylvaine to make out the details. "I'm a representative of the Principate, based in Holtag. As such, I demand that you raise the bridge."

"Demand? Demand?" Bridgemin said. "What about our demands, our appeals, our frantic letters! Do you know how many communications we have sent to Holtag asking for assistance with Raiders? Oh, you imperials like to act like you run the Wastes, but when someone actually needs the assistance of your big guns and lazy soldiers, suddenly there's nothing you can do! Why just last Anseluary—"

The man continued to berate Belona, who took it surprisingly well, only scowling horribly. Sylvaine noticed several people a ways back, working a large, rusted machine. It seemed to be a pump of some sort, she recognized some parts that looked like guild-style filtration units, welded together with a lot of pieces of scrap, including a long and winding pipe that snuck between buildings and down the hill. The machine was quiescent at the moment. A small crowd milled about it, including a few children, holding jugs, weary and desperate. A man was taking a wrench to the back of the machine, but by the look on his face, it wasn't going well.

"Something wrong with your pump?" Sylvaine asked.

The bridgeman paused his rant. "Yeah. Damn filtration gone to fritz. For the past week, we've been having to buy our water from traders, or else risk drinking ourselves a few mutations, or worse."

"Can I take a look inside? I'm an engineer," Sylvaine asked, raising her glove. It had been a good while since she had messed around inside a large machine, at least one that was close to functional. Even with the bad memories she had with filtration units, there was still a joy in mapping out the internal workings of strange slapdash inventions that she missed.

"An engineer?" Mr. Bridgemin said. "Hmm... yes, I think if you could fix it that would be a good trade, have at it."

"Fix it? I..." Sylvaine hadn't realized what she volunteered for. She glanced around at the townsfolk milling, a few of whom were staring back at her, the strange foreign ferral who had no place rummaging around in their precious, life-giving machine. Her stomach sank at the thought of proving all their horrible preconceptions right.

"I think you misunderstand her," Belona said, staring at Sylvaine with some variation of contempt, as if the whole idea was a waste of already quite wasted time. "She merely wishes to look, there is no chance—"

"Yes," Sylvaine interrupted suddenly, "I'll get it fixed."

She walked over and waved off the beleaguered mechanic, who seemed relieved to be relieved. With a tug, she removed one of the panels, its hinges cracked and rusted, and looked inside. The machine was a total mess, a hodgepodge of different parts from different places and times, shoved together with a scintilla of rhyme and reason, but no more. It was the work of a dozen different mechanics and tinkerers, none of whom had known what they were doing. Yet as nonsense as the puzzle sometime seemed, Sylvaine enjoyed piecing it together, figuring out where this pipe went, or why this engine was connected here, or how this ramshackle piece worked in the first place. She felt as though she was bringing order out of what appeared to be chaos, civilization to the wild designs of the Wastes. Indeed, despite the nonsense-design, she was able to diagnose the problem by the tail end of five minutes. An antipolarity generator was on the fritz, wasn't separating sangleum-waste from the water. With the proper parts, it was a simple fix. With some æthermantics, it was a simpler fix. With neither it was impossible.

Sylvaine raised her glove. A whisper of wind flew by, and her ætherglove sparked and fizzled. Memories flew in as well, of Lazarus Roache guiding her, so kind, so understanding, through her lessons, supporting her, praising her, all the while planning his betrayal. The blast in the exhibition hall, fire and panic, Roache's voice in her head, her professor dead on the ground. Her, covered in blood, running through Icaria, people screaming, pointing, at the beast which had pretended to be an engi—

"Are you an engineer?" came a small voice.

Sylvaine turned from her daze. There was a small girl, no more than eight, with brown hair and a matching dress. Her eyes were wide as she stared up. Sylvaine nodded mutely.

"Like, like, from the Guild?" the girl asked.

"Yeah," Sylvaine said. She rummaged through her pockets and displayed the Guild pin, the Hammer and Gear glistening in the sun. The girl studied the pin as if it were some ancient treasure.

"Where did you get this?" she asked.

"In Icaria," Sylvaine said.

"You trained in Icaria!" The way the girl spoke it was as if she were talking about the holy realm of the Demiurge, such awe was in her voice. "I heard, I heard, that it was on a mountain, and, maybe, uh ten times, twenty times as big as Bridgetown."

"Oh, it's much larger than that," Sylvaine said.

"And, and, is it true that you engineers can make things with your gloves? Like æroships, and autocars, and metal men and lightbulbs and everything?" the girl asked. It was not skepticism in her voice, but wonder.

"We can," Sylvaine said with a smile.

"And you can fix this?" she asked. "Make the water come back?"

Sylvaine looked into the depth of the machine. She sucked in her breath and emptied her mind, her glove raised. "Yes. Yes, I can."

* * *

A few metres back, Marcel was watching Sylvaine work. Belona scowled, arms crossed, clearly convinced this was all an embarrassing waste of time. The engineer, who had had a nervous quiet energy about her the past few days, suddenly seemed calm and focused. She placed her glove into the machine. A flash, barely visible. Then the machine started to clunk and clank and gurgle. Suddenly water started to flow from its far faucet, glittering clear in the late afternoon sun.

Men and women cheered, rushing forward to fill their bowls and jugs. Even the ruffians who had been hungrily eyeing their 'truck rushed forward to slake their thirst.

Sylvaine laughed and stepped back, as grateful townsfolk praised her or slapped her back. The normally bent and private woman was suddenly standing tall, an unusual smile on her face as she watched the machine do its job.

"Ain't that something, imperial?" Marcel said. "A ferral engineer. Blows your petty preconception to little bits, doesn't it?"

"Impressive," Belona said, with a tone more genuine than Marcel had expected. "I thought the woman was playing a desperate lie. She might well turn out to be the most useful of the three of you."

* * *

With that resolved, the bridgeman (begrudgingly) raised the bridge. Kayip drove the autotruck carefully over, as townsfolk from both sides took the opportunity to cross. It was slow going, the bridge was rickety as it was, but people still crowded past, scooting by the 'truck even as it passed perilously close to the edge of the abyss below. Men, women, children, even herdsfolk leading taurs over the shaking structure.

Marcel watched from the back of the 'truck, and wondered how people managed to live like this, in such squalor, with no knowledge of the world beyond their horizons, every day risking death by raiders, or troglyns, or crop losses, or dehydration. These were people the United Confederacy of the Citizen's Resurgence should be trying to help, average folk left behind. But then, a century of war does take one's attention, and these folk could offer little materially to help the cause. However heroic the Resurgence's armies were, they needed food, and weapons, and frascs. These people had a bridge to nowhere. Were they doomed then? Forever to be forgotten, ever irrelevant? Yet they seemed to survive without the aid of the Confederacy. Some had even made it to old age, like that thin-haired bent woman who was staring at him.

Wait, why was she staring at him? With her finger out no less?

Marcel moved, and realized the woman was pointing to Belona. Her mouth opened and closed several times before she could get the words out.

"You..." the old woman said. "You! At Tesakovgrad, at Tesakovgrad!"

Belona's eyes widened. "Drive faster!" she shouted at Kayip.

The old woman hobbled forward, shrieking. "Butcher! You're The Butcher! The Butcher of Tesakovgrad! Look, look, The Butcher of Tesakovgrad!"

Belona had gone pale in the face and was muttering something to herself. Where had this title come from, Marcel wondered, and what had the imperial done to deserve it? He had assumed she was just some Holtag pencil-pusher with violent dreams, but bureaucrats don't usually earn such pejoratives. *Tesakovgrad*...Why did that city sound so horribly familiar?

The old woman started to grab confused passersby, none seemed to know what she meant, or care. "The Butcher! The Butcher of Tesakovgrad!" she shouted. Most just pushed her off, though a few began to look with suspicion at the autotruck.

Kayip had reached the end of the bridge and started to speed up slightly. The woman noticed this, and tried her best to rush the 'truck, screaming as she did so. "Give me my child, Butcher! My child!"

Belona stood suddenly and pulled out a pistol.

"Wait!" Marcel shouted. The mad Imperial was about to murder this woman. But Belona didn't fire, instead unloading the bullets into her hand

and tossing them onto the surface of the bridge. Suddenly a crowd of people rushed forward, eager to grab the scattered prize.

The woman tried to push through the greedy mob, but could make no progress, merely screeching "Butcher! Butcher! Give me back my child!"

The 'truck soon escaped the bounds of Bridgetown and began to speed up, the woman desperately hobbling behind but losing ground metre by metre.

"Butcher! Butcher!" her wails went, until the town disappeared beyond a rocky bend, and her cries were lost in the winds of the Wastes.

*It is difficult to refute the recent achievements of our Naturalist's Guild, and despite my reputation, for which I have unjustly suffered, I will make no effort here to do such. Much has been discovered, in this age of inquiry, about the nature of the world and the celestial objects that surround it, (which some have boldly theorized may be worlds of their own.) I will make no comment on such hypotheticals, and focus instead on the claim, given by many in the Naturalist's Guild, that our world was not constructed by the Demiurge, but instead arose by natural process. They point to erosion and studies of volcanic activity. They postulate about the motion of "tectonic plates," and discuss the "Theory of Speciation and Modification of Heritable Characteristics," formulated by Karl Vallist. Again, I will not refute these studies or theories. Nor will I argue, as so many in The Church of the Ascended have done, that these violate sacred articles of faith. Rather, I seek merely to point out that it is empirical fact that the world we live in was, at least partially, constructed.*

*Let us begin with rivers. Guildswoman Pavo has presented many in-depth treaties on the formation of rivers through the cycles of evaporation and precipitation and the slow erosion of soil and stone. She can explain with ease most rivers, streams, brooks, creeks, and rivulets, and yet cannot account for the formation of the largest known river, the Great Delur. Indeed, it is clear that the Delur is far deeper and wider than can be explained through natural means, and its path ignores many of the laws Pavo herself sets out. Its banks contain minerals not found in its tributaries, nor in the environs it flows through. Indeed, the Delur resembles, in more ways than one, a great canal more than anything natural.*

*And then there is the issue of mountain ranges. Again, some can be understood through the motion of magma, or even these hypothetical "tectonic plates," but I dare any naturalist to explain the Skyknife Mountains, which exist without volcanic activity, and in locations that do not match any theory of underground plates. Their height is also preposterous, they cut far up into the atmosphere, and with sheer walls that should have long been worn to nothing by wind and rain. Indeed, were they formed of normal stone alone they would not have the structural integrity to resist the pull of gravity, and geological surveys have uncovered regular and orderly shafts of unnatural metal in their depths.*

*We can also look at studies of living organisms to see the Naturalist's folly. While many plants and animals appear to have a common ancestor, Vallist fails to explain the appearance of "chimeric beasts" such as the noble griffon, who bears avian and mammalian features. Or the satyrs, who Vallist posited as an alternative to apes as a common human ancestor, despite their cervine horns and serpentine eyes. Indeed, if ætheric mutations are, as some naturalists have suggested, reversions to some more primitive form, then human being themselves may be partially chimerical!*

*The solution to these incongruities? Simple. Though clearly the world is shaped by natural forces, and it is even possible that it was initially formed by the effluvium of stars, much of it is undeniably artificial. This can be seen in the grand UrWall of Muhit, the size and breadth of a mountain range yet clearly made by intelligent hands. Or we can look to the shattered ruins of the Ghost Reefs to the west, who machinework provided much inspiration to the wicked Malva. Or simplest still, the great ætherlines of Æthmach, which could never have a natural explanation! Whether this creator is the Demiurge and his Ascended, or some other race of beings altogether, it is simple empirical fact that we live in a world created.*

*—"A Refutation of Naturalism's Intellectual Excesses" By Naturalist Guildmaster in Exile Professor Stur Schreiber. First published in 1495 and republished by Phenia United Press in 1738.*

# CHAPTER 16

The screams, as always, were beautiful. Blade fell into mutant flesh, the groggy body that moments before was lost in a daze, suddenly awoke as pain flashed through it. The man, or woman, for at this point the misshapen bulge of flesh was beyond anything as human as gender, screeched out its exquisite agony. Brother Remius muttered blessed prayers as he shoved his blade deeper and deeper into the mutant's chest cavity. The creature writhed, atrophied limps flailing about weakly, fingers grasping helplessly at Remius's robes, as the Brother's Truespeech echoed throughout the sunken hall, melding with the chants of row after row of honored Unblind Brothers.

Beside him Brother Tullius pulled over tubes and pumps, shoving their sharpened ends into the mutant. Raw sangleum poured into its bleeding form. Blood of the Gods mixed with blood of the mortals, welling and overflowing into stone bowls placed below the altar. Oathblood began to fill the hallowed basins, drop by drop, vein by vein, agonize scream by stuttering moan.

The mutant bent its face in desperate, resplendent suffering, expressions like a shoat in a slaughterhouse. This thing, this piece of Tribute, had once been human. It could have been a captured scrap-merchant, or a caravan-lord, or a slave from birth, or a disposed raider sold by their own kith and kin. Now they were nothing, just flesh and pain. Namter could not imagine anything more wondrous than such a transformation. Through the precepts of the Gods, his Brothers had transubstantiated this person. Once all ego and waste, now pure sacrificial matter, pure Tribute. The mutant was purified of all the evils it had been, as it collapsed into sanctified oblivion, a punishment so miraculously complete that it left nothing behind.

Brother Tullius pulled a rusting lever, and the sangleum ceased to flow. This was of little help to the mutant, whose last twitches faltered as its eyes rolled back stained red.

Namter was silently vexed at the truncation of the sacrifice. The bowls of Oathblood were not even half filled! But he could not rightly harangue Tullius for this, it was not his fault. The unfortunate truth was that between the loss of Huile and Roache's siphoning of sangleum for slickdust, there simply wasn't much left for the rituals of the Unblind. This had been a difficult truth to relay to his Brothers. Harder still was the possibility of a delay to the Reification, a delay that Namter himself was not sure should or even *could* happen. That seemed Roache's plan, and Namter could see the logic, it was preferable to have a full Reification than a quick one. Yet try explaining that to a Brotherhood who had waited with agonized devotion the last seven years. They had not the patience of a God, nor the pseudo-playboy lifestyle of a sangleum tycoon.

Namter scanned around the caliginous hall, an old bomb shelter buried beneath the camp, decorated only with the blood-painted runes of Truespeech. He counted most of the senior Brotherhood in the room, as well as many of the lesser Brothers, and yet could not spy Brother Tacticus among their numbers. This was expected and worrying. The Brother had always been close with Verus, and Namter could not help fear that the man was having a crisis of faith. It was Namter's role as the Awakener to hold them all together in shared devotion, but that was not a role he had chosen for himself. A follower was his natural disposition, a distant administrator if need be, but never before a leader, a teacher. As he stared into his congregation, he wondered if he was worthy of the task.

Below, one of the youngest Brothers, a red-haired ex-raider by the name of Drusus, stared at the dripping blood with unease. It was an unfortunate fact that many new initiates, even those used to the brutality of the Wastes, had trouble seeing the ritual for the beatific gift that it was. Namter stepped down from the altar and grabbed the young man's hand.

"Do not fear, Brother Drusus," Namter said. "What has befallen this failure shall not befall you. Its mutations are the anger of the Truegods, it is their divine protection that shields us from the blessed mutagenic enmity that flows through the veins of the world. If these excuses for humanity are marked, if they are sick in the skin, then they deserve only contempt and punishments."

Of course, this was a simplification, *all* men and women deserved contempt and punishment, but it was easier to focus on the hatred of the mutant first, before spreading his precepts onto the proper, divinely-commanded, total misanthropy.

He raised the young man's hand towards the blood that dripped from the altar. The air bore the acrid sent of sangleum mixed with the sweet iron-tang of human blood.

"I do not know if I am ready, great Awakener," the Brother said.

"You cannot know," Namter replied, a truth with which he struggled. "You can only offer yourself to the judgement of those who created us."

He led the hand, soft with youth, stained by dust-dense winds, to the blood. A single drop fell onto the man's palms. A frisson overtook him, his pupils widened, his mouth hung suddenly open. Emotions rushed over his face, shock, pleasure, horror, despair, joy, ecstasy, disparate but all united in their overwhelming power. No doubt he would have fallen to the floor, had not Brother Tullius stepped forward to brace the boy's back.

"I... see... I..." the young man stuttered. "Towers... flesh... and gardens... beautiful arches of shimmering stone and... I see blood...and rust... and... and..."

"What else? What else?" Brother Tullius hissed with excitement.

"Shh..." Namter whispered. "Let him See on his own."

The man blinked and spat, shook and contorted, smiled and grimaced, laughed and shrieked. It was only a hint of the world beyond, the Trueworld, and as wondrous as that was, a hint was all Namter could offer. The man was not ready, could not *See* fully, eyes still corrupted by the blindness of ego. Namter ached to strip this ego from the boy, to turn him red and naked, to let him suffer so that he might know the idiocy of his own ignorance and yet... that was never Namter's skill. That had always been Verus's domain, his expertise. As Namter watched the young cultist, memories flowed of his own initiation seven, no nearly *eight,* years ago.

* * *

Eight years ago... What a pitiful thing he had been then. A butler and nothing more. An assistant to a sangleum tycoon without any sangleum to speak of. Their last contract, with one independent city of Dasht, had fallen through after an unfortunately predictable disaster involving rust locusts. They had become little more than itinerant merchants, traveling around the Border States and Outer Wastes, hawking old equipment just to maintain Lazarus Roache's faux-luxurious lifestyle. As they slept in the same motor-inn rooms, filthy despite Namter's best efforts, Lazarus would grumble lullabies of complaints, raging against his father, against treacherous snakes he had failed to scam, against the winds and the water, against fate itself for denying the tycoon his proper inheritance, his proper wealth, his proper overwhelming success that he knew was owed to him after a lifetime of 'work.' Namter too would grumble, silently bemoaning the world and his place in it, a lifetime of drudgery with no purpose greater than wiping a spoiled old brat's metaphorical ass. And sometimes it wasn't just a metaphor. A life of routine humiliation, with the only repose those brief moments when Namter looked out the window at the desolation of the Wastes and speculated how much worse it could be. But then, perhaps a quick death at the hands of troglyns or raider might be preferable to the slow *peine forte et dure* that was the crushing reality of Namter's humiliating excuse for a life.

It was a rumor that had changed everything. Just a rumor, just the ramblings of some drunk waste-wandering vagabond, barely surviving on his last sliver of liver. Roache had helped kill those few hepatocytes with a donated whiskey, as the man rambled on about some nonsense story. It was the kind of tale they had heard a dozen times a week, some crazed prophet out in the Wastes, worshiping demons and shouting out deranged sermons to his congregation of ill-bred, braindead raiders. But the twist this time was the claim the man had a special ability, a preternatural sense for æther-oil, a possible magical method of sangleum dousing. It was this claim Namter got sent out on a rusted buggy to investigate. Lazarus Roache had, of course, stayed back in the motor-inn, taken by a sudden and convenient bout of gout.

Perhaps it was fortunate that Lazarus stayed behind, he might not have survived the encounter. Namter's wastefolk guide certainly hadn't, cut down by the bullets of the very cultists they were supposed to parley with, as their buggy was ambushed in a narrow ravine. Namter was beaten and slapped in chains, barely able to explain his purpose before being dragged into a cave cracked into the side of Calamity-blasted stone.

There he found the cult, just twenty or so members, and in their middle, atop an altar built from melted frame of an autocar, was Verus, hair wild, right eye covered with a leather patch. The man screeched his homily, his voice matching the howls of the dust storm outside. At first Namter could not make out the words, gaze affixed on that altar, which had been draped with the corpse of an old woman, her blood used to paint a vivid and captivating eye. What did that eye see, Namter had wondered, why was it so piercing, so enthralling? It felt, in its simple lines, as if it were staring at him, through him, analyzing his soul, judging him for the worthless sack of flesh that he was.

"Another!" Verus had shouted. Two hooded cultists removed the body of the old woman, while a third and fourth dragged in a young man, dressed in gaudy, off-brand finery and caked with makeup. Terror mixed with gratitude that Namter was temporarily spared.

"A prostitute!" Verus said. "A whore who sucked his wages out of the genitals of stiffland perverts. A worthless piece of bone and skin."

"I'm not hurting no one..." the prostitute mumbled, mouth bloodied. "Please, I'm just trying to surv—"

Verus took a rusted rod from beside the altar and smacked the man across the face. Despite his fear, Namter found a surprising thrill in the act of violence.

"A parasite," Verus said. "Indulging the sickest desires of mankind, tempting people to egotistic indulgences, praying on their weakness to his own profit. This degenerate is rot of mankind's spirit made manifest and he seeks only to entrap others into his perversion. He misuses the flesh gifted to him by the Truegods and insults their handiwork!"

Namter hadn't a clue then what these 'Truegods' were, but the rest of Verus's short speech rung true. Though he did not know this whore, he had known many young men and boys like him, hanging out in alleyways or in the back of smoke-drenched bars. Skin peeking through popped buttons or the lace of lurid dresses. Always smiling, winking with mascaraed eyes, promising through their gaze, or sometimes their words, hidden pleasures, desperate relief, and maybe even something more, something deeper. But whenever Namter had a moment of weakness, when he had taken these rentboys up on their promises, they offered nothing but superficial sensations and devouring shame. How they would tease his heart, grab onto it, massage it with their soft voices, and then squeeze it for all the aurems and frascs they could manage. How Namter would have loved to take a rod to their faces, to make them feel the pain they had inflicted upon him. Perhaps if he had known his own death was approaching, he would have had the bravery to.

"Do you wish, man-whore," Verus said lifting a flickknife from his pocket, "for me to show the world all your secrets? To cut you open and show everyone that flesh that you sell? For me to bring righteous punishment upon you, slice by slice, until there is nothing of your vile ego left?"

"No…" the prostitute whimpered. "Please, I got money saved, I got friends who can pay ransom. Please, I was just, just trying to make a living."

How hollow his words were, what empty excuses. And yet, Namter could not help but turn the eye of judgement inward, at himself, at the worthless excuse of a man who could fall for these boys' lies, could indulge in such disgusting empty hedonism, who could wet his pillow with tears over the rejection of some whore.

Namter's thoughts were interrupted by Verus's laughter, as the man plunged his flickknife into the neck of the prostitute. The rentboy screamed death, as the blade sunk in and was forced down, toward his chest, blood spurting. True to his word, Verus cut the boy open, slice by slice, revealing what he was underneath his makeup and glitzy clothes, just flesh and bone.

As he watched the prostitute wail and choke on blood, Namter expected to be overwhelmed by horror or disgust. Instead, a shiver of excitement rushed over him. Was this sadism? Or perhaps it was something deeper, a glee at seeing the truth of the man laid bare, to see a body polluted by a lifetime of filth turned back into its constituent parts. It was like art. After such an ugly life, why could the whore not see how beautiful his death was?

Verus dropped the body and let his assistants remove it. "You see?" he shouted. "We are all, each one of us, nothing. If we indulge in our inherent nihilism, or worse, some false belief that we are better than nothing, if we embrace our raw ego, then we must be punished, we must be returned into the nothing we are. These are the teachings of our creators, of the Gods abandoned by mankind, buried under our filth and fetid monuments. Another!"

Namter held his breath, but again he was not chosen. Instead, a woman was brought forth, hair mangled and bloody, skin tanned from years of baking sun, metal arm cracked and limped.

"A raider worm!" Verus shouted. "A vicious leech who sought to scam us, to sell crippled slaves unworthy of work or sacrifice. So let her be the sacrifice. Let this woman who enacted pointless violence upon others feel that violence upon herself."

The raider woman was silent, glaring at the crowd with hate. What right did she have to this hate? Namter felt a rage building in him. The Wastes were full of brutes such as this, who found no purpose other than extracting profit from others through force and treachery. Through his boss's work, Namter had been forced to act as a manager or diplomat for many such a monster. A great number of his and his master's misfortunes had been caused by the avarice or deceit of raiders like this woman. How dare she stare out with hate as she was being brought to a just end!

"Who do you serve?" Verus asked. "Why do you mock us with your trickery, why do you plague these lands with your vile trade?"

"I serve no one but myself, troglyn-fucker," the raider spat.

"She serves herself!" Verus announced. "Can you imagine such egotism! We all must serve, must serve the true master of humanity, must make ourselves cogs in their divine machinations. Yet she serves *herself!*"

He pushed her down, onto the altar. "Do you wish for me to help you serve? To serve you up, bone and skin and blood? Do you wished to have this ego you worship cut from you, so that we might see what a pathetic piece of offal it is?"

The woman glared up at him. "Eat shit."

Verus smashed her face down into the altar. Again and again he lifted her by hair and neck, then smashed her into jagged metal. She groaned, teeth loose, blood dripping. Verus stepped onto the altar and used his whole bulk to assist in the brutality, bashing her head again and again. There was a music to the violence, Namter realized. The sonorous clang of metal again bone, the melody of Verus's grunts. The pained gasps of the raider became lyrics of the most euphonious nature. It was grander than any orchestra hall symphony or voxbox ragtime ditty. Minutes of this beauty passed; the raider's agony transformed into rhapsody. When her final breath left her, the crowd of hooded figures cheered and chanted. Namter was surprised to find his voice among the celebrants, calling for an encore.

It occurred to him suddenly, that there were no prisoners left but he.

Verus cut the dead woman's throat and kicked the body from the altar. "We all serve, we all must serve. That is the first law, the greatest wisdom

I have to offer you. Your desires mean nothing, your questions mean nothing. Only through service can you earn the punishment you deserve."

He panted a bit and slicked back his loose hair with the bloody flickknife, before causally turning his gaze in Namter's direction. "Right, right, we got one more, don't we?"

Hands pulled Namter forward, up a stairway of carved stone to that altar. He could smell the blood here, feel the breaths of the cultists who lifted and dragged him on his knees. Verus stared at the butler up and down, before turning to his congregation.

"This one's a little stiffland businessman's pet," Verus announced. "Come here to make some aurem, it seems, make a deal, ain't that right?"

Namter stared up at the man, how large he seemed, grander than a man could be. Though he opened his mouth, Namter found no words on his tongue, and merely nodded meekly.

"A deal!" Verus said, as if the punchline of a joke. "A deal with us, like we're some stiffland company. A contract with the Truegods, quarterly profits and investor meetings and everything, just sign the dotted line in Oathblood. I wonder if I should laugh." He stared up at nothing, pantomiming thought for a moment. Then, suddenly he grabbed Namter's ears, and smashed his knee into the butler's face.

Namter crumpled, and Verus turned to preach. "Make a deal! You see, this is how low humanity is, they get a whiff of the divine, and try to see how to make a profit. That's what Oathblood is to them, just a fuel, something to burn, to light up their cinegraph theatres and midnight brothels. A deal!"

Verus lifted Namter and thrust him onto the sacrificial altar. "At least this rot-brained bastard knows to serve. How sad, he knows the precepts, but only thinks to serve someone even more pathetic that he. Some old griffon-shit in a striped suit! Death is a kindness for this scraprat excuse for a man. Tell me, little butler, would you like me to slice your skin from your flesh, to show everyone what an empty piece of offal you are?"

"Y...yes!" Namter found himself saying.

Verus paused. He turned and squinted at the man on the altar. With a quiet calm, he picked up a wooden cudgel and began to beat Namter, kicking and bashing and bruising and bloodying, until, after a few minutes of glorious brutality, he pulled out his flickknife and pressed it to his victim's neck.

"Do you want me to cut you open?" he hissed. "Outline your every flaw with my blade? Slice it all away, bit by bit?"

"Yes!" Namter said. He could not imagine anything more wondrous.

With a grunt, Verus slammed Namter's face down into the rusted surface of the altar. Namter gasped, tasted blood, only some of it his. A sharpness teased his cheek as Verus held him down, the tip of the knife moving in gentle patterns along his skin, but not quite breaking it. Somehow Namter wanted it to, for this prophet, now Namter was believing in the title, to shove his blade in, and carve pitiful skin from old worn bones.

"I can flense you; I can make you as naked and red as before you were born. I can cut your ego like a surgeon, slice your soul like a butcher. If you desire it, I could turn you into nothing, into pain and blood and empty screams. Do you think you deserve that?"

"Yes! Yes!" Namter said. Let this be the end, let his sordid story finish! He had never done anything of value in his life, never served a purpose. He ate, slept, and shat, only to keep himself alive to clean up after some rich idiot's son. If there was something greater out there in the world, a beauty behind all this hideousness, let him see it, let him feel it, let him be utterly unmade by it.

Verus twisted the butler's head, then, with a smile and a flick of his knife, fulfilled Namter wish. The eyepatch fell from the prophet's head, and behind it was something... indescribable. An emptiness, but full, a void of roiling fury. He saw hurricanes made not from wind, but from the space between wind, that ineffable force that drives tornados and dust storms. Shadows and reflections, not of what is, perhaps not even of what was, but of infinite terrible possibility. In the space where his eye should have been stood hatred, pure and divine, an infinite expanse of it, a possibility space where every punishment, every judgement, every scouring condemnation lay. It was beyond anything that existed in the world of man, was far more terrifying and beautiful. Before this, Namter was nothing, a worm in human flesh, a bag of blood and ego that this storm threatened to tear open, to spin about and vaporize. This void was death, with all its overwhelming antipathy, it was life, with all its calculated cruelty. It would destroy everything if let free, and all Namter could do was shout *Yes! Yes! Yes!* until the darkness overtook him.

Hours later, when he awoke bruised and bloodied, Namter had found himself dressed in the robes of the Unblind. His first lesson had been completed.

* * *

Now, eight years later, as he watched this young man, this brother Drusus, seize and foam at the mouth, enraptured by visions of Truth, Namter could only wish he could harness the violent sagacity of his former preceptor. For there was none who knew the Truth like Verus had, who understood the rage that sat in the center of the world. He had expressed that rage, through vicious lessons, full of beatings and abuse and other wonders. Namter had never that skill, was too weak to bring his fist down upon his Brothers, to take blade and carve the beautiful sigils that Verus managed. Namter's students never walked away with gashes cut or teeth broken, and he worried if that left them empty, only half-filled with the ecstasy of pain that was the greatest teacher. How could these new Brothers judge the world if they had not yet been judged themselves?

And yet.... Yet Verus had betrayed the Brotherhood. Had betrayed the will of the Truegods. Had embraced his own ego and abandoned his service. Surely this was proof that mankind was truly corrupt, evidence beyond doubt that Verus's own teachings were true? In that sense it should be reassuring, and yet, was it too much to ask that someone was pure, that the prophet who had led them all was of strong enough will to follow the path without so great an error? And if he had failed, how could Namter hope to fare better? It was enough to lose one's faith.

Footsteps rang through the quieted hall. Several Brothers turned as Brother Avitus hurried down the stairs and past them. The worried looking man walked around the congregation and straight to Namter. He stepped close, beckoning to move away from the ears of the curious congregants.

"Watcher... Awakener..." Brother Avitus said.

"What is it?" Namter asked.

"There has been a..." the man paused, as if unsure of the proper word. "A murder," he decided.

# CHAPTER 17

Brother Tacticus lay, right hand bloodied and torso bullet-riddled, next to the corpse of his victim, who was even worse off. The shards of the raider's skull lay amongst the burnt Utarran rug that decorated the floor of Lazarus Roache's dressing room. There was no doubt who the perpetrator had been, beside from the conspicuous proximity of Tacticus's body, such a complete annihilation of flesh and bone that was displayed in the elongated red and black splotch that spread from the raider's neck several metres out and up the base of the gilded oak wardrobe could only be accomplished by the powers of the Truegods. But why had Tacticus unleashed such awful rage upon this random raider nobody?

"Strange..." Brother Avitus said.

Lazarus Roache was far less laconic. "A damned fucking disaster! Blood everywhere, ruined my rug, my dresser, need to deep clean the whole room! What cog-brained idiots are you letting into your damned Brotherhood?" Lazarus was half-dressed and covered in a thick layer of sweat. His buttons lay popped open, revealing an undershirt stained by the raider's blood. His striped jacket lay loose on the seat next to him, and his pants were unbelted. It was clear that whatever had happened here unnerved the normally sangfroid tycoon. The Lazacorp guard who stood next to him looked equally flummoxed, though instead of a flush face and furious words he simply stared off into nothing, rifle aimed at the floor, mouth hanging a centimetre loose.

"What happened?" Namter asked.

Lazarus shook his head and turned to the cheval mirror to fuss with his golden hair. "Your idiot happened. That... Brother you call him, busted into here and made a Godsdamned mess of the whole place."

"Why?" Namter asked.

"Why did he come in here, or why did he turn Gorteg into modern art?" Lazarus asked. "Well, I assumed he came in with some message from you, since you're too busy to talk to me yourself, what with all your chanting and bunker parties."

Brother Avitus stepped forward. "The rituals of the Unblind are not some petty celebr—" Namter raised his hand, and Avitus silenced himself.

"I did not order any messages sent," Namter said.

"So, you didn't send him?" Lazarus asked.

"That's what I said."

Lazarus grunted, sounding less than reassured. "Well, whatever the reason, once he came in, he got in an argument this Gorteg over here that turned violent rather quick, and well..."

"I shot him," said the Lazacorp guard.

"Yes, I think they can figure *that* out," Lazarus muttered.

Namter bent down and inspected Tacticus's body. His orb of Oathblood had been smashed in his right palm. *Right* palm. Tacticus was left-handed, odd he should use his non-dominant hand. Namter checked his left hand. It was clenched tight and empty, yet still was stained with a small splatter of blood. There was no wound, had he punched the raider before blowing his head off? Possible, but Namter couldn't help the sense that the man's hand wasn't balled into a fist, but that he had been grasping something. Something someone removed for... some reason.

"What are you looking for?"

Lazarus was staring down at Namter, eyes narrow. Namter noticed that his master was angling his head in an odd manner, bent slightly to the left, almost, but not quite, as if he were resting it in his shoulder. Namter had known the man his whole life and had never seen him hold himself in such a way.

"I'm not sure," Namter said, standing up. "Are you all right?"

"Yes, fine," Lazarus said. Then he gave the driest of chuckles. "Perhaps it is the blessing of our shared benefactor that I was unhurt by this madness. Though I shall need to change quite soon, for my speech."

The speech... Namter had nearly forgotten, so accustomed he was to overseeing every detail of Lazarus's schedule.

"So, let's be quick," Lazarus said. "What do you know about this Brother..."

"Tacticus," Namter replied.

"Yes. You did not seem as surprised as I would think when you saw his corpse."

Namter sighed. "He was close with Verus. Took the Awakener's betrayal poorly."

"Then why did you keep him around?" Lazarus snapped; his head still tilted in that odd direction. "There's plenty of Wastes to dump a body."

Namter took a moment to collect his words. For Lazarus wasn't exactly *wrong*. After Verus's horrific sabotage of their Enterprise, that wondrous machine that would have turned all of Huile into Tribute, they had been forced to execute a number of treacherous Brothers. It had been a horrible time, never had Namter's faith been as tested as when he signed away the death of those who had once been bound in purpose with him. Tacticus had seemed suspicious, with his snide remarks and unruly tone, but he hadn't done anything wrong, had not joined Verus, had done all his duties as asked. Perhaps the smart thing would have been to execute him anyways, a true Brother should be willing to sacrifice himself for the cause, but Namter had been unwilling to take such a step. Perhaps that was a weakness. Perhaps such pre-emptive judgement was required of an Awakener. It was one thing to follow the Truefaith, another to lead it.

"I will keep a more watchful eye," Namter said.

"Good," Lazarus said inspecting himself in the mirror. "We're at difficult juncture right now, we can't afford another Verus. The gangs are starting to sense that we're low on sangleum and slickdust. If we want to keep this whole thing together then we can't go pushing the raiders too far. We need their slaves for your whole Tribute thing, and once we get our extension on the whole Enterprise, we'll need their guns too. I know you're not as well trained in diplomacy as I am, but the first rule of keeping alliances together is not to have your own people going around murdering our allies! It's simply unprofessional."

"I understand," Namter said.

"What was their argument?" Brother Avitus asked.

"Gorteg here was expressing his unique theological interpretations," Lazarus gestured vaguely. "Basically, saying that The Flayed Prince was some delirious lie, and all you Unblind Brothers were just some perverts with a thing for torture and a love of wasting sangleum. Shouted some other nonsense as well, lots of rambling and foul words. Ain't that right?"

"Uh, yeah," the Lazacorp guard mumbled. "I seen it. It was, like you said. Bad words and things with the cult and stuff. And then the uh, the hooded guy got angry."

"That can be no surprise!" Avitus said. "How could you expect a Brother to sit idly by while the Truegods are besmirched!"

"I expect them to be sensible enough not to ruin everything!" Lazarus snapped. "Do you know who Gorteg was? An envoy of Mr. Crimson."

"Mr. Crimson, of the Crimson Eyes?" Avitus asked.

"No, Mr. Crimson of the Vastium Puppy Huggers. *Yes of the Crimson Eyes!*" Lazarus snapped. "The last thing we need is the Crimson Eyes starting a fuss, Inferno they would have probably already turned against us if half their number weren't addicted to slickdust. Can't seem to get Mr. Crimson himself to try it. Wouldn't think a raider would be keen on abstinence, but I guess he was once a soldier, wasn't he? And we're still facing pushback for purging those mutant-loving Hornclackers, which was Verus's idea, I might add!"

There was something off about Lazarus's voice, an insincerity to his anger. Namter was beyond familiar with the subtleties of his master's moods, and when he spoke it was not with the rambling rage from which he would sometimes lash at the world, but with a more calculated tone. An impression of anger, complete with biting sarcasm and carefully chosen shouts. It felt as if it were covering something. Fear? There was a twitch to Lazarus's hand as he idly played with his buttons, an unusually nervous tic. Why should he be afraid, he had seen bloodshed worse than this, and why should he hide his fear? To save face? And there was his gaze, which seemed always to find its way back to Namter, searching for something as he spoke. Lazarus usually did not waste time looking at his butler when muttering out orders, was this a sign of respect, or something else? So many questions, perhaps Namter was merely looking for an excuse to escape the guilt, for it was his failure to manage Brother Tacticus that allowed this whole unnecessary imbroglio.

"My sincere apologies," Namter said. "I'll make sure nothing like this happens again."

Brother Avitus bit his lip but nodded along. "Yes, we will... better manage the righteous fury of the Brotherhood. For the sake of the Truegods."

"Good," Lazarus said, patting Namter's shoulder. "See, this is what being a leader is all about. Keeping control of your people. Just, in the future, maybe talk to me directly, and don't send these intermediates."

"I did not send..." Namter sighed. "Yes, I will be sure to handle business directly. As for now, I can help clean you up before your speech."

"No need, no need."

Namter must have given a surprised look, because Lazarus smiled at him. "Come on now, Hieronymus. I'm an adult, I can take care of myself. And you are busy, aren't you? Managing Brothers, Lazacorp men, and raiders alike. I can't keep you from that."

That had never been an issue for Lazarus before, but Namter bowed his head anyway. "I thank you."

"I'm glad we reached an understanding," Lazarus said, grabbing his hat. As he placed it and inspected his reflection, he briefly tilted his head in the other direction. It was for just a moment, but through the mirror Namter caught a flash of red. A gash on the side of Lazarus's neck, which he quickly bent his neck back to hide.

"We shall see ourselves out," Namter said with haste.

* * *

After they left the building, a hodgepodge manor house seemingly constructed from the remains of half-a-dozen prewar mansions, Namter bade Avitus return to the Brotherhood, to check on the ritual. Namter, for his part, did not yet return to camp, standing at the border between the dumpyard excuse for a raider town and the Lazacorp encampment that had been growing around it. He leaned back on a chain-link fence and gathered his thoughts.

A wound. There had been a wound on Lazarus Roache's neck, one which he had awkwardly tried to hide during the whole of their conversation. Why and how? His first thought was a shaving accident, but that was certainly impossible. Despite the slew of work that had been tossed on Namter's metaphorical desk, he still maintained the most important of his domestic duties, including shaving his master. And even if there had been a nick, Lazarus's Gift should have healed that up. The fact that the wound, whatever its source, had not fully healed, meant that Lazarus's powers were waning, as the seven-year contract approached its end. Perhaps that was the cause of his hidden fear. Yet, a waning power was not a lost one, the wound *should* have healed, unless it had been made very recently, and had been much deeper than it seemed when Namter chanced his glance.

A buzzing screech. Dictaphones held on poles started to crackle to life, all around the camp and through the town itself. An installation courtesy of Lazacorp, for moments such as this.

*"My fellow raiders!"* came Lazarus's voice through the speakers. Namter stood up and stepped around the building, watching at a distance the stage set up between the junk forts and shanty complexes. There stood Lazarus Roache, already immaculate and resplendent, a high collar covering the sides of his neck. He waved round to the shambolic crowd of raiders, who cheered his name. The tycoon had a way with the raiders. It might be his unusual style, exotic to the roughly garbed raiders but without stiffland pretensions. It might be the way he always sweetened them up with well-placed compliments, flattery pushed near the verge of cloying, but somehow received as genuine. Or it could be the fact that most of the crowd was deathly addicted to slickdust. It was probably mostly that, but the man was a consummate showman all the same.

*"It's been a true pleasure being here with my people. Oh, I might have a stifflander accent, but it's out here, in the Wastes, that I feel at home. Not in those lazy excuses for cities, where people sit on silken beds and complain about their tea."*

Many in the crowd laughed. Namter always found it dryly amusing how his master could rile up hate by decrying distant elites whose behaviors he emulated so very closely. But then again, perhaps it was their distance that these raiders hated, as their own gang lords lived in excess and luxury, as least by Wastes standards. As long as Roache could find someone to knock down, some hypothetical other to rally around, it was easy for him to fit in with any crowd, in any society. Didn't matter if this 'other' was human or mutant, rich or poor, real or fictitious. Worked in Huile, worked in the Wastes.

*"Cages with pretensions, the stifflands are,"* Lazarus continued. *"A worse set of lands you couldn't craft up, not if you had all the engineers in the world. No, since I've relocated my operations here, I have started*

*living, truly living. Who else was at the Cockatrice's Nest last night? Great fight, great fight. The Savage just tore up that Sulcostan fop. Demiurge-be-buggered, you don't see things like that in stiffland towns. You know they have this thing called boxing, right? Men punch it out, but with big pillows on their fists. Who in Inferno would want that? You need some blood in your blood sports!"*

Lazarus actually quite liked boxing, Namter recalled. Opera as well, and ballet, Namter couldn't imagine those interests would earn him much cred out here, and yet the raiders ate up each hollow word.

Namter sighed and started walking back to camp. He had work to do. So much work. Always and everyday, organizing, managing, cleaning. There were raiders to pay, contracts to sign, rituals to oversee, munitions to catalog, and now, apparently, he had to keep his eye out for any aberrant behavior from the Cult of the Unblind, from his own Brothers, just to make sure no one else cracked and caused further diplomatic troubles.

*"Truly though, I must thank you for your generosity. After my losses in Huile, I was devastated, it was like letting a full and easy caravan escape my fingers or losing my favorite stud-taur. But being with you all, the Rust Thorns, the Trog-Skinners, the Crimson Eyes, everyone else, you have reminded me what life is about! You have more freedom than the Resurgence, without their pansy effeminate airs. You are stronger than the Principate, but without kissing the arse of some little jack-a-dandy in an Imperator's crown."*

And yet, as he walked the narrow streets between scrap-shacks and pillboxes turned warehouses, Namter could not help thinking of Lazarus's gash. The man had been hiding something from him, from his own butler and assistant. A wound, a serious cut, like from a knife thrust to kill.

Namter paused at the edge of camp. Two Fist-Biter raiders with their tooth-adorned gloves sat nearby on a pile of damaged tires, drinking rancid ale as they listened to the dictaphone speakers.

*"Now I know some of you are worried about the sangleum supplies, what with our losses. You need not worry, we have plenty of connections to refineries, and more than enough slickdust to go around. In fact, my, my, I've forgotten that I have a few packets right here in my pocket. Who wants a freebie? Uh, there you go! And one for you! And one for— An eager fellow there! Hey now no need to bite off his ear, there's plenty to go around."*

Brother Tacticus had had his hand clenched around something. A knife? Then had Lazarus tried to defend that idiot Crimson Eye? No. Roache was not one to stick his neck out for anyone, certainly not some replaceable raider muscle. More likely the raider had died trying to defend his slickdust supplier. Tacticus had not been enraged by some random blasphemy, he had come to that room with the intent on killing Lazarus Roache.

*"As for Huile, I am pleased to say we are currently in negotiations with the whole U-doubleC-R to regain our investments there and restart sangleum production. Weak and dumb as these stifflanders are, they know who butters their bread, and once this whole mutant insurrection thing is quelled, we will be back in those walls, getting you the sangleum and slickdust you need."*

But why had Lazarus lied about this? If he was concerned that Namter's Brothers were getting out of line, there was no greater evidence of that than if one of them had attempted to assassinate him. So why obfuscate that fact?

Namter closed his eye and tried to think, doing his best to block out Roache's voice.

*"Of course, if the Resurgence should decide to be impudent and bite the hand that feeds them, well, it's a good thing I have the best damn warriors in the Wastes! If it comes to that, I'm sure we could crush them, take back the refineries, and get us a few good slaves as well. Huile-folk are weak, but their women are quite soft to the touch. Their men too, for those such inclined. And who knows, if that goes well, we could try it on a few other cities. Trust me, raiding stiffland towns is a lot more fun than pointless, unprofitable feuds with your fellow raiders."*

Tacticus had been out of camp recently. On scouting duty, leading a small band of Trog-Skinner raiders to clear out Clan Vapulus from the nearby hills. Something had convinced him that now was the time to make his strike against Roache. Perhaps he had seen something that aroused new suspicious against the tycoon, something that pushed him beyond sulking and into a murderous rage. Something that Lazarus Roache didn't want his own assistant, no, his *Watcher*, to know about.

As the rest of the Roache's speech meandered on in the dictaphone above, Namter hurried into the depths of the camp. He did not go back to the underground bunker where his Brothers continued their rituals, nor towards his own cramped excuse for an office. Instead, he made a beeline to Lazarus's tent. For what purpose he did not yet know, but if the man was hiding something, there was no better time to search it out.

Of course, the front of the massive tent was guarded. Namter might be able to convince the armed men to let him enter freely, he was Roache's butler after all, but he did not want word of his prying to get back to the tycoon. Instead, he snuck around to the back of the tent, where a large structure had been awkwardly grafted on. A building, made of fused scrap, windowless and blocky. It was the workshop of that damned witch, Miga Veneficus, who had been working awfully close with Lazarus the past few weeks. Namter had never liked the woman in the first place, but considering the day's discovery, mad suspicions started to run through his head.

As he crept up close, he wondered if this was what it was like to be that private investigator, Marcel Talwar. Always searching for secrets, examining crime scenes with prying eyes for any possible clues. Of course, the mysteries Mr. Talwar had 'solved' were mere fictions, most of which had been set up by Namter himself to eliminate Lazacorp's potential rivals and whistleblowers. What Namter was searching for was the actual truth.

He waited there in the shadows, until he was sure that no one was near. He took a flickknife from his pocket as well as a small vial of Oathblood. He dripped just a drop onto the point of the blade, then carefully jabbed his finger. With blood mixed, he drew a circle round the scrap wall and whispered a prayer. In a second the metal rusted, and then crunched, whispering out a faint, sizzling wail as it fell. He caught the metal before it hit the ground, then he squeezed his way into the dark of the workshop.

It was, like most things Namter didn't directly manage, a mess. Tables sprawled in every direction, with no clear pathways between them. Some were new, some rusted and old, though it was impossible to tell which from which as they were all stained with layers of dried blood. Most of these tables were covered with bodies, some hanging on to the vestiges of life, most not. Near these experimental subjects were machines, pumping or creaking, or tubes-covered ones like the machine Namter used to infuse Tribute with Oathblood. The smell was awful, the viscera and blood-stench was mixed with powerful alcohol, as well as queasy, sweet-smelling chemicals that made Namter's head spin. Papers hung on clipboards, or bound in notebooks under tables, or sometimes just in piles on the floor.

Between those, the fallen glassware, and the pools of congealed bodily liquids, Namter had to step carefully as he searched.

Of course, the major difficulty was that he was unsure what it was he was searching for. He inspected some of the papers. They were written in the barely decipherable script of Miga Veneficus, but even as he made out the words, they did him little good. Some were charts, measuring vital signs over time, graph after graph of slow deaths. Besides that, the writings were so mired in technical terms like *"hemorrhagic intraosseous carcinoma,"* *"æthero-vascular contortions,"* and *"explosive hypervolemia,"* that it might as well be troglyn scratchings for all Namter could make of it. The whole room felt, despite its disorder, quite disturbingly *scientific*. Cold and obsessive, without the joy, or even the cleansing hate of his Brotherhood's rituals. The woman was studying under a microscope a force she should be worshipping.

He wondered if he should sneak into Roache's bedroom. It felt odd slinking silent into a room that he organized, decorated, and cleaned, a room he knew every nook, cranny, and semi-secret compartment. And while he felt nothing breaking into Miga's lab, to skulk around Lazarus's bedroom seemed somehow an insult to his master. Yet he had been made Roache's Watcher, had he not? Perhaps it was part of his duty to actively pry, not just idly keep watch as he had these last seven years. But what did he expect to find? A piece of paper with Lazarus's shiny signature admitting... what? There was nothing in particular he suspected, no crime to solve, no big mystery. All he was going off was an odd wound on Lazarus's neck and a half-brained chain of conjectures.

Namter shook his head and wondered if he had just been overcome by his baser emotions. A Brother had done something strange and horrible, and now Namter was trying to overturn the world to find an alternative explanation that probably didn't even exist.

At least he did not have to worry about these mutant corpses and half-corpses ratting him out. They were the same sort that his Brothers turned to Tribute, slaves pumped so full of sangleum that they were little more than bulbous bags of flesh. Besides them there were a few mutants of the other variety, *Womb Mutants* they were sometimes called, like those from Clan Vapulus. Their skinsick parents had chosen to continue their cursed lineage and so their mutations had become far more regular, with symmetrical sets of horns, smaller claws, and leathery hide a more consistent light crimson without tumors or oozing growths. Despite common misconceptions, Womb Mutants outnumbered Flesh Mutants, those unlucky idiots who had fallen into a sangleum-poisoned pool, or were part of an engineering experiment gone wrong, or who happened to enter the clutches of Lazacorp.

As for these sorry souls, they must have been caught up in a raid, perhaps the one Tacticus had been ordered to lead. Unfortunately, their chief Bladescar was not among the captured, and the rest were of little value to him. Womb Mutants were useless for Tribute, their blood already adapted to sangleum. As much as Namter hated the witch, it was actually a noble thing she was doing here, exterminating all these Vapulus brutes in a way both humiliating and—

Wait. No... not all were Womb Mutants. There in the middle was a flesh mutant, who bore the traumas of an active mutation, though not to the crippling extent as the bags of flesh around him. Namter walked over and stared at the man, single horn cracked, flesh in uneven scars of red, boils bursting from his chest. He looked much like the multitude of mutants who had slaved away in the refineries back in Huile, the sort who Verus had used in his heinous revolt.

The mutant opened his yellow eyes. His gaze was loose, his movements weak. He turned to Namter and stared with recognition. This dying figure, Namter realized, might have been there at the end of it all. Might have been one of the mob who had torn apart their Enterprise, who had slaughtered loyal Brothers. Hate flowed through Namter's veins, but was quickly replaced by something else. If he had been there, perhaps he saw something, perhaps he knew something, how the revolt had happened, why Verus had betrayed them.

The mutant's chapped, twisted lips started to move silently. His arm raised with shuddering decrepitude.

"Speak," Namter whispered.

"Lazacorp..." the mutant said. "You... Lazacorp."

"Yes," Namter hissed. "What happened there! What did you see?"

The mutant's hand reached towards Namter's face, then down towards his neck. He wrapped his fingers around Namter's neck, and tried, with a pitiful lack of strength, to choke him.

"Lazacorp... Eat... Shit..."

Footsteps echoed out from behind the thick metal doorway at the end of the room. Namter scampered back and ducked behind a groaning, dripping machine. The circular hatch at the door, which looked plunked from the innards of an æroship, turned with a creak. In stepped Miga Veneficus, hair frazzled and filth-caked, arm enwrapped in her massive, misshaped ætherglove.

The witch with engineer pretensions blinked and glanced around. With her free hand, she scratched her ass, then stumbled forward. She stopped by the flesh mutant Namter had tried to speak with. The mutant turned to her and attempted to reach up. Namter held his breath, might the mutant give him away?

Miga grunted and turned the dial on some nearby machine, which pumped some horrid something into the suddenly convulsing mutant. She took out a pocket watch, and waited until the figure stopped moving, then wrote down notes on a nearby clipboard.

Namter tried to crawl a few metres, but the woman glanced up suddenly and he froze. She stared around the room, eyes narrow, nose sniffing like some strange, lumpy animal. Miga turned suddenly and shuffled over to a bench at the end of the room. She picked up a beaker of some brownish liquid. Took a whiff. Thought a moment. Took another whiff. Then placed it down and picked up a nearby, seemingly identical beaker, and downed it. Namter took this opportunity to start inching forward, towards the hole in the wall he had come in through. With just a little bit of luck he might be able to—

"So, you have a reason why you're sneaking around my lab?" Miga asked, without turning.

Namter froze.

"Come on Hieronymus, you really want to play this game?"

Namter waited another moment. Then with a sigh, he stood up.

"Evening Miss Veneficus," he said with a nod. "May I ask how you became aware of my presence?"

The witch cackled softly as she tapped her oversized glove. "This thing ain't just for show. I can feel unusual concentrations of æther, and that storm in your eye socket gives off some wild tinglings. Reminds me of Verus."

"Yes," Namter said. "Well, I suppose that makes sense."

"And if you have any other questions," Miga said, turning. "Then just ask me. I'm as open as any book you can find. I don't lock the door for you, or for Lazzy. We're a team. You don't need to sneak around."

"I do not wish to offend you," Namter said. "My only intent is to make sure I understand everything that is happening in this camp."

"You want to snoop!" Miga jabbed her finger. "Verus was a snoop, too. One of his less attractive features. Always trying to catch me with someone's dick in my mouth. Ha! As if that were my passion not a career. Believe me, you get to an age when you tire of every odd man in town wanting a ride on this." She slapped her ass. Namter shuddered. "Anyways, Verus could never find a way to trust me, could never trust anyone. His ego always got in the way, that's how I see it. And look at where that led him! Blew up your whole damn project and got himself killed. Sad, sad, can't say I'm surprised, but sad. Don't want you ending up the same way Hieronymus?"

"I won't be like Verus," Namter said. "I'm not like him. I'm not like Verus."

Miga shrugged. "If Verus hadn't been so damn suspicious, I could have been there helping out with your Enterprise, and we'd all now be toasting in Huile. We should be working together, is what I'm saying, not fighting like wastehounds. Ain't that what your god ordered too?"

Namter nodded. It was true, they were commanded to work together. But he was also commanded to keep Watch, a task that seemed simple enough, but things always seemed messier than he could guess. "Well, I thank you, Miss Veneficus for your... kind words. Perhaps then it would be good for me to ask what, exactly, you have been working on here?"

The witch smiled. "Continuing on with the studies I was conducting before my butt was kicked to the curb. Increasing the effectiveness of slickdust, for one. Right now, you need pretty heavy doses for it to cause anything more than subtle suggestiveness. By the time you get full on control of the victim's mind, their body might be all bent and crimson. Works for some, but aesthetically pretty unpleasing."

She walked over and slapped the corpse of one of the bloated mutants. "But my big project here is working on Lazarus's whole Gift thing. You know that his powers don't come from the ætherlines, but by connecting directly to your big, buried guy, Razmi—"

"Do not speak the hallowed name!" Namter said quickly.

"Sorry, sorry." Miga raised her hands. "I knew Verus was superstitious about saying... Fine, fine, I mean no disrespect. *The Flayed Prince*. Is that better?"

"It is preferable..." Namter nodded.

"Right. Anyways. The powers come directly from him. So, you see whole system, right? Slickdust users are connected to Lazarus, who in turn is entangled ætherically with The Flayed Prince. Functional, though a bit inefficient in my book."

"I did not know it in a technical manner," Namter admitted. "Though of course Lazarus's Gift should flow through our shared Master. It is His power after all, not for a man to own."

"Sure, sure. But the connection is fraying, something to do with the whole seven-years business. I've been trying to find way to make a direct connection between Lazarus and the ætherlines, kinda like turning him into an engineer, though of a much more powerful and... fleshy variety."

"Wait," Namter said. "You mean to circumvent The Flayed Prince?"

"Circumvent? Circumvent? Now you're sounding like Verus," Miga laughed and rested her elbow on a corpse. "I'm *augmenting* the Gift. Think about it Hieronymus. Your god needs all the blood he can get, imagine the energy he's wasting on Lazarus. If we can make it easier for him, well, win-win-win."

"I suppose..." Namter said. It did make some sense, especially if they were low on Tribute. But such a dramatic action felt as though it should have the explicit approval of their Master, not overeager presumption.

"It's a heck of a task too, been experimenting with troglyn blood and these Vapulus idiots, but I think the best subjects are those who have had the slickdust rolling through them awhile, like the slaves you had up in Blackwood Row. Demiurge-be-fucked, if Verus just let me keep my up testing..." She glanced over at the flesh mutant, still shaking, foam leaking from his mouth. "Thank your brother Tacty-whatever for bringing this one in. Got some actually decent data."

"Tacticus?" Namter asked, stepping forward and accidentally knocking over a beaker of foul something. "He was here? What did he say? Did he seem angry?"

"Huh?" Miga asked. "Yeah, he was here, though he didn't say much. Your Brothers are always angry, haven't you noticed? Hate me to a man, after all the horrible things Verus said about me, some of which were even untrue. Why you ask?"

Namter paused, theories flashing through his mind. If Tacticus did indeed bring these mutants here right before his death, perhaps they had told him what had happened in Huile. Perhaps they elucidated what had twisted Verus into his horrid treachery. And if so, this knowledge may have pushed Tacticus over the edge, might have been what pointed him towards Roache with a blade in his hand. But what did the mutant tell him?

He realized that Miga was waiting in awkward silence. He tried to think to think of what to say, how to frame the events of Tacticus's death without raising suspicion. What he could leave out, what would the woman notice that he had chosen to leave out? He was spared that decision, for the flesh mutant on the table suddenly sprung up.

"Lazacorp! Roache..." the mutant shouted, eyes glazed, voice slurred. He stepped off the table, unaware of the tubes still sticking out of his torso. "Celina... Where... Have to... Lazacorp."

"Ah, this happens sometimes. Just a second," Miga said, glancing around. She bent over and a picked up a stained pipe from the floor. With a grunt she swung the pipe into the mutant's stomach. He bent over, and with another hit fell to the floor.

"Wait! Namter shouted, trying to think of an excuse for mercy. But Miga did not hear him, raising the pipe up and smashing it down on the mutant's head, once, twice, three times. With a crunch, whatever secrets the mutant had been hiding in his brain were splattered uselessly over the floor.

She let the pipe fall, leaning on the table, panting, before glancing over as if to assure herself that the mutant was indeed fully dead.

"Was, uh" the old woman said through strained breath. "Was nice talking to you, Hieronymus. Next time we'll chat at your place."

# Chapter 18

There had been a scrapstore in Taliers. Sylvaine could remember its every detail. The tall shelves overflowing with wondrous junk, each piece indiscernible in its form and function, yet organized into exact categories. The lamps, flickering and dim, buzzed along with the soft clanks of the single fan placed in an odd corner. The store had a smell of rust and musk, and the particles of dust that floated about gave her childhood wonderland a dreamlike atmosphere. She would spend hours there, after school, fleeing the taunts of bullies into its safe empty halls, knowing that the girls who would spend their afternoons strolling the shops of Roiland Promenade would never think to enter this corner shop. It was a haven, a museum of incalculable secrets, filled with hidden promises.

The old man who ran the shop was a millimetre away from decrepitude, kept up by his coglimbs and a series of iron back-braces. His eyes were covered in 3 layers of lenses, and it was barely enough. He would hobble around the corridors of his store, pointing out pre-war æther engines, tread-driller arms, gyroscopes from æroships, bits of agri-factory rotary belts, and devices whose origins he could not elucidate. He was something adjacent to a friend, treating the young Sylvaine no different than any customer, eager to answer her questions and entertain her musings, though as she got older Sylvaine wondered if his lack of discrimination was less the result of some enlightenment, and born more out of the old man's desperate loneliness. Even still, his shop was the only place in Taliers where Sylvaine ever felt fully herself, or rather, a version of herself that she didn't hate, one with a future as something more than a punchline to a lazy joke.

It was amazing, then, how much this abandoned military depot reminded Sylvaine of that store. Towering hills of metal, conetanks cracked open, warwalkers twisted around themselves, landships split in twain, and sets of autoarmor buried amongst the rubble. Despite the destruction that was ever-present in the Wastes, and despite the century of looting, so much remained untouched, protected by the excessive size of the place. An entire æroship lay sideways in the far landing field, towering gun turrets now skragger nests, its steel fuselage untouched by scrappers' hands, its lost corridors unwandered.

"Wait, wait!" Sylvaine said, scurrying up a hill and then tearing open the shell of a turtle-tank. She ignored the bones of its driver and dug through its interior until she lifted out her prize. It looked like rusted junk, and in its current state it was, but with a little work, it could be restored to its majesty.

Sylvaine slid back down the hill, to where Belona was standing.

"Unearthed buried treasure?" the imperial asked. For whatever reason, she had decided to join Sylvaine on a scouting trip around the perimeter of the scrapyard, while Kayip and Marcel made camp.

"Found this," Sylvaine said, lifting it up. "An omni-directional rotational shaft. A pre-Calamity design, able to deliver torque in impossible angles."

"Impossible angles?" Belona asked.

Sylvaine nodded and pointed to the tiny metal chips decorated with ruin-like circuitry. "Æther-circuits here apply æthericity directly to the mechanism, allowing the metal to slip across themselves like rubber, or if needed, reform themselves entirely."

"Seems a somewhat... expensive feature," Belona mused.

"Oh, extremely wasteful, and pricey," Sylvaine said. "It's a shame, now war machines rarely take such indulgences, but back before the Calamity, gear's-grits, engineers could get away with anything their hearts desired."

"I take it you long for those lofty days?" Belona said, glancing out among the ruin. "Well, you're not alone. It was a better age. I wish I could have seen it."

Sylvaine nodded, unsure what to make of the woman's tone. It was almost friendly, as if she were trying to find common ground with her.

Warily Sylvaine put her prize into her knapsack. "Well, I don't know how useful it will be for our mission."

"You can never be sure," Belona said, walking forward, past a pile of void-jumper packs, their straps ragged, metal tanks burst inward from some long-forgotten negative-density mishap. "We have the weapons necessary, but if you can find anything useful, it can't hurt our odds."

Sylvaine followed, trying not to think too hard about their upcoming assault. Truth was, during their trek across the Wastes, they still hadn't come up with a great plan on how they were going to actually take down Lazarus Roache once they reached Narida Heights. Best options were to try and snipe him as he left the building, or to find a place to sneak clockbombs in, but these were rough strategies at best, and would require careful and dangerous reconnaissance.

"Imperator's mercy, look at this!" Belona shouted. Sylvaine followed the woman's hand to a cracked metal sphere, girded by two sets of massive blades. Belona stepped over and tugged on the ends of motorguns that poked out its front, but the rusty barrels snapped.

"A shame, I don't think this is salvageable," she said. "But, dear Demiurge, look at this dathkreis! Rotating death, quick and maneuverable, can tear infantry to shreds. This is imperial engineering! None of that Guild excess, no relying on style over substance. You need a group of soldiers dead, trust me engineer, you shall find no greater tool of destruction than this!"

Sylvaine climbed up to the ball of steel and placed her glove on it. With micropulses, she could sense its innards, ravaged by time, looters, and a nesting strix. "It makes impressive use of gyroscopes," Sylvaine said. "Though to be honest, I actually think the technology has better applications than chopping up people at high velocities."

"What, you have a moral aversion to weaponry?" Belona asked, with a smirk.

"Not at all," Sylvaine said. "The Guild knows that it's not the crafter who is to be blamed for the misuse of tools."

"Well, if they claimed pacifism, it would be like a mudlion taking up vegetarianism," Belona said. "The Guild can't oppose weapons, or they'd soon run out of profits."

"It's not about profiteering!" Sylvaine said, jumping down. "It's not geopolitics either. Engineering is an art, and you can't put limits on art. We don't know where the future will take us, what the next engineering breakthrough will be, if we put blinders on visionaries based on moral handwringing, we may end up stagnating, making the same damn things over and over, no invention, no innovation, no evolution! The engineer cannot be shackled."

"Sounds like an excuse the Guild came up with so they can feel morally superior while subtly keeping two sides of an endless war equally armed and deadly, slipping drevs alongside frascs into their fat wallets."

Sylvaine grit her teeth and closed her eyes. The woman was just trying to bait her, trying to get her enraged. And yet, she could not help but notice that Belona was attacking her along the engineer axis, not make any reference to her Ferral background. A strange turn of strategy. Had her work in Bridgetown convinced the imperial to take her engineering seriously? A step up, she supposed, though not yet a fully pleasant one. The woman still followed her, still found new ways to mock her. Why couldn't Kayip have come along instead? Actually, leaving Belona together with Marcel would have been a recipe for bloodshed, but Marcel could have come! The man would have just nodded along to her eager ramblings, then add some useless detail he misremembered from a pulp to try to make himself seem erudite. His bluster was far less annoying than this woman's constant needling.

"It makes sense that you'd see it that way," Sylvaine said, with a constructed calm. "All you are is war, all you have is killing. We engineers look at the whole world, and to be honest, most weapons are just... basic. It's such a simple thing to launch projectiles at high velocities or strap a bunch of explosives together. Sure, there can be artistry, I've seen some beautiful warwalkers, but there's so much more that can be done with the same technology, with the same spurts of genius."

"All I have is war..." Belona muttered. "You're not wrong, engineer. Look at this land, scrap and dust and ruins where there were once towns and vineyards and factories. Which do you think I'd prefer? Oh, your free artistic expression? Might be nice in your city on a mountain. But in the Principate, we don't have time for fools' flights of fancy." She stepped to the side and stared off, between the peaks of metal, to the vast empty plains beyond. "But there will be a day, a day when we will need your kind's artistry, to rebuild this land, to make it what is once was. That is what I fight for, for that day to come, as soon as possible. That glorious day when people like me sit forgotten in veterans hospitals or lay buried alongside our rusting weapons. That day shall be your day, a far better day, but unfortunately, today is left to me."

There was something like silence then, only the wind rustling through the cracked machinery, and the distant whistle of a soot-sparrow. Sylvaine did not know what to make of the imperial's speech, unsure if she was still mocking her, or was, for some inexplicable purpose, attempting to reveal herself. Sylvaine had not asked for either, and was not much in the mood to muse about the future. It always seemed a grim place, the future, it was better to build something now than wait for whatever cruel trickery tomorrow had planned.

Belona sighed and turned with something like a smile on her face. "Come on now, we still have a perimeter to scout. And you may find something useful yet, engineer."

* * *

In a not-distant clearing, Marcel sat staring at the sticks of taur-beef that Kayip was slowly cooking over the fire. The supposed monk hummed as he cooked, turning the meat slowly over the embers. His expression was flat and unreadable. Between the real and metaphorical masks the man wore, what secrets did he hide?

A monk without the power of miracles... It was certainly not unheard of for more progressive churches to allow preachers without ætheric powers, rejecting the old notions that miracles were direct blessings to be superstitions and instead claiming the only requirement was to possess love of the Demiurge. But Kayip did not seem some modern Bastillian reformist, and the ability to cure wounds and purge one's enemies did seem like a job requirement for waste-wandering battlemonks. But that was hardly the oddest thing about the man. What about his reaction to the dead mutant back in that mansion? His stoic demeanor had completely caved in upon itself, over the body of some mutant he had not known. And it was not as if he hadn't seen corpses before. In fact, Kayip had mentioned that he had lost several allies in the past, an ominous detail that Marcel was now wondering if he should have interrogated a bit more. In truth there were a lot of red flags he had ignored about the monk in the chaos of Roache's betrayal and the heat of the hunt. This was not exactly becoming of a once-private investigator. Could he afford to just trust the man? Out here in the Wastes it seemed more and more that 'trust' was just a synonym for 'idiocy.'

"Is there something sitting in your mind?" Kayip asked, with a glance. Behind him Felik Rector slept, slump and snoring.

Marcel shook his head. "Tired. Just tired. A lot of driving."

"Well, be thankful that we have a 'truck," Kayip chuckled, turning over the meat. "I have walked boot over boot through these lands, and though such journeys had their virtues, I would not recommend it."

In truth, there was really one oddity about the monk that was truly bothering Marcel. That was his relationship with Belona. *The Butcher of Tesakovgrad.* That's what that old woman had shouted at her. Marcel had gone along thinking Belona was just some mid-level imperial bureaucrat with a bone to pick with Roache. But *Butcher* was no pencil-pusher's honorific. And Tesakovgrad... he had heard that name before. He faintly remembered toasting to the memory of Tesakovgrad, years ago. There had been some tragedy there he had read about in the papers, some vague imperial atrocity. Yet there were some many disasters in so many distant towns and cities with strange names, he could hardly be blamed for forgetting a few. But working with some high-ranking Principate war criminal? Yes, he could be rightly blamed for that. What would Alba say if she heard of this? Something cruel and mocking. Perhaps she wouldn't be wrong. Marcel, hero of Huile, soldier of the UCCR, somehow sleeping only a few metres from a possible enemy of the Resurgence. And here he had been, subtly smug knowing that he was a wanted man and the woman had not noticed, when the reverse could be true. Kayip had protected him by keeping his last name from her... or had he kept *her* last name from *him*?

"You very much look like there is something in your mind," Kayip said.

Marcel sighed. "How is it, again, that you know Belona?"

Kayip paused. "She arrested me."

"And you made such a good impression upon arrest that she busted you out of jail?"

"Not the first time," Kayip said. "I escaped on my own."

"What were you doing that got you arrested?" Marcel asked. "And what was her position? What happened?"

"Why are you asking this, Marcel?" Kayip stared at him, single eye soft and tired.

"I was once a private investigator. Perhaps I am naturally curious."

"You must become sensible as well. We are mere kiloms from Lazarus Roache. We cannot break down now over idle suspicions."

"Not suspicions," Marcel shook his head. "Just questions. I mean, you know so much about me, but I barely know anything about your past. Wandering the Wastes with an Ascended weapon wrapped around your wrist, I'm sure you have a few good stories."

"Ah." Kayip nodded. "You are worried that I might not be such a good person."

"I didn't say that," Marcel stammered. "I didn't even suggest—"

"Well, you should," Kayip said, blowing smoking gristle off the meat. "Because I am not a good person. I wish I were; I have tried to be, I still try. But I am not a good person, and I have not done good things."

"Kayip..." Marcel gestured without aim. "I'm sure you're a good person, that's not what I meant. I'm just, I mean, I've just been wondering—"

A scream echoed through the scrapyard. *Sylvaine's.*

Kayip jumped to his feet with a prayer, bracelet whipping round and becoming an azure blade in his hand.

"Grab Felik!" he commanded as he dashed off.

Marcel gripped the bleary raider's collar and pulled him to his feet, as he stumbled around for his pistol.

"I'm going, I'm going," Felik mumbled. "What's going... Uh, what's going on?"

"Something!" Marcel said. "An attack, or an accident, or something!"

He dashed forward as fast as he could manage while still dragging the dazed Felik, which was not very. Around scrap piles and dust-buried autocars, a skragger flying overhead, squawking wildly in the commotion.

Demiurge, why did they let Sylvaine go alone with Belona? What had the butcher done, or let happen? He dreaded what he would see, as he turned the corner into a half-collapsed loading bay of a fully-collapsed æroship.

There Kayip was standing massaging his head, sword hand limp, Belona chuckling, and Sylvaine pulling a motorcycle from a pile of canvas and dirt, eager squeals escaping her lips.

"It is, it is!" Sylvaine said. "A 1629 RestoGriffon-brand automorphic tire-slash-tread motorbike! *Cog off!* They only made a couple hundred of these, and that was back before the Calamity smashed most of them."

"What's going on?" Marcel asked.

"Nothing," Kayip said with an exhausted sigh, his blade wrapping back around to form a bracelet.

"Your engineer found herself a new toy," Belona said with some bemusement.

"It's not a toy!" Sylvaine exclaimed. "It's an antique. A better relic than half the junk the Church hoards. And it's in amazing condition."

"I've heard of it," Marcel said, walking over and glancing at the wheels. "As I thought, made of metal, but with a flick of the switch it can go into a tread-mode to handle rough terrain. I think I read about it in a textbook back in university."

"You read about it in *The Riders of the Sulcostan Wilds*," Sylvaine said, without looking up.

"Hey, you don't..." Marcel started, before realizing that that definitely *was* the pulp he had read about the bike in.

The engineer scrambled around her prize, checking each pipe, æther-tank, and fender. "I'm guessing that someone stashed it just a few years ago. I can sense some minor damage, but it wouldn't take much to fix. Must have meant to come back to it at some point, but I think it's been long enough to say that its up for grabs."

"You wish to keep it?" Kayip said.

"It's an easy repair job," Sylvaine said. "Just a few hours, if I have an extra pair of hands."

"I'm not sure that's a great idea," Marcel said. "We need to plan for our assault on Narida Heights."

"Why not?" Belona said with a toss of her wrist. "She's not a soldier, let her practice her craft. We can plan well enough, fill her in when she is finished." Marcel was quite unsure why the woman was taking Sylvaine's side. But in truth he didn't disagree. The engineer wasn't trained in military matters, and too many discordant voices could muddle any plan.

"Yes, exactly!" Sylvaine said. "I'll go grab my tools from the 'truck. Anyone want to help out?"

"*We* still have to plan," Marcel said.

"I can help," Felik offered. The rest of them glanced at the man with varying degrees of skepticism. "What? Ya think I like sitting around doing nothing? I'm bored out of my taur-fucking skull! And come planning time I'm sure you'll want to squirrel me away, even though I've only ever helped you four. So why not? Anyways, I like motorcycles."

"Sure," Sylvaine said.

"I am not so certain," Kayip said. "He is a raider, of a craven disposition."

"Yeah, a chained raider!" Felik shook his manacles and sighed. "I'm not asking ya to trust me, I'm just... Look she's an engineer and, with all respect owed, a ferral. Even if I were murderous and armed to the teeth, I'd be the losing bet. What evil magic powers do ya all think I have?"

"As much as I hate to agree with scum, I would hope our engineer can handle one raider," Belona said. "I see no issue."

"I can handle myself Kayip," Sylvaine patted the man on the arm. The monk nodded with uncertainty.

"Well, as long I'm not on his bathroom duty, I'm fine with it," Marcel said, pushing the raider forward. "Who knows, maybe a motorbike will be just the tool we need for a good getaway."

# Chapter 19

As the sun set, Sylvaine got to work. There wasn't anything majorly wrong with the bike as far as she could tell, though there were several dozen things minorly wrong with it. She opened it up with care, making sure to minimize the æthermantics. Sure, she could fix many of the issues with a snap, but there was a certain roughness to parts molded by æther alone. What's the point of having an antique motorcycle if you summoned up half of it yourself?

She and Felik did a quick bit of scrap diving and found most of what they needed in the piles of junk sitting outside. For the rest she scouted out the corridors of the æroship. Most had long since collapsed in on themselves, covered with jagged, twisted shardvines, or filled with cockatrice nests. Others were sideways, vertical shafts where moonlight cut in through distant dust-smeared windows. They found signs of habitation, but none recent, the years past measured by centimetres of dust. More than a few walls were covered in bullet holes, and some were painted brown by long-dried blood. But even more were painted with paint. Graffiti and murals, some lifelike, some abstract, some still vibrant, others long since faded. One displayed a cherub, rosy-cheeked and winged, caressing a skull with a flower growing out its mouth. Another was a simple sketch of a burning pyre, with the words *Vapulus Is Vengeance*, written ominously in smoke. Next to it sprawled a surprisingly pleasant depiction of sleeping deer in a sloppily rendered forest.

"Had a mate who did murals like this," Felik said, pointing to a cubist image of a two-headed woman, one side weeping over a fallow waste-field, the other staring straight at a rising sun, rifle in hand. "Yeah down, in Stinktown, she found some old books from before the world cracked open, taught herself."

"Really?" Sylvaine asked, glancing up from the smashed æroplane she was quickly looting. "I wouldn't think you raiders would have much time to become acquainted with the arts. What with the raiding."

"Oh, she put that past behind her to focus on the brush," Felik said with a faint smile. "Lived peacefully off the crops of her farm. Grown by the slaves she captured."

Sylvaine stared at the man with sardonic frustration.

"Well," Felik said, "I mean... no, no. That ain't fair, is it? Still cruel, to be living off the blood and sweat of others. Damn inequitable, is what it is."

"That's your big revelation?" Sylvaine said, grabbing a chunk of rotary engine. "Slavery's bad?"

"I'm learning that chains are damn unpleasant!" Felik said, shaking his manacles. "But really, this whole being-kidnapped thing, it's taught me a lot. *Y'all* taught me a lot, intentionally or not. There's a whole world outside the Wastes that I didn't for a moment understand. I can't say I've enjoyed all this, and maybe its gonna take a while, but I think I'll be doing things different, ya know, when all's said and done."

Sylvaine nodded. "That's... actually really good to hear."

* * *

The next few hours were spent productively, taking apart the motorcycle and fitting into place the scavenged parts as best they could fit. Felik actually made himself useful, holding pipes as Sylvaine welded them with her ætherglove, wielding the power drill when Sylvaine had more important tasks, and even organizing the scrap during his free moments.

"Ya know, I missed doing this stuff," he said, as he screwed on the front casing.

"Fixing up motorbikes?" Sylvaine asked, as she inspected the pistons around the automorphing unit.

"Yeah, and autocars and all sorts. Actually, far more fun to build things than smash them."

"Right?" Sylvaine said. "There's something about creation, seeing inert things comes together in your mind, and then in your hand. I don't know, its soothing."

Felik glanced around. "Do you think if given time, you could even fix this whole thing up? Make it fly?"

Sylvaine studied the ruined loading bay, the dead æroplanes still chained in place, the disintegrated crates, the elaborate floating staircase now crumbled and dust-buried. "I tried to work on a project even bigger once. Making a city fly. Though even then that was just an excuse, an impossible dream for clanking old men. But it was a fun dream."

"A flying city." Felik whistled. "Was that a war thing too? Made for dropping bombs and all that?"

"One-track mind..." Sylvaine shook her head. "Gear's-grits, I don't even thing think this æroship was meant for war, at least not initially. Look," she gestured to some fallen bannisters, made of dirtied bronze, spindles bent in the shape of flowers. "Too elaborate for a war machine, and the guns outside are awkwardly soldered on. I'd bet frascs to fruit cakes that this was once a transport æroship, some luxury deal, before being requisitioned for the war effort. Like the whole damned world. I suppose it's good business for engineers either way, but it is such an idiotic one."

She turned back to her work, as Felik scratched his chin.

"Lot to think about, mate. Maybe if I make it out of this, if ya don't put a bullet in my head, maybe I'll go into the mechanic's business. Always preferred setting up the gear for the raid than actual combat anyhow. It ain't pleasant hunting people down, you know. The sounds they make when they run, when they're shot... It don't feel good."

"But you did it. For years you were a raider," Sylvaine said.

"Sure, but where I came from, you were either a raider, or a slave," Felik explained. "That ain't much of a choice. Ya born to a raider, well then bless whatever sick taurfucker created this world, 'cause you'll be the one holding the rifle instead of being shot. Ya don't even question it, ya do what's expected of you. Raiders raid. I suspect it's the same for Marcel and that Principate bitch. Fight 'cause you're told to, 'cause if ya don't start shooting, someone gonna aim their gun at you."

"You could try doing something else. I mean, I've seen more than just raiders and slaves here." Sylvaine reached down and grabbed a wrench. She adjusted its head and began to tighten the last loose pieces of the automorpher. "You could work for a caravan, you could tend taur herds...

I'm no expert on the economy of the Wastes, but there is other work out there, another life you could choose."

Felik sighed, then bent over, and with difficulty lifted his coat and shirt over his head, until they got caught on his handcuff. His chest was tanned, scarred, and slightly poxxed, but Sylvaine immediately noticed the tattoo across his chest. It was a massive gaping maw, a cartoonish exaggeration of a taur-bull's head, teeth wild and uneven, framing an abyss that twisted beyond its flailing tongue. In all it was rather a grotesque, bestial image. Sylvaine had always too much hair to consider tattoos, but this seemed a rather abominable image to put to ink.

"These tattoos, they're supposed to be a symbol of pride, but really they're like cattle brands," Felik said, shirt still awkwardly over his head. "Reputation is everything out here, worth more than aurem. Leave your gang, and everyone knows you're a traitor. Ya think any caravan-lord would hire me, ya think any rancher would trade with someone with these markings? Your past is written on you, and anyone can see it."

Sylvaine chuckled and gestured to herself. "Yes, I can't imagine what's it's like to be prejudged for how I look."

To her surprise, Felik laughed back. "That's fair, that's fair. And you're talking as you walk, you've become an engineer. I heard of a lot of things, I heard of birds that spit ice, men that wear Vulker skulls, even stories of empires of miniature trolls living under the earth. I ain't never heard of a Ferral engineer. But here you are."

"Thanks," Sylvaine said, genuinely, as she placed the casing back on the motorcycle. It was nice for someone to see what she had accomplished, without skepticism or judgement. She turned to see Felik still struggling with his shirt.

"Might need a little help," the raider said, sounding comically pathetic. Sylvaine tried to pull his shirt back down. Somehow, through methods beyond what her engineering training allowed her to decipher, the man had gotten his shirt snagged up with the chains, and even working together they couldn't make any progress.

Felik grunted. "Maybe if you just undid my 'cuffs for a moment."

"They didn't give me the keys," Sylvaine said, pulling at a sleeve.

"Can't you... you know? With the glove?"

"Right," Sylvaine said, placed her gloved fingers on the middle of a chain. With an easy flash of focus, the metal split, and Felik was free of his shirt.

"Rusted pus, that feels good." Felik said, stretching his arms, "Thank you. Thank you! Days spent like that, it messes up ya whole back."

"Well, we'll have to reattach them once we head back to camp."

"Of course, of course." Felik bent his back, then began waving his arms in opposite directions in a manner that resembled an inept bird. "Oh, but for the moment it feels good." He gestured to the bike. "So, is it ready?"

"Yeah," Sylvaine said, scanning over her project. It was still rusted and rough on the outside, but for the most part the innards fit together. "I think it is."

"Then do the honors!"

"Oh, I was planning to wait until morning, when the rest of the group—"

"Boo!" Felik said. "Boo! Ya promised me the bike was going to transform its tires and stuff. I want to see the automorpher automorph!"

"Okay, okay!" Sylvaine said, trying to hide a smile. It was nice to have someone excited to see her craft. She walked over and mounted the motorcycle. One hand on the handle, one glove on the engine. She sucked in her breath, and focused, letting small pulses of æther dance through the machine. Then, a single burst, bright and hot, a flash of life. The moribund motorcycle suddenly coughed out a decade of disuse, smoke busting from the tailpipe, the entire vehicle shaking and humming, the motor playing a pleasant staccato. She flicked a switch, and the wheels started to clank and clunk, and then they transformed. Splitting down the middle, two wheels temporarily became four, the bike descending half a metre, before the metal slits clicked into place on either side, fusing into two long treads.

"Look at that, Felik!" Sylvaine shouted, face blush with excitement, body shaking almost as much as the bike. "Good as new! Better even! All in one evening, actually quite impressive."

The man said nothing, the sound of the bike engine echoing deafeningly through the room.

"Felik?" Sylvaine asked.

When the man still didn't respond, she turned round. He was right behind her, arm raised. She had just the time to register the wrench in his hand, as it flew down towards her head.

*Grim Salutations General Bazhinov,*

*I report that we've discovered the remnants of the missing 3rd Battalion. I had low hopes of finding them alive, and I now wish my pessimism had been validated. They still live, but not as proud soldiers of the Phoenix Rebellion. The deserters made their camp in a cave in the hills and had removed all uniform and insignia. Not as a matter of guerilla stealth, but a true repudiation of the cause! Alas, I also uncovered the location of the bandits that had been harassing our caravans. For they had joined forces and were now one in the same! Worse still, there were even Principate men and women amongst their ranks. All had united, not for any naïve pursuit of peace or brotherhood, as traitorous protesters back in Phenia might opine for, but to raid caravans and supply caches, to prey upon their fellow citizens!*

*Despite my reservations, I attempted to parley with these 'raiders.' Negotiations fell to bickering, as they complained of low supplies, poor conditions, and general desperation, any excuse to explain their perfidy. I was forced to lead an assault, and successfully cleared out the hills, though at significant loss to our own forces.*

*Still, the words of these raiders bother me more even than our losses. This war has dragged for nearly twenty years, and many of my younger soldiers cannot recall a time in their life when there was no war. Our cause, our ideals, of freedom, justice, rebirth, all that is good embodied in our grand Phoenix, these have become meaningless words to them. Indeed, there are fewer and fewer that remember our dear republic, and more and more who look only to their aching stomach or weary muscles. I fear we will soon be fighting a war on two fronts, against the Imperator's slugs, but also against those who once wore the Phoenix's red with pride...*

*—Excerpt of letter sent by Sergeant Marius Ortiz. Estimated date of writing: mid-1649.*

# CHAPTER 20

*Sylvaine... Sylvaine?*

*I swear I heard the motorcycle.*

*Damn engineer fled on us.*

*Sylvaine? Sylvaine? I do not see her!*

*Maybe she wanted to take it for a test drive?*

*Or that raider caught the girl's ear. Why did I convince you to let her mess around—*

*Sylvaine!*

Shadows and movement. Pain and aches. Voices... familiar.

*Sylvaine! Sylvaine!* It sounded like Kayip.

*Shit, Felik must have—*

*To the 'truck! We can still catch him.*

*Sylvaine! Do not leave! Stay with my voice.*

*Shit, shit. We need to hold her still. Is there any bleeding?* Was that Marcel?

The sound of an autotruck roaring, wheels skidding.

*In. In! I know where the bastard's heading.* Belona's harsh barks.

*Do you need help Kayip or— Okay, you got her.*

*Move you two! Into the 'truck!*

She felt herself floating, weightless. Sounds of a door clanking, of an engine raging, the wind squealing across a cracked window. The world shook a steady rhythm, as a large rough hand pressed across her forehead.

*Sylvaine... You must stay focused. Do not drift. We are here Sylvaine... we are here for you...*

*How is she doing?*

*Idiot girl, idiot girl... Ruined this for us all.*

*Sylvaine... You are strong. You are stronger than any of us.*

Sylvaine heard herself groan. She tried to life her head.

*She's moving. She's moving! Liberty's bloody heart, Ferrals are made of tough stuff!*

*Made of idiot stuff! We were so close and now everything is shit!*

*Sylvaine... I am here... I will not lose you...*

A face started to come into focus. Large and taunt and tanned, metal over an eye, the hint of stubble, a cautious smile.

"Kayip..." Sylvaine murmured.

"I am here Sylvaine. It is all right." Sylvaine attempted to move, but only managed a pained grunt. The monk held her tight. "It is all right... do not move yourself."

"I can see the bastard in the distance!" came Belona's voice.

"How are you feeling?" Sounded like Marcel. Sylvaine squinted to see the man in the passenger's seat, next to the imperial who was gripping tight the wheel. Beyond the windshield was the dark of the Wastes, and in the distance, she could make out a speck of light.

"What happened?" Sylvaine asked.

"What happened is you fucked us!" shouted Belona. "You fixed up a getaway vehicle and then let that raider taurshit loose."

"Belona enough!" Kayip barked. "You were ambushed, I think. It is not your fault."

Sylvaine groaned, as memory started to flow back in. Felik... He had attacked her. Could have killed her, probably meant to. After all those kind words, those stories about artist friends and wanting to change his ways. Was that all an act? Again? Played himself so pathetic, so harmless. She let her guard down and truly believed someone could treat her like... *Gear's-grits* her head hurt.

She stood up, rubbing the side of her head where there was now a massive bruise.

"Sylvaine," Kayip said. "You should stay still."

"I'm okay," she said. "I'm okay." It was to reassure the man, but she was actually starting to feel better. And though her head pounded harder than it ever had, each thump was softer than the one before it. She took Kayip's wary glance. "No, really, I'm okay."

"Just... be careful," Kayip said, still holding her hand. His face was awash with cautious relief, though she could see worry lines as deeps as ravines. It struck her that though Felik had escaped, possibly to warn Lazarus Roache and ruin their chances for revenge, the monk had focused his energy and concern onto her. The man who had just a few weeks before tried to trade his life away for a shot to take down Lazacorp was now tending to her like an anxious mother over a sick child's bed. How very odd.

"Well, I'm glad you're feeling fresh and dandy," sneered Belona through the rearview mirror. "Because we may need you to clean up this mess. We're not going to lose everything just because you decided to replace your brain with a taur's ass!"

The imperial was back to treating her like shit, so at least that was normal.

* * *

Marcel watched Kayip tend to Sylvaine, stroking her arms softly even as she insisted, in louder and louder tones, that she was fine, *really*. The monk took a wary skepticism, but it seemed, mercifully, that the engineer was telling the truth. Marcel was relieved. For a horrible second, he thought the woman had been killed. A wrench to the head could be deadly, Marcel was grimly aware of this fact. Sylvaine was the only other member of this ramshackle posse that Marcel considered fully sane. Well, mostly sane, her obsessions with machines did go a *little* far. And her taste in pulps was questionable, but at least she appreciated them. She was a good person, a friend even. Marcel didn't exactly have friends to spare, he couldn't afford to start losing them.

Relieved on this end, he could turn his worry towards Felik's escape. He squinted through the glass, the brush and stones of the Wastes rushing past illuminated by their 'truck's headlights. Belona swerved this way and that, dodging suddenly outcroppings or unexpected pits by mere centimetres in pursuit of the raider. He could see Felik, just a dot of light in the distance, possibly getting slowly closer, possibly not, it was hard to tell.

"Where's he heading?" Marcel wondered.

"Where do you think?" Belona spat. "Narida Heights."

Marcel glanced back to Kayip, who nodded.

"How far?"

183

"Not very," Kayip responded. "If we do not catch him, Roache will learn of our intention."

"And any chance of ambushing the bastard will be smashed worse that that girl's head," Belona said, pressing her boot on the accelerator. Marcel gripped the seat and dashboard, as the 'truck smashed through a patch of kilnbushes and crunched over some buried thing. The imperial was clearly ready to die if need be. But Marcel could not think of an alternative to catching Felik. He loaded his Frasco six-shooter, dropping a couple of bullets and awkwardly scrambling to pick them up as they rolled violently around the floor.

Outside they seemed to be slowly circumnavigating a large hill or small mountain, Felik's lights always threatening to disappear around the bend but never quite managing to. The 'truck thumped unto a road, unusually smooth and un-potholed for this far out into the Wastes.

"We're near," Belona said.

"I don't see any lights," Marcel observed. He imagined that if anyone would keep the lamps burning all night it would be Lazarus Roache, yet besides their 'truck, Felik's bike, and the moon above, there was only darkness. Had Felik made a wrong turn? Then they might have a chance to corner him.

Belona sucked in her breath and grunted. "Not going to catch him in time."

"What do you mean?" Marcel asked, as a sigh rushed past the window. From the glimpse he got of it, he thought he read, though layers of dust and graffiti, 'NARIDA HEIGHTS NEXT EXIT.' His stomach dropped.

Sure enough Belona made a turn up a road that twisted around the hillside. Husks of fossilized pine trees dotted the slope, strange growths of branches and vines overtaking them, creating flashes of unearthly silhouettes through Belona's beams. These sent Marcel's paranoid imagination rushing in every direction, snipers, raider ambushes, Demiurge-damned demons hiding amongst the woods! Soon he made out structures, dark and empty. Lodges, condominiums, shops, all forgotten and decrepit. They turned a bend, and Marcel could see off to the side, the glimmers of water in the dark, large fetid pools, steaming. Natural hot springs polluted with sangleum.

"What's the plan?" Marcel asked. "When do we turn back?"

"Turn back?" Belona said. "No, we're past that. All in, now or never."

"What?" Marcel shouted. He frantically looked towards Kayip. The monk had finally released Sylvaine, and the two were staring out into the darkened streets and buildings. The small armory of rifles, explosives, and other weapons Belona had brought shook against their restraints as the 'truck careened around a corner. Kayip whispered his prayer, and his blade unfurled.

"Are you insane?' Marcel said. "We're going up against... we have no idea how many men Roache has, with no plan!"

"Improvise!" Belona shouted as she turned the 'truck and slammed the brakes. Marcel pushed opened the door and jumped out, pistol in his hand. They had stopped at the base of a massive building the size of a small city block. Unlike the other structures this one seemed more intact, Marcel noticing only a handful of windowpanes broken as he hastily waved his handtorch. However, each and every window was dark, the only light being the still running motorcycle which had been abandoned a few metres in front of the structures open doors. Behind the 'truck was a field of concrete, a massive parking lot covered in small scrap structures and a few autotrucks with raider markings, but otherwise empty. Marcel could have convinced himself they were at the wrong building were there not giant letters above the door spelling NAR DA HEI HTS, with a rusted G sitting below, overgrown with weeds.

"Where is everyone?" Marcel asked.

"No idea," Belona said, jumping down from the back of the 'truck. The woman had a scattergun strapped across her back and was lugging a hefty motorgun as if it were just an unusually chunky valise. From the other side of the 'truck dashed Kayip and Sylvaine.

The monk was the first through the door, always swifter than his bulk would suggest. Marcel followed and lit up the atrium with his handtorch. It was empty, a grand hall with two twisting balustraded stairways held by caryatids, and a dead fountain in the middle, decorated with a pair of nude figures in cracked marble. On the wall above the mezzanine was painted a dim sunset, presumable to be lit up by the heavily-patinaed copper sconces. A lifetime ago, this place must have been a resort, though that purpose was long forgotten.

Beneath the peeling floral wallpaper of the first floor sat disordered rows of boxes and crates, alongside broken equipment of unclear purpose tossed ramshackle on the floor. Marcel kicked aside a wayward push trolley, as he stepped through the mess. The building now looked like a house the day after moving out, trash and forgotten baubles left amess.

"If this was Roache's base, I don't think it is anymore," Marcel said.

"Where is Felik?" Belona asked, stepping fast despite her oversized weapon.

Sylvaine sniffed the air. Marcel glanced over and when he did, she froze, and fiddled with her glove. So, he looked the other way, and after a few seconds she pointed.

"Up there, down the hall."

The rushed up the stairs in pursuit. As they passed through the corridors, following Sylvaine's lead, the purpose of the Roache's operations became more and more evident. Rusted gurneys covered in broken medical equipment, surrounded by tubes and pumps and ominous-looking vats. Scraprats squealed and skittered, and soon enough they found the vermin's meals. Bodies of human and mutants, or corpses half-way in-between, riddled with needle-tipped tubing. Many were bloated, mutations piling one on top of another, tumorous masses that merely hinted at their human-form. Some were desiccated, others actively rotting, and as horrible their number was, it was clear that there had once been many more. Empty tables and empty rooms hinting at an industrial scale facility built for mutation and experimentation. No, a slaughterhouse, an abattoir built for men and women, a factory of death.

Marcel stumbled, head spinning, nauseous. This was worse than Blackwood Row, this must have been the Inferno those poor souls had been sent to when they had acted out or ceased being useful slaves. It was terrible even in its evacuated, abandoned state, he dared not imagine it in motion.

"Hold yourself!" Belona spat, elbowing his back. "We don't have time for weak stomachs."

"Almost there," Sylvaine whispered. And indeed, Marcel could begin to hear desperate shouts.

"Klaus! Burke!" echoed the voice of Felik. "Taurshit, fucking griffon guts! Burke, Slovida, Marshall, where are you?"

The four crouched down and snuck forward, following the voice. As they approached the door Marcel could begin to hear clanging, and the desperate breaths of Felik. Then a sudden clunk, and a gasp of relief.

"Felik!" Belona shouted, jumping forward into the large room, motorgun at the ready.

The raider yelped, holding tight the axe in his hand. Next to him was what seemed to be the narrow gate to a cage, whose misshaped bulk made up the back half off the massive space.

"You've lost," Belona said. "Now come peacefully or come in pieces, make your choice."

"I know what you're thinking," the raider said. "But before ya do anything rash, I should tell ya—" he dashed suddenly to a doorway to his right. Belona roared and started the motorgun. The motor groaned and the barrels began turning, but by the time the bullets started to fly the raider had already passed through the twin doors. Kayip rushed forward and kicked the door but bounced back.

"He slotted the axe between the handles!" the monk shouted.

"Engineer, blow us a way through!" Belona commanded as she marched forward.

Sylvaine, though, was frozen, fur on edge, staring at the cage. Marcel glanced over to see what Felik had been doing. Around the bottom of the cage's gate sat a limp section of chains, which had moments before been holding it shut tight. From the depths of the cage, came a deep rumbling growl.

"Troglyns!" Sylvaine shouted.

The gate burst open, a flash of something leaping out. Marcel shined his light onto the creature, stunning it a brief moment. Deep orange it was, the shape of a parody of a man, almost ape or gibbon-like. Long muscular arms covered in layers of chiton, prognathic jaw overstuffed with razor teeth, head adorned with ram-like horns, clawed hands pawing the ground, tiny eyes staring out from a sunken skull. The troglyn roared, and its roar was match with a dozen more from inside the cage.

Belona's motorgun screeched as she fired off another round, turning the troglyn into meat. As she did so another of the beasts charged out of the cage, followed by another, and another, and more. Belona grunted as she turned her bulky gun, only for the weapon to groan to a halt in a burst of smoke.

"Imperator damn you Lechslov, clean your weapons!" she shouted as she tossed the entire motorgun into a leaping foe. Marcel aimed his pistol and fired into the mob, as Kayip rushed forward, slicing two in twain.

"Shitshitshit!" Sylvaine shouted, as one of the monsters charged her. She jumped back several feet in the air like a frighted cat, landing on a crate. The beast swiped at her, and she swiped back, drawing a deep gash across the troglyn's face.

Marcel aimed and fired three shots at the assailant, managing only to skim its shoulder, as two more troglyns cornered the engineer. Kayip screamed out a baritone battle cry and jumped forward, landing sword first into one of the creatures. Sylvaine thrust out her glove and summoned forth a burst of blinding static, dazzling a troglyn long enough for Kayip to decapitate it.

A closer roar. Marcel turned to see a troglyn beating its chest and barring its teeth just a few metres away. He aimed his six-shooter and pulled the trigger, producing only impotent click.

"Oh taurshit—" Marcel began as the monster leapt. He kicked with his cogleg in a panic. The unexpected attack slowed the troglyn, but sent Marcel clean to the ground. He fumbled for bullets as the beast made to leap again.

A blast knocked the troglyn to side, Belona aiming her smoking scattergun.

"Count your shots!" she snapped. The imperial swung her knee into a screaming troglyn, while slotting in another shell. She blasted a hole in the monster's chest, then smacked the barrels of her gun into another's face, before grabbing a knife from some hidden somewhere and jabbing it into its jugular in one swift movement. Her graceful brutality was mesmerizing—load, shoot, swing, kick, in one improvised dance. It reminded him of how Alba would spar, though his old lover had not been as viciously direct.

"Marcel!" she shouted.

"Right," he said, shoving the bullets into his cylinder, then firing off into a screeching troglyn.

Still more were rushing out of the massive cage. Kayip charged and slashed, cutting one, then two, then three down. Another raised a broken piece of piping to strike. A flash, and the makeshift club melted into its hands, the troglyn screeching with shock.

Sylvaine jumped forward, glove out. As a half-starved troglyn crawled out from the cage, the engineer sent out an arc of æthericity, collapsing the bars onto the unfortunate creature.

Marcel stumbled to his feet and put a bullet into an already injured troglyn. Kayip and Belona did a quick clean-up, finishing the last of the assailants. The room was covered in troglyn blood and smelled of gunsmoke. Marcel's ears rung from the cacophony.

"Gear's-grits..." Sylvaine muttered, glancing over the grotesque scene.

"Engineer! Quickly!" Belona barked, pointing towards the door.

"Right," Sylvaine said, jogging over. She placed her glove against the door, sucked in her breath, waited a few seconds, and then burst open the door in a flash.

"Felik!" Belona shouted as she charged forward. Marcel and the others ran to keep up. They rushed through hallways covered in forgotten scrap, rows of dense living quarters now only trashed bedframes, and up the stairwell where Felik's voice began again to echo.

"Marshall! Belka! Slovida! Burke! Damn it, damn it, rusted pus where the fuck—"

The voice stopped suddenly. The four crept forward through a room filled with industrial equipment. Though much had been uninstalled, the pipes, pumps, and æther-tanks that remained reminded Marcel of Blackwood Row, specifically that horrible slickdust infusion plant that the slaves called 'the monolith.'

Belona taking the lead, scattergun forward, they snuck around the corner into a large room, once maybe a dance hall, and long after that some sort of industrial facility, but most recently a battleground. A dozen bodies lay on the floor, raiders by their style, of several gang affiliation. Some of the machines were cut open, crust of red inside, with small bags and scrapping tools tossed on the floor alongside the weapons and bloodshed.

"Slickdust," Sylvaine whispered with a shudder.

At the far end of the room Felik was bent over a slight pale corpse, who looked to have taken the wrong end of a bayonet.

"Burke! Burke! Come on... No. No. Nonononono—"

"Felik!" Belona said, scattergun aimed.

The raider stood. He was covered in sweat and his eyes moved with desperate freneticism. He took a step towards a nearby window.

"Five floors up, by my count" Belona said. "But if you're eager for the embrace of death, I can bring it quicker than the ground."

"Okay, okay," Felik said, arms up. "I won't trying nothing. Let's just talk, like civilized folk. Look, the ferral's all healthy, no harm, no foul."

"Suck off a piston," Sylvaine said.

"Where is everyone?" Belona asked, stepping forward.

"Beats me," Felik said. "Real ghost town here, heck of a surprise."

Belona took another few steps, then bashed the grip of her gun into Feliks face.

"Fuck!" he shouted, gripping his face, blood dripping.

"Tired of your taurshit, Felik," Belona said. "Who's this Burke?"

"Just a... a guy I knew from a while back." Felik mumbled. "Was just shocked to see him here."

Belona sighed. She slipped her scattergun onto her back, then picked up the raider by the collar. With a grunt, she smashed him into the wall, then again, and again. Marcel wondered if he should intervene. This was certainly not the way one was meant to treat prisoners, even raiders. Yet the bastard did try to kill Sylvaine, and Belona seemed to know what she was doing. Felik surely had survived worse brutalities.

"Fuck, fuck, okay!" Felik raised his arms. "He's... a fellow Taur Maw."

"I could guess that. How did you know he would be here?"

"We planned..." Felik said. "Back before I was caught. Taur Maw's still new to the region, we traveled from south. I was their connection up here, supposed to hook them up, but couldn't get all the supplies we needed to start afresh. Word was that Lazacorp was moving camp, quick-like too. I knew they'd forget some stuff, equipment, weapons..." He glanced towards the cracked open machine. Marcel noticed now that the red that covered Burke's nose was not blood. "...Slickdust."

"You weren't the only one to come up with that plan," Sylvaine said, gesturing to the bodies.

"Looks like it." He glanced over, genuine sorrow twisting his face a moment. "Lots of raiders hungering for the same thing, never ones to share. I should have predicted it would be a scavengers' bloodbath."

"So, you knew from the beginning that Roache wasn't going to be here?" Marcel asked.

Felik shrugged. Belona raised her fist. "Yes, yes! I mean, yeah I knew. But ya folk were keeping me alive on for intel purposes. If I didn't give a good enough answer, this bitch would have put a bullet through my skull."

"You wasted our time, you could have gotten us all killed," Marcel said.

"Tried to, yeah." Felik chuckled dryly. "And if not, I was hoping maybe my mates here might buy me out with aurem, or info, or just have pumped ya all full of lead as you parked. But tell me what I was supposed to do, right? I'm just some raider scum to ya, if I didn't find a way to string ya along long enough to escape, I'd be dead man. And even if I brought you to Roache all right and proper, you'd have left me a dead man anyhow."

"We weren't going to kill you," Marcel protested.

"Well, who's the fucking liar now? So, what, ya'll allow me to walk free once you found Roache? Bygones be bygones?"

"Ye...yes!" Marcel said, with some hesitancy. Belona glanced back at him, with a face of pity. Marcel could not help but wonder if he had been naïve. But, he wouldn't have let it happen, even with all of Felik's crimes, he would never have allowed the Imperial to just murder him because he had served his use. Neither would Sylvaine or Kayip, right? He glanced towards the monk, who wore a dour grimace.

"She knows how it is," Felik said. "So, make your accusations, it was all in self-defense."

"Then where is Roache?" Sylvaine asked.

"Ya can understand why I'm hesitant to say," Felik said. "That info is all that's keeping me alive."

"I promise you," Marcel said, "on the honor of the UCCR, I promise you that if you tell us the truth about where Roache is, we will not kill you. We'll let you free."

The raider squinted at him, blood still dripping from his nose. He glanced at Belona, and then around at the bodies that littered the floors. Finally, he sighed and nodded. Perhaps he believed Marcel's genuine offer, perhaps he just could not see any other choice.

"Roache is where's he's always been. Stinktown."

Kayip released a sound, it was not quite a gasp, not quite a moan, something heavy with despair. His blade slunk to the ground.

"Yeah, see?" Felik pointed. "If I started with that, ya wouldn't have kept me around."

"What's Stinktown?" Marcel asked.

"A raider settlement," Belona said. "The largest in the region, by far, the one place in the Wastes where all the gangs play nice together long enough to swap slaves and stock up on supplies. If this old factory was difficult to crack, then Stinktown is near impossible. Thousands of raiders, all in one spot, all armed. You'd need an army to crack it open, and not a small one."

"Well..." Marcel said. "Shit."

"Yeah, shit," Felik said. "It's shit, it's all shit, your shit plan the most shit of all. What in the Inferno are you idiots thinking? Going to try an assassinate the richest man in the Wastes? Ya think you're the first to try? Half the gangs wanted his head when he sauntered out here seven years ago, now they all scramble to suck the man's dick. Want to try breaking into Stinktown? Ask your monk friend how that went."

"I lost... people," Kayip said. "I thought I could use the anger against Roache, but I lacked his guile."

"Got a whole gang killed, you know that?" Felik said. "Still tell stories about the mad one-eyed monk. So, you ready to turn it in? Stop this nonsense, and let me free? Or, fuck, continue this nonsense, get yourself killed, but first let me free?"

"You're not going anywhere," Belona said, pulling the raider closer.

"Hey, you promised—"

"I made no promises," Belona said. "As long as Roache is still breathing, you're not going anywhere."

"Belona, we did—" Marcel started.

"*You* did!" Belona said. "I don't give a shit about the honor of your treacherous rebellion, or the idiocy of taking pity on this raider shit."

"You vile, stick-assed, bitch," Felik muttered. "Fuck you and your griffon-shit Principate."

"Listen Felik, we will let you go," Marcel said, "just after we get our new plan together."

"New plan, new plan, more excuses, more impossible promises!" Felik shouted. "You're just gonna dump my body in some waste-ditch, stop pretending!"

"Do not forget your many crimes," Belona snarled. "Slaving, smuggling, falsifying forms, assault, and attempted murder." She gestured to Sylvaine. "You were given a death sentence; I have been temporarily deferring it."

"Now you're acting that like you're still some Justice Officer," Felik said. "Ya betrayed your own taurshit Imperator. Ya lied to your superior officer and abandoned your post. Do ya know what raiders do to traitors? We skin them and leave them to the skraggers. If you were a true officer of the Principate, you'd toss up a rope and hang yourself."

"We're getting off-track," Marcel said. "There must still be a way to sneak into Stinktown. Belona, ask him if there are any... underway passageways, or maybe nearby sangleum wells that Roache visits."

"Why trust a word of this worm?" Belona asked. "This piece of troglyn offal that has no understanding of loyalty."

"Pompous cunt," Felik spat. "Ya dare fucking look down on me? I never betrayed my own people, I never betrayed Burke or Marshall or Slovida. But first chance ya get, you abandon your duties, your people. What a fucking joke your Principate is if it's made of up selfish, spineless traitors like you."

"Tempt me more," Belona growled, "and I'll carry out your execution right here right now."

"We don't need to toss around insults and threats," Marcel said.

"I don't think your mediation is working," Sylvaine said.

"No matter what ya do to me," Felik said, "I'll die a happy man knowing that you will end your life a forgotten traitor, lost amidst the dirt and shit of this dead, empty land."

Belona grunted and hurled Felik into the wall, where he fell to the floor with a pained moan.

"You have an hour to figure out why we should keep you alive," Belona said to the slumped figure. She turned on her boot to face Marcel, Sylvaine and Kayip. "As for us, the chance for success have dropped precipitously, but as long as I breathe, I intend to do what is necessary to bring Lazarus Roache to justi—"

Marcel caught the glint of metal from behind the imperial. Felik pulled from his jacket a hidden pistol and took aim.

"Belona!" he shouted.

The woman turned and leapt to the side, as the raider shot. The bullet whizzed past, cutting the corner of Belona's jacket. She landed with a grunt, a small red line appearing on her shoulder. As Felik pulled back the hammer for a second shot, she pounced. One hand grasping Felik's pistol, the other on his neck. He groaned and struggled to aim the weapon.

Marcel and Kayip rushed forward, but Belona seemed to have a strong grip on the man. With a shout she bashed his head back into the wall. Then again, and again. It thudded in a painful manner, the man dazed and spitting blood. Belona pushed the pistol back, away from her, towards the raider, centimetre by centimetre. She muttered something, fingers around the raider's neck, pistol fully in her grasp. Felik's limp grip provided only the most perfunctory of resistance. Marcel leaned forward to make out the imperial's words.

"...by the authority endowed to me by our Imperator, Lothar Diedrev, I find you, Felik Rector, guilty on all charges. Punishment: execution by firearm."

"Wait!" Marcel shouted, as the pistol went off. Felik's brains decorated the wall.

# CHAPTER 21

The room was silent, with only the faint phantom echo of the gunshot. Felik's body slumped slowly to the floor. Belona stared down at it, as if he might move, though that was certainly an impossibility. Death had a distinct smell, even beyond the obvious blood and gunpowder. Also, the back of his skull was burst open.

"Fuck!" Marcel shouted. Sylvaine could not help but share the sentiment, though her exact thoughts were not clear. The raider had gone from a strange prisoner, to a friend, to a murderous enemy, to a corpse, in a matter of hours. Sylvaine's head was reeling, and the bruise near her temple didn't help things.

"He was our prisoner!" Marcel said. "You had him captured, overpowered!"

"This was inevitable," Belona said. "He made it inevitable, with his crimes."

"Not inevitable! Not inevitable!" Marcel shouted. "We could have tied him up!"

"And were you really going to keep your empty oath? Let this bastard go free? No, he long abandoned any path to redemption, he was only a threat and a nuisance."

"You had his pistol! You could have disarmed him easily; he was no longer a threat."

"Are you not a bounty hunter?" Belona asked. "Do you not kill your prey?"

"Not those who I have already captured!" Marcel said. "That's not bounty hunting. That's *butchery*."

The woman froze at the word. Her face bent in a new sort of fury, less arrogant and wild, more focused and bitter. She strode up to the man. "It is *justice*, Marcel. It is *duty*. Something you are not capable of understanding."

As the two shouted at each other, Sylvaine looked towards Kayip. The man was leaning on a machine, which was worrying, for as long as Sylvaine had known the monk, he was never a leaner. Standing straight, or skulking bent, or sitting with a meditative calm, but never leaning. He seemed to suddenly have trouble keeping up or still, swaying slightly. She did not think it was Felik's death that bothered the man; instead, it was the revelation about Lazarus Roache. He caught her gaze and gave a very weak impression of a smile.

"It will... we will be all ri... The Demiurge gives us another test," he finally decided. The monk pulled out his Cracked Disc and began to gently turn it around its chain. "Yes, yet another... test."

It seemed to Sylvaine that the monk desperately grasped towards religion in order to avoid the cruel mercuriality of the real world. Or perhaps that faith was just a show, for her sake more than his, to make it seem like this was just a setback, that someone had the confidence that their quest would have an end point, that this was all leading to something. Revenge, right? That was the word they were avoiding, instead preferring "justice" or "the will of the Demiurge." Yet Sylvaine had just had revenge, in microcosm. This raider bastard who had used her and tried to murder her was now just another corpse in a room full of them. Yet Sylvaine felt nothing. No joy, no relief, not even anger, nothing. Well, she did feel tired. Quite tired.

"So, what is your plan for Roache, little pacifist?" Belona spat. "Ask him kindly to repent, give him our 'truck as a getaway gift?"

"Obviously I'd take him out!" Marcel said. "Do you actually believe that is anything like what you just did? That's justice, this was a butcher's work."

"Butcher's work?" Belona said, getting in Marcel face. "You keep using that word. Well, better a butcher than a coward!" Marcel took a hesitant step back, and Belona moved in. "What sort of man are you, to stand back and do nothing? To have a friend nearly murdered and play the conscientious objector? I don't believe you are a bounty hunter; I don't believe you were a mercenary, nor a private investigator." Marcel took another step back, and Belona took another forward. "You act like you're going to save the world, as if you can do anything more than make a small mess large. You are just a little boy, drunk on bedtimes stories. A shriveled-dicked, adult child who pretends to play hero."

Marcel punched the woman in the face.

He froze. Sylvaine froze. Even Kayip was ripped from his daze.

Belona held her cheek. A drop of blood oozed from her cut lip. She wiped it with her index figure and stared.

"I... I didn't mean..." Marcel stammered.

The woman burst into laughter. Strange gurgling giggles flowed from her mouth, as she staggered back. "First blood! A strike against Belona, not blade for blade, but fist for word. There is your pacifist! The soldier all grown up! Taking a weakness exposed, attacking when unexpected. There he is, there is he! The man who will kill Lazarus Roache! Now where is his parade?"

Marcel glanced over at Sylvaine, looking as absolutely befuddled as she was.

"We cannot descend into bitter fights now," Kayip said, seeming to suddenly remember his role as the fraying rope that tied all together. "There is still hope, we cannot give up."

"Give up? Fight?" Belona continued to chuckle in a manner that was about as disturbing as any other horror Sylvaine had witnessed this night. "No, no. The man is learning! A strike against an ally. Put a gun in his hand, refocus his aim, we might make a soldier out of Marcel yet!" The woman's laughter abruptly ceased. She stood up straight and surveyed the room, as if seeing it for the first time. "Very well, it shall be daylight in a few hours, and I wish to be gone by then. Hard to know who might stumble upon this place. But we are not giving up, not yet, not as long blood still pumps through our veins. Split up and scout the area, we may yet find something that could give us a needed advantage. Lazarus Roache is still unaware of our approach; we may still have a shot."

"Yes," Kayip said, though Sylvaine could sense the uncertainty beneath his words. "We must continue on. No matter the challenge."

"Right, sure, yes," Marcel said, still eyeing Belona.

"Me and Marcel can check out the lower levels," Sylvaine offered, grabbing the man. She would have much preferred to go with Kayip, who seemed to need reassurance. But she was not sure she had those reassurances to give, and if Marcel was left with Belona a minute longer... Well, Sylvaine did not want there to be another corpse on the floor.

* * *

"That was weird, right?" Marcel asked as they walked. "She's not normal, is what I'm saying. That was not a normal reaction."

"I mean, are any of us normal?" Sylvaine asked. "Normal people don't go gallivanting off into the Wastes on the trail of some sangleum tycoon."

They descended the stairs, retracing their steps. Most of the upper floors seemed empty, living quarters left open and dead, but Sylvaine recalled passing by some locked doors on the way up.

"But she is... insane," Marcel said. "We're not just some vigilante thugs, right? We're pursuing justice, we have rules and standards and... We don't just go around murdering people, right?"

Sylvaine was pretty sure the question was rhetorical, though she wasn't sure what answer she would give were she forced. How far would they be willing to go? Kayip, she suspected, had already done things he wasn't happy about. As for herself... she was just here. She wanted Roache dead, sure, but mostly she just didn't want to be alone. Somehow, she had convinced herself that following along a makeshift posse on a suicide mission was preferable to... not doing that? But then what else would she do? Icaria was out, and it wasn't like she could ever explain things to her parents. And she did really want Lazarus Roache in the ground, that wasn't an excuse. Every time she used her æthermantics, there still felt a tug of pain, of anxiety, of horror, memories of what that man did to her, made her do, made her become, infected even the most wondrous acts of creation. It just didn't seem right that he could be allowed to live.

"The imperial just doesn't understand. Too corrupted by the idiocy of the Principate," Marcel said. He was covered in sweat, glancing around each corner as if expecting phantoms to appear. "Doesn't this place remind you of Blackwood Row?"

"A little?" Sylvaine offered as a non-answer. She wondered if the whole revenge question was moot. If the ever-faithful monk was starting to doubt their chances of stopping Roache, then maybe this really was the end. Not that she was sure she could convince anyone of that, even if they secretly knew it themselves.

The windows outside showed the usual dark. Sylvaine stopped for a moment to glance out, but the Wastes were as desolate as they ever were. For the briefest of moments, she thought she saw movement, a glimmer of metal, but as she continued to squint she found nothing more. A hidden soot-sparrow gave a shrill call, and some dog-sized snail thing chomped on rustgrass in the parking lot, but that was about it.

"I don't punch women," Marcel said suddenly. "I mean, in wartime, if they're a soldier... obviously you fight who you fight. I'm not going to dismantle my rifle if I see a woman in the opposing trench. But civilian women, right, I would never think to touch—I mean, Belona is a soldier... but that's my point, right? You understand?"

"Yes," Sylvaine lied.

"She was acting crazy, totally unhinged crazy," Marcel shook his head. "Someone had to do something. Murdering a prisoner and acting crazy. What sort of people are we working with?"

They passed by the room with the troglyn cage, taking care to avoid the pools of blood. Sylvaine noticed a wet, crunching sound. She turned and squinted to see through the bars, a troglyn bent over, another's arm in its mouth, tearing softly and chewing. Beyond it lay a pile of, presumably once kin, torn apart into mounds of bone and discarded viscera.

Marcel, due to good luck or poor eyesight, hadn't noticed. Instead, he was starting up at the tumorous growth of anarchic piping that made up the ceiling. The mass crawled down the wall towards what looked to be an oddly placed and bulky generator, wrapped in spiderweb of æther-wires.

"Demiurge," he said. "Wouldn't mind strapping a few clockbombs to that and blowing this place to Inferno."

"Agreed," said Sylvaine.

* * *

Down the hallways they found a pair of iron doors locked with a heavy chain. Sylvaine lifted her glove, focused, and split the lock. Inside was a sizable armory: scatterguns, repeater-rifles, bayonets, and a whole row of motorguns, replete for ammo for each.

"That's... a lot of guns," Marcel said. "What idiots could forget all of this?"

"Or maybe Lazacorp is so well-armed," Sylvaine mused, "that it's no great loss to leave this cache."

They stood there a moment, trying not to imagine the implications.

Sylvaine stepped over to the other door and raised her glove. A scent hit her, sudden and pungent. *Slickdust.* Unlike the scrapped crust on the machines upstairs, this smelled fresh, like the highly concentrated, liquid slickdust Lazarus Roache had once injected her with.

"Are you okay?" Marcel asked, seemingly noticing that the engineer had frozen.

"Uh, sure, yes," Sylvaine stammered. "I was just... thinking. You know, maybe we should split up. There were a few unlocked rooms a down the hallway, the faster we go through this the quicker we can get out."

"Makes sense," Marcel nodded, as he began to walk. "I want to get out of here too. Just holler if you need anything."

"Right," Sylvaine said, glove still stiff. She wasn't sure why she wanted the man gone. It wasn't like she was going to *use* the slickdust. Not after everything it had done to her, not after what it had made her do. But she could not help but worry about how she might react. She hadn't gotten close to slickdust since leaving Icaria, had never tested herself, proven to herself beyond all doubt that she was in complete control. Would she begin to salivate, like those dogs upon hearing a bell in that experiment she had once read about? No, no, of course not. She was an engineer, and her body was just another machine, she could decide what went into it, could control its every workings.

She sucked in her breath and received a much stronger whiff of the slickdust fumes than she had expected. With a panicked gasp, she unleashed an unintended bolt of æthericity that transformed the lock to smoldering slag. Trying not to dwell on that burst of uncontrolled chaos, she slowly pushed open the door, keeping her glove aimed away from herself.

Inside looked to be a laboratory of some kind, a very messy kind. Beakers and books, pipes and pipettes, scales and scalpels, desiccators and desiccated corpses. Someone had been experimenting on mutants, with grisly results. It looked as bad as anything in Blackwood Row, and Sylvaine tried to avoid staring directly into the faces of the test subjects. A dozen or more had been left behind, Sylvaine shooed off scraprats who were making the grisly scene a feast. Unsurprisingly the whole room smelled awful, yet over the chemicals and rot, the scent of slickdust still hung dense and acerbically sweet.

In a bottle it sat on a table, stoppered end near some infusion tubes. Crimson and clear, Sylvaine stared at the drug, her reflection visible in her low-glow handtorch. She could see her fur, her pointed ears, her blade-sharp teeth, her ungloved hand with semi-retracted claws. Beyond that horrid image sat the liquid slickdust, pure and perfect, memories of its warmth, of the power and purpose it gave her. Whenever she had doubted herself, whenever she might wonder if she was truly an engineer, she would take snort a little of that magic dust, and all her fears would slip away.

She placed her hand upon the glass. The liquid seemed somehow alive, reacting in imperceptible ways to her touch, wanting to unite with her. How simple it would be to open the lid. It was not as if Marcel were here, it was not as if Kayip or Belona could judge her. They were at a loss, unsure of what to do, yet Sylvaine always found plenty of ideas from just a dash of slickdust. Even her negative density generator. She may have formed the outlines of the machine on her own, but it was the slickdust that gave the design focus, streamlined it, turned it from a petty student project into the greatest invention Icaria had ever seen! Why she could remember the look on Gearwit's face when she first unveiled the working prototype. The look of Gearswit's face... The look of Gearswit's face as he lay dead on the floor of the Academy exhibition hall. The look on strangers' faces as they stared at his killer, glares filtered through the smoke of her burning creation. The screams of men and women as she dashed across the streets of Icaria, dress torn, mouth covered in someone else's blood. A killer, a monster, a beast, a damned wild anima—

Sylvaine roared and knocked the bottle off table. It shattered over the floor, the smell of slickdust billowing out like a bomb's blast. Sylvaine staggered back, some instinct inside her forcing her breath still. After a few moments she gasped, sickened and nauseated by the smell, but again in control of herself. She glanced towards the door, but it seemed as though Marcel had not heard the ruckus.

*Gears-grits.* She shook her head. It had been weeks since she had felt Lazarus's hooks, but they were still as sharp as ever.

Trying to distract herself, she scanned the room again. She noticed, in the corner, a single notebook, seemingly forgotten among the mess. On its face was written:

*Slickdust Iteration V.4.B Notes*

*M— Veneficus*
*DO NOT READ.*

Of course, Sylvaine flipped open the notebook.

*...Continuing issues with fatal mutations. Subjects C.42, C.43, C.45 dead within hours. Suffocation in the first two cases, lung tumors. Unknown cause of death for 45, need to finish autopsy. Suggestive power unable to be tested, but addiction forming. Subject 42 used last breathe to request further doses...*

Sylvaine flipped the page. Charts and graphs, all in scribbled ink, measuring varying dosages and formulas.

*...New batch 4.B52 produces low fatality rate. However aesthetic mutations still high. Crimson skin, claws, boils, can't even seem to reduce horn growth. Batch 4.B49 had even lower mutation rate, but with a corresponding decrease in suggestive power...*

Another page,

*...Nasal and oral administration still ideal for low mutation rate, but can only induce moderate suggestibility, not complete control. Mutation seems inevitable outcome if injections used, but previous tests show possibility of reduction. If aesthetic considerations were left behind, solution would be simple. Lazarus still demands control over unmarred humans, so further tests required. More pressing is issue of degeneration. Whole question moot if Lazarus himself should lose his powers...*

Sylvaine paused on that line: *if Lazarus himself should lose his powers.* The tycoon had mentioned that his blood was an ingredient to slickdust; was there something special about the man that allowed him alone to produce the substance? Something that could be lost? And if his power could be lost... No, she wasn't going down that path, wasn't even going to think it. She kept reading:

*...Tribute as model for maintaining Lazarus's current state? Slickdust-infused blood important for idiot brotherhoods' ritual, helps integrate bioætheric entanglement into ætherlines. Perhaps could also be used to connect Lazarus directly....*

Sylvaine hadn't a clue what that meant. Somehow Roache was connected to the ætherlines that ran under continent. That sounded like a loose description of the Knack, but Lazarus was never the engineering type. She caught a word on the page and froze. *Ferral.* She glanced back a few lines for context.

*...Mutation not an acceptable outcome for Lazarus. Might be possible to avoid. Only example so far is Ferral subject in Icaria, who avoided any sign of mutation. Unfortunately, Ferral's instincts prevented full control. Biology may be too divergent to use as model...*

That was her. Just an unnamed Ferral subject, an oddity left for a footnote. All her pain, her anguish, her ambition and mistakes, summed up in an inconsequential aside. It could be worse, she knew, she could be dead, most of Roache's other experiments were. She searched the notebook for any further mentions of herself but could find none. Just as she was about to put the notebook down she came upon a drawing, a doodle really, of a series of æther-circuits crudely superimposed upon a human figure. She read:

*...Is induction of Knack within subjects an intended feature of Lazarus's powers or mere side effect? Verus was unhelpful in this regard, and Namter no better. Perhaps an inevitable outcome of connection to Lazarus. Man serves as independent æthergrid, entangling those who ingest slickdust. What should happen if experiments fail, if Lazarus loses all powers, or should expire? Could those with this artificial Knack interface directly with the ætherlines? Unlikely. Primary hypothesis: result would be an immediate cessation of æthermantic abilities in all subjects...*

*...immediate cessation of æthermantic abilities ...*

*...immediate cessation...*

*...immediate...*

The notebook fell from her hand. Sylvaine stumbled, barely able to support herself on a nearby table. She tried catch her breath, which was rushing at full speed. Fears once buried now exhumed themselves with a frightening ferocity, battering her mind with that one word: *Cessation. Cessation. Cessation!*

So, she would lose the Knack if Lazarus Roache should die. So, this power that proved her unique among Ferrals, proved herself equal to humans, that made her the engineer that she always told herself she was, it would disappear. Her knack was not only artificial in origin, but completely ephemeral, dependent on the man who had abused her trust, had manipulated her, and destroyed her life. If he should die, if she would even lose this last bit, this most important spark in her life. She would no longer be an engineer.

"Find anything Sylvaine?" came Marcel's voice, as the man strolled in, handtorch swaying. "I came across a big dictaphone mic, think it's hooked up to a bunch of speakers set around the place so that Roache could have—Shit!"

The man's 'torch had lit up the face of some unfortunate mutant, more skull than skin. Marcel staggered back. "Demiurge damn it! What is this?"

"Lab," Sylvaine mumbled, staring at nothing.

Marcel groaned, and tried to keep from vomiting, jumping up when he accidentally placed his hand next to another body. "Hate this place. Hate this damned place. Worse in the dark, like the Lazacorp underway. Fuck!"

"Yeah," Sylvaine said, about nothing.

Marcel wiped sweat from his forehead. "Any way to get the lights going, just so we can see what we're doing?"

"Sure," said Sylvaine, as she walked trance-like out of the lab. The generator wasn't far, entrapped in wires. The sound of the lone troglyn crunching teeth through bone was the only ambiance. She placed her glove the generator, sent out trembling pulses. With these fingers of æther she could sense the machine, as if she were inspecting the intimacies of her own body in the comfort of a midnight dark. If she were to succeed in her task, get her justice, her revenge, she would become to blind to such pleasures, unable to feel, to work, to build and mold. Her dreams would again sit chained in her skull, her life again defined only by fur and claws and the scornful laughter of strangers. She would have nothing, be nothing. If Lazarus Roache should live, she would have his words in her bloods, have his crimes and lies crawling inside her. All her life she would not be herself fully, be an engineer only through deception, lying to herself more than anyone. Just a nameless experiment, waiting in agony for the day when her powers might leave on her own accord, joining Roache on his deathbed, surrounded by the ill-gotten riches of a life of decadent cruelty.

She sighed and focused. The generator was in fine condition, still filled with half-a-tank of æther-oil. Sylvaine could bring life to it. It might be one of her last opportunities to do so, to play the role of an engineer.

A bolt. A grumble. The roar of æthericity, the fizzle in the wires above. The room burst into a glorious golden light.

# CHAPTER 22

"Oh, thank the Demiurge," Marcel said, finally able to see. The whole of Narida Heights now glowed with buzzing ætherlamps, illuminating faded tiles, rusted metal, and troglyn corpses. It wasn't a pleasant sight, but it was a good deal better than stumbling around the dark, like they were some squad of doomed saboteurs.

"Hmm..." Sylvaine said, nearby. The engineer's gaze was glazed. Perhaps she too was disturbed by the horrors of this place. The bodies had reminded Marcel of what they were fighting for. However dangerous this 'Stinktown' place was, they could not give up here, could not stop until Lazarus was dead and buried. Even if that meant working with this Imperial murderer for just a few weeks longer. He could be the hand that kept her from future crimes, could focus them all on their task, to bring Roache to justice. Despite the brutalities around them, the light gave Marcel hope again, that every shadow could be chased from its hiding place, that Lazarus's terrors could be banished with just a little courage, that Marcel could one day return to a free and safe Huile, just as he had promised Alba.

Footsteps suddenly echoed. Marcel grabbed his pistol, as the thud of boots on wood and carpets. Belona burst through the door, Kayip not far behind, rage on her face.

"What! The! Fuck! Are you doing!"

"I... What?" Marcel asked, holstering his weapon.

"The lights!" she shouted. "We're sneaking around an abandoned Lazacorp base in the middle of the Wastes, and you light it up like a damn Santi's Night balloon?"

"We needed to... see," as Marcel spoke, he saw the potential idiocy in the move. Narida Heights was now the only lit structure for kiloms around, a bright beacon in the middle of the Wastes. But he couldn't let the smug imperial butcher grab the high ground. "It's abandoned," he said firmly, "nobody is anywhere near here."

"Abandoned for now!" Belona shouted. "There is only one road in and out this town! If any raiders decide to investigate, we will be instantly surrounded! I thought you were a soldier. Even a half-assed, pay-for-hire, idiot of a mercenary would know not to broadcast their location to every enemy in a ten-kilometre radius."

As Belona was rambling, the monk glanced over towards Sylvaine. "Are you all right?" he asked, for some reason.

"Sure," Sylvaine offered.

"Everyone who was curious about this place is up there dead with Felik," Marcel insisted, walking to the window. "The Wastes are called that for a reason, no one's out here. Look, there's not a single—"

Out on the road Marcel spotted three pairs of light winding around the base of the mountain, the glares of headlights cutting through the pines.

"Wait, shit."

Kayip walked over and stared out. "Three 'trucks,'" he said. "Could be three people, could be three-dozen people."

"Imperator damn you, Marcel," Belona muttered.

"Raiders?" Sylvaine asked, staring into the dark.

"I do not know," Kayip said. "But we cannot be confident in our ability to fight them."

"Trapped in, like scraprats," Belona said.

"No, no, we can make it out of this," Marcel said, mind racing. He had just been so confident a minute ago, he wouldn't let a small error ruin everything. There had to be something they could do. Maybe set up defenses... no it was not fortress enough for four against many. Look for a place to hide? But for how long? Maybe they could find an underway entrance, but even if one existed, Demiurge knew where it headed. Damn it, they had weaponry to spare, certainly, enough for an army, but without the hands to use it—

Suddenly, an idea burst full formed into his mind.

"The motorguns!" he said.

* * *

Belona helped Kayip heave the last motorgun into place by the window. The weapon was an aged and bulky thing, a scraped-together amalgam of Principate and Resurgence Republic design. A disgrace to both lineages, by Belona's reckoning. Its kin stood in a line down the long room, and some more in the next room over.

It was all as to Marcel's hairbrained design. Idiot was desperate to cover his obvious mistake with elaborate, idiotic schemes. Yet he was far from the only desperate idiot in the building. Belona bit her lip, cursing herself for falling for Felik's deception. She had assumed her strength would be enough to squeeze truth out of the raider. Perhaps had the facts of Roache's hideout not been so stark and grim, she could have forced honesty. When an interrogation subject sees no living path in truth, deceit becomes inevitable. This had been her error, a lack of imagination, so blinded she had been by her mission. Belona was in enemy territory, she reminded herself, she could not afford assumptions and guesswork. If she was to still take down Roache, she needed to plan, to face the harsh reality of the tycoon's fortified sanctuary and find a strategy to crack into it with her very limited resources. But to plan, she needed time, and Marcel's blithe buffoonery had robbed her of even that.

The man had not even been much help setting up the weaponry. Instead, he worked with Sylvaine, who was carefully weaving a mess of long metal wire from each motorgun to the other in one convoluted web. More than twenty of the weapons sat, loaded, as beams of light weaved closer and closer.

"This is a taurshit idea," Belona muttered, as she pushed forward the bulky dictaphone. "Even if the engineer can activate them as one, we barely have enough ammo for each gun to fire a few seconds."

"If we're smart that's all we should need," Marcel said with a twitch of his head. "Listen, these are most likely scrappers, looking for an easy job. When they see that Lazacorp are still occupying their old hideout they'll turn tail, we just need one good volley."

"And if they are Lazacorp?" Kayip asked.

"Then they'll see that raiders have taken up camp, and retreat to gather more forces."

"What if they don't?" Belona said, double-checking the dictaphone's wiring. "What if they call our bluff?"

"Then we run," Marcel forced a laugh. "We're pretty good at that."

Belona glared.

"Quiet," Kayip said, quietly.

The three autotrucks puttered through the open gate, awkwardly turning and following one another indecisively, until they slowed to a stop about fifty metres in front of the building. A pit formed in Belona's stomach as she caught the vehicles' outlines. It took a moment for their colors and insignia to come into the light and confirm her fears. Upon the blue canvas of the military 'trucks stood a symbol in gold, like a Y cleaved vertically down the middle, an inverted triangle fit in-between its bent arms. When Belona was a child, her grandmother had explained that the Split-Pairle represented the open hands of Imperator in abstract, holding aloft the radiant spirit of humanity, a mandate of prosperity and glory. Flapping upon banners it had so often given her heart hope. Now it filled her with dread.

"Shit, are those Principate?" Marcel asked, accusation in his voice.

A man stepped out from the front 'truck, tall and thin. Even at this distance Belona could recognize Lechslov from the unearned pride with which he walked. The shorter, rounder Goss awkwardly alighted from the other side, glancing around and wiping his forehead with handkerchief. She was certain this was not going at all to his intention, but the Colonel had neither the will nor cunning to stop Lechslov. Behind them twenty-five soldiers detrucked, grabbing rifles from slings on their back. They stood at the ready in two rows that were almost aligned, then, after a bit of muttering and shuffling, were exactly aligned.

"Do you recognize them?" the engineer asked.

Belona nodded mutely.

"Ok, this could still work, might still work," Marcel said, pacing back and forth. "We just need to assume... I mean if they're not expecting..."

Lechslov raised his hand and shouted something. After a moment, he shouted it again. After the third, quite annoyed shout, a soldier dashed back into the 'truck, and pulled out a dictaphone, complete with a massive brass speaker-cone.

With a fizzle and a crack, Lechslov's oleaginous baritone echoed out. "Attention, loyal subjects of the Principate!"

Belona wished such fidelity could be assumed of waste-wanderers, but the Commandants' military inaction over the past few years made it a rather ambitious claim.

"I am Commandant Harlo Lechslov, of the 1st West Bastillian Army stationed in the great city of Holtag. We are the loyal servants of the Imperator, the great lord who lives beyond the Wastes, stronger and wiser than any gang boss or petty wastetown mayor. It is by his grace that you live in safety and comfort, by his will that the laws of the ancient Imperium are upheld." He paused, glancing at the desolation around him. His was a standard, canned speech, performed poorly. After another moment, Lechslov sucked in his breath and, ignoring the obvious incongruities in his proclamations, continued onward:

"It has come to my attention that a deserter has fled to your establishment, bringing with her four criminals, who she had improperly released. I do not know the name this deserter has given you, but she is of pale skin, dark hair, one-hundred-and-seventy-seven centimetres tall and..." he gestured a bit, thinking. "Of medium build. I do not presume to know if some among have you willing collaborated with this defector, but all will be forgiven if you are to immediately hand her over, as well as the prisoners she was traveling with. If you do not, I will be forced to bring upon the full weight of Principate might upon you."

Silence returned, as his voice dissipated into the dark. Belona gripped tight the speaker of the dictaphone and stared at the motorguns. The stupidity of the Commandant stunned her; did he truly believe she had made alliance with some petty raiders? And Goss... how she wished to toss blame on him, but it was her scheme that started this all, prompted this pointless military expedition out to the Wastes.

She caught movement. Marcel had his hand by his pistol warily, staring at her. Did he think she would give them all up? Sell them out for Lechslov's mercy? The idea made her laugh silently. Resurgences rats like him might deserve imprisonment, but she would never allow herself the humiliation of crawling to a shit-stain like Lechslov. And it was not because of his vindictive hatred of her that she despised the man. No, what drove her near mad was not that Lechslov had followed her all the way out here, but that he was willing to gather his troops now, and never before; not to pacify the raiders that polluted the land, not to unite the local towns under the guiding light of the Principate, not to bring order to a land of chaos. Ambition meant nothing to the worm, but petty revenge? Of course, that alone would get him off his rump.

What wasted power, what wasted potential! Years Lechslov had sat upon his army and done nothing with it. Were she in his position now, she could transform this expedition into a crusade, march down to Stinktown and crush Lazarus Roache into the dust of the Wastes. But no, the only thing that could ever prompt the man to action was fear and personal enmity...

Yet, that was a motivation indeed...

She glanced at the motorguns, tracked the trajectory of their barrels. Hope began to rise in Belona's heart, as a plan swirled in her head.

Lechslov's voice crackled again:

"We have ruled this province with a light touch, taking a laissez-faire approach to your business. If you comply, we will continue this policy, but do not mistake our gentle hand for weakness. The fist of the Imperator is steel! This force arrayed before you is but only a small diplomatic party, mere hours away sits a military camp with numbers beyond necessary to take this... factory? And if you were to resist further, I have the authority to call upon the entire might of the 1st West Bastillian Army. Were I to do so, this... settlement? Would be turned into ash and rubble. You have ten minutes to deliver the deserter."

Yes, there was a way to make this work. A risk, but it was one she had to take. Belona sucked in her breath.

"Fire."

"What?" Marcel asked.

"Fire!" Belona shouted to Sylvaine. The engineer grasped the wires in her glove. A small flash escaped the tips of her fingers, and at once all twenty of the motorguns roared into life, delivering a sudden deafening barrage, glass flying in shards.

The soldiers scattered, rushing behind their vehicles for cover as the bullets rained down a few metres in front of their 'trucks, as she had calculated. Commandant Lechslov and Colonel Goss fled, Lechslov tripping halfway to the back, desperately trying to scramble to his feet, as the only soldier who had kept her head helped pick up the dictaphone.

Belona grabbed her own dictaphone and flicked it on. A static screech echoed through the building, followed by her stentorian voice, which boomed out into the darkness of the Wastes.

"You should have brought your whole army, Lechslov!" she shouted. "Again, missing your shot. It's pathetic."

Lechslov's voice crackled back, as the man caught his footing. "Give… Give yourself up!"

Belona's laughed theatrically, her voice echoing out from every room of the building. "As you can see, we are well-armed here. Go, run back to your camp. When you return, I will be gone." She paused a moment, letting a hint of honest disdain sneak into her deceit. "I have grown tired of the weak leadership of Holtag. The city demands true strength, strength only shown by Wastefolk. You were right to fear, Lechslov, I have made contact with the Huilian tycoon Lazarus Roache and his army of raiders. I will soon be rendezvousing with the man in his base in Stinktown. I bring with me the knowledge of all your army's ineptitudes and weaknesses, and together with Roache, we will raise a force strong enough to crush Holtag into the dirt."

"You would not dare to—"

"Fire again," Belona commanded.

Bullets flew from the shattered windows, bursting up a cloud of asphalt and dust, though no soldiers were hit.

"Now leave, Commandant Lechslov," Belona shouted, smug with the calculated humiliation she wrought. "If you wish to die on your feet instead of hiding like a coward in Holtag, then meet me. Meet me in Stinktown. And bring your vaunted army."

With that, Belona clicked off the dictaphone. A smile cracked upon on her face. Roache might be holed up too deep in Stinktown for them to weed him out under normal circumstances. But during wartime? With the chaos of a besieging army and a little ingenuity, they might have a shot. A slim shot, but even if they were to fail, at least Belona would die with the satisfaction of knowing she brought that raider hive to the torch.

Recovering from the barrage, Lechslov stood up straight. He barked out some orders, and his soldiers jumped back into the 'trucks.

"Very well!" Lechslov shouted. "You wish war, then you shall have war! Now you will feel the might of the Principate upon your back. We should have had you executed two years ago, but it is time to right that wrong. You will live to regret this ex-Justice Officer, no, Traitor, Agrippus!"

* * *

*Agrippus.*

Marcel blinked silent surprise, as the name echoed out from the Imperial Commandant's speaker.

*Agrippus*

Below, the 'trucks started to drive away, back into the darkness from whence they came. In the darkness of Marcel's mind, bounced that name, again and again.

*Agrippus. Agrippus. Agrippus.*

*Belona.* The name had struck Marcel as familiar, but he had foolishly dismissed the thought. Just some imperial busybody, just some clerk with hidden bloodlust. How had he not realized the obvious? So distracted by the hunt for Roache, that he never truly suspected Belona... Belona... Belona...

Belona turned and began explaining her plan to the engineer and the monk.

*Agrippus. Belona Agrippus.*

The two nodded as they listened, a mix of fear and hope in their gaze, as Belona Agrippus spoke. They murmured wary reservations, then uncertainty, then begrudging optimism.

*General Belona Agrippus.* Yes, Marcel could remember the songs on the battlefield. *"Oh, the Imperials do make a fuss, their wounds are all full of pus! And they cry, 'Take pity on the poor soldiers... of General Agrippus!'"*

General Belona Agrippus. The Butcher of Tesakovgrad. The Wretched She-Lion of Vastium. The Tyrant of Huile. Who took the city in a bath of blood, who slaughtered the brave men and women of General Durand's Northern Army, soldiers Marcel knew. Danel, Rada, Henri. All gave their lives to defeat that woman. That woman who was standing right before Marcel, that woman who was giving commands to his friends, the woman who had been sleeping just metres away the past few nights, all the while Marcel oblivious. She was not the petty murderer Marcel had accused her of being earlier in the night. No, no, she was far worse. A war criminal as foul as Lazarus Roache. And again, Marcel had been working with her, blind all the while.

Marcel felt a sudden burst of pain in a leg that no longer existed.

"What do you think?" Kayip asked, turning to him.

"Yeah, sure," Marcel said, agreeing to whatever craziness they came up with. The monk stared at him, concern in his eyes. No, not concern, nothing so clean. He was studying Marcel, searching for a reaction.

*He knew.* Kayip knew who Belona was, knew what she had done. Knew Marcel was being lied to again and did nothing to reveal the truth. That's why he knew it how important it was Marcel not reveal his name, lest the woman... no... No, Kayip had tried to keep Belona's surname from him. He had tried, with all his trickery, to bury the truth, to protect this butcher. All in the name of taking down Lazarus Roache.

Yet such a truth, unearthed, could never be reburied.

"Are you with us?" Belona asked.

Marcel stared at the imperial, his hand eager for his pistol. How quick it would be, a flick and a shot, then Belona Agrippus would meet her just end. To join her befouled army in the grave, as she should have those years ago. But such a dramatic move could not be made in haste. Were he to strike now, he might ruin everything. The plan Belona crafted was a poor one, but it gave them their only chance to take down Roache. And she needed to be alive for it, just for a few more days. He had to swallow his rage, hold his temper. Justice had to be patient. Not for long, he soothed himself, not for very long at all.

"Yes," he said to the monster in woman's skin. "Yes, let's finish this."

# Chapter 23

Upon centuries of fossilized trash there sat a city. Streets of beaten scrap and loose gravel, houses welded or mortared together in mockery of distant civilization. Above the raucous and rancor sat a hill, not of dirt or stone, but of buried refuse, rubbish and debris stacked and squeezed until it fused together in a sort of befouled clay. Upon that hill sat the manor houses of the gang lords of Stinktown, each an irreconcilable contradiction between luxury and squalor. In the grand library on the third floor of one of the grandest of such manors, under the yellow glow of imported, cracked ætherlamps, Namter made tea.

"The contract is all upside, really," Lazarus Roache said, sitting back in his chair as if he were the master of the house, and not just the guest.

The actual owner of the manor sat across his Vidish oak desk, an old gift courtesy of his houseguest. He stared down at the papers Lazarus had provided, face wrinkled and red. The color was not from any emotional state, though Namter could see the man was concerned. Rather it was a scar, a massive blemish, which had given him his name, as well as the name of his gang. Though to claim the etymological basis of Mr. Crimson's cognomen to be founded on a 'scar' was being quite generous to the nature of his epidermal malady. It was caused by sangleum, was technically a mutation, even if just one of the skin. To label all raiders with some æther-related deformities as mutants would be a political impossibility. They had already purged Stinktown of all the gangs that tolerate flesh- and womb-mutant amongst their rank, there was a limit to the number of people they could execute, especially as slickdust itself produced many of these skin-mutants. Still, as he stared askance at Mr. Crimson, Namter was reminded of all the compromises he had had to make in the name of expediency. Would that he could turn Stinktown into one great sacrificial altar, let the Truegods' punishment fall upon this house of filth and ego. Instead, he sucked in his breath and began to pour the tea.

Mr. Crimson sighed, placing down the contract.

"We raiders value our independence," he said. The man wore an old Principate uniform, a reminder of his past that sat at stark odd with his current status.

"Of course," Lazarus Roache said. Namter could see hints of gray hiding amongst the roots of his master's well-combed hair. "But alliances are not shackles, my dear Crimson. We have the Fist-Biters, Britta's Bloatbeasts, and the Skinrenders signed on, and more still. With the gangs united, you won't waste resources on petty feuds. I'll admit my own faults here. I have been busy, traveling all around, haven't had the chance to play peacekeeper. Have you visited Icaria by chance? A wonderful city, I should take you sometime! But I am off-track, with the gangs united we will have the force necessary to take any sangleum fields we desire. You shall have all the fuel and slickdust your men and women would ever need. We are both managers, of a sort, we both know how hungry our people can get. You would be doing right by them, and that is what matters."

Mr. Crimson sighed and bent his elbows, gaze down. He had been one of the most intransigent of the gang lords, perhaps due to his own suffering at the hands of Lazacorp's machinations. But that was all the past, water under the bridge, or so Lazarus Roache claimed. But grudges were deep things, and personal ambition could be even deeper.

"Tea?" Namter asked, bringing over the tray.

"No," Mr. Crimson said, not looking up. "I'm a coffee man."

"Come now Namter," Lazarus said, taking his cup, and pouring in a baggie of slickdust. "Grab yourself a seat."

"Sir?" Namter asked, turning.

Lazarus got up and dragged over a chair. "My dear Namter, you represent the interests of the Unblind. Your voice is most valuable."

Namter cautiously sat.

"You know, with an official alliance," Lazarus said, "it would be much easier to initiate members into the Cult of the Unblind. And you've seen the powers that Namter's followers wield."

"Indeed," Namter said. "Though our members have their duties, the gifts given to them can be of value to men like you. I know Miss Bloated Britta has been pleased with the combat applications her initiated men can provide." They also provided eyes inside the various gangs, but best not to mention that.

"My people are already stretched with their work," Mr. Crimson said. "I can't well afford letting them take time off to pursue... spiritual edification."

"Of course, it is merely another opportunity." Lazarus sipped his tea. As he did the strands of gray in his hair started to regain their golden color. The restoration was remarkably fast, perhaps Miga had made some breakthrough? "These difficult times won't last. Soon we will have slickdust production at max capacity again. You and your people will want for nothing. Assuming you are interested in signing the contract."

Mr. Crimson sighed. "I do not deny the benefits. I have seen war, and I do not love it. We should be rich here, and yet it is always like scraprats fighting over a meal." The man spoke with a weariness that would suggest age. Yet Namter knew this was put on. Despite his deformities, the man was still healthy and spry, and far younger than his wrinkles would suggest. A young man in the body of an old, he was near the opposite of Lazarus Roache. He was different from the tycoon in other ways as well. His library, for instance, was filled with bent-spine books that looked as though they may actually have been read, and not simply purchased for display purposes. And his floor was uncarpeted, displaying veins of grout between a mishmash of tiles. The only things in his room that seem truly luxurious were gifts from Lazarus himself, which included a gild-leaf orrery and a fine oak-and-copper voxbox. Silent, of course, there were few voxwaves that made it this deep into the Wastes.

"Still," Mr. Crimson said, "the price you demand is ridiculous! Have we not given you enough slaves? I'm starting to think the rumors are true, that you're dragging these slaves out into the Inner Wastes and cutting their throats in some sort of massive, daft, demonic ritual."

Namter wanted to chuckle as the term 'demonic.' It just showed how blind most people were, how willing they were to trust the lies of their eyes.

"Slickdust production can be a somewhat bloody affair," Lazarus admitted. "I won't bore you with pretensions that it is a vegetarian process.

But you have to admit your men are more pliable, are they not? And not one of us came to Stinktown to weep over the corpses of some slaves."

"Indeed," Mr. Crimson said. "But for all the bodies you need, we don't seem to be getting much of the red powder. Just last week we sold you sixty-five slaves—"

"Fifty-five," Namter corrected.

Mr. Crimson paused and scratched at a fissure by his chin. "No, I'm quite sure it was *sixty*-five."

Was the man cheating them? "I can check the records to see—"

"Namter!" Lazarus interjected. "There is no need to interrupt a good discussion with some minor bookkeeping discrepancy."

"I counted them myself, I can find the receipt," Mr. Crimson said. Namter was equally as sure *he* was correct. With the chaos that seemed habitual among Stinktown, he was sure to check that any numbers claimed matched reality. Indeed, he had overseen the set-up of the infusion station himself, had sent away the Tribute. Namter did not make errors.

"There is no need." Roache smiled and gestured. "What's a body or two among friends? We received the goods requested, and you the payment, there's nothing else to discuss. Oh, Namter? Don't you have another one of your rituals to oversee?"

"I do, but I had planned to let my Brothers handle it, as we have important work—"

"There is no need," Lazarus Roache said, with a smiling wave equal parts affable and dismissive. "I can handle the rest here. You are a busy man, and I don't intend to keep you from your duty."

"If that is your wish, sir," Namter said, rising. He gestured to the two men. "May you come to an amicable agreement."

* * *

Down in the streets of Stinktown the conflict between luxury and filth fell firmly in the latter's favor. Namter stepped out of the gate of Mr. Crimson's manor onto a narrow alleyway posing as a major thoroughfare. Decrepit tenements bent over to cover the late-night sky, the sounds of fighting and awkward sex wheezing out their cracks, matched only by the groans of a moribund autocar squeezing past a one-armed beggar, who had more fingers than teeth. The road was made of cobblestones and cobbled-together trash; it oozed. Oozed with what, Namter could not guess. If there was one positive thing he could say about Stinktown is that it was honest. Most cities pretended they were something more than rotting monuments to mankind's vanity. There was neither the pretension of greatness he had seen in Icaria, nor the thin veil of civility that Huile wore.

Brother Avitus stepped out from the dark, two other Brothers following.

"Awakener," he said. "You are early."

"Roache had no more need of my services," Namter explained.

Avitus glanced up towards the yellowed window. "He's hiding something."

"I will not speculate," Namter lied. Lazarus Roache had, in the past few days, been much more respectful of Namter's time commitments, particularly at moments when the tycoon wanted his assistant gone and busy. "Brother Vitan."

A blond-haired, child-faced man stepped forward, large knapsack on his back.

"Do you have last Gotday's transactional records?" Namter asked.

"Of course, Awakener," Vitan said, pulling out a binder from the bag, and handing it over.

"I do not trust this place," Avitus said, staring up at the manor.

"I can read and walk," Namter said, scanning the scribbled lines under the light of a handtorch.

Brother Avitus nodded and led the quartet down the road. Stinktown never slept, but most of the raucous debauchery happened closer to the bars, fight-rings, and brothel complexes. Still, they passed by a number of drunkards, and an even greater number of slickdust-addicts, many who mixed begging with threats, but were silenced by a quick brandishing of a pistol by one of the Brothers.

For his part, Namter squinted through pages and pages of minutiae, trying to filter out all the distracting sounds of the city. The buzz of the ætherlines above, the moans of whores down alleyways, the echoes of distant hacking coughs, the sputters of unseen machinery beneath the earth, the growl of wastehounds in their iron-chain leashes. He finally found the line he was looking for. *Crimson Eyes: 55 bodies sold. Number 1: A woman of middle-age, fair skin, minimal muscles or fat, missing one leg. Number 2: A man of youthful demeanor, exact age unknown, large muscles..."* Namter scanned the list, counting them, making sure the number was right. Fifty-five, undeniable. Had Mr. Crimson made an error? Possible, but he did not seem the type to double down unless he was certain. Then where had the ten went? Lazarus had been keen to change the subject, though that could be simply due to it being a distraction from his schmoozing. The tycoon was never one to let details or facts get in the way of a deal. But he and Miga had already been syphoning off a quite a number of slaves on the book, for slickdust and experiments. Could there be even more off the book?

Namter sighed and played with his pen to calm his mind. Perhaps this was how Verus started. A fear here, a theory there, questions morphing into paranoia. It was not hard to go down that path with Lazarus Roache, he was a profligate liar, a maestro of duplicity. That's why he had been chosen for his Gift in the first place. It was all too easy to suspect the man. Yet would following that path lead Namter to some buried truth, or just drive him mad, turn another Awakener into a deranged maniac? It was his duty to follow his master. It was his duty to spy on his master. It was his duty to keep everyone together. It was his duty to root out any possibly traitor. Always at odds, always self-contradicting. Why was it so hard to be a good man?

Perhaps that's what the problem was, there were no good men. Just men who had the decency to know they deserved their own suffering.

"Watcher," Avitus hissed, grabbing Namter's elbow.

Namter glanced up. Across the width of the narrow road stood half-a-dozen raiders, wearing tattoos of rusted brown, identifying them as Rust Thorns. In their arms were pistols and bludgeons, the tools of common muggers. Did the idiots not realize who they stood before? If they harmed a hair on a Brother's head, the united might of Stinktown would fall on them.

Yet, as a raider staggard forward, old revolver in his hand, Namter noticed something in his countenance. A desperation in his eyes, teeth clenched, spots of red skin around his noise, sign of a slickdust addiction, his twitchy movements evidence enough that it was a long-unsatisfied dependance.

A tug from Avitus. Namter glanced back. Five more men in the other direction, members of Britta's Bloatbeasts, by the look of it. The Bloatbeasts and the Rust Thorns working together? Something was very wrong. Avitus grasped his orb of Oathblood, while Namter flicked a button on his pen, a tiny blade jutting out from its end.

Brother Vitan stepped forward. "Out of the way, imbeciles! This is Hieronymus Lealtad Namter, leader of the Unblind Brotherhood and liaison of Lazarus Roache. Go ply your parasitic trade somewhere else you—"

A gunshot went off. Vitan fell to the ground. In that instant that followed, Namter ducked down, bullets whizzing above. Behind him Avitus smashed his orb and whispered a vicious prayer. Namter used his bladed pen to cut at his eyepatch, shouting words of command as he did so. Even in the dark of midnight, his eyeless gaze caught the Rust Thorns. Their gun-hands went limp, entrapped in the world that sat in his eyesocket. Namter whispered out a prayer, and a whirl of black fire flew from his hand, engulfing one of the assailants, as the others stood dazed.

Behind him Avitus had summoned up a wall of flame and smoke. The third remaining Brother, Edik, stood holding a gunshot wound, firing his own pistol into the hidden enemy.

"Look away you idiots," shouted one of the Rust Thorns, who had had the foresight to cover his eyes with his arm. Or perhaps it was not an act of ingenuity, perhaps he had been warned about Namter's power. Either way he rammed his fellow thugs, knocking them from their stupor. Namter could not give them a moment to regroup. He screamed a prayer to the Truegods, and from the flaming corpse of a Rust Thorn burst out blood-soaked wings of rust.

The being looked, to his human eye, like a mass of twisting metal and viscera, a dozen bladed ring surrounding a beating heart made of offal and iron. But with his True vision of his Eye, he could it as it was, a beautiful piece of divine craftmanship, golden wings surrounding a body of glowing celestial clockwork.

This numinous automaton struck with a holy fury, Namter had to call it back immediately to keep it from turning all the raiders into ground meat. It spun round, past Namter, into the flames. Screams burst out from behind the smoke, and then silence.

"Fuck!" came a voice.

Namter looked down, to see some terrified panhandler lying terrified on the side of the alley.

"What was that? What was that?" the bum shouted.

Brother Avitus holstered his weapon and checked Edik's wounds. He nodded; the man might yet survive. Brother Vitan was not as lucky, his blood pooling in the street.

A moan. Namter walked forward and picked up a dropped pistol. With his other hand he grabbed up the sole surviving Rust Thorn, who was slowly dragging himself away, his stomach cut open. He pulled the dying man up and against the wall.

"Who sent you!" Namter hissed, shoving the pistol under the raider's chin.

"I didn't... it was just... she promised..." The man's face was tinged red, not from his blood. How long had he been desperate for a hit of slickdust, days, weeks, more? Namter pressed his sharpened pen into the man's guts, who was still lucid enough to moan in pain.

"Who? Why?" Namter said.

"She promised... slickdust... makes it... just a simple job... She promised..." The man's mouth fell limp, his last life draining from him. Namter let the body fall. There were a number of women with power in Stinktown, but it was hard to imagine why the heads of Britta's Bloatbeasts or Iron Strixes would go after him. That left one obvious possibility. Miga Veneficus.

"Shit, fucking taurshit, shit," rambled the beggar. Namter raised the pistol and put a bullet in the vagabond's head.

"Awakener?' Brother Avitus asked. "Should we retreat back to Roache?"

"No," Namter shook his head. "Clear the bodies. No one will know of this." He stared down at the eviscerated corpse. Maybe Verus had gone too far in his paranoia. But he was right about one thing. Someone inside Lazacorp was sabotaging the work of the Unblind Brotherhood. And no one could be beyond suspicion.

*"I saw two dustsnakes entwined*
  *Tight upon a fat brasshare.*
  *Biting with a hatred maligned,*
  *Towards each other, cut and tear.*
  *As they fought, scale-kin against brother,*
  *The hare slipped away, safe into the brush.*
  *And with that hatred they would ever suffer,*
  *The two fell dead, upon the Wasteland's dust..."*

  *—"Poems of the Wastes" Collected by Bengard Stranik.*

# Chapter 24

The trip to Stinktown was remarkably uneventful. Something had convinced Marcel and Belona to quit their bickering. Sylvaine wasn't sure the cause, but she was thankful for the silence, she had enough on her mind already. The whole of the 'truck, now decorated with the black cloth and garish emblems of the Taur Maw gang, felt eerily quiet. As they drove through the Wastes, Sylvaine could hear the distant skragger caws and roars of mog-lizards over the puttering of the surprisingly well-maintained raider engine. The journey took only a couple of days, and would have been quicker had they trusted the main roads, but they weren't that confident in their disguise.

It was also surprising how, after devolving more and more into wild chaos for uncountable kiloms, the regions around Stinktown started to again resemble something akin to civilization. Forests of unruly coppershard trees were replaced into clear-cut fields, full of palewheat and what Sylvaine assumed were some sort of tubers. Stinking mudlion mires had been replaced with taur ranches, ordered in neat rectangles and delineated by wastewood fences. There even appeared new industry, mines cut into mesas, watermills built beside fresh canals, refurbished factories, both agri- and industrial, lit by blazing ætherlamps. Even the roads were relatively well-paved, and despite their fears, no errant raider tried to run them off or hold them up. Yet this was not some Wastes-hidden utopia. As Sylvaine stared into the fields she could see the glimmer of iron chains upon the ankles of the field hands. Slaves, sun-scarred and emaciated.

They entered the city at night. Despite its name, Stinktown was much larger than a town. The *Stink* part of its title, however, was entirely accurate, as Sylvaine was quick to notice. Many of the buildings and much of the infrastructure seemed to have been built from old junk and scrap. By the smell of things, centuries of organic trash still festered beneath the streets.

Sylvaine wrapped her black scarf tight around her face, an accoutrement she had taken from one of the dead Taur Maw raiders. The other three were equally disguised, in a mix of stolen clothes that still had the odor of death about them. Marcel wore a black leather vest with a poorly painted linen undershirt and an awkward bowler hat atop his head. Belona wore a leather coat, cut and re-sewn countless times, and patchwork trousers. She kept her military boots, which did not much stand out among the crowd. Kayip's outfit was the most absurd. To keep his identity hidden, he wore stitched black leather from head to toe, including a tight mask that covered everything but his single good eye, with a few additional airholes cut roughly around his mouth.

"Remain careful," the monk whispered, almost subaudibly. Amongst the ruckus of the late-night crowds none without Ferral hearing would even know he was speaking.

Sylvaine nodded. Though she had raised concerns that their costumes might be too ostentatious, she quickly discovered that they were, if anything, prosaic. The styles of Stinktown folk were diverse and maximalist. They seemed to ape every fashion of the civilized past all at once. Top hats and biker jackets, riding goggles and filthy petticoats. Men wore military jackets alongside workpants cut to the crotch, women mixed patchwork tweed with glittering jewelry. Sylvaine caught a glimpse of a tanned man with shades over his eyes, his limbs all clinking steel. He stepped into an alley, as a tattoo-adorned woman passed by, riding a bulky mog-lizard, the beast using its sharpened horns to push through the crowed.

"Blasphemy," Kayip whispered. Sylvaine noticed him staring side-eye at a golem. *Auto-homid*, she corrected herself. The metal mimic of a man seemed to be selling pornographic ambrotypes, though Sylvaine suspected that his outrage was less about the product, and more the machine. The Church had taken a hard line against any sort of mechanical imitation of the human form. Apparently in ancient times a bunch had gone haywire and nearly destroyed humanity, but Sylvaine thought it silly to give up after a single failed experiment.

The neighborhood they were in appeared to be a bazaar of some kind. Shops and stalls with blaring lights and hanging bone-charms bore painted signs like 'Scrapstuff and Other Antiques,' 'Quality Taur Leatherwork,' and 'Bethany's Flechettes, Hollow-Point Express Bullets, and Landmine Emporium.' The atmosphere was almost carnivalesque. Men and woman both human and other-folk hawked their wares, or else gawked and shouted. A gray-skinned salvi walked past, dragging along a pet troglyn, who gnashed its teeth through its heavy iron muzzle. A short kortonian piloted on a two-legged walker, towering over the crowds as he hollered the praises of his inventory of clockwork knickknacks, useless inventions, and cruelly creative weaponry. There was even an ember-dripping ifriti, leaning on a corner, hair smoking, her hands twitching with elemental æthermantics. Sylvaine had only ever seen her kind once, on a trip down south to Muhit, though this one did not look to be handling her migration well. Sylvaine could relate, losing control of the æthers might to some be an abstract problem, but for people like this tweaked out immigrant and herself, it was near existential.

There were no mutants in Stinktown, Sylvaine realized suddenly. An oddity considering how deep in the Wastes they were. Though there were signs of minor mutations, a hint of crimson skin, especially around the nose, mouth, and eyes of several of the more ragged-looking passersby.

"How much ya charge for this old sketchpad?" Marcel asked one of the vendors, an unfamiliar twang in his voice as he picked up, seemingly at random, a faded pamphlet.

"Sixty aurem for the map," the old stall-keeper said.

"Sixty? That's like 500 frascs," Marcel said, instantly catching his error. It would be odd for a raider to instantly translate prices into Resurgence currency, but he spoke quickly to cover it. "Utterly absurd prices! Could buy a heifer from my local taur-wrangler for that dough. Look at the rambling wiggles of the coastlines, and these islands? All wrong! Won't pay any more than ten."

"Ten, ten!" the vendor said with outrage. "That is a genuine *Petrius Brother's Map*, pre-calamity. It is a relic, I found it in great condition, buried in a dusthome south of here. Fifty Aurem."

"Well, it's a taurshit map," Marcel said. "Probably drawn for idiot children. Fifteen at most."

"We are looking for a man called Lazarus Roache," Belona cut in suddenly.

Marcel glared at her. It was clear he had a plan, maneuver around the subject, and sneak the question in, as an innocuous aside. It was equally clear the imperial lacked his patience.

"Lazarus Roache, Lazarus Roache! Of course, I know Lazarus Roache," the vendor said. "Well, I mean, I don't *know* Lazarus Roache. But I know him. Everyone here does."

"We're trying to meet with him," Sylvaine said. "We're from the Taur Maw gang, heading up from Sulcosta. One of our members had made a deal with Roache, but we don't know where either is."

The man turned to her. "Hey, are you related to The Savage?"

"What?" Sylvaine said, taken aback.

"Listen," Marcel said, placing down a few coins, "we've traveled a long time, feet as sore as a waste-keffel's hooves. Be kind a moment and point us to where the man hangs about."

The Vendor looked at the coins as if they were some strange insects, then with a sudden alacrity grabbed and pocketed them, as if afraid they'd scurry away. "Don't know how to meet with Mr. Roache, but he often speaks on that stage up by Pig-King's Square. Just keep on and take a right at the collapsed tower, you can't miss it."

"Many thanks," Marcel said, tipping his hat.

They continued down the road, past vendors selling everything from grisly blood-soaked trophies of past raids, necklaces made of human bones and preserved organs floating in liquor, to candied nuts and discount trousers. Of the four, Belona seemed to be the most uncomfortable in her costume, hand hanging awkwardly close to her holstered pistol. Marcel kept his distance from the woman, glancing at her with open contempt whenever she wasn't looking. Still, the first part of her plan did seem to be working. A few times on the trip over they had spotted Principate scouts on the horizon, trailing them. Now, amongst the crowd, Sylvaine could hear nervous whispers above some roaming imperials. For now it just seemed one rumor among many, intermixed with tales of gang lord's sexual misdeeds and possibly fictional boasts of glorious raids or successful troll-hunts. Still, if Belona's estimations were correct, the army would be here in just a few days. Just a few more days, then this would all be over.

Sylvaine idly reached into her bag and stroked her ætherglove. Just a few more days.

They came across what looked to have been the tallest structure in Stinktown, turned horizontal. Amongst the collapsed ruins of some fool's ambition, a couple sat sharing a clope. Above them people had made dwellings out of the sideways, half-collapsed tenement rooms. This seemed to be the Stinktown attitude, every past disaster was just some scavenger's new opportunity.

They took a right and soon found themselves in a wide square. Near the entrance stood a statue of a man in an antiquated robe, standing tall, chipped arm raised with half-sword in hand. On the plaque beneath was written, beneath layers of graffiti: *Lord Imperator Opus Diedrev*. On the shattered neck was tied a decayed hog's head, complete with a crown made of barbed wire.

"Bastards…" Sylvaine heard Belona whisper.

In the middle of the square, past a middling crowd, stood a stage of wastewood, and on it, a bald man with tattoos of lurid eyes stood screaming.

"It is all fake! False! A lie told by the ego of man! Civilization and all its excuses are but the toys of a petulant child! Turn away! Renounce the filth you call your ego! Pray to the Gods buried, and through their punishment be reborn!"

As the man shouted, Belona scanned sightlines. Sylvaine could see her finger twitch, as the woman glanced from building to building. They had some scoped rifles in the 'truck, which they hadn't even had to smuggle. It would have been odder for new raiders in town *not* to be bringing in weaponry. Though she was no soldier, Sylvaine imagined it wouldn't be too hard to make the shot from one of the nearby buildings if they could find a way to sneak in. But the escaping bit, that was less obvious.

"I saw a bar a ways back," Marcel whispered. "Bars were always a good go-to for intelligence gathering, back in my private investigating days."

Sylvaine nodded, Belona shrugged, and they turned back. On the street, beneath a buzzing æther-lit sign for 'Fresh Taur Sausages' loitered two young teenagers, already covered in gang tattoos of bulbous monstrosities. One was showing off to the other an armored boot, sabaton and greave made of pale blue metal. Kayip froze, staring at it. As Sylvaine squinted she notice on its side were strange runes, ones she recognized from old Church artifacts, relics of the Ascended. One of the young men poured a drink into the boot, and took a swig, much to the amusement of the other. The first glanced over to look at Kayip.

The monk suddenly stumbled off in the other direction, down into an alley. Sylvaine hurried and worriedly followed, with Belona and Marcel not far behind. Kayip stopped halfway in, bent and panting.

"It is not right, it is not right," he whispered.

"Kayip?" Sylvaine whispered back.

"Do not say my—" The monk sucked in my breath. "My apologies. I should not— I was just not expecting…"

"Everything all right?" Marcel asked, too loudly. "I mean, it's not exactly sanitary, but I've seen university students drinking from boots during—"

"That armor," Kayip continued to whisper. "It was from my order."

"How did it end up here?" Sylvaine asked.

"I… do not know. It should not be."

Kayip stood. He turned and silently nodded to Marcel and Belona that everything was okay. Then he froze, staring behind them. Sylvaine turned to see a man blocking the way they had come. He was scrawny and bedraggled, covered in rags and filth. Around his mouth were splotches of red, becoming a deeper crimson in circles around his eyes, which she quickly realized were actually tattoos. In his hands was an old revolver, rusted and grimy, but aimed straight at them. Sylvaine began to reach for her bag.

"Not so fast, not so fast! Don't move, don't move, don't fucking move!" the man said, his voice interspersed with frantically quick breaths.

"Hey now," Marcel began, accent dropped. "We're just—"

"Newbies," the man said with a frantic shake of his head, scraggly hair flapping. "Out-of-towners. Rich ones by Hort's bet. No don't tell them Hort's—" The man shut his eyes tight in a grimace. "Don't tell them your name. *My* name. So come on, empty those pockets, let me see what you got. Aurem, Frasc, fucking drevs. Give 'em to Hort, I mean *me*, I mean shit, shit, shit! Give 'em. Or slickdust, yeah slickdust, you been by the market, pretty expensive but you can still buy. Come on, come on."

"Are you seeking death?" Belona asked. "Because there's four of us, and one of you."

"Want to check, want to check?" The man possibly named Hort stepped forward, gesturing with his pistol.

"Hey," Marcel said, hands up in casual placation. "We all got off on the wrong foot. Listen, we're new and could use a guide. Why don't you help us out, and we can get you paid, all fair and square, no need for threats, just scratching each other's backs."

"Oh no. Oh nonononono. Hort knows how it— I mean *I* know how it— fuck!" Hort spat. "You send me off, then disappear. No, no, Hort has the upper hand. So you'll give Hort, give me, all you got. Now. Nownownownow!"

"Hort!" came a shout. A large, middle-aged man rushed forward, similar crimson markings around his eyes. Hort turned, face pale, his gun hand went limp. The middle-aged man strode over, and socked Hort across the cheek. He went down quick, dropping the gun. The middle-aged man growled, then kicked the prone Hort in the stomach, once, twice, three times.

"Taurshit on a stick Hort! Now what in all Infernos are you doing?" the man asked.

Hort merely groaned and curled up like a baby.

The man turned to face them. "My apologies, my most sincere apologies for the actions of my compatriot here. That just ain't how you treat guests in your city. The name's Utber, Utber Bastillicizek, but my friends don't care much for surname formalities."

"It's a pleasure to meet ya, Utber," Marcel said, twang re-entering his voice as he shook the strange man's hand. "Name's Marshall. Marshall Zweihänder."

A smile stretched over the raider's face. "Marshall Zweihänder. Now ain't that a good, fine name-and-a-half!" he said, before glancing expectantly over to Sylvaine and Belona.

"Belka," Belona said.

"Slovida," Sylvaine said. "And this mute giant is, uh Klaus."

Kayip snorted.

"Well, as a representative of the Crimson Eyes, I welcome you fine folk to Stinktown!" Utber said. Beneath him Hort groaned. "Once again, my apologies. Hort here is a good kid in his heart, he really is, but you know how it is with slickdust. They get hooked on the stuff, and it leads them all sorts of detestable places. Come on now Hort, get up. Get the fuck up Hort!"

Hort pulled himself slowly and shamefully up the wall, avoiding their glances.

"Now what do you say?" Utber asked.

"...sorry."

"Sorry for what?"

"Sorry... for trying to rob you."

"Now there we go, first step, isn't it?" Utber grinned. "But let's take a second one. Why don't I treat you folks to a round of drinks? Least I can do for the trouble my comrade here caused you."

"Why that just sounds swell," Marcel said, with a perhaps exaggerated smile.

# Chapter 25

"And across this little bridge here is Scrapper's District, though it's really more of a general factory hub ever since The Steel Claws started digging those mines."

Utber talked as he walked, pointing to various monuments, some putrid and decaying, others surprisingly well-kempt. Hort sulked behind him, twitching occasionally and scratching odd places. Overall things were going quite well, Marcel thought. They had made contact with a local, and a garrulous one at that! This is how you made progress with investigations, it wasn't about threatening and forcing your will, it was about making connections, and letting the information slip from your interrogee's mouths without them ever noticing that they were being interrogated.

"You know, Stinktown used to be a dump, I mean literally a garbage dump, back before the whole Severing War. Which is why it survived so long, made it through the Calamity untouched, because what fool would attack a dump? Deserters from both sides would make camp here, just to try and survive. Ending up forming little groups amongst themselves, started taking to raiding other survivors, and there you go, you got yourself the gangs. The town built up bit by bit after that, I think, one gang then another grasping for control, until they realized they needed some neutral ground."

"Fascinating," Marcel said. "Yeah, us Taur Maws, well down south kind of similar story. Tired of fighting for dumb stiffland ideals, like some mules with flapping flags stitched over our eyelids. Decided, 'ferno, let's just take what we want when we want, am I right?"

"Law of the Wastes," Utber laughed.

Marcel glanced back to Belona, who was glaring. She motioned with her head to leave, as if this were all some waste of time. Of course the imperial butcher couldn't understand things more complicated than wanton slaughter. Marcel glanced away; afraid his face would give away his rage. It has been a struggle and a half pretending everything was normal these past few days, acting as if he didn't know the monster he was sharing a 'truck with. Every time he looked at that woman, he could only see the faces of his fallen comrades, Henri, Rada, Danel, the members of the Huile Sewer Rats who had given their lives fighting the cruelty of the Principate, fighting *her*. He had never any notion that the foul General Agrippus had survived the battle, to live in obscurity in some nowhere town. If he had, he would have gone to Holtag years ago and put a bullet through her head. He had no doubt Desct would have done the same, or Alba, or Lamber— Well no, obviously not Lambert, that cowardly traitor. Everything that had gone wrong in Huile, every death, every lie, it all traced back to her invasion. He let his hand idly slip by his Frasco six-shooter. The model as named after Vincent Frasco, the hero that had founded the long-mourned republic on the blood of tyrants like Belona Agrippus. Just a few more days. Then Roache would be dead, and he could start on his second dose of justice.

"You know you've come in at a fortuitous time," Utber explained. "I'm not saying a good time, necessarily, for just a few years ago Britta's Bloatbeasts and the Rust Thorns were in full out war. Would have been an Inferno of a time trying to enter the city as some unknown gang, each half of Stinktown would have thought you a spy to the other half. Then, a tycoon by the name of Lazarus Roache help mediate things, and the city's been calmer since."

An explosion went off down the street, home-made fireworks bursting into colors, catching a nearby drunk on fire. The man screamed and ran, while passersby laughed and shouted. This was apparently Stinktown calm.

"Lazarus Roache," Marcel said. "Know a bit of him. One of our fellow Taur Maws was supposed to meet up with that tycoon, but we haven't heard head or tail of him in over a week."

"What's the fellow's name?"

"Felik Rector," Marcel said. "Meant to make a big sangleum deal with Lazarus on behalf of our other Taur Maws down south. Any chance you know how to find the gentleman?"

"A man like Mr. Roache don't have many free minutes to spare... Ah, here's the place!"

They turned the corner, and the building that appeared looked like giant abstracted bird's nest, rusting girders bent all around themselves and interwoven. The glowing sign that hung above the door pronounced it, predictably, as *The Cockatrice's Nest*. Utber waved to the bouncer, and the woman gestured them through with a steel thumb. Inside they were hit with a wall of sound. Shouts, singing, a random scream, an ætheric guitar competing with a set of drums over who could create the greatest cacophony. It took Marcel's eyes a few moments to adjust, full bar tables sat on disorganized scaffolds, the floor beneath all pipes and wires, in the middle stood what looked like a bloodstained boxing ring, ensquared by chains and lit by the glare of too many ætherlamps. In that ring a half-naked maniac threw axes and blade against a man in a suit of clanking autoarmor, complete with a whirring drill which splattered blood in every direction, much to the glee of the crowd.

"Colorful," Belona said.

Utber led them to a table in the back, where the noise was merely overwhelming. Marcel was already drenched in sweat when he sat, the cool of the night replaced by a dense humidity that smelled of armpits and beer. The raider sent off Hort to grab them drinks. When he returned, Utber asked: "So there was some sangleum you were talking 'bout?"

"Right," Marcel said, grabbing his mug. "Just some old Resurgence refinery we raided awhile back. Trying to make a deal, sell it off, ya know how it goes."

"I wish I did. Haven't had an excess of sangleum in quite some time. Lazarus Roache used to be the main supplier, but not anymore it seems. And whenever anyone else gets a drop, the man buys it out with slickdust. Same story with slaves, can barely get enough people to manage the Crimson Eye's farms this year, and you do not want to see hungry raiders."

"Sounds like you bear enmity with this Lazarus," Belona said.

"Oh no!" Utber said quickly. "I would never—Listen, maybe you've heard rumors that the Crimson Eyes aren't close with Lazacorp, but I can assure you that we are loyal and—"

"Of course ya are," Marcel said. "Ignore her loose mouth, the girl hunts drama with the frenzy of drunkard seeking hooch." The two shared a quick hateful glare, before Marcel turned back and continued. "I understand what ya mean. Times are hard. But hard times breed hard men, that's what my pops always said."

"I can drink to that," Utber said, slamming his glass against Marcel's. He chugged some down and glanced expectantly. Marcel raised his cup and sipped. He had barely drunk more than a sip for two-and-a-half years, booze always infected his nights with endless nightmares. That night under Huile, the sangleum gas spurting, clouds of crimson closing in, the screams of his friend in the distance, a burst of pain in his leg.

"Come on, now!" Utber said. Marcel silently cursed, then tipped the glass back and sucked half the spicy liquor down. It stung his throat and he blinked, trying not to guess what it was made from.

"There we go!" Utber laughed. "If ever there was a drink to put hair on your chest."

"Ya know," Marcel said, holding his mug up as if it were some rare gemstone, "we had something like this when I was doing mercenary work down on the Sulcosta coast. Called it the Ab'Ghelud Gutpuncher, a southern drink from across the Interra Sea, made from some tropical fruit mixed with jungle snake venom."

"How was it?" Utber said.

"Kicked even harder than this!" Marcel said. "We used to drink before charging the enemy. Anyone with the courage to down a glass was someone you could trust in battle. Weeded out the cowards pretty quick that way."

Utber laughed again, and waved Hort to get more drinks. Sylvaine glanced over at Marcel with concern, asking with her eyes why he was making all this stuff up. But the woman was a gearhead, was never one for the subtle art of conversation. And it was easy enough to fabricate stories about distant events and faraway lands. Marcel was a worldly man, and he had seen plenty of relevant cinegraphs about raider drama and Wastes politics.

"Mercenary, eh?" Utber said. Then he gestured to Belona. "I don't think I heard your story."

"I—" Belona began.

"Ex-Principate" Marcel cut in. He didn't trust the woman's tongue. "Actually, a deserter, traitor really, abandoned her own unit in the middle of a battle, left them to die." The woman shot a look of hate, and Marcel continued with a subtle smirk. "Don't get me wrong, she's a fine raider. Learned cruelty in the imperial army, butchered her enemy, men, women, and children. I think the career switch really worked out for her. In her heart she's always been a raider."

"As long as you get the job done in the end!" Utber clinked his glass against hers, prompting Marcel to take another sip. The drink tasted truly of rubbing alcohol, and Marcel was already feeling tipsy.

"Similar stories with us," Sylvaine said, clearly disinterested in adding anything more.

"Now the sangleum?" Utber said.

"Just some spoils of war we're trying to offload," Marcel said.

"So we're talking just a few barrels?" Utber said, disappointment threatening to take over his features.

Marcel laughed. "Ya think we came up here to hawk a few barrels? Nah, our new refinery is still pumping out the red stuff fine and good, but we need to find new customers. Heard Roache might need a refill."

"It ain't easy reaching him, as I've said." Utber drank. "Perhaps you could do a deal with Mr. Crimson. He leads our gang, a good man, a damn fine man if I may say so myself. Personable, I could set up a meeting."

"Behind the back of Lazarus Roache?" Marcel said. It was seeming like the tycoon might not have as tight a grasp on Stinktown as he had on Huile.

"What? The man doesn't have monopoly right or nothing. It's just business. And it might be nice if some of that sangleum was going into our 'trucks and æthericity generators, and not just to produce more slickdust."

"Slickdust?" Hort said, as if awoken from a daze.

"See? See what that stuff does to them?" Utber shook his head. "I like the peace that Mr. Roache has brought, but his drug... at least back when it was just stimjuice and zippowder they killed you if you got too addicted."

"I keep my vices limited to booze," Marcel said, realizing a moment too late that that would elicit a toast.

"Here, here!" Utber said, clanking classes. The last time he had drank this much was the night Alba had left him, another unpleasant memory drinking brought back.

"But really," Marcel said, "our old comrade was supposed to have made a deal with Roache. We need to meet with the man directly."

"This Felik guy, he disappeared right?" Utber said. "Maybe... well I hate to say this, but it can be dangerous wandering around Stinktown without allies. Maybe he tried to talk to Roache, but someone got to him first. Could be for nothing more than change in his pocket, if it's known that no one will bother avenging his death."

"Not here to avenge anything," Marcel said, "and I hope I'm not hearing a threat in your words."

"Not a threat!" Utber said, ordering another drink. "We are friends, I am genuine here. We Crimson Eyes won't touch you, but other gangs might."

Hort seemed to disprove that assertion, but the man had a point. An idea slipped into Marcel's mind. "Perhaps we can make this whole deal mutually beneficial. You're right, without Felik's connections we're a school of freshwater carp trying our luck out in the ocean. Maybe you fellows could organize this rendezvous of ours. We get a friend in the city, and an in-person meeting with Roache, while ya and your Mr. Crimson get yourself fat finder's fee."

Utber tapped his cup. He stretched his jaw this way and that as he mulled over Marcel's words.

* * *

As Marcel spent the night babbling and drinking, Sylvaine sat bored. Marcel seemed to have some plan going, and if it were following his usual pattern, it was probably equally slapdash, inventive, and dumb. Still, it was less likely to be suicidal, so she let the man blather.

She stretched her neck and tried to avoid the stares. There were a lot of stares. There had always been a lot of stares, but for some reason in this specific bar people seemed even less subtle than usual about gawking at the ferral. Some were whispering, though in the din even her ears couldn't make out their exact words.

There was at least one table nearby who were completely ignoring her. Four men poured lines of red powder on the dirty table and took turns snorting it. Slickdust. Somehow, despite the stench of the building and the whole city, Sylvaine could still smell the drug as sharp as if it were smeared under her nose. She hated how she ached for it. Her hand went instinctually down towards her bag, rubbing her hidden 'glove. It comforted her, the touch of brass and leather, but for how much longer? Soon would it be only a mockery, a reminder of what she had lost, what she would soon lose. And even during these last days she couldn't practice æthermantics, had to hide her engineering skill, because there were no Ferral engineers.

Yet... yet... the powerful dose Lazarus had given her. It had activated her Knack to a far greater degree than merely drinking his tea or snorting ever had. It kept her abilities potent even when she dropped the drug. Perhaps her Knack *could* be made permanent. She just needed to take a larger dosage. Or a series of larger dosages. Even in those notes she read, this Miga woman clearly didn't fully understand the mechanism of the drug. Perhaps slickdust could maintain its power even after Lazarus's death. What made that man special? If she could just smuggle some of the drug away before they left, maybe she would never lose her powers, would always be an engine—

Kayip grabbed her arm suddenly. Sylvaine turned and her vision went dark a moment. When it had passed, she realized she had been hyperventilating, sweat dripping down her hair onto the table. Luckily Utber hadn't noticed, caught up trading pointless anecdotes and drinks with a flush-faced Marcel. Kayip was staring at her, eye bent with concern, not judgment.

Sylvaine slowed her breathing, and quickly wiped her forehead with a rag. "I'm... all right," she mouthed to Kayip, which wasn't exactly true, but then were any of them particularly all right? The monk had nearly lost it earlier at the sight of that boot. She had to get control of herself, and knock away these idiotic, panic-inducing thoughts. Look at Hort. The haggard man was picking at a sore while staring lustfully at the slickdust-devouring raiders. Is that the future she wanted? Was that dignified?

Seeking to find a distraction from her own hunger and the increasingly raucous laughter of Marcel and Utber, Sylvaine turned to the arena in the middle of the structure. There a man covered in metal beat a prone figure dressed like a walking taur. The victorious fighter seemed more machine than man, all coglimbs and autoarmor. He bore a giant mechanical arm that Sylvaine recognized as a modified ætherglove, and his other arm had been replaced by a whirring drill, which he used to emulsify his leather-adorned victim.

Grotesque, but it *was* distracting. The crowd, at least those not obsessed with their drink, drugs, or licking up the bodies of their fellow bar-mates, roared with excited. A spike-haired announcer stepped into the ring, shouting into a bullhorn.

"Let's hear it for this metal-monstrosity. The manufacturer of your demise, the mechanic who can make you panic, the engineer of pain. Give it up for our victor, The Gearmaster!"

"Gear! Gear! Gear!" came the shouts of a table, who wore tiny, rusted gears as necklaces, and had painted their cheeks with rough imitations of the Icarian Guild's Insignia. It was disgusting, a mockery of the noble science of engineering.

"And for our main event, we have last month's champion!" shouted the announcer. "Claws of a tiger, teeth of a wolf, fur covered in the blood of his enemies, that's right it's the beast of the east, the Nemori berserker, the cave man with a pain plan, the one, the only, *The Hirsute Savage!*"

"Savage!" came the shouts of two dozen fur-coated drunkards. On cue the fighter jumped into the ring. Claws out, ear's tufted, eyes gleaming in the light. The Savage was a ferral, lanky and cocksure in his struts, his eyes marked with crimson tattoos, his fur shaved in strange irregular patterns. Besides a simple loincloth, he was entirely naked. Sylvaine shook her head in disgust. The Savage dashed around in a mock frenzy, grunting and shooting spittle, before leaping up onto the chains and howling like a dog. His idiotic fanboys howled back, and Sylvaine instantly changed her opinion on The Gearmaster. She wanted more than anything for this metal man to smash the unearned wild smirk off The Savage's hideous snout.

"Gearmaster," The Savage said, "It's time for you to join the rust pile! I've eviscerated The Skragger King, disemboweled The Imp-Smasher, tore the guts out from The Masked Maverick of Malevolence. But I'd love to impale your head on a stick outside my hut."

*Hut, what fucking hut?* Sylvaine wondered. She was sure the man slept nice and sound in a normal room, in a normal bed, like everyone else. But of course he would play up his bestial, primitive, tribal heritage.

"You are uncivilized and illogical," The Gearmaster said, in a faux-mechanical drone, like how auto-homids were imagined to talk in mediocre cinegraphs. "I will break you down into your constituent parts and recycle your bones."

"I will take your big, smart words and shove them up your arse!" The Savage said, which didn't strike Sylvaine as all that inventive a comeback.

The Gearmaster whirred his drill, and The Savage charged. He swiped at The Gearmaster's face, who blocked with his ætherglove, jabbing erratically with his drill. The Savage dodged nimbly, getting behind The

Gearmaster and shoving his claws into his armor. With a yowl he ripped off a chuck of the metal, The Gearmaster screaming as the bloody hunk fell to the floor. Apparently, the armor had been grafted on.

The Gearmaster rushed around, retreating to cut off any assaults from the rear. The Savage ducked and dodged, back and forth. The Gearmaster tried to tentatively jab, his drilling whirring and groaning. Suddenly The Savage tripped. The roaring crowd went deadly silent. The Gearmaster lunged forward, smashing down with all his force.

But it was a feint, The Savage jumped back up, as the drill smashed into the ground, tearing cloth and wood and muck. The drill groaned to a halt, caught in the debris, smoking. The Gearmaster tried to pull his weapon out, but The Savage got round him and started biting at the exposed flesh of his elbow. The Gearmaster screeched, pulling his naked arm out, as The Savage slashed at his face. Desperately The Gearmaster thrust out his ætherglove, sparks flying, as he lifted up the drill into midair. He chucked the pile of levitating junk, but The Savage dodged, the broken machine flying into the crowd, where it crushed one of the spectators, to the hooting laughter of the rest of the bar.

"I will... skin you," The Gearmaster said.

The Savage simply howled and charged. The Gearmaster shot forward an ætherspark, but merely singed his assailant, who leapt onto him. The Savage's claws found meat. As he latched onto The Gearmaster he fell into a berserk fury, slashing and biting and slashing and biting. The Gearmaster screamed, as skin was torn from face. Blood flew everywhere, to the cheer of nearly all except The Gearmaster's horror-stricken fans.

"Ugh," Sylvaine said, turning away from the carnage. The Savage ripping apart human flesh and machine bits in a wild fury... there was obvious symbolism there, but Sylvaine did her best to ignore it.

In the meanwhile, Marcel had managed to get genuinely sloshed. He swayed back and forth on his stool, relaying stories that were neither true nor entirely consistent, yet the near-equally drunk Utber still sat with astonishment in his eyes, listening to tales of impossible and barely comprehensible heroics.

"...and then, then when we didn't even think it could get worse, what do we see? Yes... Vulkers. Big ol', mean ol' Vulkers. Each fours metres tall, if I'm one... metres tall. Which I'm more. I'm more than a metres tall. But! But! The Vulkers' beards. Big ol' fluffy, and on fire. Yes, they were shooting fire! From their hands and mouth and outnumbered us two to one. With axes... and spears... and big icey lizards that you don't even know!"

"Wow," said Utber. "You know, me and my buddies once fought a troll. But there were like ten of us!"

"No, no, no!" Marcel said, waving his finger. "Vulker's are much worse than trolls! They're smart, is what they are. Set us up in an ambush! Surrounded us! And I could see why. Since in that valley, there was a skull. A skull of a dragon."

This was starting to sound to Sylvaine a lot like a mediocre fantasy pulp she read once. Though that pulp took place in frosty Anklav, she wasn't sure why Marcel had transported a tribe of northern Vulkers all the way down south to sunny Sulcosta. But that wasn't the detail that grabbed Utber's attention.

"A dragon! I didn't think those were real."

"Well, their skulls are. 'Cause I saw 'em," Marcel said.

"How'd you survive?"

"Yes... Marshall," Belona said. "Do regale us again with your heroic escape."

"Not escape!" Marcel said. "We beat 'em! Because, Vulkers you see. They're dumb, is what they are. The mines. The landmines we set up! For the ghuls remember? Well, I told him, I told the Vulker... chief. Yeah, that's what they have. I told the chief that if he was so tough, to take a step to his right. Kaboom! Blew up into a thousand pieces. Now them Vulkers, they didn't know about the mines, couldn't see 'em, or any weapons, so they think, why they think I'm magic! And I run with it, threatening to blow them all to pieces if they didn't obey me. By the time they figured it all out, why we had taken the skull and put ten kiloms between us. Just like that! Sold the skull for five hundred aurems."

"Demiurge... Demiurge..." Utber said. "Ain't that a tale. Now this was before or after you joined the Taur Maws?"

"After!" Marcel said. "Remember, I told you the day before we were getting our tats."

Sylvaine froze. Tats. Tattoos. The one part of their disguise they had not been able to fake. *Gear's-grits*, Marcel had gotten too drunk and was about to blow their cover.

As if reading her panicked thoughts, Utber tapped his crimson eyelids and said: "Where are your tattoos anyways? A taur's maw, seems like something a bit more exciting than red eyes."

Marcel paused. Sylvaine held her breathe. Then the man burst into laughter.

"You ain't heard?" Marcel asked. "We do it Sulcosta style."

"Inferno is Sulcosta style?" Utber asked.

"Below the belt!" Marcel grinned.

"Below the—No!" Utber said, honestly scandalized.

"It's true! I can prove it if you want to." Marcel attempted to stumble to his feet, but either to inebriation or quite convincing acting, failed to lift himself up.

"I believe you; I believe you!" Utber said. "It's just... really? Like you have to get naked?"

"It's what you do on Sulcosta beaches," Marcel said. "Everyone knows where you stand there, ain't no questions about that, or nothing else."

Utber laughed, and Sylvaine finally took a breath. "You all are a riot-and-a-half. You need to tell all this to Mr. Crimson sometime."

"Yeah," Marcel said, lifting his near-empty cup. "Love to meet your boss. Sounds like a swell fellow."

"Then let's meet up and make a deal," Utber said. "You sell the sangleum to us, we sell to Lazarus, we both make a hefty profit."

"Nah-uh," Marcel said with a smile. "Ya make the deal, and we meet, all of us. You guys, Lazarus Roache, us, all at once. And not here. Out in the Wastes."

"What, you don't think it's safe?" Utber said. "We can't protect you?"

"If Stinktown is safe, then you have a griffon in Vastium to sell me," Marcel laughed. "I ain't dumb. I'm sure you're honest, I know ya are, but so much can go wrong here. No, we meet on our terms. Out there, far away, where we're comfortable. Or else... well plenty of other gangs we could talk to. Love for ya to be our buddies, but business comes first, Utber, business comes first."

The raider stared at Marcel, cold and hard. Marcel, despite his inebriation stared back. Finally, a smile cracked Utber's lips.

"Ah, Inferno-be-damned! Okay, I tell you what? I can't promise it this way, but you talk to Mr. Crimson tomorrow, and maybe we can work something out."

"Out in the Wastes?" Marcel asked.

"Tomorrow here, but I won't ask you to bring the sangleum to Stinktown. I get it." Utber nodded. "I'm sure Mr. Crimson will too. I'll get a meeting set up for tomorrow. Maybe day after we can do the hand-off. In the Wastes. But for now, one last toast to a new business partner, and buddy."

"I can drink to that!" Marcel said. And against any better judgement, he did.

# CHAPTER 26

Ubter offered them a Crimson Eye-aligned autotaxi to their motor-inn. Sylvaine, Belona, and Kayip silently agreed that this would be marginally safer than trying to drag the well-past-drunk Marcel through Stinktown at two in the morning. They arrived without too much trouble, except for when Marcel vomited out the 'taxi window, which did not much bother the driver. What did bother the driver, and Sylvaine for that matter, was Marcel's insistence on singing the whole way through.

*"So dream those days, and dance away! Under the moonlight! Of Bastillia! Oh my love! Sweet Ophelia!"*

"How has he not lost his voice yet?" Belona grumbled, as she helped Kayip drag the man out of the taxi and through the motor-inn. Sylvaine carried Marcel's hat, his head seemed no safe place for it.

*"Cause she's a Phenia girl! That's right, a Phenia girl! No pretenses or condescension. Just your humble, salt of the earth... mistress of home and hearth. That's right, just a normal, good old-fashioned, Phenia girl!"* Marcel seemed to have moved on to show tunes as they lugged him up the stairs and into their room. Kayip helped him into a chair, as the man kept up his off-tempo melodies.

"Fool's liable to get us killed if he keeps up this cacophony," Belona said.

"Fool. Fool?" Marcel said. "I just... I made us a connection, and now we have a shot, have a good chance to kill Roache. Get him out into the Wastes and put a bullet in his head, and run, run, run!"

"Keep it down!" Belona snapped.

Kayip took off his mask, then knocked on the layers of metal that functioned as walls. "I have been here before. Very thick. You could kill someone, and the person in the next room over would not hear their screams." This was not just some morbid observation. The innkeeper had told them this directly. It was their promise and unofficial tagline. It seemed they knew their cliental.

"What plan did you have?" Marcel asked, words slurred. "Send in the army? Make chaos and everyone's shooting around at everything? Now that's a fool plan!"

Sylvaine picked up her ætherglove from her bag and slipped in on. It was a comfort, after being denied its touch the entire night.

"So now we're meeting this Mr. Crimson guy," Belona said. "Who knows what he'll do? Could easily hold us hostage as a negotiation chip in order to convince our fellow Taur Maws to sell their sangleum cheap, all of which is just one insane fiction you've roped us into."

"No, no. They might be raiders," Marcel said. "But they're honest. About this. Has to be, have a reputation to have. Unlike you. So many secrets little miss Belona."

"I don't even know what you are accusing me of. But if I have to find a way to make this work, I will. Cleaning up your messes Marcel, somehow that has become my pitiful duty."

"Cleaning up your messes," Marcel said with a strange smile. Something about the man's tone unnerved Sylvaine. "Oh, I've cleaned up your messes. Real big messes, real big cleaning."

"Do you know what this idiot is on about?" Belona asked Kayip.

"I know we have been having a long day," Kayip said. "And that we should rest. We can figure out the details in the morning."

*"Oh, let's rest the night away, you and I,"* Marcel sang. *"Let's rest, for the best, forget about the rest, we'll pass the test, oh let's let the night just slip away…"*

"More show-tunes?" Belona asked. "Dear Imperator, you really are just some bourgeois city-boy."

"Just some city boy, eh? Playing at soldier?" Marcel said, bobbing his head back and forth.

"Full of taurshit," Belona said. "Mumbling off tall tales to drunken raiders to feel like you've done something. Inferno did you do as a mercenary? Ramble at the enemy? Or is all that just another lie, and you were just some bookkeeper who got big dreams of hunting down some dangerous criminal, like the heroes in your children's books?"

"Not a soldier, that's what you think? Can't do anything. All pretend." There was something off in Marcel's voice, a subtle coldness. He glanced up at the imperial with a gaze Sylvaine had never seen in his face. Belona hadn't seemed to notice the change.

"Have I hurt the drunkard's feelings?" she asked Kayip. "Imperator's mercy, how did you two manage to drag this nuisance all around the Wastes? He wouldn't last a day in the imperial army."

"The imperial army..." Marcel said. Then he began to sing again. *"Oh hail, hail, the imperial army. Hail them with bombs and shells. Hail, hail the imperial army. Hail them a bloody farewell!"*

Sylvaine glanced at the man, who continued to stare at Belona. What was he doing? He had kept his identity hidden from the imperial so far, why taunt her with hints.

"Beautiful," Belona said, unimpressed. "Some Resurgence tune?"

"The night is getting on," Kayip said, trying to hide his concern. "We should sleep and deal with—"

"Here's another," Marcel interrupted. *"Cry, cry, cry for her boys in blue. Cry, cry, there's no one left to cry to. Cry, cry, cry for her too. There's nothing left for her to do. Just bones and stones, for General Agrippus."*

Belona froze. "Where did you hear that song?"

"We have done enough singing—" Kayip started, panic breaking through his calm façade. Sylvaine felt as if she should to do something, but hadn't a clue what that something was.

*"General Agrippus, General Agrippus!"* Marcel sung without a hint of joy. *"Let the chorus of Inferno hear her name! General Agrippus, General Agrippus! Let's give her her foul-won fame! So go grab your bayonet. We will never let her forget. Oh how the ground grew wet, with the blood, and the guts... coming from the holes, and the cuts, in the bodies of those silly little boys who followed their dear... General Agrippus!"*

"How. Do you know. These songs." Belona spoke with a voice empty of everything but force.

"I'm sure he heard them over the voxbox," Sylvaine tried to intervene. "These kinds of tunes were everywhere back in the day. I'm sure you have the same sort of thing in the Principate."

She waited for Marcel to nod along, to agree with her plausible lie. Instead, he kept staring at Belona.

"You want to know, don't you, if I was there?' Marcel asked. "If I fought in Huile?"

"You're not a fighter," Belona spat. "Maybe some cowardly bureaucrat who watched over my fall. But you are no soldier. Just some useless idiot who took pleasure in my tragedy, like so many others."

"No soldier... no soldier... You think I was in the backline, you think I was just some useless civilian observer?"

"Marcel—" Kayip tried one last desperate time.

"You know where I was, Miss General?" Marcel asked, pushing himself from the chair. "I was right beneath you. Right under your fucking camp. Clamping tight those clockbombs. Click. Click. Click. Boom. SSSsssssss. Red gas rising. SSSsssssss. Soldiers one by one by a thousand. Little boys in blue covered in red. While you ran away, I was ending your army."

Belona did not move. She did not scream. She did not dash forward. She did not crease her face in fury. She did not rip a hidden knife from her jacket and swing it at Marcel. For a long, silent moment she did none of those things.

Then she did them all at once.

"You fucker!" she screamed, rushing forward, blade out.

"Shit!" shouted Sylvaine, as Kayip swung out the blunt edge of his sword, knocking Belona's knife from her hand. The woman did not miss a beat, whipping out a hidden pistol and taking aim. Without a moment for thought Sylvaine sent a spark of æther into the pistol, turning its barrel to slag. Belona tossed the gun and, still shouting, pulled out a second knife. Kayip charged into her as she tried to throw the blade, which flew centimetres close to Marcel before embedding itself into the wall. Kayip brought the woman to the floor, but she managed to twist out of his grasp, and jumped to her feet. Sylvaine sent another ætherspark flying, pulling up a chuck of metal from the floor, and melding it into Belona's boot. The imperial fell, a third knife in her hand. She turned and started to pull her foot free, as Sylvaine rushed over and kicked the knife. Kayip rushed over to grab the woman hand, where there had appeared a fourth knife (how many hidden blades did the woman carry?)

"No!" he commanded, as Sylvaine ran over and pulled manacles from one of their bags. Together, with some difficulty,' they pushed Belona back, and handcuffed her to a sturdy pipe. She tried to tug herself free three times, drawing blood from her wrist before accepting that she had been incapacitated.

"Woah," Marcel said, blinking slowly.

"What idiotic madness has infected you!" Kayip shouted at him.

"Me?" Marcel said, swaying. "She just... She was the one... She tried to kill me!" As if the effort of saying that was too great a task, he fell back into his chair.

"I have tried to keep your secret from her! For your safety!" Kayip said.

"Fuck you too monk," Belona spat. "You claim the moral high ground that is the Demiurge's Church, yet you suffer this murderer within your ranks."

"Murderer?" Marcel said. "I'm not the one with the epathe... epithe... pithet... with the name 'butcher.'"

"You murdered thousands. Thousands of soldiers. In the most horrendous way," Belona said. "Do you know what happens with sangleum poison? The flesh melts, the skin boils. Your lungs bleed into themselves and you drown in your own agony!"

"Shut up, shut up!" Marcel said with a stomp. "I know, I saw it. Saw it in my friends. They died in the line of duty. Heroes, like me! Martyrs! To free Huile from your oppression. I know what the gas does. Lost my leg to it. I gave what I needed to, did what I needed to, suffered as I needed to."

"Don't you dare compare your suffering to mine," Belona snapped, lunging out as far as her chains would let her. "You have no idea what I lost, who I lost. What are a few terrorists to an army?"

Sylvaine groaned silently. This was the shitstorm Kayip had tried to keep from forming. Perhaps it was a losing battle from the beginning, but they had gotten so close. All they had had to do was keep it together for two more days. Sylvaine had always hated Belona, but Marcel had been the one to open the feud. Who in Inferno brags about using chemical warfare? Was this some man thing she didn't get, a need to respond to any emasculation with absurd escalation? Alcohol clearly hadn't helped things, either.

"I don't compare, there's nothing to compare," Marcel told Belona with a snarl. "Criminals, bastards, brutes, every one of your soldiers. I know what you were going to do. You were going to do the same as we did, but not to soldiers, to Huile! Going to punish the city, let the gas burn through the citizenry, condemning every last man, woman, and child for defying your dumb, idiot Imperator. I saved them, I saved them all!"

Some mockery of laughter escaped Belona's lips. "Is that what you believe? Are you so deluded? And who told you this fable? Do not answer, it was Lazarus Roache."

"I..." Marcel began, taken aback. "It was... the whole intelligence staff knew that you were..."

"Because of what Lazarus Roache told them," Belona said. "Because of his lies. Lies which were easy to believe. Or, who knows? Maybe the only one fool enough to believe that tycoon's fabrications was you. So that you could play hero instead of monster."

"No," Marcel said shaking his head. "You were going too... going to use the gas. That's why we had to do it first."

"Why? Why? It was my city. I had already conquered it, why would I do that? You know who suggested using the gas? Lazarus Roache. Told me we could load it into artillery and rain it down upon your traitor camp. But I would never befoul my victory with such barbarity!"

"Lies," Marcel said, but there was a crack in his voice. "You were going to... the Principate is evil, they were going to purge the city, already murdered people. We were using your own weapon against you."

Belona leaned forward, as far as she could manage. "Let me tell you some names. Private Anna Seidel. Kaimark-born, daughter of a baker, loved poetry, had a book of verse on her even on the battlefield. Saved my life, one of the finest soldiers to wear the Imperator's blue. Dead, because of you.

"Shut up," Marcel mumbled.

"Sergeant Juliann Zervas. Family came from Tyrissa, grandparents killed in Resurgence purges. Had a wife and daughter, now widow and orphan, because of you."

"Stop it!"

"Major Hans Krimme. Once just a Wastefolk wanderer, came to the Principate to make a better life. Found purpose in the army, found a family. Rose up the ranks, showed heroism and bravery in the face of adversity. Dead, thanks to—"

"Henri!" Marcel shouted, stumbling to his feet. "Henri Schmidt. Was a merchant from Ordone. Wanted to open a shop after the war, couldn't, died under Lazacorp, fighting you. Or... Or... Rada. Rada... Volkov. Kept to herself. Said she was... well, she worked as a mercenary, I think, before joining the Huile Sewer Rats. And Danel... shit. I don't remember his last name, he joined the squad last minute, but uh, also gave his life, martyred himself."

"You're puttering out at three?" Belona sneered. "I could list those murdered by your hands for hours. I was their general, they were my soldiers. Each deserved victory, or at least an honorable death

"Fuck... fuck you Agrippus," Marcel said, but he would not look the woman in the eye. "We did what we had to. We were heroes, saved Huile..."

"And delivered it to Lazarus Roache. What happened there? Is the city so much better under your watch than it would have been under mine? Flames and bloodshed and mutant slaves. This is what you fought for; this is what you murdered for."

"Had to," Marcel said, voice weak. "After you forced your tyranny onto Huile. Had to do the right thing, the hard thing..."

"So these are the lies you have been telling yourself. The empty words you need to repeat like prayer in order to sleep at night. I'll tell you what I hear. I hear their screams. I hear each and every one of their screams, you worm-hearted bastard! I feel each of their deaths. I'll feel yours by the end of this."

"And then what!" Sylvaine suddenly shouted. All three turned to her. "You both go on about wanting to take down Lazarus Roache. He betrayed you, Belona, got your army killed. He used you Marcel, and fucked over Huile. So what, now, you guys are just going to try and kill each other?"

"She tried to kill me," Marcel said, pointing like a furious child.

"And what were you going to do when this was all over?" Sylvaine asked. "Because something tells me you weren't going to let your old enemy walk away."

"And I won't let him leave this room alive," Belona growled.

"Really?" Sylvaine said. "Because right now there's three of us, and you are chained to a pipe. Your plan is to kill Marcel and then let Roache escape."

"No," Belona said, pulling against her cuffs. "I will not let Roache escape his justice."

"How, how? Going to burst in, a one-woman army? Or are you going to meet with Utber and explain how his friend had a sudden case of bullet-in-the-head. You have nothing!"

"Sylvaine is right," Kayip said. "We must either fight together, or we are doomed."

"You ask me to tolerate this murderer—" Belona began.

"Don't you take the high road," Sylvaine said. "You were a Demiurge-damned Principate general. I know you've caused thousands of deaths. And I also know what the Principate's Ferral policy is, and yet I've somehow managed to not murder you."

"We did what we had to do…" Marcel muttered. It sounded as if he had given up arguing with Belona and was now just arguing with himself.

"You don't understand war, engineer." Belona shook her head. "It cannot end until one side is defeated."

"And you have to resolve it now?" Sylvaine asked. "When we're finally almost at Roache."

The Imperial stared down at the floor, thinking. Marcel continued to mumble things, vague empty reassurances. After a long minute, Belona grunted, and nodded to herself.

"A duel," she said, turning to Marcel. "We'll finish this properly, the fair fight you denied my men. You and me."

"That… beside being stupid, doesn't solve any of the problems," Sylvaine said.

"It can wait, my vengeance. A few days more," Belona said. "Until we kill Lazarus Roache. The day after he's put in the ground, we will finish what we started Marcel—"

"Talwar," Marcel said suddenly, catching her eye a second before glancing back at his feet.

"What?" Belona asked.

"My last name. Talwar," he mumbled. "No point in hiding it. I know who you are, you know me."

"I wasn't asking… fine. Talwar," Belona said. "If you want to work together, then this is how. I swear on the Imperator I will honor our ceasefire. Then I will bring you to justice, in honorable combat."

"This isn't what I meant—" Sylvaine said. She turned to Kayip. The monk just shrugged. "Really?" she asked.

"Fine," Marcel said. "I'll do it.

"Marcel—" Sylvaine said.

"Kept things buried too long." His voice was distressingly sober. "No more secrets, no more childish games, tossing petty words when we should be… Do the right thing, we need to do the right thing, not for us, for all of them. All of those… those we left behind."

Marcel put his hand out towards the woman. Belona stared at his fingers, as if they were rotting offal. Then, suddenly, she grasped his hand, firm. Sylvaine was certain the imperial was about to pull the man in, to summon up another knife and stab him in the chest. Instead, neither meeting the other's gaze, the two shook hands.

"We will take down Roache," Marcel said. "And then... we'll settle things, like we should have from the start."

# CHAPTER 27

The truths of the Unblind were many. Some obvious, like the depravity of man and the falseness of the Church of the Ascended. Others were buried deeper, revealed only to those who had proven their deference and bore the proper self-loathing. Namter could still remember the moment when he had learned the true fetid nature of mankind, and his disgust had grown from a vague detestation born from the bitter scars of his ego, to a true, divine revulsion.

Verus had been beating him. With leather switch and barbed wire, with subtle blade and thumbscrew. He had shocked him with æthericity and suffocated him with rags and water. And for every cut given, he had his servants pour curative Oathblood and whisper prayers, so that no scar marks would remain to give Namter pride. As other Brothers in the basement of the dusthome had cried for mercy, had crawled away and asked for release, Namter had only requested more, more. To be carved, to have his flesh stripped from him, to seek death, not as a release from his well-earned suffering, but as a true, final climax.

With a sigh, Verus collapsed onto a fossilized oak chair, dismissing the other Brothers with a simple wave of his hand. Namter panted on the flood, the taste of blood in his mouth.

"You know, one might guess you get some sexual kick out of this," Verus said.

"No!" Namter protested. "I would not... nothing so vile."

Verus stepped over, and with a swift kick knocked the man to his back.

"I have suffered the presence of many such degenerates," Verus said, pulling a pistol from his loose folds of his stained robes. "Stiffland nancies who like the idea of pain. It gets them hard, false humiliation, agony as a game. They carry with them some foppish decadence, thinking our rituals some sort of namby-pampy fucking orgy. There's an easy way to correct these preconceptions, and it is a savored part of my duty."

With that he pulled back the hammer of his pistol and fired. The bullet blasted dirt just centimetres from Namter's head.

"I'm not... Never..." Namter said, with the horrified fear that he might secretly be such a man. The precepts of the Brotherhood were precious to him, but could his own corruption be too deep, his motives as impure as his flesh?"

"I think I know what you are," Verus said. "So, I'll let you do the honors."

With that he tossed the pistol. It smacked Namter's temple, before settling on the blood-marred dust beside him.

"Take it," Verus commanded.

With a shaking hand Namter grabbed the gun.

"Cock it."

He did.

"Now pull the trigger."

Namter's hand was wet with a sudden cold sweat, his grip weak.

"Or you can leave," Verus said, gesturing to the door. "I won't stop you. You can go back to the world you crawled from, prove your oaths false, and live like the rest of them. Or you can admit your decadence, accept your perverted ego, do what you're told, and blow your fucking brains out."

This was the death he had asked for. The true destruction of the self. Not in some great ritual, not by the power of the Gods, but by his own hand. As sad and pitiful as if he had hung himself in the backroom of some half-aurem brothel. Namter realized that there was no choice. There could never be a choice, not for a servant of the Unblind Brotherhood. He hated that his heart beat with fear, that sweat poured from him, that he couldn't will forth the gratitude that he should be feeling. Perhaps that was why this was inevitable, a failure, as always. He sucked in his breath, held the gun tight, and pressed his forefinger tight around the trigger.

It clicked, and nothing happened.

Verus laughed, his greasy curls shaking with a grim mirth. "If only all of taur-fucking humanity had the guts to do the same. Come on, get up. Get the fuck up!"

Namter scrambled to his feet and returned the empty gun to his master. He felt both relieved and disappointed in his relief. It had been a test, only a test. His life would continue, in all its fetid inadequacies

Verus studied his pupil. "Here, I have something to teach you." He stepped over to the stone bowl of steaming Oathblood that sat in the center of the room. Beside the improvised scrap dais, lay the body of some idiot caravan driver, who had made camp in the dusthome. "Tell me, Brother Namter, what is Oathblood?"

"It is not as the false priests say, a gift from the Ascended, corrupted by human sin," Namter said. "Nor what the idiots engineers claim, a naturally forming, æther-attuned liquid."

Verus slapped him with a quick backhand. "I asked what it was, not what it wasn't!"

"It is... the blood of the Truegods," Namter said. "Left behind, so we can commune with our forgotten masters."

"That is what we tell our initiates," Verus said. "But it is only a half-truth. Tell me why humanity in its ravenous hunger has not yet drained away all sangleum? Why does more Oathblood ooze from the earth, why did the Calamity summon up such torrents of it?"

"I do not know," Namter admitted.

"Because the Truegods did not give us their blood willingly," Verus said. "It is no gift. They lay buried, even now."

Namter blinked, he could not bring himself to understand, even as simple as it was. "Then, they are..."

"They are suffering! They lie underneath us and bear the weight of our putrid excuses for civilization. We cut into them and drain them, like leeches. Do you not see? Humanity is nothing but parasites! We, once the children of the divine, had turned against our masters, and suck at them like mosquitos!"

An image flashed through Namter's mind, of Lazarus Roache, beaming proud over an array of newly built sangleum pumpjacks, a young Namter standing loyally by his master's side, as they tore new wounds into the hidden flesh of the Truegods.

With a sudden nausea Namter wretched, vomiting crimson bile onto the floor.

"Correct," Verus said. "There is only one proper reaction to the truth, long hidden by the false gospels of the Demiurge."

"We must be purged, destroyed, eliminated…" Namter muttered.

"Some of the Truegods think this way," Verus said, narrating with his hands. "Such was their fury during the Calamity. They could have crushed us into the dust of the Wastes, but their fists were held back by their gentler kin. But we serve such a kinder Master, one who merely wishes us to suffer what they have suffered, to repent with a few centuries of pain for the millennia of agony they have endured. And it is our duty, our sacred duty, to release him, to awaken him from his nightmare."

"I am not deserving of such a task," Namter said.

"None of us are," Verus said, patting Namter's back. "And yet we shall do it anyways, for there is none other. You think those stifflands fucks will ever get it through their skulls? They're the ones burying these truths under lie, after lie, after lie. Us, the Truegods' chosen, must be the first to pay penitence, to bring forth a future where humans are proper servants, not just taurshit-writhing flatworms wearing the twisted masks of our creators. We shall all have our roles, our duties. You, I, even that oaf of a tycoon shall have his part to play, whether he understands it or not."

Namter did his best to nod, to balance the horror of this hidden truth, with the determination of a new purpose. As he did, he stared into the cold eyes of the corpse beneath, face now splatter with his vomit. Even seven years later, he could remember that blank, purposeless stare, it was not unlike the corpse he was examining now.

* * *

This corpse was still warm, though the blood had stopped pooling. Namter studied the body splayed out over the wooded bench, like some sort of slapdash autopsy table. But no autopsy was needed, the cause of death was obvious. A bullet to the head, as well as three to the stomach.

"Hort shot them good, Hort means, *I* mean, I shot him good!" the bedraggled raider apparently named Hort said. He stood, hunched really, arms shaking, eyes twitching, next to Brother Avitus, who was one of several Brothers present in the darkened tent-turned-office. The raider had brought in his prize straight to the Unblind Brotherhood, as word has been spread that the Brotherhood was buying bodies. The implication was meant to be *living bodies,* but such subtleties had been lost on the addict.

"I did good, right? Hort got one," the strange raider mumbled on. "Saw this soldier-man, scout, spy, skulking round alleys. One of the invaders right, right? Princapeople? Got him, got him, Hort did! Deserves a prize,"

Namter nodded noncommittedly. It might be worthy of a small reward if the man had killed a Principate scout, considering the worrying reports of some ambiguously hostile imperial force marching on the city. But the thing with *Principate* scouts is that they usually wore *Principate* uniforms. The corpse in that lay before Namter was instead decorated with the red and browns the Resurgence. The idiot raider had murdered a UCCR envoy.

Namter made a silent gesture to his Brothers, before reaching down and inspecting the contents of the envoy's pockets. A pistol, a lighter, a pack of clopes decorated with a faded illustration of a smoking raccoon, several coins, a key to some autocar, some brittle chewing gum, identification papers smeared by blood and...

A letter. In fine stationary, its borders decorated with subtle ink linework that skirted the line between stoic militaristic minimalism and flamboyant ostentation. On the back the letter was sealed with wax, stamped with the emblem of the Phoenix. The front declared, in perfect penmanship, *For The Eyes of Lazarus Roache.*

A private letter for his master. As his servant, he should swiftly deliver the message. As a Watcher and Awakener, he had other duties.

Namter hesitated a moment, then another. There had never before been such a conflict between his roles. But if he had to choose between serving a lesser and greater Master... Namter sucked in his breath, then pulled out a knife and cut away the wax. It would be simple enough to reseal it, if need be, he had much experience with forging official documentation and seals.

The letter opened, predictably, *"Dear Lazarus Roache.*

*As a representative of the United Confederacy of the Citizen's Resurgence, I wish to share my sympathy for the series of unpleasant events that have led to....*

Namter skimmed quickly.

*...we have taken the testimony of trusted UCCR officials, and have come to believe that your account of recent events is factual. We apologize for these past difficult weeks as you have waited....*

More fluff.

*...we are prepared, upon pacification of the revolt in Huile, to reinstate you as sole proprietor of the Huile sangleum refineries. If this is agreeable to you, please contact us as soon as you are able.*

*Sincerely,*
*General Antoine Levair*

Namter carefully refolded the letter. So they had bought the lie. Unsurprising, it was in their interest to buy the lie. Namter had found that convenient untruths were quicker to spread than any statement of fact and verity. This was good news. This should be good news. Then why did Namter feel like his stomach was dropping out into some unseen void?

Lazacorp would return to work. The Enterprise could resume. Of course, it was a bit late for all that, the seven years were nearly up, the deadline did not allow for such dallying. Still, it couldn't hurt, right? A reconquered domain to be delivered to their true Master. Unless Lazarus Roache used it as an excuse to try an argue for his 'extension.' Which he would. Of course he would. The logic was clearer than spring water. Verus had ruined everything, and now Lazarus Roache has a chance to create the mass Tribute promised, if only given a little more time, a little more power. Would the argument fly? It was hard to know, the mind of a God is beyond human comprehension, would the petition please The Flayed Prince, or condemn them all for their faithlessness?

Namter carefully folded the letter back into its envelope and slipped it into his pocket. He could not give that choice to Lazarus, not yet anyways. For there were more extenuating circumstances than the loss of Huile alone. The supposed Principate army, for one. After nearly three years of inaction they had suddenly mobilized in force, intentions unclear. Was this about Huile, striking at a potential ally of the Resurgence before they could regroup? Seemed an odd choice, as the Resurgence would still have control of the city and refineries even if Lazacorp were taken out of the picture. Then there was the increasing nuisance of Bladescar and his Vapulus brutes, who had in recent days burned down several caravans and farms in acts of surprising brazenness. And of course, there had been the attempt on Namter's own life. This was one of the few mysteries where he felt he had a solid theory. One shaped like a certain geriatric, horrendously promiscuous engineer.

"So, what's Hort get? What I get? Slickdust, aurem, slickdust?" Hort asked, with a stuttering eagerness. "Mr. Crimson don't like Hort spending all on the 'dust, but if he don't know, he don't know."

Namter glanced at the twitching addict, then at the Brothers behind him who were already setting up the infusion device. He gave the signal. With a coordinated alacrity, two Brothers grabbed and gagged the raider. As the wiry man panicked and struggled, they chained his limbs to a tilted gurney. They did not bother to sedate him before jabbing him full of large needles. The sangleum worked its quick ways down the tubes, into his veins. Even through the dirtied rag hastily stuffed in his mouth, the raider screamed.

"Do you think it will work this time?" Brother Avitus asked, as Namter bent down to the corpse of the envoy.

"It's a matter of numbers," Namter said. "Miga will ignore most bait, but eventually she'll need more test subjects. I trust in the Truegods, they will give us our opportunity"

As the raider shook and gave muffled wails, his skin reddening and flesh bloating, Namter got to work on the envoy. He took his knife and cut into the corpse's stomach. The smell was awful, the filth of humanity hid poorly within the flimsy sacks of degenerate flesh called bodies. There was always a subtle excitement to revealing this truth, no matter how disgusting it was.

Namter reached in and pulled at the guts, using his blade to cut away at a small tube of offal. He held it in his hands, limp, oozing. With care he removed his eyepatch. Brother Avitus wisely averted his gaze, but the writhing raider happened a glance, and seized with even greater horror and panic. Namter let his Eye That Wasn't fall upon the sliver of gut, as he whispered words of piety and adoration. As he spoke, he pulled from his pocket a vial of Oathblood, and began to drip it onto the offal. It began to shake and shudder, undulating with rhythms of impossible life. Now came the difficult part. He needed to see it as it should be, to See it, See what was needed, See the gift he requested in order to better serve his True Masters.

With a blink of his not-eye, it was there. A creature that was real and whole, a spirit of the Gods made manifest in the crude medium of human meat. It looked, to his corrupted vision, like a long maggot or worm, but with his Truesight he saw that it was closer to a celestial serpent, scales glittering like a weave of stars. But to all his sights, the entity had one common feature, an eye, colored with the same dark brown of his own eye, the one he had given up. Perhaps it was that very same eye, for he could see through it as if it were in his own head, could see himself through the gaze of the numinous, dripping being he held.

He lifted up the creature as Brother Avitus helpfully cut open an incision in the body of the rapidly mutating raider. This 'Hort' would not be missed, just another lost addict in a city overrun with them. One more body for tribute, or, if the Truegods willed it, an eye into the secrets of Miga Veneficus.

As the being slithered its way into the flesh cavity, as Hort screamed and thrashed with his fading strength against his restraints, Namter felt a spark of hope. For so long he was worked passively as a Watcher, only seeing what others allowed him to see. Now he had realized his error, realized that his duties demanded action, that the powers gifted to him were not meant to stay idle. There had been truths hidden from him, but they would not remain hidden for long.It is imperative when on campaign and elsewhere, that all officers in the Imperial Army are ever cognizant of the Articles of Tolerations, so as to properly bring to order reconquered territory, and to know which other-folk are acceptable or even welcomed in imperial territory, and which are not to be tolerated in the Principate.

*Other-folk are organized into three Classes:*

### Class 1:
*Full Toleration*

*Only the Kortonians and the Malva fall into this rank. The short, square-headed Kortonians have been long integrated in human society since the days of the old imperium, and their skills of engineering are vital to industry, commence, and the war effort. The Malva Thalassocracy has been a long ally of the Principate since its support of Imperator Franz Diedrev's restoration of the throne. Malva are gracile, with hair of metallic tints, and rarely settle in continental Æthmach.*

### Class 2:
*Conditional Toleration*

*This is the most complex category, as each member within has its own rules and regulations. For example, the hearty, gray-skinned, horned Salvi are to be tolerated only when working as servants for their Malva masters. Free Salvi are considered Rank 3. The flame-haired Ifriti, the photosynthetic Oawhti, and the masked El'Fasay, whose monochromatic skin fluctuates like a swirling bowl of oil and milk, are to be tolerated if able to present Integration Form 10-B, signed by both proper Principate officials and representatives of the Kingdom of El'Helmaud.*

### Class 3:
*No Toleration*

*This includes all other groups of other-folk, whose natures are barbaric and violent. They have no place in the Principate and must be removed from reconquered lands by any means necessary. Crimson-skinned Mutants, furred Ferrals, giant Vulkers, flesh-shifting Vilkolak must all be considered enemies of the state, and the laws of the Imperator do not protect their lives or property. Follow local protocols for more specifics.*

*Failure to abide by Imperial Law can result in dishonorable discharge or imprisonment.*

*Glory to the Imperator!*

*—"Articles of Toleration" informative flyer given to Junior Officers in Drevstad Imperial Academy.*

# CHAPTER 28

*Danel... Danel Lu...something. Lu...Gouffe? No, that was the old mayor. Le...May? Le...Moi. Something with a L then a M? Damn it, what was his last name!*

Marcel sighed and rubbed his temple. Demiurge, his head really fucking hurt. Felt like a full marching band had come through on parade, then stayed the night dancing and pissing, leaving nothing but a layer of boot-dragged grime and stubborn, thumping echoes. He had felt this way for the better part of twenty-four hours, hungover even as they met back up with Utber to share glasses of the hair of the dog that had mauled him.

The atmosphere hadn't helped things. They had met in one of Mr. Crimson's 'Pleasure Parlors.' It seemed like a mix between a bordello, a night club, and a cheap cafeteria. On the far wall women and men gyrated around oiled poles, clothes ranging from too-thin strips of leather to intricate and flamboyant costumes mocking the pomposity of civilized life, back to absolutely nothing at all. Some did more than dancing, but Marcel avoided staring too close at the sweaty piles of flesh in the distant dark corners and did his best to filter out the moans. What was less filterable was the music, heavy throat singing amplified by a frizzing dictaphone, the vocals provided by a man with more scars than skin. There was gambling, of course, and a buffet line, and even some old men playing catur, an Utarran board game played on a monochromatic grid that Marcel had fancied himself a master of in primary school, before dropping out in the second round of a city-wide tournament and never playing again. Which was fine, the game was old imperial propaganda anyways, figures of Imperators and their guardsmen in ebony and ivory, though these raiders seemed to have replaced many of their cracked pieces with scrap and wastewood stand-ins. Near them a group of young women took turns snorting slickdust, Sylvaine glancing over now and then with an odd look in her eyes that Marcel was far too hungover to think about. Next to the engineer sat Belona, who stared at Marcel with a look beyond hatred. Marcel tried to return the look but couldn't muster the antipathy.

*Danel… Danel Lemire? Lorette? Did it even start with an L?* The man had been a gruff one, not quick to talk, brought into the squad late, didn't train with them, never had a heart-to-heart, a man-to-man. Marcel tried to come up with more excuses for why he couldn't remember his squadmate's surname, but each rung hollow. He had apologized to Danel after his death, called upon his name to curse the Principate, to curse General Agrippus, to prove to the world the depth of his own losses, what he had had to give up in his heroic quest to rid Huile of the Imperator's tyranny. And yet he couldn't even remember the man's damned name! How could he glare at Belona with the enmity she deserved, if he couldn't remember who he had claimed he had lost?

The woman continued her stare. He didn't mind the hate, he wasn't even that terrified about the duel he had drunkenly agreed, though he knew he should be. No, what he truly despised was the way Belona had tried to make him feel bad, feel guilty, feel *sorry* for her. For her loss, *her* loss, as if an authoritarian sociopath could feel grief. He tried to shoot a look of loathing, but couldn't meet her eyes, imaging again and again the melting faces of Principate soldiers.

Kayip watched the two of them warily. Near their table Utber chatted on a vocaphone, bragging to someone about the massive influx of slickdust they were about to purchase.

Marcel tried to plan out what he would say to Mr. Crimson when the gang lord finally arrived, but his mind kept circling back to Belona's absurd accusations the night before. The Huile Sewer Rats had done what they had to do; he had done what he had to do. It hadn't been pretty, it hadn't been nice, but war wasn't nice. It wasn't like in cinegraphs or in pulps, war involved deaths, and deaths were never pleasant. Was it all that much worse to be killed with sangleum gas than by gunshot? The screams that echoed his dreams and the aching phantom pain in his metal leg suggested it might be, but at the end of the day, that had been the goal of both sides, the elimination of the enemy. And the Principate had started it, had invaded, he had only done what they had forced him to do. General Agrippus was going to unleash those same weapons upon Huile. To stop her wasn't a crime, it was the opposite, it was heroism, stoic and brave. Belona tried to obscure the issue with her ludicrous claims of her own side's innocence, as if the Principate wouldn't use any weapon they had their hands on. Of course she was going to use the sangleum gas herself, General Durand had reported it plainly! Sure, he had received that intel from Lazarus Roache, who was a profligate liar, but the Resurgence command believed it for good reason. And not just because it was in their direct interest to believe it, but because... because... well, because of course the Principate would do that! The Principate was evil, could they really wait and see? They had to strike first, they had to, it was a heroic sabotage, not terrorism. But the woman was cruel enough to sow doubts in his mind, as some petty revenge. Belona knew he was a moral man, took advantage of that fact to bite at him. Isn't that what Alba had told him? *"...people will use anything they can on you, any weakness. Don't let your ideals be a weakness..."* That's exactly what Belona was doing! Using his ideals as a weakness, his sense of justice, his heroic nature. He couldn't let her win, couldn't let her get to him. But what in all Inferno's was Danel's last *fucking* name!

Kayip grabbed Marcel's hand and squeezed. Marcel glanced over, unable to tell from his hidden expression whether the monk was expressing sympathy or trying to tell him to get his shit together. Either way, Belona grunted.

"I'll use the bathroom," she said, getting up with one final scowl. She huffed off into the dark. Perhaps she had recognized the tension her presence brought, that if she stayed either she or Marcel would muck up this whole endeavor. Or perhaps she was just off planning some future cruelty. Either way, Marcel was glad to be rid of her. Mr. Crimson should be here any minute.

Utber gave a thumbs up from the vocaphone. "Sorry for the delay!" he shouted. "Hort fell through, my mistake to rely on the lad. But soon, soon!" He then returned to his idle chatter.

Marcel wished he could make out the details of the raider's conversation, but between the strange throat singer (who was in the middle of an impossibly long solo) and the raucous shouts of the parlor, it was impossible. He had heard some murmurs earlier in the day of an approaching imperial army, but the details had been vague and uncertain. The air was growing thick with concern, though not yet with panic.

Still, Marcel worried the imperial's gambit might come to ruin everything. They were too close to Roache now. Marcel could take the man down, remove the last threat to Huile's safety and freedom. It was the tycoon's fault everything had gone to shit after the war. Not Marcel's fault, not the Resurgence's fault, *Lazarus's*. Marcel had to remind himself of that. The noble UCCR government had been poisoned by slickdust. Even Lambert had drunk the substance, Marcel had seen the red tinge of his tea. If not for Lazarus's terrible mind-bending drug, Lambert, flawed as he was, would have never tolerated Lazacorp's crimes, would have never allowed corruption to seep into City Hall. Marcel just had to keep his mind focused and finish the job. Then he could return to the city, welcomed back as the hero he always was, and all would be right again. All he had fought for, all he had suffered for, it would all be worth it. And he *had* suffered. That's what heroism was, suffering for a good cause. Suffering for Huile. He lost his leg, the love of his life, his friends... Okay so maybe Danel wasn't a close friend after all, maybe Marcel couldn't remember his squadmate's last name. Maybe he used Danel's name to highlight the depths of his loss even as the man's face faded from his mind. Might someone see that as hypocritical? Sure, such an accusation could be made, but it would be ignorant. Danel was a symbol, which in many ways was better than being a man. A symbol of sacrifice, of duty, of freedom, of heroism. He was a stand in for all those other men and women who died saving Huile, all those men and women who sacrificed in any way for any quest of justice anywhere. Marcel wasn't emptily honoring a man he happened not to have known well, but was paying tribute to all the brave soldiers of the Resurgence.

Alba would have understood, even if she had not the resolve to stay and defend the city they had won, stay, and protect what they had all sacrificed for. Of course Belona could not see any of this. She had rattled on the night before about soldiers she had lost. But those had been Principate thugs, they had stood for nothing, symbolizing only tyranny and viciousness. They had been human only in the loosest, most literal sense, not people truly worth mourning. It was gauche how Belona had trotted their names out, as if tiny knives. The real tragedy was their indoctrination into the cult of the Imperator. They had all been lost long ago, Marcel had only done the merciful thing in finishing them off. It was heroism, it was heroism, it was heroism, it was—*Demiurge damn it Marcel, keep it together!* Now was not the time to get lost in solipsistic doubts. This was bigger than him, he had to keep himself together.

It was the alcohol. That was it, just the alcohol. It blurred his mind, confused him, let the imperial's words poison him. It was just the damned alcohol, soon he'd feel better.

"Mr. Zweihänder. Slovida, Klaus," Utber said, walking over. "I am pleased to introduce you fine folks to my boss, the honorable Mr. Crimson."

Marcel stood as a man hobbled over from the dark. He looked smaller than Marcel would have though a gang lord, spindlier, bent, though not necessarily old, at least judging by the rich youthful curls that framed his face. The face did confuse things. As his alias would suggest, it was a bright crimson. Sangleum-poisoning, no doubt. A mutation technically, but one largely localized to his skin. The man bore neither the horns nor the wild disfigurations of a full mutant. Still whatever had happened to him had left its mark, in his deep wrinkles, his hanging misshaped jowls, and the limp which he compensated with a gilded cane, replete with gemstones so bulbous Marcel had to wonder if they were fake.

Mr. Crimson was wearing a beat-up and heavily patched Principate officer's uniform, as if to taunt Marcel, though he reminded himself that plenty of raiders wore old military uniforms. They liked to tell stories of the stiffland idiots they murdered to get their new outfit, though based on the number of shops Marcel had passed selling secondhand uniforms and forgeries, imagined that many of the stories were pure ego-boosting fiction.

"So you're the Taur Maw representatives," Mr. Crimson said with a smile.

"It's a right good pleasure to meet ya, sir," Marcel said, removing his hat and shaking hands.

"Oh, the pleasure will be in the profits, if Utber here hasn't been telling fibs," Mr. Crimson said, shaking Sylvaine and Kayip's hands in turn.

"It's all as I said." Utber pulled out his boss's seat. "What was the number, Marshall? A hundred and twenty kilolitres of sangleum?

"A hundred and twenty-five," Marcel said. "And that's just the count when we left. Boys down south got the pumps working all day, so we just need a market."

"Well, you'll find one here, I assure you," Mr. Crimson said, sitting down. "I'm mighty pleased that you have chosen the Crimson Eyes to work as your intermediary on this deal. And I'm quite sorry that I kept you three fine folks waiting... there was a fourth, wasn't there?"

"In the bathroom," Sylvaine said.

"Ate some bad meat-sticks," Marcel cut in. "Otherwise, she'd be here."

"Oh, I take no offense," Mr. Crimson laughed. "You have to be careful with your choice of vittles out here. Ain't the stifflands, unless you know the vendor well there's no promise the meat will be fresh, or the species advertised. Anyways I was in the middle of explaining my absence. You might have heard about that Principate army wandering about."

"Just... rumors," Marcel said.

"Well, don't get too worried about them," Mr. Crimson said. "We're getting a delegation together; no doubt they just want to get paid off. Ain't no profit in attacking Stinktown. And I know their leader, this 'Lechslov.' Avaricious and an inveterate coward. Wouldn't risk his neck to save his own daughter if he had one."

"All news to me," Marcel said.

"Well, worse comes to worse, I sent a message out to reputable gang called the Death Skulls up north. Boss is a real nice woman, though hard to wrangle, I'll admit. But with your sangleum we can bribe them down with some slickdust, and that should be more than enough if talks fall through. Which they won't. But in the meanwhile, I'm sure you can understand how the presence of Imperial blue-caps might complicate your unusual request."

"And which request might that be?" Marcel said, though he suspected he knew.

"Meeting out in the Wastes," Mr. Crimson said. "I know you don't feel it's safe in Stinktown, but we can make it far more secure here than out there."

"And we can find a different gang to work with," Marcel snapped.

"Hey now, I didn't suggest that." Mr. Crimson's raised his hands, as if to slow the conversation. "How about this? We meet up in the hills at the back of Stinktown. At the far side, long past where people are making shacks. It's cut through with ravines and gulleys and plenty of places away from the eyes of the other gangs and the scopes of any overeager imperial soldiers."

Marcel glanced at Sylvaine and Kayip. They shared subtlest of nods. "We can make that work," Marcel said. "Assuming we can choose the spot."

"All right, that's a start," Mr. Crimson said.

A door in the back of the room flew open. Sylvaine groaned. Out walked a half-shaved and almost nude ferral, his two arms handing off the shoulders of young woman wearing even less clothes than he.

"The Crim-man!" the ferral shouted, walking over. Mr. Crimson got up to greet him, arms wide. They shared a surprisingly long hug.

"This here," Mr. Crimson said. "Is the greatest ring-fighter Stinktown has ever seen. The Savage."

"Savage to my enemies, sweet to my friends, ain't that right ladies?" The two women giggled on cue. Sylvaine groaned louder.

"And this here," The Savage continued, smacking Mr. Crimson's shoulders, almost knocking the man down, "is the greatest damn gang lord who ever stepped foot in the Wastes. Can you believe he's been a raider for less than three years? Rose straight to the top, and took me with him."

"Ain't no reason to go stroking my ego like that," Mr. Crimson said. "But this guy here, a real gut-slasher. Did you folks catch his match last night?"

"Unfortunately," Marcel heard Sylvaine whisper.

The Savage turned to Sylvaine. "Well, I was going to say, I thought I smelled another one of us fine furred folk. We don't get many Ferrals out here in Stinktown."

"Can't imagine why..." Sylvaine muttered.

"So where you from?" The Savage asked. "You grow up out east, or you one of the Rat Tribe-ers like me."

Marcel assumed east mean the Nemori Forestlands, but was less clear on the rat thing. "Around," was all that Sylvaine replied.

"Right, right, wastefolk then?" The Savage asked. "Better out here than in those stiffland cities. People are real stuck-up arseholes there, you know? Stifflanders ain't even want to know you, they take a look at your fur, your claws, and bam! Think they got you all figured out, like they have a whole book written about you, except all the pages is full of smeared taurshit, you know?"

"I don't. Never been," Sylvaine said, sticking to her story, and doing her best to display concentrated disinterest.

"Folk out here are better, don't judge so much, and even when they do, they like what they see. Slashing a man's face off with your claws, why you'd get cheers here! And the dames, the dames!" The Savage leaned on one of the women, who kissed his cheek. "They know the way of the world. Know that skills in the ring translate right into the bed. And that bed is large enough for four..."

"Okay, I think that's enough for now," Mr. Crimson stepped in, politely but firmly shooing The Savage away.

"Right on," The Savage said. "Hope you folks make a great deal. I'll catch you later Crim!" With that he walked away, two women in tow. Another raider howled as The Savage passed, and he in return he howled back. Soon half the establishment was howling. Sylvaine slunk down into her seat, so deep that it looked as if she might just well slip off onto the floor.

"So Lazarus Roache," Marcel said, trying to re-rail the train of conversation. "Ya can get him there in person? You're friends with him?"

"Not friends with him," Mr. Crimson said, sitting back down. "Can't say I like the man one bit."

"Oh." That was not the answer Marcel was expecting.

"It's better this way," Mr. Crimson said. "He needs me, needs the Crimson Eyes as allies. In truth, we need him too. Either we join together or fall into war, and he'd win that war. But I can still drag out that process of confederation, get what I can before falling in line. Got this gift from him, for one," he tapped his gilded cane. "But no, I do not like the man. Slickdust... hate what it does to my men and women. Can be useful I admit, I sell it as much as anyone, but its nasty stuff. And, to be truthful, I've never forgiven him for this." Mr. Crimson said, pointing to his skin.

"What do ya mean?" Marcel said, a strange anxiety forming in his stomach, as he again noticed Mr. Crimson's ragged principate uniform.

"Battle of Huile," Mr. Crimson said. "Was a Major, if you can believe it. Was close to being a Colonel by battle's end. Then Lazarus Roache switched sides, sent some UCCR terrorists after us, released sangleum gas." The man paused, staring off into the distance, as the blood drained from Marcel's face. "It was... horrible. I managed to find a gas mask just as the red smoke started to rise. Filter worked fine, but the lens was cracked. Like a thousand scorching claws slashing at your skin, digging at you, pulling, twisting, melting. I shut my eyes tight, and managed to stumble away, trying not to scream, trying to ignore the screeching wails of the soldiers under my command, the men and women I had to leave to their death. I wandered blind the underway, until I found some tunnel with ventilation, Inferno knows from where, but it kept the gas at bay. The damage was done, of course, the pain constant. Hasn't gone away since." The man sucked in his breath and winced. Marcel could not look him in the eye, did not want to see the agony, did not want the man to see his own reaction. His cogleg burning with the buried memories. The screams, he could hear them too, his own just one of thousands.

With great effort, Mr. Crimson smiled. "But in the end, maybe it did me good. Taught me the folly of following other people, the folly of theses lies we call ideology. The Principate, the Resurgence, what's the difference in the end? Law, freedom, order, democracy. All just words, nothing to them, just little sounds to decorate your songs with. After I escaped, when I studied my oozing features by the oleaginous glimmer of a waste-pool, I knew I could never go back, never be again the man I was. So I buried Hans Krimme, out there, forgot my old life, took on a new one. And look where it's led me!"

Marcel tried to nod, emotions roiling in every direction, too chaotic to even define. Mr. Crimson had gone from a man to a ghost, a spirit haunting him. One of the many Marcel had tried to kill. Scum, true, he was even a raider now, and yet Marcel couldn't look him in the eye. This person, this name, Hans Krimme, it was too real, not a number, not just a uniform. Thousands of ghosts, thousands who did not escape... It hit him suddenly. And that name... why did it sound familiar?

He reached for his glass to give a toast, to Mr. Crimson, or the Taur Maws, or Lazarus fucking Roache or anything, anything to distract him, to give Marcel's mind time to calm. The glass slipped from his finger, rolling off the table and smashing on the floor.

"Drunk already?" came a voice. Belona's voice. A horror suddenly rushed up Marcel's chest. "My apologies, I'm late," the woman continued. "But I assume negotiations are underway."

"Indeed they are," Mr. Crimson said, turning. "I was just telling your colleagues about—General Agrippus?"

The woman froze. Mr. Crimson froze. Sylvaine whispered a panicked "Shit!" Utber looked confused. Kayip reached into his pocket.

"Agrippus," Mr. Crimson repeated, "why are you—?"

And then Belona shot him.

# CHAPTER 29

The gunshot cut through the racket of the parlor, which seconds before had been overwhelming Sylvaine's ears. Everyone stopped what they were doing, drunkards stopped drinking, pole dancers stopped pole dancing, catur players dropped their pieces.

Utber whipped out a pistol, but the imperial was quicker.

"Run!" Belona shouted, as the raider's corpse slumped to the floor.

It was good advice. They rushed forward, chairs flying, smashing past people as they fled for the door. Bullets began to fly. A hulk of a man stepped in their way, fumbling to load a shotgun, but Kayip swung his sudden sword and the raider's torso flew from his legs. Belona kicked open the door, bullet whizzing past her hair, and they all dashed out into the street.

The night was cold and full of voices. They were at a square filled with people, shopping and drinking and fighting and all the usual Stinktown stuff. No one seemed to have notice the ruckus from the parlor.

"This way!" Marcel hissed. They quickly rushed past the crowd and down an alleyway, as men and women burst out the scrap-lattice parlor doors, guns out, gaze franticly searching.

"What was that?" Sylvaine asked Belona.

"I was... our cover was blown..." she said. There was a creakiness to her voice, an uncertainty that she had never heard in the imperial's tone.

"And there wasn't a subtler way to extricate ourselves?"

"You're not a soldier! When you have the initiative... there's no time to think, you just have to strike," Belona said.

"Shh!" Kayip shh-ed.

Outside a group of Crimson Eyes were searching the square without much success. The crowds were distracted by drinking and slickdust snorting, and those sober enough to be useful were enthralled by a heated debate taking place in the middle of a square. Well, less a debate, more a shouting match, two raiders arguing about the incoming Principate forces, whether they should negotiate (like cowards, according to one) or fight block by block (like fools according to the other.)

Only one man was looking in their direction. He had metal arms and wore a familiar pair of shades. Hadn't Sylvaine seen him in the crowds last night? The man turned and put two steel fingers to his mouth. He whistled. It sounded uncannily close to the call of a soot-sparrow.

Before Sylvaine could think on that, a horrible shrill shriek erupted from the depths of the parlor. The Savage burst through the doors, tears streaming down his face. He glanced this way, then that. With alarming speed, he vaulted up the side of the parlor building, all three floors within seconds. He frantically sniffed the air, ears turning, gaze methodically covering every inch of the square... until he locked his distance gaze on Sylvaine.

"Shit," she whispered.

"There they are!" he roared, pointing.

Belona did not have to repeat her previous advice. They fled down the alley, the shouts of dozens of angry Crimson Eyes echoing behind them.

"To the 'truck!" Marcel said, as someone shot off his hat.

They turned up a narrow avenue, bent in the direction of the nearby hills. Boot to cobblestone, to scrap-brick, to mud, to fossilized trash, they dashed through uneven roads, pushing past confused passersby as screams of rage echoed down the streets.

"There they are! There they are!" The Savage howled, jumping from rooftop to rooftop, brachiating over flimsy powerlines like a monkey, keeping a close pursuit. Belona fired off a few rounds, but this did little to deter the ferral.

"You murdered him! You taur-fuckers murdered him!" he shouted.

They came across a bridge made of fused scraped and rusted chains, hanging over a ravine in the middle of the city. Down below was a raw bedrock of trash, with a fetid river cutting through, flowing from some unknown place. Figures in ragged clothing dug through the garbage or rested in small nooks carved from the sedimentary layers of refuse.

"Not sure that's steady..." Marcel began, before a crowd of Crimson Eyes dashed out from the corner, replacing his hypothetical fears with very real ones.

They staggered across the bridge, avoiding holes and jutting nails. The chains swung precariously as they did, creaking and groaning and tossing specks of rust, but not quite giving. Violent vibrations announce the arrival of the raiders, who stumbled forward, pushing past each other on the narrow bridge, pistols aimed over heads firing wild shots.

One bullet whistled past Sylvaine's ear, and some instinct inside roared for her to follow The Savage's example, to get on all fours and scamper away, to climb and dig and hide. She could rush far ahead of the raiders, sprint quicker than anyone, quicker than her friends and Belona for certain, leave them all behind in a burst of panicked speed. Of course that was just the instinct of flight, there was also that of fight, to turn and charge claws out. These were the contradictory impulse of that growling thing inside her, but she pushed it down as deep as she could manage, trying to keep her breath stable and mind clear as the bullets flew and the bridge shook.

Finally the four reached the end. Kayip was last, and as his boot touched cobblestone, he twirled his sword, slicing the chains behind him clean as butter. With horrid screams the raiders fell into the ravine, crunching or squelching into the wet refuse.

This victory was short-lived, as the remains of the pursuers simply ran down the street, towards a more secured bridge not too many metres distant. The four used what little time as they had to get distance, all the while The Savage taunted them from the rooftops.

"We'll cut your fucking eyes out! We'll, we'll skin you quick and make coats out of you... that's what the Crim-man would have wanted." As The Savage chucked a hunk of shingle, Sylvaine heard him let out a deep, wailing sob.

They were getting close to the garage now, close to freedom. The only issue was if they could get their 'truck out before being surround. And if they could manage to navigate the city while being pursued. And if they could lose their pursuers somewhere in the Wastes. And then even if they survived the night, there was the question of how they could now possibly catch Roache. So there were a lot of issues, an overwhelming number, so many that their force rose back up that buried panic inside of Sylvaine, but she tried to push them out, to focus on the most pressing issue, simply putting one foot in front of the other faster that the raiders did.

Again whistled the call of a soot-sparrow. A woman rode down the street towards them, atop a horse-shaped golem shining in chrome. Her blonde hair was cut short, and upon her face sat a pair of shades similar to the metal-armed man. In her free arm was what looked like an explosive of some sort. All this Sylvaine saw in a second, then the woman was past them.

"Wait, was that—?" Marcel began, slowing his step.

"Move!" Belona shouted, pulling the man with her around a corner.

As they passed that bend an explosion ripped from where they had run from, followed by screams.

"Wait, wait!" Marcel said. But they hadn't the time to wait. Ahead was the entrance to the garage, a massive concrete block of a building that looked as though it had once served a military function. The guard there took one look at Kayip's gleaming sword, and jumped out of the way, as the monk cut open the door.

The inside was lit by rows of buzzing 'bulbs, shadows dancing among the bodyshells of hundreds of vehicles neatly packed in rows. There were autocars, some finely kept with fresh paint, others piles of rust. There were motorcycles and caravan-trucks, thin-legged warwalkers and svelte monowheels. Rushtanks, and autoarmor, and landships, and miniature mopeds, and goliaths of twisting metal that Sylvaine had no words for. In the very back, was the 'truck they came in on, with the blackened markings of the Taur Maw gang.

Between them and the 'truck, stood about two dozen Crimson Eyes.

"Shit!" Marcel said. Sylvaine shared the sentiment.

The sounds of sobbing. The Savage flung himself down in front of the raiders, face soaked with tears. "You... you mog-lizard shit, griffon-fucking bastards..." he wailed. "He found me, that man found me, when I had nothing. Sold myself in slavery to pay loansharks, treated like an animal! Like some fucking dog set to do tricks, until he found me, and he saved me. Gave me a job, gave me a family. What kind of man has a heart like that? And you put a fucking bullet though him, through the one man... a man I loved. I fucking loved him, and you... you..."

He glanced behind him, at the crowd of Crimson Eyes who were giving strange looks at his outburst of emotion. With a deep breath, he started to gather himself.

Sylvaine for her part studied the autotruck that stood between him and the raiders. It was a Crimson Eye's transport 'truck filled with metal boxes, and what looked to be a few barrels of sangleum. She reached slowly into her bag, slipping on her ætherglove.

"I... I..." he began. "I mean, *The Savage,* will not let this go unavenged!" he shouted with a showman's cadence. "I will rip your bones out and use them to clean my teeth. I will cut off your head and decorate the walls of my hut with your scalps!" The raiders cheered this speech as if watching a ring-match. Sylvaine felt out and could sense not only sangleum within the fuel barrels, but some sangleum-products within the boxes as well. An explosive combination.

"Now, now, I think there's been a been misunderstanding—" Marcel began, as Sylvaine lifted up her 'glove and focused a bolt onto the autotruck. It burst into flames, sending a shockwave that knocked The Savage to the ground and nearly sent Sylvaine flying. With this blast came spreading a thick red mist of—

Sylvaine suddenly realized what was in the boxes. The payment Mr. Crimson had mentioned earlier in the night. Roache's poison in unfathomable quantities, all her desires and self-hatred manifested into one horrible, alluring, overwhelming powder. There was no choice left, no room for will in the milliseconds that remained, no continence or abstinence possible. As the cloud of roiling slickdust rushed towards her, Sylvaine screamed.

# CHAPTER 30

A pain in the back of his head. The world was dark and dizzy. Screams and shouts and gunshots. Marcel could only guess where he was. Under Blackwood Row. Clockbomb in hand, or maybe already placed. Gasmask tugging tight his face. Above him the countless soldiers he would condemn. Hans Krimme, face youthful and unscarred. Near him, somewhere, his squad.

*"Desct..."* he tried to moan. *"Don't trust... Lazacorp... they will... they will."*

How did he know? How could he know if he was there? But he smelled it. The stench of sangleum. Felt it. Felt Lazarus Roache, felt his words, somehow. He coughed through his gasmask and could taste the sangleum as well. Must be a leak, a crack, the end of him. His leg burned. He needed to find her. Needed to find his captain. He had just seen her, on top of a gleaming steed, running through the streets of... the streets of...

"Get up Talwar." A woman's voice. He reached out. A hand grabbed his tight, and pulled. Pulled him up from the darkness, from the nightmare.

"Get up Talwar!"

"Alba?" he asked. She had returned, finally, to save him.

"Who in Inferno is Alba?" Belona Agrippus asked, covered in blood. No, not blood, slickdust. The whole room was covered in a layer of red, like a winter's snow viewed under crimson moonlight.

"Was that poetry?" Belona asked. Marcel realized he had been speaking. And as he straightened his vision, he realized that not all parts of the parking garage were covered in slickdust. Some were on fire.

"What happened?" he asked.

"Besides you hitting your head?"

A roar echoed through the room. A slickdust-encrusted animal jumped over a 'truck, hurling a molten ball of 'car parts at a crowd of panicking Crimson Eyes. It took Marcel a second to realize it was Sylvaine.

"She happened," Belona continued. "Imperator's mercy, I did not know the girl had it in her." The woman spoke with pride.

"You stayed to help me," Marcel said. He had assumed the imperial would take the first opportunity to abandon him, or even put a bullet into his unconscious head. He felt an uncomfortable sense of gratitude.

"Of course." Belona nodded. "I need someone to drive the 'truck."

A raider rushed out from behind an autocar, axe in hand. Belona put two bullets in him, as Marcel fumbled with his Frasco. With a war cry, Kayip rushed into a crowd of Crimson Eyes a few metres away, hewing them in twain. He did not hesitate a moment, but continued his rampage, as a hidden Sylvaine howled up a storm of ætheric lightning.

Belona pulled Marcel forward, half sneaking, half running, until they made it to the 'truck. Marcel couldn't recognize it, like everything else it was covered in red, but Belona's key worked fine.

"Why aren't you driving?" he asked, feeling the need to convince himself the imperial's assistance was purely crude utilitarianism. Perhaps it was, for she pulled off some tarp to reveal the gleam of a motorgun.

She set the weapon up in seconds. On a tripod stand, with a heavy belt of bullets hanging. She turned on the motor and the barrels started to spin. Of the crowd on Crimson Eyes, only one noticed the weapon's groans. As he screamed and pointed, Belona let loose a fury of bullets. Red painted red, the raiders fell to the ground. Belona cackled as the gun revved.

"Feel free to take some shots yourself!" she shouted to Marcel

It seemed almost unnecessary. Autocars were flying, motorcycles exploding, raiders fleeing, as a berserk, ætherically-empowered ferral raged throughout the garage. Claws went to face, bodies were tossed. Blood and smoke and flung debris and arcs of æthericity. Raiders ran, they begged, they tried to defend themselves with whatever they had on hand, but she was quicker, deadly, moving faster than any eyes could track. Marcel had never seen Sylvaine like this, all bestial fury. It was so unlike the engineer, usually quiet, bookish, snarky at most. She looked like something out of the cinegraphs, the monsters of the eastern forestlands, a blood-soaked blur of fur and claws. She was terrifying.

"She's beautiful," Belona said. "Why did she hide such potential? Can you imagine, Talwar, an army of these? Better than the Imperator's own guard! There'd be no city beyond my grasp."

Tactically useful as it was, Marcel did not find the sight so heartening. Sylvaine was roaring, screaming, she was not herself, had fallen into some pit inside her and he was not sure she could dig her way out.

"Sylvaine," he tried to shout. "Sylvaine!"

"The Savage will put a stop to this!" The other ferral appeared, blade of sharpened scrap in his hand. He jumped down at Sylvaine and swung. Sylvaine pivoted and grabbed his blade-hand with her 'glove. With a growl, she sent force a burst of æthericity, turning the weapon into incandescent slag which fell upon The Savage, scalding him.

"Fuck! Fuck! I give up!" he shouted, but Sylvaine would not relent. Her free claw tore into his chest, she bit and tore and scratched and gored. The man screamed a horrid cry as she took him to the ground, ripping flesh from blood in a wild, unhinged, rage. Her ferocity did not let up even after the man's voice faded, even after his limbs fell limp. Blood flew in ribbons, mixing with the slickdust on the floor. Smoke gathered and spread, Marcel coughing and squinting to keep his sight upon the terrible scene.

Finally Sylvaine started to slow. Her grunting and growling faded, her breath getting deeper, as she stood up and stared at the corpse before her. She took a step back, her mouth moving as if she wanted to say something, but no words came out. A look of absolute abhorrence appeared upon her face, growing even greater as she stared down at her own dripping claws.

She screamed. Loud and horribly human. Æthericity flew from her glove in chaotic arcs, this way and that, melting motorbikes and turning autocars into sudden smoldering wrecks.

"Shit!" Marcel said, as one of the untamed bolts exploded a nearby warwalker. Belona just went back to cackling. Sylvaine was the center of an ætheric hurricane, devastation snapping out in all direction.

Out from the smoke and billowing slickdust walked Kayip. His sword had bent itself back around his wrist, his leather head-covering had fallen off as some point during the battle, his metal mask glimmered under the flickering lights. He stepped towards Sylvaine, as the woman screamed out erratic strands of æthericity, fizzling and crackling through the air. Kayip kept walking, not flinching as a bolt flew centimetres near his face, landing in an explosion far off. He approached Sylvaine without saying a word, and when he reached her, the ground shaking around them, he put one hand upon her shoulder.

Sylvaine froze. The æthericity calmed. She turned to Kayip. The man stared at her, and then embraced her tight. She paused. Then she weakly placed her hand around him.

The storm abated. With raiders dead, the garage had become strangely silent, only the crackle and sputter of a few small fires. Marcel could even hear Kayip's soft words.

"You are Sylvaine. It's going to be okay. You are Sylvaine."

Sylvaine nodded back.

Kayip helped the dazed engineer stagger to the 'truck, over the bodies and the wreckages, leaving great red footprints behind him. As they reached the 'truck Marcel offered his hand, but the monk did not need it, lifting first Sylvaine, then himself into the back.

"You should drive," Kayip said, laying Sylvaine down, and sitting beside her.

"They'll be on us soon," Belona agreed.

Marcel took one glance at Sylvaine, who seemed at least physically okay, then nodded and ran to the front of the 'truck.

* * *

It took less than a minute for Marcel to navigate the disordered garage and make it out into the streets. He had hoped that they had dealt with the bulk of their pursuers, or that the confusion wrought by their flight to the garage would give them amble time to cleanly escape the city.

These were overly optimistic hopes.

As soon as he turned a corner, he heard the shouts. "It's them!" There was no need for explanation or context. Killing a gang boss had made them the unambiguous *them*.

"Floor it!" Belona shouted as Marcel floored it. Their 'truck skidded over muck-grouted cobbles, as half a dozen motorbikes and one heavily armored wartruck vroomed into pursuit. Bullets started flying, decorating their cabin with of bullet holes.

Belona returned fire, sending one of the motorcycles hurtling into a meat-stick stand. The 'bikes slowed some, aside from one which raced forward, a raider in the sidecar menacing a grenade in his hand. The first one he tossed fell short, eviscerating an overly curious bystander. As he unpinned the second, Belona shot a spray of bullets right in front of their pursuer. A burst of earth and filth crashed over them like a wave, the raider dropping his explosive into the sidecar, with predictable results.

"Running low on ammunition here!" she shouted.

"Which way do I go?" Marcel shouted, doing the best he could just to keep on the narrow streets and make the sharp turns without careening into the ramshackle buildings that made up the outskirts of Stinktown.

"Go left, then right, then straight forward until you pass the broken statue, then another left," Kayip said, without looking up. He was still tending to Sylvaine, one hand on the frame of the autotruck to steady them, the other holding her head as she drank from a canteen. She groaned as Marcel made the first turn.

Marcel, for his part, didn't have the time to guess how Kayip got such an encyclopedic knowledge of Stinktown's backstreets, but followed the directions as best he could, managing to maintain a consistent distance from their pursuers. He wondered if he might have had a career as a racecar driver.

"What's going on?" Belona said. "They're so slow. They can't all be cowards."

As Marcel made the final turn, he found the answer to Belona's question. The large western gate to Stinktown had been slammed shut.

"They have us trapped!" Belona shouted, firing off another round at their slow pursuers, as Marcel awkwardly tried to turn the 'truck into one of the side streets.

Suddenly, a shrill birdcall rang out. A woman appeared atop a steed, leaping across the building tops, blonde hair streaming, as she dropped something into the raiders below. Marcel got only a second's glance at her, less time that he had when he saw her earlier, but the sight made his heart jump.

An explosion ripped suddenly, taking out the 'truck and two motorcycles. As this happened another motorbike burst out of a street. This one was cleaner than the others, made of a similar chrome to that of the horse-golem. The man riding it wore a pair of shades and had gleaming cogarms. Belona twisted the motorgun to aim at him.

"Don't shoot!" Sylvaine said, grasping at the woman. "He's a friend!"

It was the first cogent words she had said since leaving the garage, and Marcel was certain the imperial would ignore her. Surprisingly, Belona let her gun cool.

The bikers stopped for a moment in an alley, waving for Marcel to follow. Marcel twisted his wheel and pressed the gas, bursting down the alley, as the last two raider bikes pursued after.

"Who are these people?" Belona asked.

"No idea," Marcel shouted, which was a lie. He was far from certain, but he did have one idea. After all these years... to appear so suddenly, like a ghost or a sharply timed punchline. This was certainly not the city he expected to meet her again. He wasn't sure if he should cry or laugh, not that he had time for either.

Though they were out of the frying pan, the fire was still burning. Specifically the fire was burning out the back of one of the raider's rocket-hurlers. The missile blew up the second floor of some shanty tower. Marcel swerved wildly to avoid the falling debris.

"Shitshitshitshitshitshit!" Marcel said.

The mysterious biker was leading them up above Stinktown, into the sandstone hills that sat behind the city. Tenements were quickly replaced by shacks, and shacks by nothing but raw rock and shrubbery.

As the raider reloaded his 'hurlers, another chrome horse appeared. This was ridden by a salvi, his horns covered with hanging charms which clattered about. He pulled out a pistol from his jacket and with a single shot, took out the one of the raider pursuers.

The last pursuer rushed forward with fearsome determination. Belona aimed her motorgun and fired, but the man leapt out from his bike and grabbed onto the back of the 'truck. He hung on tight, legs trailing behind. Belona twisted her gun as far as she could, but realizing he was beneath its line of fire, started to kick at the man.

The raider ducked back, and then lifted out a grenade from his pocket, sans pin.

"I may not make it, but I'm gonna take you taur-fuckers out with—"

A slash too fast to be seen. Kayip held out his sword, the other hand still on Sylvaine.

"—me!" the raider finished, not realizing he had lost his hand until it exploded some metres behind them. He stared at the stump and screamed, before finally being removed by Belona's determined boot, tumbling behind.

"That's the last of them," the imperial said. "But we need a place to hide out."

"I think that's where they're leading us to," Marcel said, slowing the 'truck, but keeping pace with the cog-armed man and the salvi, as they lead them through increasingly narrow passes.

The sandstone walls grew taller and taller, the last hints of Stinktown's filth disappearing as they drove. The salvi was riding on the ridge above them, the metal-armed biker just in front of them, until, suddenly, his bike transformed. In a flash the wheels split out into two pairs of limbs, clinking together before even touching the ground. The headlight bent forward and split into twin eyes. In the back its exhaust pipes spun out into a tail. The chassis raised up upon its sudden legs of metal, and the man's bike had transformed entirely into another chrome horse.

"Woah!" Sylvaine said. Marcel silently echoed her sentiment.

He slowed as he squeezed the 'truck round a bend, eager to make distance between them and Stinktown, but no longer afraid for his life. Instead, he took every moment he could sneak his eyes away from the misshapen excuse for a road to look up at the riders. Just the two of them, the man with the metal arms and the salvi. Where was she? The woman that... he did not want to lend credence to his own theory, his own active imagination, did not want to put a name there, in case he was wrong. It was dark, he had only seen glimpses, and yet who else could she be, who else would come to save him again? And stranger still, why was he so eager to see her again? She had abandoned him, had abandoned Huile. She had been cruel and dismissive in their last moments together... But now he was desperate to see her again, desperate to believe this strange woman on a horse was—

They turned into a sudden dead end. It was so covered in brush and scrap, that Marcel did not even see the cliff slope until he was almost on in. He slammed tight the breaks, and the 'truck skid to a halt.

"What in Inferno is this?" Belona asked, pulling out a handtorch and pistol. "An ambush?"

"I don't think so," Marcel said, stepping out of the autotruck. They appeared to be mining pit of some kind, old mineshafts with rusted rails and rotted wood cut into every direction around the cliff face. The riders trotted down from the clifftops, disappearing into separate shafts.

"Hey!" Marcel shouted.

"Be wary with your voice," Kayip said, helping Sylvaine down. "We are not so far out to be reckless."

"I don't like this…" Belona said, glancing this way and that.

"We can trust them," Marcel said. As the words left his lips there was a sudden buzz of æthermantics, and from where they had entered the gulch a great scrap gate rushed across the entrance, slamming shut.

"It is an ambush!" Belona said, pistol searching desperately for a target.

"No, no," Marcel said. "It's… I think…" he was suddenly quite unsure what he thought. He glanced around frantically for the woman, but could see no one.

A metal cannister was chucked from one of the mineshafts. As it landed at their feet it began to vomit out smoke. Belona began firing at nothing, as Marcel stumbled back, coughing. Another smoke grenade was flung in, blocking the moon a moment before landing right behind Marcel.

"Shit! Shit! Sh—" Marcel couldn't speak, could do nothing but desperately cough. The smoke-shaded gas tasted odd, earthy, and musky. A headache hit him suddenly, with a strong dull force. He tried to call out, but only succeeded in sucking in more gas, as grenade after grenade fell.

Marcel fell to his hands and knees, trying to crawl for air. He lungs forced his mouth open, and as he sucked in the gas, he realized it did not burn as he thought it might. The dullness in his head spread to his arms and legs with each desperate breath. He struggled to keep his mind focused, did not realize he had stopped crawling until he felt dirt upon his cheeks. The sound of Belona's gunfire ceased and, though maybe it was a mirage, he thought he saw a woman step out from the smoke, face a black leather skull with great glass eyes. He knew he should be terrified, should be furious, but with each breath, he found such emotions more and more distant, felt the whole world tiptoeing away, centimetre by centimetre. The smoke fell upon him more like a blanket than anything else, he felt warm, and his muscles ignored his increasingly lackadaisical requests to move. As things went dark, he could only muse that at least it wasn't sangleum gas this time.

*Bloodshed in the streets of Huile! Reports are still coming in on what appears to a violent riot staged by the violent mutant workers of local Huilian sangleum firm, Lazacorp. Though the motives are still unknown, the mutants were reported to have acted with "unspeakable cruelty" according to one witness, having captured not only the Lazacorp refineries, but City Hall itself. There they murdered a number of local politicians, including one Gaspard Levair, nephew of famous General Antoine Levair, who is currently organizing a detachment of his forces in Fim-Niuex to put down this violence.*

*Yet the brutality does not appear to have been limited to politicians and notables. Early reports on civilian fatalities places the number slain in the high hundreds, if not thousands. Women cut to pieces in the streets, men slain protecting their children, police burned alive by mobs of rabid mutants. It is a butchery reminiscent of the Principate siege that just three years before wracked this Border State city. A horrific tragedy made all the more shocking due to the peace and prosperity the city had been experiencing, a city which this very periodical referred to as "...an oasis of Phenian civilization and comfort, in an uncomfortable, uncivilized land..." mere weeks ago.*

*As to the motivations of these murderous mutants, that is still unknown. There have been speculations that it arose due to a labor dispute, but the leading theory is that many of these mutants may have had raider loyalties, and their employment was just a ruse to get behind the walls of Huile. Indeed this theory had found great support in the Society for the Uplift and Integration of Mutants (SUIM). Jean Desvaux, the SUIM spokesman for its Phenia chapter, gave a statement to the press this morning.*

*"We are as horrified as any other citizens of the UCCR at the disgusting violence displayed in Huile. Mutants are like any other citizen, loyal to the values of the Resurgence, and eager for peace. It is important to remember that these Huilian mutants are not like those of Phenia. They are wastefolk, unused to civilization and close to barbarism. I have previously praised Lazarus Roache for his philanthropic outlook with Wastes mutants, creating jobs and opportunities for mutated men and women who had none. Tragically, it seems this generosity and kindness have been taken advantage of, at a horrible cost. We weep alongside the rest of Phenia for our fellow citizens in Huile, and will join our voices in a*

*united cry for justice! We express full support and faith in General Levair, and hope for a swift return to order."*

*As of the time of writing, the whereabouts of the Executive of Lazacorp, war hero and philanthropist Lazarus Roache, is currently unknown, but sources in the military have expressed hope that he may still be alive.*

*—Front-page article from the evening edition of The Phenian Post, Noth 26th, 1749.*

# CHAPTER 31

The Junta Council of the Gang Lords of Stinktown was as orderly as the city itself. Shouts and insults were thrown wildly, objects as well. Pens, aurem, chunks of jagged rocks snuck in for this purpose, none with velocity great enough to do more than sting, but which together gave the whole affair a sense of petty puerility. That was not to say serious work never happened, Namter had been present at enough of these meetings to know that fortunes were routinely transferred in intricate business dealings, that military campaigns were organized and financed, that complex alliances were formed, broken, and reformed within these shouting matches. It didn't make it any more pleasant, especially considering that he would be responsible for cleaning Roache's sizable drawing room when all their guests had left, guests Namter noticed, had not removed their grim-caked boots before stepping on the griffon-fur rug. Between their bouts of shouting and lewd invectives, Namter could hear the rat-a-tat-tat of clockwork rifles outside, as pretenders to the leadership of the Crimson Eyes fought it out.

"It's a rat-fuck mess, it is," spat Gillie Strixheart, of the Iron Strixes, though the young woman's scoliosis-twisted back gave her a look closer to a skragger hunched over a meal than a strigine strix. "Been dealing with Crimson Eye punks running wild round my territory, like spikefowl with their heads cut off. What we need is to slaughter the lot of them."

"What we need is order," said Yimur Broken-Tooth, the knuckle-scarred lord of the Fist-Biters. "Give my men permission, and within half a day we'll have this civil war buried under rubble and lead."

"Tea?" Namter asked, tray in hand, the fumes of slickdust thick in the air. Roache's drug was, of course, complimentary. Yimur took the cup with caution, giving a muffled "thanks mate" while shooting nervous glances up at the butler. Despite Namter's servile duties, the gang lords were well aware of his power in the Brotherhood, and treated him with, if not reverence, then an appropriate amount of dread.

"We don't have half a day," said Stefanus Silverlips, of the Silverlip Slavers, his feet on the large scarwood table, his hair tied in an oleaginous gray bun. "I'm not sure if you're all aware, but there is an imperial army a day's march away, and not slowing. If I may suggest—"

"We are all aware," Lazarus Roache interrupted, sitting on armchair that was just ever so subtly taller than all the others, "of the military situation we find ourselves in. That is why I gathered you all here in the first place. Though we have sent an envoy to negotiate with blue-caps we cannot assume their success. We must prepare for the worse, so it is vital that we work together to secure the defense of our joint interests."

"My interests are currently being plundered by idiot raiders who no longer have a lord to teach them manners," said Erik 'Trog-Face' Weissman, master of the Trog-Skinners. As was to be expected, the man wore a mask of troglyn leather, giving him rough approximation of a troglyn's face, if that troglyn had been run over first by a tread-driller. "We can't even reach our armory, as there's been a three-hour shoot-out between some wannabe gang lords pretenders. The only other Crimson Eye who had a chance of keeping things together was that Utber fellow, but he's as dead Mr. Crimson himself. And I know who's responsible!"

"You about to point fingers at me?" Yimur Broken-Tooth spat.

"Only because you're obviously guilty!" Trog-Face shouted, pointing and jabbing.

"Lazacorp is currently investigating the assassination," Lazarus Roache said. "But we do not believe that any Stinktown Gang was involved. Some claim to have seen members of southern gang known as the Taur Maws, but it seems very possible to me that the whole thing was a ploy by the imperials to weaken our resolve. We mustn't let them succeed."

"Agreed there, mate," Yimur said. "I've already lost dozen shopfronts to Crimson Eye looting. Which is why us Fist-Biters must be given authority by this council to crush this whole chaos mess and take control of the remaining Crimson Eyes."

"Bah!" Trog-Face shouted. "Is that the claim of an innocent man! Let us Trog-Skinners have a crack at it, Crimson Eye territory was already rightfully ours."

Shouts and vituperations were fired across the room, the lords greedily arguing over who should get which piece of the blood-soaked pie now that Mr. Crimson had met his end.

"I have begun to partition out territory in a manner fair and equitable for all," Lazarus interrupted. "Once the situation is resolved, we will be able to tally up other captured capital and spread the wealth to all of you. There is no need to make this some vicious squabble, the only question at hand is how best to quell the current unrest."

"Just ignore the bastards," shouted the bulbous Britta of Britta's Bloatbeasts, as she swung a large tankard of slickdust-infused booze. "They'll sort themselves out in time, by talk or blade. We have bigger beasts to butcher."

"Oh, the high and mighty lady Britta giving out orders again," snorted Red Rust Ronnie, leader of the Rust Thorns. "Ya want us all to cower, to don't ya? To tuck in our dicks and run, letting these gangless hooligans make of mess of the place? Well, Red Rust Ronnie don't run!"

"And no one's brought up Vapulus!" shouted Stev Clawsfolk of the Steel Claws, smashing his impractically oversized gauntlet on the tables. "Been harrying us for weeks, as I've mentioned council meeting after council meeting. And now with all this shit spinning, that Bladescar brute's taken down two of our caravans!"

"Drown in piss!" Gillie Strixheart cackled. "Little whiney Stev can't even handle some mutants."

The arguments continued on in this manner, with no clear direction or focus, but a lot of cursing. Lazarus kept a level head and an equanimous tone that occasionally restored order, but never for long.

Namter knew there was a place for his own subtle interventions, but his focus was not as complete as needed. It hadn't been since he had started inserting those celestial spies into the flesh of mutants. Part of his mind, his soul perhaps, was elsewhere, sometime kilometres away, buried deep into fetid tissue. It was more than a little distracting. He was starting to wonder if the whole scheme was even sensible. So far, each body he had implanted found itself overlooked by Miga. Perhaps the woman had found a way to sense his interventions and—

Something overcame him suddenly. Namter gripped a nearby chair, as a vision, no, an *embodiment* assaulted him.

*The pumping of blood, the squelching work of intestines, the labor of two lungs and halting winds that emanated therewithin. Viscera, bone, warmth. From the wet darkness that surrounded him, Namter felt sensations of pain, of panic.*

*A blade cutting into flesh. Light streaming in, past epidermis and muscle. Namter peaked his single eye and saw beyond the blinding light, a face. Tired and bloodstained, scowling, Miga Veneficus stared into the corpse in which Namter was hiding, like some monstrous giant.*

*Sounds escaped her vast lips, primitive grunts that Namter struggled to translate into words. "Heartbeat steady, vitals good," she said, before scribbling something onto paper.*

*The giant moved, and Namter took the opportunity to make his escape. He wormed his way out, unaccustomed to the body of the divine parasite. He squirmed and slithered, up past the opened ribcage, out onto the skin of the mutant once named Hort.*

*How strange the laboratory looked from this new vantage point, how vast and hostile, more a landscape than a room. Gurneys as plateaus, great forests of test tubes, the crackling ætherlamps above seeming horrid suns. There in the corner hunched Miga Veneficus, jabbing an infusion device into the neck of the still groaning mutant.*

*Working on instincts that were not his own, Namter moved, sliding off the body of the mutant, onto the hard, dark floor below.*

Namter fell onto the chair, with a thump, able to orient himself in time to keep from sprawling gracelessly onto the floor. Fortuitously Red Rust Ronnie and Bloated Britta were caught in a quite distracting screaming match, fine porcelain dishware flying as punctuation. Only Yimur Broken-Tooth chanced a nervous glance in the butler's direction.

"Enough!" shouted Lazarus Roache. "It has been decided. Lazacorp will lead a quick and decisive assault to pacify the remnants of the Crimson Eyes."

"But—" Britta began

"And part of this assault!" Lazarus continued, sweat heavy on his forehead, his face a deeper red than Namter had seen in many weeks. "Will be composed of raiders from Britta's Bloatbeast and the Trog-Skinners, with compensation from captured spoils."

This seemed to calm the woman down. Erik 'Trog-Face' smirked at Yimur. Namter took a step back and started another, unneeded, kettle of tea, as he calmed his nerves. He could still feel his other body, a kilom away, metamorphosizing, other-flesh liquifying and reforming in an altogether uncomfortable manner. It was strange to be in two places at once, stranger still to feel both human sized and as small as a rat. Yet he could not give himself away, not hint to Roache or anyone any clue that something was amiss.

"What about the Iron Strixes?" Gillie slammed the table. "My girls want blood!"

"You will be kept as backup," Lazarus explained, with as much calm as he could force. "And duly compensated."

"And—!" Stev Clawsfolk began.

"Yes, yes," Lazarus grumbled. "Remaining forces will be organized to protect other investments from Vapulus thieves, or loose Crimson Eyes, or… scraprats if need be. Order will be restored, I promise you this."

For the briefest second everyone was calm. Stefanus Silverlips snorted laughter over bent arms. "There's one detail you are so conveniently leaving out. Who is getting Mr. Crimson's slickdust?"

This summoned forth a new round of angry murmuring.

"Lazacorp will take *temporary* control of any slickdust acquired," Lazarus said, with a sip of his tea meant to evoke an ease he clearly did not have. Namter stepped over and quickly refilled his master's cup. "Might I remind you all that we are in the midst of a potential military emergency. We cannot afford internecine squabbling at a moment such as this. You may all be great warriors, but you are used to being the attackers. You've never seen a *siege*. Artillery shells falling night and day, the thumping of thousands of soldier's booths, the blasts of tanks and screeching motorguns of dathkreis."

Namter could hear it, could feel it, the heavy thumping, the world shaking beneath him. He realized, almost too late, that it was not the *him here* that was shaking.

*Thump. Thump. Thump. The horrid giant lumbered above him, striding from table to table, mutant corpse to mutant corpse, each one a universe. Namter stared up from his single eye, as his vermicular body completed its shuddering metamorphosis. From what he might call his back he felt an agonizing burst of pressure. He writhed on the concrete, as two sharp, diaphanous sets of wings sprouted. From his bottom grew a set of legs, thin like an insect's, but with human toes. Small hands appeared, not his human ones, but not of the creature he inhabited either. Slender and feminine, with jagged nails, ethereal in form, not quite physical, gasiform and shimmering, the shade of blood or sangleum fumes.*

*Miga muttered something and strode over, her boots quaking the earth. Namter skittered away. Following hidden whispers emanating from his numinous, rotting flesh, he ascended a bench and towards the side of a mutant. The figure, a woman once, moaned, saliva and pus escaping her mouth. Namter could sense the soul inside of her, so pitifully human, so agonized and confused. How sweet her pain was, how right and correct. He wished he could prolong her suffering, but she was not long for the world, and he could make use of her yet. With his arms that weren't he carved a Truewords sigil into her side. Then, on fluttering wings, retreated.*

*The Truewords flashed a brief black light, and the woman's skin and flesh began to rot. Subtle at first, but within second her figure had shrunk a notable few centimetres, her face slumped, and her breathing ceased.*

*"Ah, what taurshit..." Miga began, as she noticed the body. She checked its vitals, then spat on the ground. "Gear's-fucking-grits, Lazarus, really giving me the pick of the damned litter here..."*

*Lazarus. Well if Namter needed proof of his master's involvement, here it was. The man was siphoning off mutants for his own personal projects, even as the deadline for Tribute approached. This was beyond irresponsible it was... well he didn't want to say betrayal.*

*"Now I'll have to restart the fucking infusion..." Miga muttered, unhooking the mutant. "Ahck! Can't be helped."*

*She pushed the corpse and gurney out towards the back. Namter hadn't the time to mull over his thoughts. Now free of the giant engineer's wandering gaze, he took flight.*

Namter blinked himself awake. Yimur was staring at him, as the rest of the table sniped snide asides to each other, beneath the grandiose oration of Lazarus Roache.

"We are at a turning point in the history of Stinktown, a challenge unlike any your forebearers faced. No longer are we at the edge of the world, the world has come to us, and we must show it the strength of the

Wastes!" Lazarus spoke with his hands as much as his words, exaggerated gesticulations meant to grab the attention of the squabbling lords.

Namter was still in two worlds, two bodies, and he knew he could not allow himself to fall completely into one or the other. He walked as well as flew, though the effort was quite taxing.

"While we crush the remnants of the Crimson Eyes," Lazarus continued, hair messed and graying. "We will build grand defenses. The Fist-Biters will secure the south, while the Rust Thorns defend the east, the Steel Claws will provide support where needed, and all the gangs will unite to—"

"This is absurd!" Stefanus Silverlips shouted, standing suddenly. "We are raiders, not stiffland grunts who build trenches and cower behind rubble."

"Yeah, them Imperials supply lines are thinner than a starving whorehouse harlot," Red Rust Ronnie said. "If they chose to attack, then let them have the city for a day or two. Stinktown can survive the mess. Meanwhile, we'll cut them off and starve the stiffland bastards of fuel and food!"

"That sounds like running," Britta said.

"Not running, not running!" Ronnie shouted. "I already done established that I don't do that!"

"Running will leave our backs open if Clan Vapulus tries to shove us with a shiv," Stev said.

"Not! Running!"

"Who's afraid of some half-wit mutants?" Stefanus added. "We can drive circles round them; we can drive even bigger circles 'round these imperials."

The conversation was derailing. Namter could see twitches of fear hidden in the corners of Roache's lip as the raider's rambled. The city was practically Lazacorp's, but the Wastes were still the Wastes. No better way for these raiders to regain their independence then to achieve their own victory by their own methods. Namter needed to intervene, yet all his focus was spent on trying to keep both bodies conscious.

"The losses would be far too severe." Lazarus shook his head. "We still have slaves here, and sangleum, and slickdust. You don't know the damage these imperial ghulshrews could do if allowed to have their way with our fair city."

"Yeah, Mr. Roache is right," said Erik. "We need time to evacutate, evaculade, evac—to get all our stuff out of the city."

"We can get a shit-ton out if we start now," Stefanus said. "And what's a few lost galleons of sangleum, eh? We can earn that back in a week! Especially if those Imperial idiots leave their own city open! How about that, finally taking down Holtag!"

Interested murmurs popped up around the table, some silenced by Lazarus's gazes, others disturbingly persistent.

"We have great defenses here, tremendous." Lazarus smashed his fist on the table. "We'll be giving all that up, for what? To attack some meagre stiffland slumtown?"

"I heard they've been hoarding all their taxes up there," Stev Clawsfolk said. "Drevs, Aurem, palewheat, sangleum, hoards of it. Maybe we'd gain more than we lose."

"Not to agree with Ronnie, but I'm thinking tactically," Britta said. "How many of us are trained for defensive warfare? If we keep on the move, we nullify all their fancy smancy artillery."

"It's obvious what we should do," Stefanus Silverlips said with a haughty laugh. "The only thing stopping us is some stiffland nabob who's afraid of losing his precious 'investments.'"

"I am the only one keeping this city together! I am the only supplier of slickdust, and do not think your men will choose you over slickdust!" Lazarus shouted. His voice still inspired some fear, but less and less it seemed. A few of the gang lords, slickdust addicts, were swayed instantly, nodding along with the man's words, and yet many lost their certainty as soon as his voice faded. More and more Namter could hear whispers in agreement with lord of the Silverlips. Lazarus turned a quick glance to Namter. A decisive intervention was needed, and yet Namter felt himself a cripple, unable to exist in both realities at once, his mind still stuck in the head of the buzzing spy. In order to do his duty, to help his master, he had no choice but to abandon his espionage. To give up his chance to learn the truth. It was what Lazarus was silently commanding, even if he did not know it.

So Namter closed his eyes, sucked in his breath, and made for the lavatory.

He slammed the door and locked it tight, giving himself just a moment to safely slump to the floor.

*And then he was back, fully and true, wings flickering, legs twitching, somehow more himself in this divine insect than ever in his own skin. Yet here was no time for relief. Miga could return any minute, and Namter could not long hide his human vessel in the bathroom. With his sanctified form he flitted about, desperately searching the notebook laid haphazardly around Miga's room. His astral hands assisted him greatly, able to manages pages far larger than he, as his single eye dashing from word to word. How horrid her scribblings were, and not just from her terrible handwriting. In this celestial embodiment, Namter was overcome by immense disgust at the fouls marking humans dared to call language.*

*Much of the work was mere medical records, technical notes recording sangleum doses given and effects measured. Yet their extent was prodigious, piles and piles and piles and more. He found the records going back months, then years. Many of them making reference to Lazarus, hypotheses printed on what exact concoction might prolong the man's powers, might maintain his youth, even if his 'Gift' should fail him. Miga had made mention of this project, but portrayed it as something recent, a necessary response to the failure in Huile. But these notes extended seven years, back through her exile, all the way back to the very beginning. Did Lazarus know about this? Her continuing experiments, even when she was supposedly banished? He had to, there no reason she would have worked on this project without his orders, could not have without his funding.*

*Lazarus had agreed to serve. Agreed to serve for seven years, and for seven years be given the powers needed to serve. And yet, from the very beginning, he had been secretly seeking to extend the contract. That was no simple adjustment to a deal, this was... the word betrayal came to mind again, and this time Namter buried it less deep.*

*As he was about to place the notes down, to remove his mind from this furtive avatar, he noticed a familiar set of abstracted shapes. He pulled them over and recognized the schematical outlines of the slickdust infusion-plant back in Huile, what the workers had colorfully named 'the monolith.' Why did Miga have a copy of these plans? By the sketchwork they were drawn by her hand. She had no involvement in its construction, was it purely engineering curiosity that cause her to—*

*No... these were not quite the same schematics. It was her own draft, focused on the addition Lazarus had made, the one that modulated ætheric frequency of the slickdust flow, the one based off that foul ferral's invention. Except in this version, it was not simply reducing mutation rate, as Roache had claimed, while maintaining the ætheric frequency necessary to commune with The Flayed Prince. It was altering the slickdust to match a new frequency, one labeled with a single name.* 'Lazarus.'

*What had Miga said about Lazarus's blood? That it was like a set of ætherlines, connecting slickdust to The Flayed Prince, with Lazarus as the medium. The monolith was supposed to simplify this procedure, bind the Tribute of Huile to their divine master directly. But this schematic, it wasn't cutting out Lazarus. It was removing the Prince himself.*

*An outline of a horrid plot arose in Namter's mind. No longer Lazarus as the intermediary, but alone he would stand, no longer powered by their shared master's Gift but by himself. He could abandon his contract, wield power and everlasting youth while their god sat starving under the earth. Could such perfidy truly be—*

A gunshot.

Namter returned to consciousness, letting his ætherial spy dissolve into Oathblood a kilom away. He pushed open the door, one hand on a hidden blade, the other ready to tear his off eyepatch.

There, lain sprawled beside his chair, was the body of Stefanus Silverlips, head decorated with a new crimson cavity. And on the other side of the table, pistol in hand, stood Lazarus Roache.

The room was, for the first time in the night, truly silent.

Lazarus pocketed his pistol. He looked around the room, and then towards the grandfather clock in the corner. He clapped his hands.

"Well, seems to be getting late," he said. "Let's say the matter is decided. Oh and Namter, please tidy up after our guests. It seems one of them made quite the mess."

# Chapter 32

The water felt like ice, but at least it was clean. Sylvaine scooped another bowl from the cavern pool and splashed it over herself, suds forming from the soap her maybe-captors had generously provided. She didn't mind the cold, even as she shivered. The shock gave clarity to her vision, dispelling any last vestiges of the sleeping-gas. It made her feel in control of herself, just a little, just a bit, and she needed that as she washed the slickdust and blood from her fur.

*Fur. Yes fur.* What else could it be? The mane of a wild animal. Humans, for all their potential for evil and depravity, did not do what she had done, did not go berserk, did not scratch and rip and bite into flesh. In the garage, something inside her had rejected the slickdust. But it had not been Sylvaine herself who had resisted the drug. She had not denied the force of the narcotic with a steady head and a determination built on logical analysis. Quite the opposite. Her conscious mind had given in fully to the slickdust, had surrendered instantly to its sweet acrid tang. The rejection came from something else inside of her, something animalistic, a deep instinct, something more true and more powerful than she had ever been. The real her, the beast with fur and claw and fangs. She did not dare thank this horrid thing, even if it saved her life. Better to die than become *that*.

Yet she was *that*, was a beast, an animal, a feral thing that wore human clothes and played pretend. She always had been *that*. What more proof did she need?

"You okay in there?" came a shout from behind the scrap partition set up to hide her privacy.

"Fine," she lied. She had gotten quite proficient at lying.

When she had cleaned herself as much as she reasonably could, she got back into her clothes, a fresh set washed by her ambiguous captors, and stepped out into the cavern. It was a wide room with a coarse ceiling, a few chairs, some old crates, a table, a broken minecart, and a set of cots lit by an ætherlamp.

The metal-limbed biker was there as well. He had introduced himself as Diego when she had first awoken. The man had seemed causal about the whole kidnapping thing, no locked doors, no chains, though he did have a pistol hanging upon his belt. Resurgence model, Sylvaine recognized, though she was unsure if that was a comfort.

Currently, Diego was wrist-deep in the side of his chrome horse. Sylvaine could feel the subtle pulses of æthericity and see sparks flash from the man's metal hands. As he turned to face her, she realized what she took for simple cogarm prosthetics had the intricate piping and sparkpoint fingers of æthergloves.

"You like 'em?" Diego smiled, splaying his metal fingers, letting their minute mechanisms glitter in the lamplight. "Lost my left hand taking down some slavers over by Hottart's Hogback. Some Icarnian gearhead helped set me up. As for my right... well I like myself some symmetry, you know?"

Sylvaine nodded. For a maybe kidnapper, he was fairly affable. She stepped around the man and inspected the horse-shaped golem. "This is a transmorphic two-wheeled autoequine right? Is it a 1620 model? From TwinPiston Inc., before they went under. You must have a wealthy patron, even before the Calamity these were never on the open market."

Diego laughed. "That's the most technical eloquence I've heard spoken about Frizzy since I trotted her round a Guild outpost. Most folks just say 'wow, that's a big metal horse.' I can tell you've done your research."

Despite herself, Sylvaine smiled, though she wasn't sure reading through old, browned engineer's catalogs for fun counted as 'research.'

"But no, it's not an original, it's a re-creation. Based on some rusted-out wrecks I found in a dusthome."

"Wait, you made these?" Sylvaine asked.

"Oh yeah, us Wastefolk ain't all club-dragging barbarians," Diego said, with a sass-infused inflexion. "But feel free to take a look at it. I'd love to hear an Academy-trained engineer's opinion."

"You saw my ætherglove?" Sylvaine said, surprised the man would consider her an engineer, even with the evidence.

Diego laughed. "I've heard about you, Sylvaine! Your work on negative-density generators, your analysis and sabotage of Blackwood Row. All impressive stuff."

"Not all impressive..." Sylvaine said, thinking back to that horrific moment in Icaria. Her invention a smoldering wreck, her professor dead, slickdust tearing through her veins, Lazarus's word echoing through her skull, mocking her, commanding her. In response came a fury roaring, a rage, a wild something from deep inside of her. It had now twice saved her life, and she despised more than even the tycoon.

Diego waved the statement away as if a buzzing fly. "Gear's-grits, what engineer worth their pin hasn't blown up an invention or five?"

"Sure," Sylvaine said, wishing it were all that simple. "And you've figured all this through your own... research?" She had been under the impression that she had more or less successfully fallen off the map after Icaria. It was concerning that this random someone was aware of her past.

"Well, I've also stalking y'all for the last few weeks," Diego said.

"Ah, so those bird calls?" Sylvaine asked.

Diego whistled out a soot-sparrow trill between his metal fingers. "Yeah, just me calling Frefis."

"Frefis?"

"Freedom's Fist," Diego explained. "That Salvi gentleman you probably saw. Soft-spoken, but a good lad to have in a scuffle."

"Ah."

There was an awkward silence, water drip-drip-dripping into the cavern pool, as she pondered how to ask the question that was on her mind. Finally, she just asked it blunt. "So, are we prisoners?"

"You and the hot monk?" Diego asked. "No. There's not bounty on your heads. Just unfortunate that you happened to get roped all in on this. Once we got everything sorted, you'll be free to go."

"Oh," Sylvaine said, half-relieved, half-very-much-not. He had not mentioned Marcel's name. If the Imperial got her just desserts that was one thing, but Sylvaine had already invested immense amounts of sweat and stress to keeping Marcel from getting himself killed. She'd rather not lose all that to the avarice of some bounty hunters, regardless of how impressive their rides were.

"As for the other two," Diego continued, reading her expression. "Well, that's up to the boss-lady. Things have gotten complicated, politics and all that, not a simple smack-and-drag job, lots of things to balance, if you understand."

"I do not," Sylvaine said honestly. As she did a figure walked past the open doorway, gray and horned, a salvi, tall for a human, but short and slender for a man of his own kind. The salvi snapped his figures and gestured down the direction he was walking. Diego nodded, and as the salvi passed, Sylvaine noticed a familiar odor.

"Kayip!" she exclaimed, as the man wandered into the room, dressed in a clean set of linen clothes.

"Sylvaine!" the monk said, as she rushed up and embraced him. She would have been taken back by the brashness of her own excitement were she not so damn happy to see the man.

"Are you all right?" Kayip asked. "Are you unharmed?"

"I'm okay, Kayip," she said, and she almost meant it. The man embraced her back with careful tenderness, as if afraid she might shatter at a wrong movement.

"They did not do anything to you, yes?" Kayip asked, with a hint of genuine fear.

"No, no, it's really been fine," she said, calming herself with Kayip's comforting warmth.

"I'm glad ya'll having a heartwarming reunion and all that," Diego said, walking towards the doorway. "But we should get going. Boss-lady's almost ready,"

"Ready for what?" Kayip asked.

"To wake your friend."

* * *

They followed Diego down a winding pathway, past crevices cut into the walls, dust-engulfed vents, rooms filled with fungus-encased crates, and old mine tracks which disappeared down darkened distances that even Sylvaine could not see the end of. Finally he took them to a carved-out grotto, a bit larger than the one she had awoken in, though of even simpler decorations, just lamps and canvas bags. There sat Marcel, in chains, on the floor, snoring. Across the room sat Belona, also in chains, but very much awake. She glared up with suspicion as Sylvaine and Kayip entered.

Sylvaine wondered what the imperial knew, what she had assumed. That they had sold her out to buy their own freedom? An insulting presumption! Sure, Sylvaine would be happy to sell the imperial were she given the opportunity, but she hadn't yet.

In the far corner of a room a woman was hunched over, grinding something in a mortar. "Thanks Frefis," the woman muttered, as the clean-shaven salvi handed her some herbs. She stood and turned, pressing pestle against stone, as she walked forward. The woman was tall, with tanned skin and off-blond hair. She wore a taur-leather jacket, heavily patched, with a military medal sewed in around the sleeve, of UCCR design by the look of it. Her eyes were a dulled blue, weary but still sharp, a half-smile upon her lips.

The whole situation perplexed Sylvaine. Usually bounty hunters were rougher with their prey, even when going for the alive half of 'dead or alive.' But there was a strange, inexplicable cordiality to the three. Sylvaine might have guessed that the bounty hunter captain knew Kayip, the monk did seem to have a past with many shady wastefolk, but neither had made any indication of familiarity. Perhaps the bounty hunters wanted something out of them, and thought the friendly approach the wiser. Then again, getting knocked out by noxious gases hadn't exactly felt 'friendly.'

"Sorry about all this," the woman said as she grinded the herbal mash. "Compressed chokeshroom fumes can spin someone silly, and most people I use it on actually deserve the surprise. Nonfatal, usually. But you three seem to be doing well, and I don't intend to lose this one."

With that she bent down and placed a few dabs of the green gunk on top of Marcel's lip. The man groaned and tilted his head.

"Come on..." the woman muttered, as she spread some more.

*"Leave... me..."* Marcel moaned. *"Slow you... slow you..."* he tossed his arm down in the vague direction of his cogleg, and let out a groan.

"Come on, get up Talwar," the woman said, a hint of genuine fear in her voice. "You're safe. Get up. Get up Talwar."

Marcel blinked his eyes open, face swaying, gaze unfocused. He glanced around, not seeming to see anything in particular. His hand went up to wipe some of the drool from his lips, and he caught the ointment. He stared at the green marking his finger, and then up at the woman kneeling in front of him. He blinked again, this time in disbelief. His mouth moved, slow and silent, until he swallowed something back, and was finally able to find his voice.

"Alba?"

The woman chuckled. "Who else would it be, Mar?"

"You left... you left and now you've..." Marcel reached up, as if to touch her face, but his chains clanged taut. He stared down at his handcuff. "I don't underst... what?"

"Protocols of the trade," Alba said. "I finally got the whole bounty hunter thing going. Sorry, I never had the chance to update you, but you know how two years can just slip by like—" she snapped her finger.

"Then that means... I would..." Marcel began, words still awkward on his tongue, but getting less so.

"Yes you have a bounty on your head, Mar. A big one. 70,000 frascs. Shit most gang lords don't get bounties that chunky. Placed on you by our good old Citizens' Confederacy."

"The UCCR?" Marcel said with genuine shock. "No, no that doesn't make any sense."

"Talk me through it Talwar," Alba said. "Because from where I'm kneeling it makes all the sense in the world. One of the biggest sangleum refineries in the Wastes goes up in violent revolt, a city once the prize of a hard-fought war finds it's dial set from peaceful productivity to violent riot, and in the middle, striding through a trampled city hall? One Marcel Talwar, the only full-blooded human to be seen walking free with the rebel mutant insurgents, making deals with their leader while the rest of the Resurgence-loyal government is chained and bruised, if not dead."

"That's not—!" Marcel began, trying and failing to stand up, face red. "I wasn't— Desct! Desct! Not some insurgent leader, not some riot, Demiurge damn it, it was Desct, and I was fighting for his freedom!"

"Calm yourself Mar. I'm just saying how Phenia's representatives explained it, how the story's been told. I'm not saying it's the truth. And yes, yes I know it's Desct. I saw him. *Fuck.*" The woman paused, bit her lip as she stared off a moment into wall. "Fuck, I saw what the bastards did to him. So, I know it's not that simple. But I got to ask, as part of my job, as my duty, I have to ask you, in your own words, what happened?"

Marcel sighed. "What happened? What happened is it all went to shit, after you left, just as you said. Used me as a decoration, like you said, turned my ideals into a weakness, like you said. You were right, you were always right. I never cleaned up the city, just wasted years as the mess grew bigger, even when I couldn't see it."

Alba shook her head. "Don't recall prophesying all of that. Just thought it wasn't the right city for me. Smelled too artificial, too Roachey. But half the Border States smell foul in one way or another, most don't go this bad. If I had the power of clairvoyance to see this shitstorm, I would have dragged both you and Desct out kicking and screaming. But give me the details, Marcel, the step by step. Please."

Marcel leaned his head back, staring up at the shadows sent by the ætherlamp as if they were not mapping the topography of the cavern, but that of his mind, his memories. His eyes flickered back and forth, his forehead wrinkled, he opened his mouth to speak, then didn't, then tried again, words coming out in ones and two, but without any direction. Finally, after a minute of this, he sucked in his breath, and just started talking.

The story came out, not all at once, not all in a linear and sensible fashion, but in its fullness it did reach some coherency. Most of it was familiar to Sylvaine, she had been present, but there were details to his telling that she didn't know, small facts and personal tidbits mostly, fragments of the man's past she hadn't been aware of. There was his experience in war, which he spoke of in an inconsistent manner, sometimes presenting it as a tale of heroism, reported by some cinegraph announcer. But then he would halter, unsure, as if he didn't quite know what had happened, or rather, what it meant. He fluctuated between portraying the loss of his leg as some noble sacrifice in the line of duty, or an ironic tragedy, some deserved punishment for a deep moral transgression. Or maybe, he mused, it was just a thing that had happened, a piece of lead wandering without purpose into his leg, a roll of the dice that meant nothing.

When he got to Lazarus Roache more certainty returned, alongside rage. Strangely enough, much of the anger seemed focused on himself, how gullible he had been, how idiotic. This fury burned quick, shouts and curses, gestures tossed as far as chains would allow, until Marcel sighed and slumped down with resignation.

"It was... simpler for it to all be true, right?" he muttered, shaking his head. "Everything just fit together, for the most part. Lazarus constructed this whole world, this whole painted-fucking-backdrop, and there was just no way to tell it was just a play. Except... there were holes in it. There were always holes, hints, threads I should have pulled. If I had taken the letter... if I had pushed further, in different directions, questions some of the... It was just... all built around me. That's what it was. In all his lies I just fit in so perfectly. I was the champion of Huile, a great private investigator keeping the streets safe. If it wasn't true, all a lie, then I was a lie..." he paused on that thought. "Yeah, I guess that's what he was counting on. And Demiurge knows if left alone when I would have seen it for myself."

Part of Sylvaine wanted to chide Marcel for failing to notice the wool placed so blatantly over his eyes. And yet the greater part of her felt sympathy for him. Sylvaine could find parallels with her own experience, how Roache had played a similar game, building up a narrative where she could be who she always wanted to be, needed to be. Marcel's tale may have lacked slickdust, but Sylvaine realized that had not been the central ingredient to the man's deceit. It was not money, nor power, nor slickdust, the man offered, but a sense of purpose, a fantasy of self-fulfillment, an escape from despair, whether hers or Marcel's. Such was too great a prize to scorn easily. Marcel had been an idiot not to see the trickery, but she had been an idiot as well. It was easy to be an idiot when the alternative was to be a monster.

As the narrative went on, it reached the point of revelation, the truth of Huile revealed, the shanty towns, the corpses, the mutations, the lies, the murder. It was how Sylvaine recalled it, told with a mix of fury and poorly-buried guilt. Some of the details were a bit off, Marcel acted as if searching for Kayip during the revolt in Blackwood Row had been his idea, when Sylvaine recalled quite clearly that he had been prepared to leave the monk. Still, most of his telling was close enough to the truth. He finished as they left Huile, the city aflame, off to bring Lazarus Roache to justice. Of course, that part of the story hadn't ended where he hoped.

Silence fell upon the grotto, for a moment, at least.

"Well, that's a real mog-lizard shit of a situation," Diego said.

"It does corroborate with what we were told by Desct," Frefis added.

"Don't tell them that!" Diego nearly shouted. "You never tell prisoners what other prisoners said, they might change their story up."

"He already told his story," Frefis protested.

"Yeah, but maybe he got more to say, and now he knows that—" Diego's rambling was cut off by a single raised finger from Alba. She nodded, thinking. Finally, she let out a deep sigh, one that sounded as if it had been building for months.

"I'm not sure what I hoped you would say, Mar. It's not that I thought Desct was a liar, or wanted to believe that but…"

"So, you believe me," Marcel said.

"I know you, Marcel." Alba nodded softly. "You do a little thing with your eye whenever you lie. So yes, I believe you, I believe Desct."

"Then tell the UCCR. They must see the truth, they have to! We're soldiers, war he… war heroes." Sylvaine noticed Belona scowl and grunt. "I mean, we're reputable. And the facts are all there, Desct has the evidence, the pictures, hundreds of firsthand accounts. We have the truth!"

Diego laughed. "Kid's naïve," he said, though Sylvaine was fairly certain the man was younger than Marcel.

"Lambert's testified the exact opposite," Alba said. "Desct gave him over, as a sign of goodwill. Would have stopped him had I been there, but once I got to the city, the damage was already done. Lambert cooked up a real good story, and there's plenty of City Hall folk eager to follow his telling. And there's the corpses, of police, of officials, of the General's damn nephew, and plenty of civilians too. As far as the UCCR is concerned, Desct ain't even Desct, Desct is dead of wastelung and that mutant claiming is identity is just some rebel terrorist, holding a city hostage. Well, Desct *is* holding Huile hostage, technically. Only let out a few people as part of negotiation, even executed a couple who were trying to coup him. I vouched that Desct was indeed Desct, for what little good that did. Things were not going well when I left. Inferno I even heard talk that they had already sent messengers out to find Lazarus, hear his side of the story, with quite friendly ears. Mar, if things don't turn around, they might well attack the city, reinstate Roache."

"They can't!" Marcel said, lunging forward, strugglingly against his restraint. "That's not—That's insane, they have to see the truth, they have to! They—shit can you please just let me out of these fucking cuffs!"

Alba pulled out some keys from her pocket and stared at them. Diego started clicking his tongue.

"Oh, no, no, come on boss-lady, don't get soft…" he muttered. "We have a job. A contract. 70,000 frascs!"

"They were in love," Kayip offered.

"Every single one of my exes would have tossed my corpse out to the Wastes for 70,000 frascs!" Diego shouted.

"Would you have done the same?" Frefis asked.

"For 70,000? Inferno-be-frozen, of course I would!" Diego folded his arms. "I ain't dumb. Half the bastards would have deserved it, anyhow."

"There's only one small detail that's confusing me." Alba said, shaking the key. "Desct's story mentioned you three. He didn't say anything about her." She gestured towards Belona.

"I'm—" Belona began.

"She just a mercenary," Marcel interrupted, eye shifting to the corner of his socket for a split second. How had Sylvaine never noticed that tic before? Alba turned to him, and the man caught himself and kept his gaze steady as he talked. "Picked her up in a place called Bridgetown. Had an old feud with Roache, screwed over her squad way back when."

"So, no bounties on her head?" Alba asked.

"Not that I'm aware of," Marcel said. "You get yourself into trouble, Christina?"

"Uh." Belona paused. "No, no. I was working then as... a bartender. Did not think I would have a chance for revenge until I met these three."

"A bartender eh?" Alba said with a chuckle. "Christina... let's make up a surname as well, Avenarius, Aquila perhaps?"

"Weber," Marcel said.

"Christina Weber," Alba said, pacing. "Now I went through this Miss Weber's... it is Miss, correct? There is no Mr. Weber?"

"Unmarried," Belona said.

"Ah, of course, it's a busy life, mercenary work. I was just wondering, you know, as part of my *due diligence* why a random mercenary would have this." Alba pulled from her pocket an emblem. On cracked wood, covered in faded velvet, stood a lion in glit-bronze. Underneath it was written, in shining letters, *Agrippus*.

If Marcel was panicking, he hid it well, the imperial only slightly worse.

"That's one of your trophies, right Christina?" he said.

"Yes," Belona said. "Found it on an imperial... bitch's corpses."

"I recall you telling us that," Kayip interjected.

"Now don't you start!" Alba snapped at the monk. She turned and walked uncomfortable close to Marcel, waving the emblem as if it were a weapon. "Come on Mar! For her! Really?"

"What?" Marcel said.

"You think I don't know what General Belona Agrippus looks like?" Alba shouted. "Inferno, I've been trying to think of a way to assassinate this monster for the past two years, it just never worked out. Do you know what's she's done, Talwar? They don't call her the Butcher of Tesakovgrad for nothing! Do you know how many she's killed? Our men and women, fuck, our friends even!"

Sylvaine couldn't help but agree. The imperial had already ruined their chances to catch Roache, which was the only reason they were keeping her around. Why stick their neck out for the woman?

"I... she's not," Marcel began, eye flicking rapidly. "There's been some misunderstanding."

"Do not waste more breath," Belona said. "I am her, she is me. General Agrippus. The Conqueror, The Lioness of Vastium. I bear no shame for my actions. You wished to capture me, to kill me? Well, you have succeeded. Consider yourself lucky, Talwar, it seems I shall not have my vengeance upon you. Do what you will, let your excuse for justice fall upon my head. But I will apologize for nothing."

Alba laughed, deep and free and bitter.

"Yeah, I wasn't asking for one. You think I asked every murderer, rapist, and slaver to say they're sorry before I put a bullet in the back of their neck?" She kicked the woman to the floor, before turning to Marcel.

"Hey—" he started, but Alba ignored him. With a grunt, she unchained him from the wall and began pulling him, though pointedly did not unlock his handcuffs.

"You two are free," Alba said, gesturing with her chin to Sylvaine and Kayip. "Rest a little, and come morning Diego here will guide you out." Belona glared from the floor, face covered in dirt, not bothering to push herself up. As Alba pulled Marcel out the room, she glared back at the imperial with matching enmity. "We have much more to talk about, Mar. And we don't need enemy ears listening in."

# CHAPTER 33

As Marcel followed Alba through the winding corridors and twisting caverns, he tried to organize his thoughts. This was easier to attempt than succeed at, for they swirled around at an impossible pace, bouncing off the concavities of his skull. Alba was alive, but she had left him, and then she saved him, and then chained him. He was so ecstatic to see her, but bitter memories sat on his lips. She could help them take down Roache, if she didn't sell out their last chance, and his freedom, for a few thousand frascs. The woman was everything she ever was, but not a bit like he remembered.

Then there was Huile. The city he had saved, the city he had doomed, the city Desct liberated and covered in blood. He was relieved to hear his friend was alive, terrified about what happened, furious at the evils of the Resurgence, which stood for all that was good, confident that they would see the error of their ways, and equally certain they would never realize their mistake.

And Belona... That was another storm in of itself, the contradictions there too convoluted to even try to unravel. When had everything become so complicated? He was a good guy, did the right thing, always had. It should be that simple, and yet he couldn't shake the feeling that he had, in some manner concrete or abstract, messed everything up.

What struck him most, as he kept pace with his captain/ex-lover/captor, was how he was keeping it all together, relatively speaking, not falling apart in the hurricane of incongruities that was his mind. He even noted the odd resemblance between this moment and the wartime horrors of the Huile Underway without breaking out in a cold sweat, the only symptom being a dull pain in his cogleg. Perhaps his calm was thanks to the fact that each idea that ricocheted round his head collided with equal force, balancing out in a perfect cacophony of roiling emotions that left him just vaguely dissociated. Or perhaps that was just the lingering effects of the chokeshroom gas. His tongue felt oddly numb, and his nose was itchy and warm.

Finally, after what might have been many minutes, or perhaps just a few seconds, Marcel couldn't keep track, Alba pushed open a door of scarwood into a pleasantly lit and surprisingly lavish room. Bronze sconces and a violet rug, bookshelves, and cabinets, and an old dusthome armchair in faded leather. On the wall hung a portrait of a crimson-skinned mutant, garbed in fine robes, rifle upon his back, half-naked mutant women by his feet, portrayed not in simple oil paint, but upon a closer glance, a collage of colored metal flakes glued with care to produce an image equally artful and tasteless.

"This is your base of operations past two years?" Marcel asked.

Alba scoffed and gestured to the man in the painting. "Not my style. Was this guy's. Tiberius Hornclacker, one of the greatest raiders in all Stinktown, terror of the Wastes, until I finished him off here. A king abandoned in his grand castle, nowhere to run. His execution echoing through its ennobled halls."

Her voice was as melodious as Marcel remembered, but also rougher, more bitterly sardonic.

"Sounds like you've been keeping busy," he said. "Alba's adventures out in the Wastes? I'd read that pulp."

Alba studied the chipping façade of the dead man. Marcel found he couldn't stop staring at her, her short-cut hair, her dimpled chin, her soft bent lips, beautiful even as they had become chapped and scabbed from wind and sun. He tried not to blink, as if she might somehow disappear should he stop looking. Then Marcel felt the weight of his manacles and reminded himself that her sticking around was maybe not such a great thing either.

Finally, she shook her head. "Truth be told, I'm overselling it. Tibbie's star had already faded by the time I had caught him. Sad sack was piss-drunk, blubbering at the end. You know, the Hornclackers nearly ruled Stinktown before that cult moved in. They killed off near all the mutant raiders, chased the rest into the arms of petty, waste-wandering clans.

Theses mines and tunnels were the Hornclackers' secret hunting grounds. I think I might be the only one now who knows their full extent, their contortions and convolutions."

"Cult?" Marcel asked.

Alba nodded. "That Unblind Brotherhood deal. Thought they might have some connection with Lazacorp, wasn't positive until Desct told me the whole tale."

Marcel nodded. Memories of Verus and his vaguely religious and distinctly mad rantings came back. He would have dismissed the ravings wholesale, were not for the disturbing powers the foreman had summoned forth, that whip of black fire and that horrible, horrible eye, that nightmare void in the man's skull that seemed a portal to Inferno itself.

"We took down their leader," he said, suppressing a shudder.

Alba nodded. "Yeah, Desct told me, said one of his fellow mutants stabbed Verus."

"Yeah, and I was," Marcel paused thinking, images flowing through his head of Sylvaine blowing up the tread-driller, Kayip swinging his azure sword, and himself... "Well, I was there. I threw something."

"Sounds like a fun time," Alba said, almost smiling, but catching herself. "It's not been so *fun* since you left."

"I can imagine," Marcel said. "Wait, before, did you say before that Desct was *executing* people?"

"A few dozen, yeah," Alba said blithely.

"A few dozen!" Marcel nearly shouted. "What in Inferno happened in Huile! Desct can't be... He's supposed to be bringing peace!"

"Shit happened, Mar." Alba leaned back on a crumbling bookshelf decorated with carved animal bones. "Sounded like he was fighting a small-scale insurgency even before the Resurgence army started knocking at his gate. Old cops, Lazacorp workers, city hall bureaucrats, mobs of Huile citizens who were pissed about dead relatives, or the fires, or just wanted to bash some mutant heads. So yeah, there's been some summary executions by the sound of it."

Marcel sat back, onto an old chair that gave a strange crunching noise he chose to ignore. "*Summary executions?* Demiurge Alba, that sounds like a euphemism to murder."

"Of course it is. 'Execution' is a euphemism for state murder, 'bounty hunting' is a euphemism for paid murder, 'war' is a euphemism for mass murder. That's how things are. The man isn't wanton, isn't arbitrary. I don't envy Desct's situation, or what he's had to do."

"Maybe if he surrendered peacefully..." Marcel began.

Alba laughed without humor. "I was in the room with some of those Resurgence officers, playing a pitiful diplomat. They promised all sort of clemencies when talking with Desct over the voxbox, but when they're alone with only humans, they speak their blunt, bloody truth. Desct has people to protect, and he can't do that by surrendering what little he has."

Marcel opened his mouth, and then just sighed. He didn't know if he could judge Desct, wasn't sure why he so wanted to.

"Lazarus. He's the cause of this..." Marcel mumbled, more for himself than Alba. "He's the monster at the center of everything."

"Perhaps," Alba said, a soft touch to her voice. Then it sharpened suddenly. "But it seems to me that you're already fine with monsters."

"What do you mean?"

"Belona griffon-fucking-Agrippus is what I mean," Alba spat. "How long? How long did you know?"

Marcel stared at the floor, and said nothing, willing for the subject to change itself. When it didn't, he just shrugged. "I'm not sure what you want from me."

"What, I w—I just told you! Are we talking from Holtag, or last night? The context changes things."

Marcel scratched his chin. "A few days ago, in a place called Narida Heights."

"I'm familiar," Alba said. When Marcel glanced up, she snorted. "I had Diego trailing you. So I know wasn't a few days, Mar, it was a week. A week with—"

"The Butcher of Tesakovgrad, I know, I know."

"But you're defending her," Alba said, with a jab of her finger.

"I'm not defending her!" Marcel protested, chains shaking. "I'm just... You'd put bullets in her and take her head in for a bounty."

"Yeah, and make a clean fifty-k too," Alba said. "Not that I wouldn't put her in the earth unpaid."

"She's part of our... our team, our posse, our whatever you call it. Our squad!" Marcel finally decided. "Would you let Desct die, or Henri, or R—"

"Lambert? Absolutely," Alba cut in. "Listen, I know you never had the stomach for killing people, so just let me take my—"

"That's not it!" Marcel stood suddenly. "I've... killed people. I don't enjoy it, but I'm strong enough to do what I need to do."

"Then what?" Alba's eyes widened suddenly. "Demiurge, please don't tell me you're fucking her."

"What?" Marcel stumbled over his words, stunned at the absurd accusation. "Is that what this is about, jealousy?"

"Not jealousy," Alba said. "You can do what you want, you're a free man, I'm a free woman. More the mindset. You have a type."

"A type?!"

Alba shrugged. "It might not even be sexual, you know. Again, I don't care, but if she's used her... charisma, or whatever to convince you that she's somehow changed."

"It's not about that! It's not about me being unwilling to pull a trigger, and it's not about her being a decent person secretly, or... or..." Was he crying? He felt a wetness on his cheeks. "Fuck Alba. After everything we did. To her?"

*"To her?"*

"Under Lazacorp, what we did to the imperial army there." His metal leg wobbled, as he felt two limbs compete for the same brain space, neither quite real, both in pain. "The sangleum gas. Thousands of them. Not in some heroic battle, not standing on their two legs, gun in hand. Sleeping, screaming, drowning in their own fucking blood, not knowing what had happened to them."

"After killing plenty of our own," Alba said. "Forgive me for not weeping over some blue-caps."

"I told myself that we had to do it, because if we didn't then the Principate would just do the same to us, to civilians, unleash their own gas-fueled massacre. But was that true? Or just a convenient lie to wipe away our own moral qualms?"

Alba rotated her wrist indecisively. "In this instance? Who knows? The Imperials are no strangers to massacres, but it doesn't make much tactical sense to slaughter the civilians you intend to use as your labor base. And the whole story came from Roache's mouth... I had my doubts then, but you never know the truth on the battlefield. 'Fog of war' they call it, or just the brass lying out their ass. All I knew was what the imperials had already done was unforgiveable. Is unforgivable."

The two were silent a long moment. Alba glanced up at the buzzing ætherlamp in the corner. Her gaze was distant, her cerulean eyes fainter than he recalled, ringed by weariness. Her tongue tapped her teeth as she searched for words. "You don't remember Tesakovgrad, do you?"

Marcel tried to come up with a reasonable answer, but the truth was it had slipped from him. So many cities with so many problems had smothered the pages of Phenian newspapers and strained the voice of newsboys and caravan gossipers. There was always some new tragedy, some massacre somewhere.

"About eight months before Huile," Alba said. "Up by the border of Anklav and Videk. North of the Atsols, so Phenians didn't much care, might as well have been on the other side of the planet. But I saw what she had done. Tesakovgrad had been a city, a real one, not a town with pretensions like Huile. History and culture, and people, Mar, tens of thousands of them. When I got there, it was a graveyard of rubble and smoke, bodies buried under a millennia of grand architecture and clustered apartments. The city had survived the Calamity, but not her. No one ever have a count to number of dead, but it wasn't just soldiers, Mar, it was innocent men, women, children. All of them sacrificial lambs for her ambition. Even if Huile were to be torched brick by brick it would not come close to matching what I saw that day. So, if you want to know why she has to die, it's not for my revenge, it's not even for Huile's sake. If you claim to believe in justice, even imperfect, flawed, human justice, then I think the logic is pretty clear."

Marcel stared at nothing, trying to weigh the horrors he'd seen with Alba's words. He didn't want to believe it, even though it was so very plausible, even though he knew it was true. Why was it suddenly so hard to hate Belona? He had hated her just a day ago, would have gladly given her over for her just execution. Did he feel like he owed her, somehow, for helping them escape, for pulling him up out of the ash and slickdust in that Stinktown garage? It had been her fault that they had been there in the first place. Or in Holtag, she had broken them out, but it was her Principate who had captured them. Yet she had never abandoned him, and so he felt he couldn't abandon her. But why should he be bound to her, just because they had fought the same enemy? It was all so easy when he was good, and she evil, but now he didn't know what he was, and that somehow blurred things. She deserved whatever happened to her, perhaps, but then what did he deserve when all the scales were balanced?

"I haven't forgiven her," Marcel said finally. "Once this is all said and done, we're agreed to fight it out. Me and Belona, a duel."

"A duel?" Alba said, a smile sneaking onto her lips. "Marcel, you're a terrible shot."

"That's my problem. But we can't just kill her, after everything, and I mean, we're so close to Lazarus now and she could... I don't know." Marcel sighed. "I just don't fucking know anymore. I'm just... trying do the right thing. I didn't think it'd be so Demiurged-damned complicated."

"Yeah, well, welcome to the world," Alba said, stepping near to stare at him, studying his expression. Marcel studied her back. Two years, nearly three, and all the while he had kept the memories, of them together, of that night, under the moon, clothes tossed free, Alba under the moonlight, skin a pure snow pale. Except it wasn't, was it? It was tanned deep, cut with a dozen small scars. Was this new, the price of her new career? Somehow he didn't think it was. He tried recalling that night again, in all its little details which he had cherished like pearls. There was a hazy doubt now, as if what he recalled was more a cinegraph recreation, than the real raw, and slightly muddy truth.

"You know, they want me to bring you back to Huile," Alba said.

"Go back?" Marcel asked. "Wait, who's 'they?'"

"General Levair and the UCCR command overall. My patrons, if you will. Desct too, sort of. He thinks it's a terrible idea, but he's reached the point where all ideas are terrible."

"No, no," Marcel said, chains shaking. "We're still so close! Roache is still a threat, right? If the Confederacy is reaching out to him, he could muck everything up, twist their minds. I have to stop him first!"

Alba put up her hands in a plaintive gesture. "I'm just the messenger here. I'm not saying you should go. I'm not saying you *shouldn't* go either. Things are bad Mar, real bad, and probably have gotten a lot worse since I've last checked. On the other hand, Demiurge knows if you'd actually make a difference, I couldn't. But you Phenians were always better at talking posh, so maybe?"

Marcel shook his head. He had made the right choice, he had to have, he needed to take Roache before he started brewing more chaos, that's what they all agreed on. Or, well Desct hadn't been so confident, but once Marcel took down the tycoon, he could return swiftly to Huile. That's what he had told himself for the past month, and yet Roache was still very much untaken down. And the flames of Huile had burned all the meanwhile.

He stared down at his handcuffs, and then back at Alba. "So do I have a choice, then? These say I'm still your prisoner."

Alba sighed, then pulled the keys out of her pocket and tossed them to Marcel. He unchained himself, then rubbed his wrists. They felt almost naked now, not that he was complaining.

"I wasn't going to drag you down there, unwilling" Alba said softly. "Half the reason I took the job was to keep other bounty hunters off."

"You could have fooled me," Marcel said, with a slight chuckle.

"Well, it was the Agrippus thing that fucked me up," she spat on the ground, then rubbed it in with her boot. "Shit, I almost believed you had turned traitor. I mean I know you wouldn't, but damn it Mar... *Her?* Never mind. There's more pressing matters, I suppose."

"So, what do you think then? About Huile?"

"Might be a mess if you went back, honestly," Alba said. "Lambert's been trying to convince the brass that they should execute you on the spot for treason should you pop up your head."

"Lambert?" Marcel asked. He had once considered Huile's Minister of Justice to be one of his few true friends. Then Lambert had tried to murder him. Yet somehow this new betrayal still surprised Marcel, twisting his stomach one knot more.

"I guess slickdust stays in one's system longer than I thought," Marcel finally said. "Lambert's still taking Roache orders after all these weeks."

"Slickdust?" Alba said, with odd incredulity.

"Yeah, saw him take some in his tea."

"Maybe he did," Alba snorted. "But let's face it, that slug-ass didn't need some ætheric drug to corrupt him."

"It's how Lazacorp was controlling City Hall," Marcel explained. "How Roache was able to blind them to what was happening in Blackwood Row."

Alba laughed, then tried to catch herself, and failed. She rubbed her weary eyes as the bewildered giggles left her. "Somehow I've forgotten how... naïve you can be Marcel."

"Inferno are you talking about!" Marcel shouted, taken aback at a sudden fury that burst from him. "After everything I— was the Battle Under Huile not enough?! Was losing my leg not enough? I'm just a naïve little man who can't take care of himself despite everything I've—"

Alba raised her hand in a military scout's signal for silence, and despite his rambling rage some drilled-in instinct from training silenced Marcel, though his thoughts rushed onward like a unrailed train.

"I shouldn't have said naïve." Alba spoke carefully and slowly. "That's not what I meant, not exactly. You were always idealistic, and that's not always a bad thing. You really do believe in the cause, genuinely, whatever that cause is. Don't meet many folks out here with that sort of... moral conviction."

"But ideals can be a weakness," Marcel said, repeating bitter wisdom Alba had once shared with him on a chilly night outside Huile.

"Sure, maybe," she said, as if it were the first time the idea had been tossed. "Demiurge knows the Resurgence loves to squeeze all it can out of big words like 'freedom' and 'liberty.' That hypocrisy is everywhere, but not with you, you're not hypocritical, in that way at least. But sometimes that hypocrisy shows hints of itself, and you don't seem to want to see it. You want to believe only in those beautiful ideals."

Marcel let himself fall back into the chair. He was still angry; he just couldn't tell in which direction. Fury at her tasted so similar to rage at himself. "And because of that blindness, I wasted myself in Huile, just like you said."

"I never said that."

"You did! Just before you abandoned me," Marcel protested, and his words somehow sounded so petulant.

"I never abandoned you." Alba shook her head. "Inferno, I tried all I could to get you to leave that damn city. But it wasn't my choice to make."

"If I left..." Marcel let the idea hang there, in the air. If he left, then he would have never discovered all of Lazacorp's crimes. Except he didn't, that was Kayip. Still, he was the one who used the schematics to sabotage the Lazacorp facilities... well actually that was mostly Sylvaine. But without Marcel they never would have gotten the schematics necessary to take down Blackwood Row. Unless Desct had just sent them elsewhere. And then there were all the people, the faux criminals he had arrested, under the machinations of Lazarus Roache. All that suffering for his blindness... except that Roache would have likely just found another patsy. Marcel had fantasized about confronting Alba again, proving the necessity of his decision, how it had changed everything, how he had proven himself the hero that he knew himself to be... or had been told he was. And yet now, thinking back, he could not for the life of himself decide if he had been central to everything, or just a gear that could have been swapped out for any other.

"Maybe I did waste myself. I was certainly a shit private investigator."

"Well, you got the whole idea from a pulp," Alba said.

"Hey that's not—" Marcel let the protest fall before finishing. It wasn't exactly *untrue*.

"In fairness, you three did blow up a hefty chunk of Lazacorp's slave-fueled refineries. That ain't a waste in my book. And all of this as well..." she gestured vaguely. "You got yourself a crew together, and you've gotten damn close to taking out Roache."

Marcel turned and studied the irregular grains in the wooden bureau beside him. "Yeah, except now everything's turned ass-end up, with our cover blown."

"There's that imperial army marching in," Alba scratched her chin. "Might not be a bad distraction."

Marcel shrugged. "Belona's idea. But who knows, they could just as well make peace when they realize her provocations were all empty taurshit."

Alba thought on this, foot tapping. "Surprisingly devious for an imperial. I kind of like it, the two monsters of the Wastes tearing each other down. Just might need a little spark to get things going... Then you three would have your shot, you chance at revenge."

"Revenge?" Marcel said. "This is about justice! About protecting Huile!"

"Justice is just revenge with more paperwork," Alba said dryly. "And I want some too. I don't know what will happen with Huile, what the U-doubleC-R will end up doing, but I know I'll be a little more at peace with that swine-souled tycoon in the dirt."

For not the first time that night Marcel sighed deeply. "If you think the Resurgence is going to end up... attacking Huile, if you truly believe they're that vile, why did you enlist?"

Now it was Alba's turn to sigh. "It's all relative. The UCCR at its worse is what the Principate are like on a normal day. And truth to be told, I like the Resurgence. I'm just not daft enough to think it's actually something as simple as... good."

"So you think it's a lesser evil," Marcel said.

"It's *my* lesser evil, my occasionally corrupt home. The Citizens' Confederacy executes more monsters than saints, it frees more cities than it burns. At the end of the day, there's a power vacuum out here, and when it's not filled you get, well you get Stinktown. Demiurge knows even with as much graft as Phenia allows they wouldn't have let Lazacorp go as far as they did if they truly understood what was happening. I know General Levair, he's not a bastard by nature, at least not any more than any other general. He just can't accept the truth of what's happened. If blood flows on the streets of Huile again, it's going to be from an inability to understand their Confederacy's own failures, rather than any sort of pure malice. There is some good in the Resurgence, sometimes, occasionally. So I sometimes, occasionally fight for them."

"But what if you didn't leave?" Marcel said, standing and then pacing as he spoke. "I mean after the war, you were the talk of the town. The hero of the hour, the leader of the Huile Sewer Rats. If you rode that wave of acclaim, you could have been a general, or a mayor. Could have helped fix the UCCR from the inside."

"The inside?" Alba picked up a dust-encrusted bottle from the floor. She turned it, and out dripped, viscously slow, some black fetid liquid which plopped, blob by blob, onto the floor, releasing a sharp, horrid stench, like wet socks left out to spore. "That's how they all start, don't they? Wanting to make some changes from the inside. But then comes the scramble to stay on top. You need soldiers, arms, money, *dear Demiurge always more money,* and sangleum. And how do you get it? Not by following your principles. And if you decide you want to be the martyr for your ideals, they're always someone to replace you. Some people are born bastards, some chose bastardy for convenience, others... well, sometimes that the job, ain't it? To be the right kind of bastard? Let that be someone else's job for once." She let the bottle drop. It cracked, but didn't shatter, held together by some fetid internal adhesion.

Marcel crossed his arms, leaning back on the wall. It crunched a little at the touch, dust crumbling onto his vest. "Maybe we just decide to compromise ourselves, decide to allow bastards to rule us with the complicity that they're somehow the lesser bastard." He snorted, a bitter taste rising from the back of his throat, flavoring his words.

After a long silent moment, Alba sighed. "I never wanted you to come with us. Under Huile."

"Alba, I'm strong enough to—"

"Mar stop with this faux masculinity, this need to prove yourself, that you're some tough soldier guy. Most soldiers are just kids with a gun. It's not noble, it tragic, it's agonizing, its war. I didn't want you to go. Not just because I didn't want you to die. Because I knew that if you lived you were going to start moralizing yourself into a pit of self-hatred and misery. I hate the Principate, it's easy for me. You just hate the idea of the Principate. I can say, 'woops, the Huile thing went to shit, let's try something else,' and sleep well at night. I can do the math and realize one city is a small cost to pay to stop a war that might have burned down dozens more. Maybe that's strength, maybe its sociopathy, but we have to live with our choices. Regrets are wounds we cut ourselves. And if you don't figure that out soon, you're just going to keep bleeding yourself fucking dry!"

"I missed you," Marcel said suddenly, to his own surprise.

Alba blinked. Then her voice went soft. "Yeah, Mar, I missed you too."

It was comforting to hear, though he couldn't help but wonder if she felt the longing he had. Whatever his angers, whatever his regrets, whatever heavy memories dragged down his bruised ego, he had gone to bed every night missing her. Sometimes he wanted to prove himself to her, sometimes he wanted to apologize, sometimes he wanted her to beg her own apology, but not matter how he framed his desire, he just wanted her to be there.

"You never wrote," Marcel said. The words hurt as they left his mouth.

"You didn't either."

"Well, of course I mean you were off wandering the Wastes with no..." Marcel began to say, before remembering suddenly, as if finding a lost photograph dropped behind a file cabinet, that Alba had left him a piece of paper with mailing address, to some mailbox in Petram that she checked a few times a month. Marcel had crumbled it and tossed it the night she left. "I guess... I didn't want to come crawling to you."

"I never asked you to crawl," Alba said. "I just was waiting... until you were ready to move on. I could see that the war took something from you. A lightness you had. A wonder about the world, a joviality that was masked by a thin layer of sardonic wit. You became sullen. If you needed space to get through it, if you didn't want me in your life, so be it."

"Seems a bit hypocritical to say that," Marcel said with a small laugh. "Considering you just kidnapped me."

Alba chuckled as well. "I'll admit it wasn't how I expected things to go."

"None of this was," Marcel said, gesturing at everything.

Alba nodded. "Well, it's not over yet. You can go in the morning. I mean, you can go now if you want, but these tunnels are a maze, and my men need their rest. I'll be heading back to Huile, you're more than free to come with. I suspect the engineer and the monk will try one last strike at Roache, sane or suicidal, I don't know, but maybe we can help them out."

If felt too big of a choice for Marcel to even consider now. The thought of letting Alba go was painful, even just leaving her for the night felt agonizingly premature. But then again, this wasn't like in his fantasies. She wasn't here to rekindle their romance, and he certainly didn't have the time to try. And he was tired, so damned tired.

"What about Belona?" Marcel said, rubbing his eyes.

"I'll figure that one out," Alba said, with a half snarl. "You get some rest. Whatever you decide to do about Huile or Lazarus, it can wait until tomorrow."

"Right," Marcel said. "And are you..."

"I have things to do. Diego and Frefis are going to be curious what's up. I have a squad to take care of, some orders to give. It's a straight shot back. There's a bathroom if you need it, or rather a hole and a barrel of water, just beyond the mineshaft."

"Okay," Marcel said. He waited a moment to see if Alba had anything else, a reason for him to stay a few minutes longer. It seemed she did not, and when he couldn't come up with a good excuse to stay, he slowly staggered over to the door. The world swirled in his head, in different patterns than before, but not less wild. He had imagined this reunion ten thousand times. Sometimes it ended in triumph, others in misery, others with reconciliation and consummation. In all of his fantasies this reunion answered the questions that had dug at him the past two years. Now it had happened, and nothing was clearer.

"Stay safe, Talwar."

Marcel nodded as he opened the door. He paused at the threshold.

"Alba..." he said with hesitation. "What... was Danel's surname?"

"Lautrec," Alba said. "Always wanted to call him Lau-prick, since he was such a pain in the ass, but then he went and died, so it felt in bad taste. Why you ask?"

"No reason," Marcel said, letting the door shut behind him. "No reason at all."

*Hark, speak to me muse, of the great lands of Æthmach,*
*Imperium long built upon its sacred rock.*
*And ever it was both split and unified,*
*In separate lands, whose destinies be tied.*

*Come, speak to me muse, of the king-realm of Kaimark,*
*Upon whose dark hills Imperators made their mark.*
*Great cities of men arise from its peaty soul,*
*Its ancient woods cut, for industry to toil.*

*Now, speak to me muse, of Bastillia's fertile fields*
*Where wheat flourishes and grapevines yield,*
*Much wine to drink for Tyrissian Philosophers.*
*On their Golden Isles, relax proud Imperial Officers.*

*Let me hear of wild Videk, in whose forests life renew,*
*And in whose hills are born, Delur, our river true.*
*Through bend and turn it travels, to far torrid Tor,*
*In whose horizonless bay abound a great many sailor.*

*Or muse, talk instead of frosty Anklav,*
*Protected by the peaks of Eishohn, and mankind's resolve,*
*Whose valleys are warm with the heat of steel,*
*Civilization to barbarity never shall kneel!*

*Then in the north, sits Sveln hibernal,*
*Where clans once feud in wars eternal.*
*And in the south tropical Sulcosta lay,*
*Whose hot summer breeze leads idle vacationer astray.*

*No no! Speak Muse of only one land.*
*In the heart of all Æthmach it stands so grand!*

*Grand Vastium, Imperium's soul!*
*Culture and state as one, it embodies mankind whole.*
*Glory in every banner, every street, every stone,*
*Of its wonders, it stands alone.*
*If all our enemies should make bloodshed their wish,*

*One would not fear, for Vastium could never perish!*

*—"An Ode To Lands Of The Ancient Imperium, And to In Their Persistence In The Grand Modern Principate, Of Whose Glory We Relish, And For All Days Hereafter!" By Wilbart Lugmann, High Propagandist of the Central Vastium Office for Ideological Dissemination, 1625.*

# CHAPTER 34

Smoke billowed from the charred barn. It floated up to the late afternoon sky and waved in the wind, as if a one large, blackened banner. A flag of victory, a grim victory, a pointless victory. A dozen dead raiders lay on the field around it, just as many imperials as well, the latters' bodies now gathered up by their comrades and given impromptu burial rites. This was war. Goss felt no nostalgia.

"A glorious sight, isn't it?" Commandant Lechslov beamed, staring over the first military encounter of the campaign. That's what he had been calling it now, 'a campaign.' As if they were back three years ago, fighting under General Nikolai Sovanov. Back when Belona Agrippus was just a commandant herself, back before her rise and back before her fall. Goss found he missed the woman terribly. She was always calm, always sure of herself, and unlike Lechslov, her confidence didn't smell of arrogance.

"Was it necessary to attack this farmstead?" Colonel Goss asked.

"Indeed, this structure could give the enemy a foothold in our rear," Lechslov said. "Anyways, they ignored our request to parley."

The 'request' had been shouted through a dictaphone half-a-kilom away, and the Commandant had not given them even a full minute to respond before launching the assault. Now soldiers lay dead. The sight spurred waves of nausea.

"It's good to give the enemy of taste of what's to come," Lechslov said. "Spread fear among the ranks, let them know the might of imperial lead."

"And what do you recommend for the slaves who survived?"

"They will be set free!" Lechslov exclaimed. "Free to fight for their Imperator! We'll give them some old rifles, use them to draw away the enemy fire from our main assault on the city."

"Hmmm..." Goss hmmm-ed.

Nearby, frustrated shouts were tossed about. An artillery team prodded at a captured raider motorgun, unable to figure out how the strange scrapped-together machine worked. Behind it, up amongst some hillside ruins, lay their own half-deployed mortars, which had proved utterly unnecessary for the minor skirmish.

"Victory is sweet, is it not?" Lechslov said. An awkward silence sat in the air a moment. "Of course, Colonel, I only serve your authority. If you ever find my manner of command disagreeable, I would instantly step aside to allow you direct control—"

"You are to continue in your duties," Goss said, glancing back at the soldiers who were interring their comrades. One wept at the sight of her squadmate, another stared disdainfully at the pair of officers. A third idly picked a boil on his neck. No, Goss had no intention of taking command. He was not going to take direct responsibility for the lives of so many men and women, take the fall if things should go wrong. Even more wrong, that is. It would be like reliving the nightmare when General Sovanov had died. If the General had not appointed Belona his successor... what a horror that would have been, Goss in the middle of Resurgence territory, with thousands of lives decided by his uncertain orders. It is why he had never blamed Agrippus for the loss at Huile. He knew what a burden it was to command.

Well, not a burden to Lechslov, he seemed to be having the time of his life. "Look!" he said, pointing at the horizon. "There, Stinktown. Soon it will be ours."

"I think that's a hill," Goss said.

"Is it?" Lechslov squinted,

"Yes," Goss pointed. "It's covered in some fossilized trees or something, but I'm pretty sure it's just a hill. I believe Stinktown is the blotch right next to it? Unless that's just a mudlion mire."

"Well, we can have the scouts resolve this issue," Lechslov muttered. "Whatever its exact location, Stinktown will soon be—"

"Colonel! Commandant!" The two turned to see Corporal Sofia Pulcher rush up. The once-private had earned both their favor by maintaining her composure during 'The Battle of Narida Heights' as Lechslov had taken to calling their encounter with Belona. Goss still didn't understand what Belona was planning. She couldn't truly be working with Lazarus Roache, right? Yet she said in no uncertain terms that she was, and that put Goss in the most damnable position.

"What is it, Corporal?" Lechslov asked.

Sofia saluted. "There's a caravan approaching, in raider colors."

"An attack?" Lechslov said.

"They are waving a white flag, so I think it's for parley," Sofia said.

Goss heart jumped. Perhaps these raiders might not prove entirely unreasonable. Peace would still be more than preferable, if he could just figure out the truth, or a workable lie, about his ex-general.

"Hmm, well we can't assume benign intention," Lechslov said. "They could well be setting up an ambush, an attempt to cut off the head of our army. Gather the 1st Company, we'll respond to any bellicosity by blasting them into the dirt!"

* * *

They watched the coming caravan, which kicked up dust as it traveled the winding raider roads. Goss noted that the road was actually better upkept than most around Holtag. In fact, most raider infrastructure seemed in superior condition compared to their holdings. Goss had not traveled far outside their town and accompanying base and thought its decrepitude an inevitable part of living in the Wastes. Still, decrepit or not, he very much ached to be back in Holtag. Whenever the possibility of combat arose his stomach did summersaults, and even now his guts were practicing their acrobatics. Perhaps his mother had been right all along, he should have just been a dentist.

Lechslov studied his soldiers, standing in rows at attention. Rifles up, bayonets gleaming, three solid lines of blue underneath the flapping banner of the Principate, abstracted golden hands holding up a half-sun. An almost intimidating sight, perhaps they really might be able convince the raiders to sue for peace.

"This is how it always should have been," Lechslov said. "If that dustsnake Agrippus hadn't jumped rank and stolen our glory, why think of what we could have achieved! Wouldn't have wasted our chance on some quixotic campaign down in fucking Bastillia, I tell you that. Imperator's mercy, we would have done something great, made a name for ourselves, a fortune, all the honors and prestige that we deserved, not stuck out here in the Wastes. General Lechslov, I like the sound of that. After you got your generalship, of course. *General* Goss."

Goss snorted an ambiguous response. He buried ambitions like that a long time ago and had no desire to dig them up.

"There is still a chance," Lechslov said. "A conquest under our belt, the hated Agrippus in chains... or dead. There's quite a few back in Drevstad who will be pleased to hear that our trigger-happy ghulshrew is gone."

"Let's hear what they have to say before drawing up invasion plans," Goss suggested.

"I suppose that is the proper order of things..." Lechslov's tone was that of a begrudging child. "We shall see what these Wastefolk barbarians have to say for themselves."

The caravans slowed to a stop. Seven autotrucks in all, each with different markings. A bird made of iron, a swinging blade, a turgid slug-creature ridden by an equally corpulent woman. In the back he even notices the simple LC logo of Lazacorp. Only the foremost 'truck was absent of any icon. From each a colorful man or woman stepped out, flanked by guards. The emissary from the first 'truck took the lead, a gray-haired man in a strange robe with a lowered cowl. Beneath his neck hung an orb of some crimson liquid.

"Greeting," the man said. "I am Emilio Travert, and I bring with me a delegation of peace from Stinktown." In order he introduced the six other members, delegates of various gangs. One, a giant who had somehow procured green hair dye out in the Wastes, stared at them with unconcealed hatred. The last man, in an oddly normal uniform, was introduced as a representative of Lazacorp. This set Lechslov off.

"Lazacorp!" he spat. "Those are the bastards that betrayed us at Huile. Resurgence rats!"

"I understand that there is some bad blood between the Principate and Lazacorp," Travert said. "I assure you that this organization maintains no relation with the UCCR, and bears no ill-will to your noble Principate. Indeed, if I may set the example, I will gladly overlook the... incident here at this farmstead, and pay from my organization's own pockets for the damage to both sides here. Though I do wish to ask, why have you brought your army into Stinktown territory? We have kept the peace for nearly three years. We have not raided Imperial land, nor have you prevented us from our business. There is no need for us to come to blows."

"That's a kind fucking view," said the man with green hair, who had been introduced as Gregor BloodyFist, liaison for the Fist-Biters. "Once again, the Principate comes prancing in our territory, burning, and shooting. This is the same taurshit you pulled three years ago, rambling on about order and law and your fucking ponce of an Imperator as you just piss on everything. And now you've gone and burned one of my fucking farms down! My fields, my men, my slaves, my fucking barn that I just fucking built!"

"Gregor, please!" Travert snapped, before turning back to face them. "Obviously, your aggression has not gone unnoticed. But we in Stinktown respect power. And we ourselves are powerful. We have kept our hand light as you trample our fields, but our gangs are united, far more than they were three years ago when you had a much larger army. Test us and you will know, but leave in peace and we will continue as we have. Continue to bring trade to Holtag and—"

"Trade?" Lechslov said, glancing back quick at his soldiers. "There is no raider trade in Holtag. Never! Never allow such corruption."

Travert paused. The other raiders tried to stifle their laughter. "Yes... I must be... mistaken. We have never traded in Holtag. And we will continue that... not trading."

"This all seems... reasonable," Goss started to say, but if Lechslov heard him he made no indication of it.

"The 1st West Bastillian Army will not leave until our demands are met! You must turn over to us, immediately, Lazarus Roache and that damned traitor."

"Lazarus Roache?" Travert said. "That's not possible. We can't—Wait, who is this traitor?"

Lechslov laughed. "Do you have so many that it's not obvious? See Goss, they're just wasting our time."

"Perhaps they are genuinely confused," Goss said. He turned to the envoys. "You see we were told—"

"Wasting your time!" Gregor interrupted. "What imperious arseholes you are. This is just like with your last fucking general. That bitch Agrippus. Razed our hideout up by Mogheads's Pass. For what? Doing a little slaving? We weren't even bothering you none."

"If you hate the bitch so much," Lechslov said, "then why did you invite her into your city? Why do you protect her?"

"Protect her?" Travert asked, stoic continence belied by a look of utter bewilderment in his eyes. "We're not... is that the traitor you're talking about? I have no idea where Agrippus is."

"See, they're playing dumb," Lechslov muttered to Goss. "Buying time. They know they can't stand up to us in arms. Maybe they're trying to give her time to flee the city."

"Agrippus is not here!" Travert said.

"It's possible they are telling the truth," Goss said. Perhaps Belona had been lying, as he had hoped. And this was all just some... well he didn't quite understand it, but it might mean there was no need for war.

"It is also possible they are sneaking enemy forces around on our flank as we are distracted!" Lechslov said, a bit too loud.

Goss glanced around, but saw no tattooed or scarred men sneaking through the underbrush. The Wastes were as they always were, mostly empty. *Mostly.* Indeed, as Goss glanced towards the imperial artillery, he made out a figure, not clearly imperial, nor wearing raider colors. He seemed to be riding something, something chrome.

"Sneaking?" Gregor spat, stepping forward. "We don't sneak here. If you want to be dumb enough to fight, then let's have at it now. You and me! Man on man!"

"What sort of waste-worm thinks he has the right duel an officer of the Imperator?" Lechslov scoffed. "Your body odor is more threatening than your blade."

"Wait, I think there's someone out there..." Goss muttered, still squinting at the strange figure. Was he riding a horse? Yes, it looked like the man was on a metallic horse. He moved now to place his hands on the side of one of the imperial mortars. "Hey, there's someone out there!"

"Gregor calm down!" Travert shouted, as some of the other raiders tried to hold the raging brute back, Lechslov too distracted taunting the idiot to listen to Goss. "If we could just take a moment—"

And that is when the explosion went off.

As the ground burst in front of them, as shrapnel flew and fire burned, as Lechslov screamed "They're attacking!" and gave the command to counterattack, as the raiders shouted in confusion amongst themselves,

Goss turned to see smoke rising from their own mortar, the mysterious man gone.

"Down sir!" Sofia smashed into Goss, and the two rolled behind a ruined wall. The corporal jumped up and helped him to his feet, as bullets flew through the smoke and dust.

"Wasn't them, wasn't them..." Goss muttered.

"Sir?" Sofia asked, as she fired off rounds into the confused enemy lines.

"We need to... stop..." Goss couldn't get the words together. People shouted, rifles cracked, rubble flew. Principate infantry charged forward, bayonets out, into the remains of the raider delegation. Gregor rushed forward, berserk, blade in one hand and pistol in another. He killed two soldiers before being taken down in a hail of gunfire.

Goss crawled to the end of the wall, though would not leave its safety. "Lechslov!" he shouted. He spotted the man crouched behind a large rock, shouting commands. "Lechslov! It wasn't them!" he tried to cry, drowned out by the din of chaos.

Strange syllables echoed through the air. The hair pricked up on Goss's neck, his fear and panic replaced with a greater, unplaceable terror. Shaking, he glanced out to see Travert dragging himself across the dirt, left leg shredded by shrapnel, blood oozing from a dozen wounds on his body. As he pulled himself, he spat those horrid words, in a language Goss had never heard, the crimson orb in his hand. When he reached Gregor's body, he smashed the orb in his fist, lacerating his hand, his blood mixing with what looked like sangleum, though Goss couldn't be sure. The moribund man's chanting rose to a deafening clarion, as he shoved his bloody fist into the raider's corpse. His last horrid whispers left his mouth as he collapsed onto the ground. Just as he stopped moving, the corpse of Gregor started to shake. It bulged up, deformed, vibrated, then suddenly burst in a shower of red.

Something crawled out of the corpse. Long and gangly, fingers the shape of knives, arms with too many joints, covered in a fetal slime. The creature's human-like face was stretched three times too long, it's teeth shards of rusted scrap. Its legs were stitched together into a snake-like tail, and on its emaciated back burst a set of pipes, spewing black exhaust which spread like a pair of ashen wings. The battle stopped, Principate soldiers staring in horror, unable to think or move. The monster was not so constrained. It rushed out in a fury, slicing the arms off the nearest soldier.

The man's screams were enough to shock everyone from their trance, as they began to fire into the monster. It roared as bullets splattered through it, charging a squad of soldiers, tearing one in half, before vomiting a blast of burning bile that turned another into a mass of steaming flesh.

They unloaded round after round into the creature, as many soldiers falling to friendly fire as to the maw and claws of the creatures. It writhed and screeched, meaningless words escaping its shapeless mouth as it disemboweled any who were unfortunate enough to find themselves range of its impossibly long arms.

The unrelenting spew of bullets did eventually slow the monster. Steaming blood burst from its side, its roars growing pained, as soldier fired everything they had. With a final horrid scream, both unearthly and unnervingly human, it collapsed, dissolving into a sizzling pool of sangleum.

The battlefield was quiet, besides the moans of Principate soldiers left dying. The delegation's autotrucks had been peppered with bullets, or blasted by grenades, not a single raider left alive. Goss stumbled over to Lechslov, who stared at the crimson puddle.

"A demon... she's allied with demons," Lechslov was mumbling.

"It wasn't them," Goss said.

"What?"

Colonel Goss gestured back to the mortar. "Another man. Not a raider, on a chrome horse. It was our mortar he fired."

"What? That sounds like a raider to me," Lechslov said. "Sabotage! So they could blame the Principate for starting things!"

"But why not target us? It hit the raiders worse than our forces..." Goss's mind spun. Maybe it had just been a raider with bad aim? But it seemed such a daft plan, and the envoys were as shocked as they. Was he just desperately clinging to any lie that might preserve peace, or was there something more going on?

"They summoned a fucking demon!" Lechslov shouted.

"I think they're called ætheric aberrations," Goss said weakly.

Lechslov gripped his hair, his cap had fallen sometime in the battle. "Demons, Goss, demons. Do you understand?"

"We don't need to; I mean shouldn't we figure out..." Goss tried to get his thoughts together. "What if it's a misunderstanding?"

"A misunderstanding, Colonel?" Lechslov was slowly gathering his wits back, which was far faster than Goss could manage. "What's to misunderstand about a demon from Inferno! Look what it did to our troops!"

Goss tried not to; the sight was nauseating.

"Agrippus had made her alliance with these demon-wielding bandits. I will do as you command, but I must ask you, can we just return home while we know that a traitor is in league with raiders who have made some sort of demonic pact and... and can summon up.... that?" Lechslov gestured.

Goss looked around. The soldiers were staring expectantly, wanting a command, needing some sort of response. He felt as if everything was wrong, as if someone had cut a deck of cards and dealt strange hands to their own design, only he knew not who, nor why. Peace had been cheated away, yet he had not even a suspect to call bluff. But that monster... he had no idea the raiders had such nightmarish capabilities; it was like out of stories of the Calamity. Such horrors could not just be ignored, could they?

"Colonel?" Commandant Lechslov asked. "I recommend a full assault on Stinktown before they have a chance to attack again. Do I have your permission to proceed?"

Goss glanced from face to face, from body to body, from smoldering wreck to pool of demonic æther. He should say something, argue something, slow thing down, cool temperatures. Things were happening he didn't understand, things were happening Lechslov didn't understand. He needed to trust his gut, to trust Belona, to stop everything from spinning further out of control. He needed to be the leader, needed to make the tough decisions, needed to say the right things to convince his men and women to take a step back, to be rational. He needed to accept his responsibilities, no matter the difficulties, to command his troops hold back and figure this all out, even if that move was unpopular, even if it would override and infuriate Lechslov, even if it would seem insane to his troops and risk a mutiny. He needed to take a risk and accept its consequences.

"Commander, your orders?" Corporal Sofia asked.

Goss nodded. "Yes...Yes we attack."

# CHAPTER 35

*"Twenty... Twenty-one... Twenty... Twenty-one..."*

Sylvaine opened her eyes. Not that there was much to see. The cavern ceiling still looked as it had when she had first tried to go to sleep. Rocky.

*"If nine hours then... It would be... Twenty-one... Or twenty?"*

Sylvaine turned on her cot. Diego had been sent off on some mission hours before they had gone to sleep, so the only one in the room with her, if it could be called a room, was Kayip. The monk was bent over, hand on his Cracked Disc, as if praying. But the words didn't sound like Church prayer, since she could actually understand them.

*"But then, ten hours... Twenty-one."*

"Twenty-one what?" Sylvaine asked.

The monk looked up. Embarrassment flashed over his face. But there was something beneath it to, a concern, a fear maybe. After a moment he mumbled, "Days."

"Days?"

"What is the time?"

Sylvaine reached into her bag and pulled out her watch. "Two-thirty. In the morning," she added since it was impossible to tell. They had been here a full day.

"Then twenty..." Kayip said.

"Twenty days until what?"

The monk shook his head. "Just until... until there is no more chance to redeem my sins."

"Can you stop turning every basic question into some ominous riddle?" Sylvaine said, sitting up.

"I do not mean to make riddles..." Kayip said. "I just... if we are not able to stop Roache and his allies in the next few days... Things will be bad. Perhaps it would be better for you to head back east, then."

"Oh, no." Sylvaine jabbed an accusatory finger. "Don't you try and get rid of me! After everything we've gone through, you're not dumping me off."

"That is not... what I mean." Kayip shook his head. "You have risked your life already. I should not have asked you to do that, but I have. If you stay... things will get bad, death will not be a risk, but a certainty."

"What do you mean?"

"What Lazarus tried to do in Huile, and what he is trying do to here, is part of something... very large. It will occur soon, and you should not be around if it does."

"What will occur?" Sylvaine said. "What are you talking about?"

Kayip paused. "Something very bad."

"Kayip you..." Sylvaine sputtered with exasperation. "You can't keep talking like some coy oracle. What's going to happen, how do you know?"

"I cannot tell you."

"Yes you can, it's easy! You open your mouth and let words come out!" Sylvaine acted out the process in exaggerated detail. "And you keep alluding to these other people you've worked with who've died, and all this terrible stuff that has happened, and might happen... we're a team! You can't leave all this a secret. We're not some set of catur pieces for you to move around."

"Do not ask me," Kayip said, "please."

There was enough pain in that 'please,' that Sylvaine found she could not force the question. Instead, she leaned back on the wall and sighed. "What do you expect me to think then? That you no longer find me useful, that I'm too erratic and wild, and now you want to get rid of me. I get it, it makes sense." She stared up at the ceiling again, its jagged edges devoid of pattern or meaning. "You're not even wrong. I'm dangerous. Whatever I try to be, whatever I pretend to be, I'll always be *that*. That beast in the garage. In Lazarus's penthouse. That wild animal who can only tear and bite and destroy."

"Sylvaine... It is not, that is not, not what I am saying." Kayip glanced up as she had done, his one eye darting, as if searching for an answer in the stoneface.

"I was more honest," he said, finally, "with those who came before. I told them of my sins, and what the consequences would be. I told them, because I knew they would take on that responsibility my knowledge gave, that they could not say no if they knew what they would condemn the world to. They stayed with me to the end, to their end, somehow never mine. It was my burden to bear, it was not right for me to foist it upon others, to let it drag them to their grave. If I tell you everything, perhaps you will stay when instead you should flee. And you, you are not like others who have fought with me, you have not chosen a path of violence in your life, you should not be consumed by it. You have already done far more than it is fair to have been asked. If we should fail, it is not right that you should perish. No, I would not like that."

Water dripped into the pool as Kayip's words sat in the silence. Distant winds moaned soft and something small skittered down a hallway. The dim light of the one hanging ætherlamps flickered subtle patterns across the scratches and chinks of Kayip's mask.

"It doesn't matter," Sylvaine muttered. "Safe or not, doomed or not. What else would I do? I'm not here because of some duty, some ideals, I'm not even here for revenge. I'm only here now... because where else would I be? There's not a place for a thing like me. Not that there should be. A counterfeit excuse for an engineer, a beast wearing clothes and an ætherglove, playing pretend. That's what I've always been. The more I crawl towards this fantasy, the more I'll just fall back into the animal I am, and the more people who will get hurt."

So there it was. The truth out in the open. Whenever she admitted it to herself, it felt as though she was stabbing her own beating heart out with her claws. Now that she let the words free, they felt... dull. Less sharp blades, more blunt sticks, hitting tired and numb flesh.

"Why," Kayip said after a moment, "do you place such hate upon yourself, Sylvaine?"

A sudden spasm of laughter overtook Sylvaine. She grabbed the side of the cot as she shook and wheezed, shuddering and releasing strange chortles. Kayip's question was such an absurd statement, so obvious in its answer that she could do nothing but laugh. It took half a minute for the attack to subside, the sounds of her hoarse cackling echoing down the stone hallways.

"Why do you think?" she said, when she could, words intermixed with strange chuckles. "Look at me! I've been trying to prove that all this," and she gestured to her fur and claws and ears and everything, "doesn't matter. That there's something inside of me, the same as everyone else, that it's all just aesthetics, just a coat of unseemly hair, some sharp nails, nothing important, nothing real. But I've failed. Of course, I've failed, how can you disprove that which is demonstrably true? This is what I am, what I've always been! A beast, a monster, an animal. Everything else, my studies, my application to the Guild Academy, my 'glove!" She went to tear it off, but found that even now she could not bear to do so. "It's all just a story I want to tell myself. Like those pulps I read as a kid, fantasy."

"Sylvaine... that is all untrue. You are grabbing daggers to hurt yourself."

"Is it? Am I? Because everyone's been quite keen to remind me of these facts. Kids at schools, teachers, people on the street. In cinegraphs Ferrals are always the enemy, or at best, wild and wacky primitives, idiot allies used for comic relief, gawking at radiators, thinking autocars are big scary metal bears." She stared up at the ceiling, still unable to find patterns in its savage cracks. "And I can't prove them wrong. Even in Icaria when I was given a chance, all I did was kill the only person who even temporarily believed in me, and revealed to the rest of the city a bloody, murderous animal. Then there's Belona, of course. Tossed me in chains meant for dogs, mocked my engineering pretensions. And you've always so quick to defend her!"

"I do not..." Kayip began, his voice strained. "I do not mean to defend her. Not when she does such things. It is wrong, and hateful. I only seek to keep her alive, so she may help us. And to sin does not mean she should die."

"It's not some abstract sin, Kayip, it's against me, me personally," Sylvaine said, knocking a pebble with the side of her foot. "What is it about her?"

"Pity," Kayip said, after a moment. "She has suffered. And much of it due to my failures."

"Suffering doesn't make a shitty person good. It doesn't give her a fucking excuse."

Kayip scratched at his mask. "Perhaps pity is not exact. It is a need for redemption. For her, I tell myself, but truly for me. If she can be redeemed... no. It is greed to ask for such things. To demand forgiveness."

"I'm not demanding forgiveness," Sylvaine said. "But it's not just Belona. Your own church treats Ferrals as nothing more than bestial abomination to be casually smote."

"The Chronicles of the Ascended say very little definite on Ferrals," Kayip protested.

"Of course. Because we're an afterthought, unimportant, some strange anomaly of man-bones and beast-flesh. What am I supposed to think when you follow that creed with such devotion? What am I supposed to think if my only friend doesn't even protect me?" She shook her head and groaned. "It's not you, not really. Let's just look at thing empirically. Humans build. The cities of Æthmach and Muhit, the roads, the buildings, the trains, the æroships, all Human work. Kortonians build, even Malva have their Ironship cities. What about Ferrals? We've spent the past two-thousand years sittings under trees, stomping about in the mud, building nothing but stick-woven huts and waving our spears at anyone with a hint of civilization about them."

"Ferrals were not the ones who destroyed the world."

"Of course not!" Sylvaine stood up. "Because they couldn't, we can't! Can't engineer our way out of a pit. If all ferrals disappeared one day, the world would look no different."

Kayip closed his eye and sucked in his breath. He stroked the side of his mask idly, as he thought.

"You do not need to prove yourself, Sylvaine" he said. "But if you did, you would have succeeded. You wished to become an engineer, and you are one, Guild recognition or none."

"It's not the recognition," she said, which was at least partly a lie. "I would think that you of all people would judge an artificially injected Knack, given to me by Roache's slickdust, by unstable æthermantics that your Church would call demon-magic."

"Perhaps we would." Kayip nodded. "And in spite of that origin, you succeeded. Your will to choose your own fate overcame all boundaries, of biology, of prejudice. There are many humans who seek to be engineers, or priests, or many other things, and yet when faced with the insurmountable, give up. You persevered. If proof was truly needed, what more proof could be offered?"

"It's all empty. Even if I could believe it was real, it's not sticking around." Sylvaine stared at her ætherglove. Despite all the ugly traumas it had witnessed the 'glove was still beautiful, with its intricate interlocked piping, its shining sparkpoints, its gauges with perfect, sensible measurements. The world was chaos, she was unworthy, but the ætherglove was as it was meant to be, would continue to work as it was designed to, even when she couldn't. "I found some notes in Narida Heights. By an engineer, must be involved in slickdust production. My Knack is tied to Lazarus. Apparently once he croaks, that's it. Just back to a normal Ferral, all my studies, my struggles, my pain, none of it matters."

Sylvaine fell back on her cot, her gaze down at the ground. Kayip quietly studied her. With what expression, she did not bother to check. What was there for him to see anyways?

"You knew this," Kayip said finally. "And yet you continued to hunt the man anyway? Even if it would cost something so precious to you? Sylvaine... that is noble."

"Who cares?" Sylvaine thrust out her hands in exasperation. "A noble human without a Knack doesn't suddenly become an engineer. A noble animal is still a damned animal. And it doesn't matter if I help kill Roache or not. One day he'll die, and then I won't be an engineer, not even a pretend engineer. I'll just be me."

"I know how you feel, but ask yourself, is that truly such a bad thing?."

Sylvaine sighed. "You have no idea how I feel. You can't. Give thanks to your Demiurge that you will never have to."

"Perhaps..." Kayip's voice trailing out into nothing.

Water dripped in the nearby wash-pond. A simple plop, plop, plop in the silence. Not quite silence, for Sylvaine never had silence. There was always some distant sound others could not quite hear, a gust of wind on a single leaf, the squeak of some near inaudible animal, tiny movements of things too diminutive for the human ear to make out. But she could, and she could smell as well, nauseating wafts of hidden filth, whether human, animal, or industrial, unceasing in their assault. These useless senses did nothing but remind her in every waking moment that she was different, was other. Was alone. Alone in the false silence, in the hidden smells, in her inner loathing, and buried dreams. That was the fate of creatures like she.

"Sylvaine," Kayip said suddenly. "There was a time, not too long ago when I also had… powers. Æthermantics, you would say, our Order did not use those terms. Miracles, blessings from the Demiurge. There was a time, when I could…" he pulled up his Cracked Disc and stared at it. There was something in his eye, a gleam condensating into a tear. It was a gaze of adoration analogous to how Sylvaine admired her glove. She had not realized she shared that with the monk.

"There was a time when this relic listened to me," Kayip said. "But it has been silent to my pleas. Silent for years now, seven years. Seven years in twenty days."

"I didn't know…" Sylvaine said. She had always assumed the man a believer, but not a true æthermantic priest. It had not occurred to her such abilities could be lost, she thought herself a unique exception. But the way he spoke of his loss was almost as she did. But no, it was not precisely the same. There was something else behind his tone, a pain of a different sort. *Guilt*, she realized.

Kayip let the Disc fall to the end of its chain. "I do not claim to know your life, only my own. But I know that the shame you claim to bear lies with no fault of your own. Mine is well earned. I have hid the truth at times. Not with the purpose to deceive, but because it is difficult. I have seen things, done things…" He sucked in his breath; the words stuck in his throat. The single tear was joined by many. "I have hurt people, Sylvaine. Innocent people. I wielded my righteousness as a brigand whips his knife across a child's throat. There was, is, a Clan, they call themselves, out in the Wastes. I knew little of them, and yet felt I as if knew everything, could judge them. I was young, and I… and I… I…"

His voice faltered and faded. Sylvaine had always thought Kayip a strong man, but there seemed something inside him he could not lift out. When he spoke again it was in the softest of tones. "Perhaps I thought the mutants in Huile might redeem me. But it is not right to demand redemption. There are some who are beyond its grace, and yet we must struggle anyways. Sylvaine… I am sorry that have left evil befall you, I am sorry I have kept secrets, I am sorry for so much more as well."

"Kayip, I was never asking…" Sylvaine said, matching his softness.

"There is something I would like to show you," he said suddenly. "Perhaps it will make things make sense, perhaps it will only add confusion. Yet is not something to be explained. Because there are few others... no others, who I care for as you, as I trust as you..."

As Kayip spoke his tremulous fingers had crawled their way up his face, until they grasped the edges of his metal mask. They paused there a moment, then started to drift down, second thoughts leading his hand away. Kayip swallowed, and lifted his fingers back up, until they reached all corners of his mask. Then with great care, he removed the curved sheet of metal.

Sylvaine noticed the skin first, red, not flushed, but naturally crimson. Its surface was hard, rough, almost scaley, though faded and blotchy by the borders of mask's depression. Next, she noticed a bump, the width of two knuckles, scarred and pale above the man's unveiled eye. The base of a horn, she realized, though grinded away in a manner that looked horrendously painful. Finally, his eye. Close tight at first, the same flakey crimson as the skin, until it blinked open, yellow, and slitted, like a lizard.

"Kayip..." Sylvaine said, touching soft the edge of his mutation.

"There is no shame in being a Ferral," he said. "And there should be none for mutants. But this marking, it is not accident... It is punishment. It is sin! It is what separates me from the Demiurge, and it is deserved."

"Shh..." Sylvaine said, staring into his eye. "It's okay, Kayip, it's okay."

She pulled his head close with her gloved hand. With gasping breaths, the monk wept into her fur.

# Chapter 36

Marcel hadn't slept much. Or maybe he had, it was hard to tell. In the subterranean dark, thoughts merged with dreams, and Marcel could not quite differentiate the wails of his conscious anxiety with the slumber-born poetry of his id. But he was awake now, probably.

He leaned his head back against the wall. The cavern was empty, besides Belona of course, still slouched, still chained. There wasn't a guard watching them. Did Alba trust him not to bust the imperial out? Or were that metal-armed guy and the salvi just around a corner, waiting for any excuse to put a bullet through Belona's head. Or his head. Alba wouldn't do that, right? Probably? Marcel groaned silently.

There was a hum he noticed, a murmur. Was it Alba talking? He put his ear against the wall and listened in. Sounds definitely, possibly even words. He concentrated, squeezing tight against the wall, ear flat against stone. There was certainly a voice, two voices, or maybe just water leaking through some hidden pipe, or some mechanical something churning in the wall, or maybe...

Marcel let his head fall. He had no idea. Had nothing to do but wait around, his only company that nagging question in his head: go back to Huile, or continue his quixotic quest to take out Lazarus? Go back and try to talk down a furious Resurgence General, mind poisoned by lies? Or attempt to break into the roiling chaos of a homicidally-inclined raider town, again? Face his past fuck ups, or fuck up once more?

He could see why Kayip kept alluding to past mistakes with sullen words. The vigilante path hadn't done any more good that his career as a faux private investigator. Maybe that meant it was time to stop both, to head back with Alba and try to fix what was broken. He had always condemned her for abandoning Huile, but wasn't that what he had done? Just with more excuses? Always with the delusion that somehow taking out Roache would fix everything, that he'd ride back into town like a hero. His journey finished, the people cheering round, every wrong righted, every hurt mended. A childish dream. He needed to do the mature thing, and head back.

Or was it the other way round? He had gotten this far, and paid the cost to do so. To turn around here, to not attempt with every ounce of sweat to execute a monster who might still be a threat, was that truly the wisest option? Even though he felt guilty about his past mistakes, returning to Huile as some penance would do nothing to stop the danger. What if he went back, explained everything, and then Lazarus Roache returned, tricked everyone with subtle words and slickdust, and then brought it all to ruin? And did he even have any reason to believe he could convince the UCCR of their mistake if Alba couldn't? On the other hand, did he have any reason to believe he could actually take down Roache? His track record on that front was pretty shaky.

The worse part was, even if he made a decision now, it would make no difference. He would have to wait around until morning all the same. He hated waiting, hated it with every centimetre of his being. Hated the empty time, and the darkness, and the nothing he could do. Maybe since he was awake, he could try and sneak a message to Sylvaine and Kayip about... about what? Inferno, he could probably just walk over to their room if he really wanted to talk to them. But then what would he say? They'd want to know what he talked about with Alba, and he wasn't much in the summarizing mood. They'd be curious what his plan was, and Demiurge knew so was he.

The hum was back. Not quite the same as before he realized, and not from the wall. It was softer, clear, and gentle.

*From the bright shores of Kaimark,*
*To the eastern mount peaks,*
*No land stands untouched,*
*By the light of our glory.*

It was Belona, Marcel realized, head still low, singing to herself.

*Our roots spread in the soil,*
*Laid down by the first men.*
*Our branches reach out,*
*To unending horizons.*

The tune was like that of a lullaby. It was so unlike the woman, though the lyrics... they sounded familiar.

*So Hail, Hail the rising stars,*
*Who shines brightly on borders and hearth.*
*So Hail, Hail, the rippling banner,*
*As it leads our soldiers to glory.*
*So, Hail, Hail, Imperator,*
*Whose grand word brings law to his children.*

"It's the Anthem Imperial," Marcel said, with some shock. It was the sort of horrid refrain usually belted out by marching soldiers or cheering crowds of the Imperator's most loyal sycophants. He hadn't recognized the anthem of his enemy, so strange was Belona's rendition. It had almost sounded... soothing.

"I'm surprised you know it," Belona said. "Does that make you a traitor to your rat's-ass excuse for a Confederacy?"

"I went to University," Marcel said simply.

"Yes," Belona chuckled. "Yes, you most certainly did."

"It's not usually performed with such..." Marcel said, tapping his foot on the stone as he tried to find the right word.

"It's how my grandmother sung it. Every night, as I went to sleep. Even as I got older, and she drifted towards infirmity. Even when I would come back from school with a black eye or oozing scabs from... well I was not a pacifistic girl. Even then I would go to her, and she would sing to me, and the world was, for a moment, healed."

"Huh," Marcel said. He had never thought about Belona's family. Presumably, she had one, sort of a biological necessity, but it felt too normal, too prosaic. "You get along with your folks?"

Belona's laugh echoed throughout the cavern. She reared her head back, and then buckled forward. "No. Fuck, Talwar, no I do not. Not my mother, not my cousins, not our maids or butlers, certainly not my dear patriarch, Mr. Gerfried Handler. Only her, only grandmother, Agrippus."

"Wait, Mr. *Handler*?" Marcel asked.

"Yes, Belona Handler, the accursed birthname of a scion of profiteers," Belona said, wrist turning in her manacles with disdain. "While my grandmother and her daughter bore a matronymic title of an ancient and noble lineage, our household was named after a corpulent hog of man who overcharged the Imperator's own soldiers for second-hand autotrucks. But my grandmother... she had been a soldier, had given everything for the Principate, youth, arm, even her husband. She believed that the Imperator would reunite all of humanity, bring order back to the world, combine the ancient and the modern into one grand eternal Principate. Instead, her daughter married some paper shuffler, a scam artist who managed to loophole his way not only into legal legitimacy, but lavish luxury. And I was supposed to continue that line, serve my Imperator with not my fist and rifle, but with my womb. Heated words were tossed when I enlisted, as were several pieces of antique porcelain. So no, I do not get with the *Handlers*." She turned her head to finally look him straight on. "What about yourself, Talwar? You've traveled far from your homestead."

"Oh," Marcel said, tapping his foot. "Yeah, I have a mom. Two brothers too. Shit, I should probably send them a letter, last message was a postcard for Bell Day."

"So, they don't know you're a wanted criminal?"

"I haven't really figured out how to explain everything," Marcel said. "Been kind of keeping correspondences limited to vague pleasantries the last few years. I think this might give mom a heart attack."

Belona nodded, then was quiet for a moment. "It was idiotic of you."

"What? To not write more? You should talk, you just said you haven't—"

"No," Belona interrupted. "To cover for me. That was pure foolishness." She scratched at the skin under her chains. "You're protecting an enemy combatant from an allied force whose loyalty is valuable and trust uncertain. Giving me up would have proven your fealty, ensuring her cooperation and potentially helping you clear your name with the UCCR. You are now doubly suspicious and have gained nothing for it."

"Uh." Marcel gestured. "You're welcome?"

"Why?" Belona asked, staring straight. "You're not an idiot, Talwar, at least not that big of one. And you don't want me to survive, I still have a vendetta, we still have a duel planned. You could have removed me with ease, and without the interference of the engineer or the monk."

"You still want to fight me?" Marcel said, with snort of frustrated bewilderment. "Even after I tried to save you?"

"I have not forgotten my loyalties, even if you have. You have a duty as a soldier of the Resurgence, to remove all threats to your homeland by whatever means available, to avenge all slights, retake all losses. Perhaps I flatter myself as a 'threat,' but there is certainly much to be avenged."

"I haven't forgotten a single damn thing," Marcel said. "What about our loyalty? The loyalty to squad, or posse, or traveling group, whatever we're calling us four. We look out for each other, whether out in the Wastes, or in Stinktown, or here. Would you abandon your soldiers? We're in this, together, for better or not, we can't just leave one of us out to die. When we were fighting those raiders, when Sylvaine was busy turning that garage into a bloody æther-storm, you found me and pulled me up."

"I needed a driver," Belona said, looking away.

"You could have driven yourself, or found Kayip, and put a quick bullet into me if your revenge was so damn important." It felt a strange argument to make, but Marcel felt the need to convince her, or himself at least.

Belona sighed. "You're an idealist Talwar. It's a noble trait, you just chose the wrong ideals."

"Is it so hard just to say thank you?" Marcel asked, with a stomp.

Belona paused. She turned to face him and nodded. "Thank you, Talwar."

"See?" Marcel tossed out his hand. "You're welc—well I already said that, but yeah."

"Does it change anything?"

Marcel slumped on the wall. "Lazarus Roache is still alive, Huile is burning, an army is marching overhead looking for us, and you still want to kill me, so, fuck."

"You still have a shot at taking him down," Belona said. "Even if I'm dead. You still have a shot."

"We'll... get you out of this," Marcel said, with a hollow conviction. "Alba will see reason. She knows that Roache is the greater threat."

"I am a fowl in her hand, and Roache is still chirping in the bush." Belona rubbed some dust between her fingers, and let it fall. "She's not the type to let a sure hunt slip by on the faint promise of another. But don't let me haunt you, Talwar, it was my past that doomed me, not yours. To think Hans Krimme survived, only to go native with these bandits..."

"Is that why you killed him? For betraying the Principate?" Marcel asked.

Belona scoffed. "Deserved or not, no. We had a mission, Talwar, I did a calculation and decided the longer he lived, the less of a chance we would have to escape. If we, you now, are to take out Roache, he had to die. In war, one cannot wait to feel, must do their duty no matter the pain. But now, now that I have time, time I do not want, time alone with nothing to do but feel?" Her face twisted up suddenly, her gaze turned away. For a moment Marcel thought the woman might weep.

With a deep breath Belona composed herself, and spoke again in a stoic tone. "It was a grim thing, Talwar. Terrible. A soldier should die in battle, not by the hands of his officer. I had mourned him years ago, for I had felt responsible for his death. Then I discovered he was alive, and swiftly removed all ambiguity about my guilt. I suppose I must mourn him again. It is as the priests say, our sins will always stalk us."

They were both quiet for a moment. Marcel closed his eyes and could see that raider lord's face, recognition, surprise, then pain, as Belona's bullet flew through his chest. That glimpse of agony joined its kin in Marcel's memory, soldiers under Blackwood Row, civilians bleeding upon Huile's streets. Enemies and friends united in that moment of death, all blurred together.

"Is it true?" Marcel finally asked. "The Butcher of Tesakovgrad?"

Belona thought on this. After a long moment she moved her head in a manner not quite decisive, but closer to a nod than a shake. "I conquered Tesakovgrad."

"And killed everyone? Men, women, children?"

"Not quite everyone," she said softly.

There were many things Marcel knew he should say. He should tell her off, insult her, condemn her, shout out his lungs, or coldly conclude that he was wrong to save her. Instead he just asked, "Why?"

Belona shook her chains idly and stared up at the dark. "I don't want to give you an excuse. I don't believe in excuses. Tesakovgrad was my first major campaign after I ascended to the rank of General. Our last General, Sovanov, had been killed in a Resurgence autocar bombing. He was... a gentle man, if such things can be believed, though not exactly a gentleman. Boorish at times, as far from nobility as one could find, but concerned for his soldiers and with a keen wit. I was there when he died. It was a slow thing, guts perforated, legs bent back like paperclips.

"I took command in a precarious situation. The Resurgence's campaign of bombings and guerilla ambushes had plunged several local settlements into chaos. We hadn't the troops to protect every supply caravan, and bread riots were becoming a near daily distraction. I don't blame the people for this, most had no interest in partisan bickering, they were just hungry. I needed to cut off the enemy's head if there was to ever be peace, but I was inexperienced and timid. I took the city in a slow, cautious manner, focusing overwhelming force, moving block by block, minimizing causalities, both my own and civilian. This was a mistake. Tesakovgrad, you see, is a two-tiered city, the main metropolitan area below on flat plain, the smaller industrial district raised up on a plateau by the mountainside, only a few roads in and out. My delay gave the enemy time to fortify, to pull back all the artillery in the city and rain Infernofire down, upon my troops and their own people alike. Worse still, they had made a big show of gathering all the civilians they could, friends, family, some even forced by bayonet point up into their fortifications. They knew if I were to fight fire with fire, it would be a bloodbath, a stain on the Principate's name and a rallying cry for future battles."

"What did you do?" Marcel asked.

"First I tried to fight them nobly, taking the main roads and assaulting them head on with armored squadrons. No success. I tried to negotiate with them, but was met with either silence or bullets. I tried to cut off their supply line, but the passes through the mountains were too numerous, the underway systems too labyrinthine. They were a fortress that could not be sieged, and all the while they could coordinate terrorist activity throughout Anklav and Videk, supply insurgent cells, export their brutality to every corner. They knew the quandary they forced upon me, give up on the region entirely or unleash the Imperator's superior artillery. You know what I decided, my epithet is clear enough on that front."

Marcel kicked his boot as he thought a moment. "You said you weren't going to give an excuse. I heard nothing but excuses. How you had no choice, how your hand was forced. If I were to believe your excuses, then everyone is just a butcher who has been lucky enough to not yet be forced into an abattoir."

Belona shook her head. "I remember, when the bombardment was over, when the last shell has torn the last structure into rubble. When I had surveyed what I had done, I noticed something through the smoke. A small hand, partially buried in debris, her body just visible in the haze. The girl could not have been more than six years old, had certainly not understood what was happening, nor why. She was guiltless in this, as were thousands more that day, as were uncountable millions throughout this war. They were guiltless, I am not."

She stared at Marcel, eyes tired.

"I did have a choice, Talwar. I will never deny that. I chose to do my duty as a soldier, knowing full well what it would cost. I live with that, right, wrong, or something else. We all must live with our choices."

*All must live with our choices.* Seemed pointed, trying to turn it around on him, and yet her tone didn't make it sound like an insult. Isn't that what Alba said too, that they had to live with their choices? Except she meant to leave them behind, to let bygones be bygones, regardless of the body count. Belona did not seem so blithe. It was clear what she had done had haunted her. Maybe she deserved the haunting. Maybe he also deserved his own.

"I thought it would fix everything," Marcel said. "Huile. A few bombs, and it would put an end to it."

"Trying to fix war through war," Belona said. "We share that instinct. That is why I sent my armies over the Atsols, down into Bastillia. The Severing War started over a century ago, and yet we are still fighting it, even after all the deaths, even after the Calamity burned Vastium into these horrid Wastes. I didn't want revenge, not for my general, not for my Imperator, not even for my homeland. I just wanted it to end. One decisive victory, a victory whose peace would wash away all the blood of a century, including that I spilled. The first thing I can remember is war. War in its splendor, soldiers marching, banners held high, the Anthem Imperial on every dictaphone. I believed in it, until I experienced it. War is evil, Talwar, such is obvious to anyone who's seen it. We are evil, a necessary evil, but evil still. I thought that if I could just end the stalemate, then there would be no more artillery bombardments, no more 'car bombs or gas attacks. There'd be no more middlemen scamming and growing rich in the chaos, no more engineers Guildsfolk playing both sides to their profit, no more corrupt bureaucrats in distant provinces, no more raider brutes crafting kingdoms of cruelty. You want the same, I know, you believe truly that your

Resurgence will do what I wish my Principate to do. I admire the purity of your vision."

Marcel sighed. "Not sure such 'pure visions,' have done anything but muck things up further."

"I know. And yet I cannot give up on them."

They were alike in that sense, he had to admit. Alike in many more senses as well. As he thought of all Belona had done, he tried to convince himself he would never have done the same, and yet he found himself uneasily uncertain. As a child he had been told stories, in pulps and voxboxes and cinegraphs. Stories of noble Resurgence heroes and brutal Principate tyrants. As an adult the stories had grown with him, but had not changed in content. Yet he had loved them all the same, had followed them. Followed them out into the Border States, into the ranks of the army, under Huile and to a new life in the city, had followed them all the way here. He did not know if these stories had led them in the right direction, only that he had not expected the twists in their paths. He did not know if his journey had made the world better, only that each step had felt right, had seemed in line with the stories he could not bear to give up. But what if the stories had been different? What if they had led the opposite direction? What could he have done, been convinced to do, convinced himself to do? The questions sat heavy in his stomach, and he knew they would sit there a long time still.

"So," Marcel said, leaning forward, "what do you think you would be doing, if there was peace, true peace?"

Belona scratched at her manacles again. "Most likely... I'd be in prison, or dead, perhaps in that order. A good world should have no place for women like me."

"I don't think that's true," Marcel said, surprised at his own earnestness. He stared at Belona, her ragged, short-cut hair, her scar-ornamented chin, her sharp hazel eyes now suddenly soft. "At least, I don't want it to be true."

Belona stared back at him, and chuckled. "Maybe I was wrong about you Talwar. Maybe you are that much of an idiot."

# CHAPTER 37

Namter stood motionless before the chipped oak door, tea tray in hand, as the distant screams of artillery shook the world. The outer world, that is. His inner world was wrought by something much greater. A question, a revelation. Lazarus Roache, his master, was a traitor. That was not a surprise in itself. Treachery was the man's business, but that he would betray the cause, betray Namter—No, he must not let get his ego in the way. The fact that Lazarus would betray their shared master, The Bleeding One, The Buried Sovereign, The Flayed Prince, that Lazarus would betray a God...

Yet Namter could think of no other explanation for what he had read. The schematics had been clear, Lazarus had made alterations to their Enterprise, a hidden adjustment to their slickdust-infusion device. The original device would have turned a Huile into a city of Tribute. With the alterations the city would have been useless to their Master, but enthralled completely to Lazarus Roache himself. There is no reading of their contract that would have allowed this, it's only purpose would have been for Lazarus Roache to attempt to break away from his duties, to hold tight his Gift, and never pay his debts. Of course, this is why he had Miga working so hard experimenting on mutants, he needed an alternative to the numinous power of The Flayed Prince. Could Roache have even been behind the witch's assassination attempt? Had Roache fallen so far as to even bring blade against his own butler?

Perhaps Verus had discovered this all. It would explain the old Awakener's apparent betrayal, though to have also destroyed their

Enterprise as well seemed excessive... unless that was an accident, the doing of that monk, Kayip. After all these years of waiting, he finally got his revenge in Huile, only for Roache to blame it on his foreman. And now... now Lazarus Roache wished to buy himself time, to get another chance at betrayal.

The roof shook and dust fell, as the blasts continued. A clear reminder that there was no more time. As Roache schemed and gang lords bickered, the Imperials invaded, threatening not just this worthless junkyard city, but the Tribute still held within. If only Namter had forced the transport earlier, had them safe for Reification, and not dallied as Lazarus tossed about his seditious notions of 'delay.' What other plans had he crafted in this stolen time?

A grandfather clock in the hall groaned, a hand-carved copper stymph dove popping out to announce the coming of seven a.m., as another distant boom rattled the windowpanes. Namter had gotten too used to being a puppet-master's assistant, now he must walk ever wary of the invisible strings that might yet hang over him. Whatever conspiracies Roache had sketched in secret, Namter could not simply wait with his unease and uncertainty. There was too much to do, too much at stake to dally. The butler sighed softly, and opened the door.

Lazarus Roache stood at the far end of his office, staring out silently over the city, columns of smoke in the distance. On his black-timbered desk sat relics of a past life, a broken shaft from Lazacorp's first well, an unused ætherglove with silvered pipes and platinum sparkpoints, an iron griffon statuette gifted by imperial insurgents alongside to a medal of heroism with the Resurgence's Phoenix in silver, and several other useless bibelots. On the wall hung a faded photo of a young, flaxen-haired man, eyes full of hope and avarice.

Nearer the tycoon himself was a small side-table where sat his pistol, handle of pearl, barrel inlaid with abstract geometries of gold. For a frightful moment Namter wondered if Roache might turn the weapon towards him. Instead, he glanced back with disquieted smile, then shook his head.

"I've never had to shoot a man before."

"Sir?" Namter asked, placing his tea tray down, and beginning to pour.

"I mean, I have had men killed, certainly," Lazarus said. "But never had to pull the trigger myself. It's such a wasteful thing."

"What about that monk?" Namter asked.

Lazarus chuckled. "Fair enough, my Namter. But there's something classy about a dagger in the back. A pistol? So crass, and to have to do it in front of all the lords of Stinktown, it's simply embarrassing."

"I can imagine, sir," Namter said, pouring in slickdust, and then offering the tea.

Lazarus took the cup with a sigh. The wrinkles round his eyes were deeper than Namter had seen in seven years, and liver spots were starting to reappear. Miga's experiments were not working as well as the tycoon had hoped.

Out the window Namter could see a glittering of gunfire between dust clouds. It seemed a storm was brewing. He wondered if the imperials had planned their attack to be covered by a dust storm, or if their assault was simply as reckless and shambolically planned as it seemed. Occasionally he espied movement, sunlight off motorcycles or raider buggies. A shell flew wild over the fray and landed on the outskirts of the city, turning some small tenements into rubble.

"It's like Huile again," Lazarus said. "What cruel fate it is that we keep finding ourselves under siege."

Namter studied his master's tone. It was congenial and slightly wistful. Nothing to suggest any plans of perfidy. Was he even now planning a way to remove Namter? After all these years serving, Namter felt as if he should be able to tell, and yet Roache betrayed the cause at Huile and Namter was not the wiser. Could the tycoon's soft sadness itself be a ruse?

"I know what it is," Roache said. "It's the work of that bitch Agrippus."

"Agrippus?"

Roache nodded. "Our men got our hands on some Crimson Eyes, apparently they heard Mr. Crimson call his assassin 'Agrippus.' Once I heard her name, I knew there was no chance this imperial army would parley. It must all be her doing, part of her petty, vicious vengeance."

"I was told the assassins were Taur Maws," Namter said, unsure if Roache's words were some a further deceit, though for what purpose he could not surmise.

"A clever disguise," Roache mused. "No doubt she was sent ahead to sow chaos. I assumed she had fallen too far to ever have the clout to lead an exhibition. Maybe it's some deal, she goes off on some suicide mission to take me out, in return for, what's-his-name, Lechslov's assurance of power. Something like that... I don't know, we should have spied more on

Holtag. I simply feel as if we are standing amidst a great puzzle, but are missing half the pieces."

"I know just the feeling, sir," Namter said. "I've still been wrestling with why Verus would betray our cause."

"It's these questions that haunt us," Lazarus nodded, idly tapping the glass. "I wonder if I am partly to blame. I antagonized him too much. The man was a taur's asshole, but maybe he wouldn't have turned traitor if I better kept up our détente. I thought he recognized we were all on the same side in the end, but people are complicated, Namter. I'm sorry that put you in an unpleasant bind."

There was almost honesty there, just enough to cover the obvious lie that Lazarus knew exactly why Verus had done what he had done. Though to admit fault, even in such a deceptive manner, was unlike the man. Perhaps things really were spinning outside Roache's control.

"What's the plan, sir?"

Lazarus sighed. "The plan *was* to reconnect with Huile. But even there plans fail me. I have heard nothing from our friends in the Resurgence, and with the raiders on edge, we're starting to run out of allies here."

Namter found his hand drifting towards the letter in his pocket. He had kept the message from his master, and now the specter of guilt began to haunt him. If they had been coordinating with the UCCR, perhaps they could have scared off the Principate invaders. There was too much to lose here, too much Tribute, even if he didn't trust Roache. Yet that was also far too much power to give the tycoon. If he had his refineries back, and no Verus to challenge him, he'd have even more reason to remove his butler and any among the Brotherhood who opposed him.

Another blast, metal legs gleaming in the morning sun. It seemed that the imperials had brought a few spidertanks, Truegods knew from where. They really were serious, desperate even. Lazarus turned away from the grim scene.

"It's like... It's like the day my father died," Roache said. "After all those years waiting, a youth wasted, I finally inherited my birthright, only to find that my dad had frittered away my dear grandfather's sangleum empire."

"Ah yes, the inequity," Namter said dryly. Roache never brought up his grandfather, except to complain about what had been denied him by his own father.

"Years wasted, trying to rebuild, trying to fix what had been broken," Lazarus muttered. "A lifetime wasted. Two lifetimes, I suppose, I know it is not glamorous to serve a vagrant."

"I certainty would not call you a vagrant, sir." Namter pulled out a duster and started to work on the man's desk.

Lazarus waved him stop, "I've been treating you like a domestic for too long. It's easy to believe those roles, even when they are naught but for show. Were you but a simple valet for hire, you would have left me years ago, when I had nothing and no prospects."

"Never sir," Namter said, though he had thought about it many of times. Truth was, his loyalty had been something closer to depression. Before he had joined the Brotherhood he had lacked all purpose, his only training being in the Roache household. He had seen the filth that was the world of men, at least Lazarus Roache was known filth. He would have never left his master, though on occasion he had considered slitting his wrists and draining himself in some stained motor-inn bathtub.

"I never realized that you were greater than any fortune I could have been left with," Lazarus said, patting Namter on the shoulder. "Even as we barely scrapped by, even as our skin burned pink in the Wastes sun as we struggled to squeeze sangleum from dry dirt, even as the years turned to decades and more, you stayed by me. You found our salvation in The Flayed Prince; you've kept everything together even as the world conspires against us. You were never my servant, Namter, you were my partner, my friend."

Namter studied his master, trying to find the lie. And yet he could not find one in the man's slightly wrinkled, very tired face. It occurred to him suddenly that Lazarus Roache could never have been behind the assassination attempt. Despite his faithless nature, the tycoon needed Namter. Needed him for practical reasons, of course, to keep the Unblind loyal, to manage the dull routines and paperwork, to clean up after himself. But there was more to it than that. Lazarus, despite all his viciousness, despite his celestial Gifts and occasional sociopathy, needed human connection, or rather, a convincing approximation of human connection. The man had never known the true thing, neither had Namter until he had joined the Brotherhood. Lazarus needed someone he truly thought of as a friend, and though he may lie to Namter, may use him, mistreat him, undermine the very cause for which he lived for, Lazarus could not get rid of his butler. And now he needed him more than ever.

"Of course, Lazarus," Namter said with a wary smile.

The tycoon smiled back, disturbingly genuine. Outside the blasts continued.

"I suppose, we wait now." Lazarus turned back to the window. "This battle is out of our hands."

"Perhaps it needn't be." An idea suddenly birthed in Namter's mind. There might still be a way to play this to the Brotherhood's advantage. "I wanted to confide something in you, sir."

"Yes?"

"You mentioned the possibility of getting an extension on the contract with The Flayed Prince." Namter walked as he talked. "I was initially hesitant, but more and more I began to think this the wise course of action. Then I had a vision."

"A vision?" Lazarus asked.

Namter nodded as he lied. "From The Flayed Prince himself."

Lazarus scratched his chin. "That's not... Verus was never able to—"

"Verus lacked the faith!" Namter shouted, interrupting his master for perhaps the first time ever. It was a thrilling act. "He failed The Flayed Prince, and now that the day of Reification is coming, the divine one has made himself known to me. And he has told me that if we can get him the Tribute we have, then we shall have another seven years to build him an empire. And your Gift will, of course, be renewed."

"That's..." Lazarus almost stumbled on his words. "That is excellent news! But why haven't you mentioned it before?"

Namter sighed and stepped aside, allowing his faux exasperation to cover for himself as he fabricated an excuse. "I did not know if I could believe it myself, was I just so desperate to believe every dream a vision? Could it just be my Eye playing tricks on me? But no, The Flayed Prince has a way of making himself known. He has seen everything."

"Everything?" Lazarus asked, with a subtle hint of fear buried in his casual tone. Namter cursed himself.

"Yes everything." He nodded as if nothing was amiss. "Everything that I see through my Eye, as the Watcher, he can see. Alas, he had been blind to Verus's gaze for many years now. Verus coveted his own power, his ego would not allow him to share even with a God. Can you imagine, being blinded by your own follower? The Flayed Prince was thrilled to make contact with me, pleased by our loyalty. And if we continue our faithful service, we will be well rewarded.

Lazarus nodded, fears mollified. "That means, if we win the battle here—"

"No, we cannot risk it!" Namter said, which was the first part of his story that was true. "If we lose the Tribute we have here, all will be lost. We must take the opportunity afforded by the battle and retreat, with all our sangleum, refined æther-oil, and prisoners."

Lazarus furrowed his brows. "If we did that we would be abandoning—"

"Those gang lords who now question your authority," Namter concluded. "While withholding the resources they desperately need. Win or lose, the remnants of the gangs will be forced to pledge their loyalty to you, simply to survive. And this imperial army shall not follow us so deeply in the Wastes, it would stretch their supply lines to a breaking point."

"I'll have my extension and de facto control over what remain of Stinktown," Lazarus said, eyes wide. "My dear Namter, after all these years you are starting to think like a businessman."

Namter gave a short bow. "I learned from the best, sir."

"We shall get started at once. I still have a tanker-truck that can hold the remaining æther-oil from Huile. Then we need to get the slickdust loaded, pack up my tent, rally our guards, ah too much to do, so little time, but we have a shot, Namter, we have a shot!" Then the tycoon did most unexpected thing, rushing forward to embrace his butler. Namter hesitated, then returned the embrace.

Yes, Lazarus could never get rid of Namter. The betrayal stopped there. But there was a betrayal, to something much larger than mere men. Namter would bring his true Master the Tribute promised, even if that meant harvesting raiders. He would fulfill his duty as an Awakener, to the best that the grim circumstances would allow. Then, with Lazarus there, Reification at hand, Namter would fulfill his duty as a Watcher, and reveal to The Flayed Prince every single dark truth he had uncovered.

*I've stopped praying that anyone can hear me. I've tried rewiring the speaker on this [muttered explicative] thing, and my only hope is that I've failed. The alternative is that there's no one left to hear me. I have to believe that's there's someone out there, that what happened here... Demiurge...*

*[Silence for a full minute.]*

*Captain's dead. Gregor's dead. Sigrid's dead. I buried Hanz this morning. Thought he had been spared the blast, no signs of mutation, but his lungs looked crimson enough as he coughed them up. City's a necropolis now. The great bridge of Latapons is just a couple of pilons over baked mud. Food's low, not that there's anyone to share it with. Before Captain got his head blown off, we were going to make contact with some civilians, but last I heard from the voxbox was their screams as... those things they got to them. But I think they were saying... [sounds of static]*

*My grandma loved to drink at the Vinsmann watering hole. When she'd come home, she'd tuck me in and tell me stories not about fairies or princes, but about demons. Yes, demons, fuck that 'ætheric aberration' nonsense. She told me of men with the face of pigs, balls of living bile, angels with rusting wings, and walking factories made of flesh. Bless her bibacious soul, now I realize she was censoring herself, making them seem like mere storybook monsters. These things, they're not like beasts, they don't hunt for food. They're not like men either... Not even asylum maniacs take that kind of pleasure in killing. They're more like— [strange noises interrupt]*

*There! Can you hear them! Over the storm? Demiurge, I swear they sneak up to the bunker door and whisper. Whisper things just below conscious hearing, sneaking ideas into your head, can't be sure what thoughts are your own. Maybe that's why Gregor went mad, why I had to put a bullet in his head as he slept, before he tried anything.*

*Oh Demiurge, that's them. Listen! Tap, tap, taping. Hear it? Makes you wonder if it's just a rat, but I don't think even rats survived all this. Their breath... You can hear it right? How do they do that? It's like they're right in your fucking ear!*

*[The signal is lost for a minute. Static can be heard, alongside classical music from an unknown source.]*

*...on the door! They're banging on the door! Thud. Thud. Thud. Thud. [Manic laughter.] Must be tired of playing. Well I'm tired too. I'm so damned tired. If there is someone out there, someone else who made it, know that I was here. Tell the world I died fighting. Tell the world about Private—*

*[Signal lost.]*

*—Voxbox message from unknown soldier. Recorded by imperial recon forces sent by General Varma, one week after the Calamity.*

# CHAPTER 38

Groaning echoes of gunfire and the sonorous thunder of uneven fusillade, distant and stretched, rushing through winding caverns and the reverberations of buried pipes. Marcel worked clearing rifles and setting clockbombs. Preparing weapons, underground, while a siege blasted above. It brought back memories of that night, the night of Crimson Death, the night they had gone under Blackwood Row and—

*Demiurge damn it!* Marcel shook his head. Why did he keep finding himself in situations that dug up that memory? Again and again and again, like a rotfly drawn to mog-lizard shit, he kept going back, finding new ways to relive that night. At this point it was beyond tiring and just a tad absurd. Whatever happened, here and in Huile, when all was said and done, he was going to take a train and spend the rest of his damned life on some sunny hilltop far away from any sewers, or underway passages, or clockbombs, or anyone whose names rhymed with Razarus or Loache.

The room shook with an artillery blast, chips of rock falling from the ceiling.

"Sounds like a big one," Diego said, with an accompanying whistle. The metal-armed man placed his æthergloved hands onto one of Belona's broken scatterguns, and with a flash, transformed the shabby, cracked, rusted thing into merely a shabby and rusted thing. As he worked, he hummed to himself. For a second Marcel thought he heard the Anthem Imperial in the man's tune, but that might have been his imagination.

"So, you're going to show Sylvaine and Kayip the way to Roache?" Marcel asked.

"That's the plan," Diego said, yawning and waving a rolled-up map. "I'll leave the actual shooting, or, uh, swording to them. Not about to risk my hide or sweat for your revenge. Already down 70,000 frascs on this job, *thank you*. Boss-lady's might be more willing to indulge in some target practice if she had the time, but she's got to head back to Huile, make her report, check if those proverbial embers we saw hadn't yet turned blaze-like. Which way you headed?"

Marcel sighed. That was the hundred-aurem question, wasn't it? And it was coming time to answer it. There was only one responsible choice. Marcel had to stop running, had to stop assuming that everything would miraculously turn out okay if they only took down Lazarus Roache. The man was just some shithead tycoon, pushed out to the Wastes, about to watch the remains of his empire crumble. Belona's plan of dragging the Holtag army into war seemed to be working. To put Marcel's own personal desire for revenge above the needs of Huile would just be childish.

"So's that monk a bachelor or what?" Diego asked suddenly, slipping a freshly polished bayonet onto a clockwork rifle.

"What?" Marcel asked. "Uh, he's a monk?"

Diego laughed. "Yeah, I've met enough monks and hierophants and priests and all sorts to know that the Church's chastity vows aren't worth the spittle spent mumbling them."

"Oh," Marcel said, unsure of what to make of that. A question popped into his head; one he knew he should ignore. "Does, Alba... I mean has she, uh, been seeing any other men?"

"Men? Hmm... No, not men."

"Okay," Marcel said, embarrassed by how relieved he was. Then, after a moment: "Wait..."

Footsteps and the sway of an handtorch announced the sudden arrival of Sylvaine and Kayip, who turned round a bend in the stone.

"Marcel!" Sylvaine said. She was wearing one of Alba's old Resurgence scout's jacket and had on her hip a pistol. The militarized look didn't suit the engineer. Even Kayip had a scattergun slung, though Marcel suspected he would be relying more on his bracelet.

"I am glad to see you are well," Kayip said. Marcel felt a pang of guilt. Going back to Huile meant abandoning them two, right at the very end of their journey. How would they take it, would they see it as a betrayal?

"You two okay?" Marcel asked.

Sylvaine nodded. "The bounty hunters gave us decent cots, and Kayip made us some omelets."

"Omelets?" Marcel said. "I was only given some old ration bars."

"Yeah, well you don't cook," Diego said, giving Kayip a overly familiar slap on the back. "Delicious!"

"Wait, did everyone else have—"

"We do not have time for frivolities," Kayip said. "Alba has called us to gather."

"Must mean Frefis is back from his scouting," Diego said.

* * *

It did indeed mean Frefis was back. The young salvi man sat on an old crate, panting, horns resting on a rock cropping. All of them had gathered in the room Marcel had spent the night, including, of course, Belona, still chained. Frefis took a sip of water from a canteen held by Alba. His jacket was open, his chest bound up tight with sweat-soaked linen.

"They're on the move," Frefis said. "Retreating?"

"The whole army?" Alba asked.

Frefis shook his head. "Just Lazacorp forces. As far as I can see, they aren't coordinating their movements. The raiders are fighting, while Lazacorp is closing shop and fleeing into the Wastes."

"One last betrayal," Belona chuckled darkly. "As it always goes for friends of Roache."

"I saw him head into his tent," Frefis said.

"Then you all don't have much time to strike," Alba said. She gestured down a crooked tunnel. "This way will lead you under the Lazacorp camp, Diego can take you. No one else knows these paths, excepting a few grumpy mutants, but they haven't caused us trouble in quite some time, and they're certainly no friends of Roache's."

"Wait, I have to lead them all the way myself?" Diego protested. "But I got a map drawn up and everything."

Alba nodded. "Not enough time to let them wander the underway following your strix-shit handwriting if Roache's already preparing to flee."

"But why not Frefis?" Diego protested. "I risked my life last evening mucking around with last-minute sabotage. Could have gotten shot up by raiders or imperials, and now you want me to—"

"Orders are orders," Alba interrupted. "Just get them into the camp, and then you can rendezvous with me."

Diego grumbled and groaned, but finally nodded. Alba turned to Sylvaine and Kayip. "Sorry I can't take you myself, but Huile calls. I've been out here far too long as it is."

Marcel sucked in his breathe. It was time, he knew, to announce his decision. To accept responsibility for what had happened in Huile, and to tell his friends that he couldn't be joining them. He looked at them all, Kayip, grimly determined, Sylvaine, nervous and dour, holding tight the monk's hand. And then there was Belona. She looked as if she were staring death in the face and remained unimpressed. If Alba did follow through and executed her... Demiurge what sort of awkward autocar ride would that be back to Huile? Marcel couldn't help but feel he had failed the imperial, as strange an emotion as that was.

Finally he glanced at his old captain, his lover from a not so distant, yet impossibly far life. She had become, in her few years' absence, a ghost, a wisp of longing, a specter of judgement. Alba turned her eyes towards him, idle curiosity in dim blue, skin rough, eyebags heavy. She was, as she always was, a person, whose life had gone on regardless of the past, but who, like himself, could not fully escape it. On some level he still wanted his announcement to prove something to her, his strength were he to follow Roache, his maturity if he went home. Yet this couldn't be about her, it was about doing the right thing regardless of its cost.

"I—" Marcel began.

"I must tell you all something," Kayip said, slightly quicker and louder. Marcel tried to get a word in, but the monk continued: "There is more to Lazarus Roache and this cult than I have told you. I must apologize for my secrecy, I thought it would be wrong to... No, there is no place for excuses, I will simply tell you the truth. Lazarus Roache had done more than dabble in demonology. He has found a being of pure sin, buried deep within the earth, and seeks to manifest it into reality. You may call it an ætheric aberration if you wish, but its name does not matter, it is kin of those abominations that crawled out of the depths of the Wastes in the first horrid years of the Calamity. But unlike the blind, wild hatred those demon-gods bore, this one is subtler, he seeks to corrupt and control. It is his power that allows Roache to bind others' minds through slickdust, and if he is awakened, he will wrought far more devastation than Lazacorp or any army of the Principate, or raider hordes. And it is in a mere twenty days that he shall come into being, shall reify, if Roache and his cult allies are able to gather the requisite blood, which it seems they are even now extricating from this battlefield."

"What?" Alba said, which seemed a sensible reaction.

"A demon-god?" Diego snorted.

It did all sound absurd on its surface, but then again, if true it put into perspective a lot of what Verus had raved about to Marcel back in Blackwood Row, 'truegods' and 'oathblood' and 'people serving through death' and all that nonsense. Also the fact that the foreman had possessed a hypnotizing eyeless eye that invoked madness and could summon up whips of blackfire seemed to Marcel to be solid evidence of the monk's claims.

"He's telling the truth," Sylvaine said. "I found notes mentioning how Lazarus Roache was functioning as an independent æthergrid. I know most of you aren't trained in æthermantics, but to put in simply, that's really not a normal thing for humans to do. Having some sort of direction connection to an ætheric being would explain it, and any aberration powerful enough for that could be incredibly dangerous."

"Why did you not mention this sooner!" Belona shouted, Marcel silently agreeing. If true, this changed things very significantly, Roache was not some criminal on the outs, he was the key to some horrid terror. Marcel had been right to try and take him down! Despite the objectively awful news, he felt almost relieved by this sudden vindication.

"I thought it my burden to bear," Kayip said with a sigh. "But that was a weakness of mine. This is greater than myself."

"I've seen the devastation even lesser ætheric beings can unleash, in my time in bondage out by the great Ghost Reefs," Frefis added. "Malva Ironship cities ravaged, sent to the bottom of the sea."

"I've never seen anything in the Wastes that can't be felled with a good handful of lead," Alba said, pacing, "but it might be worth nipping this one in the bud. Not that it changes much for me, I have a report to make back in Huile. What do you think Mar?"

"I, uh," Marcel's tongue stumbled. He had everything prepared, but a sudden wrench had been tossed in the gears of his mind.

"Talwar is no coward," Belona snarled. "He will not abandon his duty to take down Roache."

"Your opinion wasn't asked, imperial," Alba said with dismissive disdain. She turned to Marcel, arms crossed. "I could see it going either way. What's your call?"

Marcel shut in eyes in frantic thought. If he did take down Lazarus Roache and escape, he could still rendezvous with Alba. Two birds, one well-placed stone. If things went poorly, then all could be lost, Huile abandoned to the mortar-fire of General Levair… No, that was a defeatist attitude, an excuse for inaction! There was still a chance to make everything right. He had despaired when faced with failure, but his instincts had been correct. He could strop Lazarus Roache, prevent these horrors from awakening, and go back to save Huile. He had been right all along. He could still fix this.

"I'm not giving this up, not at the end of it all," he said, with a nod to his friends.

Alba nodded, her eyes saying something her lips wouldn't. She had to understand, Marcel reasoned, she had to see this was the sensible, even heroic path. Finally, she gave a small smile. "Just don't get yourself killed, Talwar."

"Haven't so far," Marcel said, trying and failing to laugh. "But if we're going to take down Lazacorp. Then we need all the help we can get, including Bel—"

"Not your decision," Alba interrupted. She squatted down and stared the imperial, eye to eye.

"I'm ready to face my death, even at the hands of terrorists," Belona said.

"Great," Alba said, "because you will."

"Alba, I know she did some horri—" But his old captain raised her finger, and despite himself, Marcel shut up.

"You know what I did right?" Alba smirked. "Led the Huile Sewer Rats under your army, strapped clockbombs, let the gas drown your men in blood."

Belona growled.

"Marcel might have his trousers in a twist about it, but I don't," Alba continued. "Set out the same scenario, I'd do it all again. I'll never get tired of Imperial corpses. Will never pass up an opportunity to force you to bury your mistakes."

"Alba don't—" Marcel began, silenced again by his captain's finger. Whatever their hatred, this was just cruel.

"You can kill me, so kill me," Belona said. "But why play this game of mockery? I foolishly thought you a professional."

"Because though I will kill you, it doesn't need to be today," Alba said, flashing a key. "You're an honorable woman, in your own fucked up way. Give me your word and we can make a deal."

"What sort of deal?" Belona said.

"A deal you might actually want to fulfill. A chance to take down Roache with your own hands. But succeed or fail, you'll come back to me, immediately. No dallying, no running, swear it on your damned Imperator."

Belona thought on this and nodded. "So then we'll finish things, woman to woman. A duel."

Alba laughed, her voice echoing down distant tunnels. "What absolute taurshit. I beat you already, imperial, I beat you twice." She held up the commensurate number of fingers. "You're my prisoner, I'm giving you a stay of execution, not a pardon, and I'm certainly not going to trade fair bullets when I could just as easily end you now."

"All this talk of death and revenge," Marcel cut in. "Why not put aside these vendettas and—"

"Stay out of this!" Alba and Belona said in unison.

"So after I fight Talwar—" Belona started.

"No dueling Marcel either," Alba said. "Let's face it, you beat him a thousand drevs to a half-frasc."

Diego burst out in laughter. Marcel started to mumble a protest, but it sounded pathetic.

Belona shook her head. "I cannot agree. I am your prisoner, you say? Well, he was mine. And Talwar agreed to our combat freely, you have no right to take that from us."

"If Marcel survives, he'll need to return to Huile," Alba said. "I can't let your feud risk the city's peace."

"Then after Huile," Belona said. "I have no desire for the city to burn, even if it bears the wrong banners. I can find the patience to wait. If Talwar is not executed by his own people, then I will have him."

"This is all just stupidity," Marcel said, pacing as he tried to act the very needed voice of reason. "There's no reason we need to be trading lives."

"This doesn't involve you," Belona spat.

"It *literally* does!"

"Fair enough," Alba tapped her boot as she thought. "You're right, it's not my place to save Marcel from each and every predicament he constructs for himself. If you two want to fight it out, fight it out. So, do we have a deal? I mean, you're dead either way."

Belona was silent a long moment. She sucked in her breath and sighed, before glancing up at Marcel, and then Alba. Her gaze was not full of hateful fire, not even embers, but what remained long after a flame, something sintered and worn.

"I died three years ago, by your hands," she said, quiet. "Since then, I've been only a specter, walking about in someone else's uniform. To trade a ghost for a chance at vengeance, twice over even? Oh how I desire for your head too, bounty hunter... but I suppose I cannot get greedy. So yes, I agree to your terms."

"Swear it," Alba said.

"Belona, Alba, don't—"

"I swear it," Belona raised her shackled arms. "On the life of our Imperator Lothar Diedrev, on the honor of House Agrippus, I swear to you I will honor this agreement."

Alba didn't shake, but instead shoved a key into the woman's hand. "I look forward to cutting your throat, Butcher."

# CHAPTER 39

As they followed Diego down the irregularly sloped passageways, Sylvaine could begin to smell violence. It was funny, but violence did have a smell, mostly the pungency of sulphur and oil from a distance, the tang of blood a little nearer. Close up she could smell sweat, fear, and panic, pheromonic screams that seemed inaudible to most. The odor was strong enough to cut through the ever-present putrefaction of Stinktown, which itself was growing in strength with each anxious step.

They were panting, each one of them, not quite running, but certainly not walking, aglow in the lights of their handtorches. Somehow, they had all made it out of Stinktown alive, and were each dumb enough to try and break back in. Even the imperial had come with, as unfortunate a surprise as that was. Sylvaine thought she could rely on the vengeance of the bounty hunter for one good thing, but even that was asking too much.

"There's a shortcut through here," Diego said, grasping at a rusted metal door. It cracked as he pulled, but didn't move. "Nuts. Just a sec," he said, taking a step back and raising his metallic hands.

"Got it," Sylvaine said, pushing her ætherglove forward and knocking the door to the floor with a single spark, before continuing on. In a few hours, her Knack would be gone, so she might as well use it while she could, while Lazarus still breathed. Or perhaps Lazarus would survive the day, and she would die in some idiotic attempt to assassinate the man. Was it weird that she didn't view that outcome with any more dread than the alternative? Lose her Knack, lose her life, it seemed about the same either way. Was that what this was then? Some strange, dramatic attempt at self-annihilation in the face of—

Sylvaine tripped over some unseen thing, blinded by her desperate thoughts. An arm rushed out and steadied her. Kayip offered a quick smile in the dark, as they kept moving. Sylvaine shook her head. Of course she cared, of course she wanted to take down Roache and survive the day. If not for herself, then for the monk. Her friend had given so much on his quest, she would see it through to the end with him. He had once had powers too, and lost them, yet found a way to live with himself and his mistakes. Maybe she could too.

Also if they didn't take down Roache, he was going to summon up a horrendous ætheric aberration of mythic power and malice, who would unleash a new Calamity upon the world, which should probably factor into her decision-making at least a little.

"Okay," Diego said, map in hand. "We turn right here, then go down this old bunker, should lead us into a series of basements that converge into an old sewage plant, don't worry long inactive, with pipes that should lead directly into a power station in the middle of the Lazacorp camp where—"

The man paused suddenly. He whipped out a pistol.

"What was that?" he said.

"What?" Belona asked, rifle raised. Kayip unraveled his blade from his wrist, and Marcel glanced around. Sylvaine hadn't noticed anything and found it odd that a human would first. She placed her glove on a nearby wall and tried to sense out the area with pulses of æther. The walls were dense with rusted mechanisms too messy to quickly make sense of.

Diego inched back the way they came, pistol at the ready. "Thought I heard something. Movement?"

"Someone following us?" Marcel said, too loud. Belona and Kayip both gave a quick *shh!*

"I don't hear anything," Sylvaine whispered. Well, nothing large, just a—"

A scraprat scurried past. Diego swore and lowered his pistol.

"Y'all and your suicide mission got me spooked," he said turning round and shaking his head. "Jumping at every damn—"

"Tripwire!" Sylvaine said suddenly, as she noticed its glean off Diego's hanging handtorch.

The man jumped back, but not quite in time. A snap, a click, and then a blast all in quick succession. The rotting supports gave way instantly, and stones, dirt, and fossilized trash poured down. Sylvaine leapt down to avoid a flying jagged something, panic coursing through her veins. Her instincts roared over her, senses sharpening, mind dimming. She felt something on top of her, a person. He claws raised up to strike at—

*No!* she snarled her instinct back. The man above her was Kayip, trying to shield her from the blast, though now that she had taken a moment to calm herself, she realized it was a relatively small one. She could smell the musk of mining explosives, as well as spilled oil, but no blood. Right as she was about to try and stand, another blast went off, distant this time, and another, and another, the last one collapsing the right junction of a split in the tunnel some thirty metres forward.

"Is everyone okay?" Marcel shouted, after the last explosion echoed away. He also had fallen, not far, with Belona standing at the ready, rifle aimed at the dark. Diego was nowhere to be seen, in his direction was a pile of rubble near to the top of the half-collapsed passageway. A fit of coughs was the first evidence that the man was alive, though distressingly it came from the other side of the wall of debris.

"Taurshit smeared over toast," Diego swore. "That was too close."

"We can move the stones," Kayip said, standing up and starting the task.

"No time!" Diego said, half his face appearing in a gap between the fallen earthwork. "Anyways, I didn't get off completely clean." He pushed forward his left arm, and only left arm, as the metallic hand once attached to it was now just a few wires and cracked rods.

"That ain't good," Marcel observed.

"What's worse is that we cleared out these passageways years ago," Diego said. "Demiurge knows who's been retrapping them..."

The ceiling shook, tossing bits of stone and muck. Sylvaine could hear the distant muffled roar of war engines.

"Not sure we have time to solve that mystery," Marcel said.

"Right, right. Well, I think the rest of me's going to take this as an excuse to head on back," Diego said. "But don't worry, path's simple enough, just take the next right and—"

"Right's blocked," Belona shouted. "Left's clear."

"Well fuck. Just a second." Diego lifted up his bag and pulled out his map. With more than a little difficulty, he took out a pen, uncapped with his mouth, and began scribbling. "That's fine, that's fine, that's completely, absolutely okay. You just have to reroute to the abandoned scrap-warehouse, you know Kayip, the one with the... uhh murals. There's a path in the basement that goes straight into the power station right by Lazarus's tent. Here!" The man shoved the crumpled map through the hole.

Kayip took it and squinted. "How do we access the warehouse?"

Diego laughed nervously. "Well, the underway don't go everywhere. I suppose you can try the front door."

# CHAPTER 40

"It is a beautiful day for a battle!" Commandant Lechslov shouted, his neck bent out the side window of the command wartruck, scanning the carnage through a set of binoculars. Before him blots of blue dashed forward, or sometimes backwards, firing shots at the no longer distant city. Warwalkers followed, the lanky machines firing their motorguns into the dirt and occasional enemy troops below. Tanks of all sorts rushed onward with uneven bravado, rushtanks svelte and quick, spidertanks crawling on clanking legs, conetanks spinning madly as they fired. Their shells tore through the outer buildings of Stinktown as if they were made of papier-mâché, which perhaps some of them were. It would hardly be strange for a city of trash.

"It is certainly a... dusty day," Colonel Goss said, staring out at the storm that had gathered behind him. The artillery that had early on struck enemy positions with precision were now firing far or short, their targets mere theory. The only strategy now was to blindly barrage the city, and they even missed that wide target on occasion. Goss had suggested early they delayed the invasion, but Lechslov had ignored him, or perhaps had simply not heard him. It was closer to a mumble than an order, and it was very windy.

"Look at our men go!" Lechslov cheered. "Those raider brutes don't know what to do in the face of Imperial steel!

Goss was not so confident in his commandant's assessment. Though the initial assault had gone surprisingly well, overwhelming armored assaults do tend to overwhelm, the raiders had adapted quick. They had burst in their hundreds on motorbikes and warbuggies from every street and alleyway of the city, like a swarm of rust locusts. Darting this way and that, strafing imperial lines and cutting between squads like snakes through fingergrass. Imperial tanks had little clue on how to respond, they were firing upon their squads of blue about as often as raiders. Several tanks and warwalkers had been lost, and not just to enemy fire, but to unseen mud pits or their own untrained incompetence.

Glass burst in the truck, Lechslov ducked down. A motorbike whirred out from behind some ruins, a raider in the sidecar firing off a repeater-pistol. They were driven off only by the return fire of the commander's chauffeur, Sergeant Sofia Pulcher.

"And… stay away!" Lechslov shouted, with unconvincing ferocity. He laughed, also hollow. "Perhaps we should move back?"

"We may lose visual of the battlefield in the dust storm, Commandant," Pulcher said. "But if your order is retreat…"

"No retreat! Never flee a battle you are winning, my good sergeant!"

"Of course, Commandant."

The raiders were even making superior use of their infantry, Goss silently noted. Hiding in the outer structures of Stinktown, taking potshots from hidden windows, or firing down with motorguns, as the imperials moved back and forth inconclusively. The plan had been to breach the city by… half an hour ago. The walls of Stinktown were flimsy scrapmetal compared to Huile, or any half-fortified city, and yet they seemed impenetrable to the disorganized offensive.

Goss had been through enough battles to know that a decision was need. Decisive vision could turn a stalemate into victory, or a loss into a strategic gain. And he was the commander, technically. He could order a full-on assault! Straight into the enemy stronghold… with little exact intel and no clear goals. Yes, what a grand plan. He imagined a weeping soldier in front of him, holding tight a squadmate, friend, brother, bloodied, dead, beseeching Goss, asking what it was the man had sacrificed for, what was the plan, *Dear Demiurge, what was the Colonel thinking?*

No, no, perhaps a retreat was in order, a 'strategic regrouping' if Lechslov opposed the terminology. But then, what if that gave the raider's time to rally? They could be facing a fiercer foe, and retreat would open the question of why they had even attacked in the first place. And those ætheric aberrations, if they let the raiders be at peace, they very well might… summon more? Maybe? Goss didn't really have a first grasp on anti-demon tactics, but it seemed like something that could not be allowed to fester. But then, if the imperials did strike and made an error, they could be caught up in block-to-block fighting against an enemy with homefield advantage and—*Blessed Imperator*, why was Goss's handkerchief so wet with sweat?

As the Colonel worked to dry himself, Lechslov cried out with glee. "Retreating! The cowards are fleeing!"

"What?" Goss said, as he pushed himself around the Commandant to get a better look. Indeed, it seemed that a large portion of the raider force had started to move back, rushing as fast as they could into the largest thoroughfare of the city. He grabbed the binoculars from Lechslov to get a closer look, but could make out nothing in the blur of dust and vehicles that gave him a hint as to *why* they were retreating.

"I told you, did I not, Colonel?" Lechslov said. "And now they open up a chink in their armor, a cut in their stomach, a pustule in their—"

"Yes, Commandant, I understand" Goss said.

Lechslov pulled a voxbox from the front seat and flicked it on. "Soldiers of the 1st West Bastillian Army! Your heroism is rewarded, the enemy flees before us! Now is the time to push the attack! All troops in vicinity of... the main Stinktown Street, your orders are to—" He paused, as if realizing it wasn't technically his right to send such orders, and glanced expectantly at Goss. Something was wrong, the Colonel felt, something odd about the raiders' move. Why would they break so quickly, and so easily? He felt as if he had studied similar maneuvers, but his mind buzzed, and he could not summon up the memories. Yet the chance to strike would not last long, if they did not take the opportunity now the enemy could regroup, and the battle could slip from their fingers...

"Colonel?" Lechslov whispered, staring, demanding with his gaze.

"Attack, yes, attack," Goss said, glancing away, at the approaching dust storm, wishing more than anything his General was here to take all this horrid responsibility from him.

* * *

Over the scope of a mounted clockwork rifle rose smoke, wisping up from the clope in the half-toothed mouth of Red Rust Ronnie. One the gang lord's flunkies, a bald raider whose Namter had not bothered to learn (as it

372

would not matter soon), had up a scraped-together motorgun on the next window, and was trying to get loosen a stuck belt of ammunition, assisted in this struggle by Brother Tullius.

"Are they coming?" asked Namter to Ronnie, as the gang lord squinted through the scope with his bloodshot eye. In the wide street below raiders rushed back in motorbike and buggy, around the bend where Namter had ordered prepared a large gate to cover their faux retreat. In opposing windows across the street, as well as many parallel to their own, sat hidden raider gunmen, motorgun nests, and grenadiers, all in wait. A few windows down Namter could even see an overeager servant of Bloated Britta, torso jutting out for a better look. The idiot could well give them away, but with some luck by time the imperials noticed anything was up, it would be several hundred metres too late.

Red Rust Ronnie chuckled, a gravely, unhealthy sound.

"Oh those blue-caps took our bait. Swallowed the hook and sucking down the line!" He squealed with excitement. "Guess they never heard that Ronnie's boys don't ever run! Not for real, not for cowardice."

"They shall discover the truth soon enough," Namter said sagely.

"Great idea by the way," Ronnie said with an unasked-for slap on the chest. "Classic raider move, can't believe we didn't think of it! Feigned retreat, get them pursuing, hit them with the old 'Vastium five-and-a-half caliber hello!'"

"I would think it best to get on the voxbox and assure that your men are in position, sir," Namter said. "If the counter-attack should fail, you'd leave the heart of Stinktown open to the enemy."

Ronnie laughed and waved away the fear. "Be like shooting ghul-shrews in a shoebox," he said, as he sauntered over to the voxbox.

"Ah, and I will take no offense if you fail to mention us," Namter said quickly. "Battlefield glory is of no interest to the Brotherhood, and I would not want my presence to undercut your authority to your men, or to Britta's boys."

Ronnie tapped his forehead knowingly, then flicked on the voxbox to ramble crude encouragement to his ersatz troops. Namter's plan was last-minute and hasty, but proceeding well. As the gangs fought the invaders, Lazacorp extracted their resources and made flight. Already caravans were leaving Stinktown, westward. The only concern now was that the raiders might actually win. Namter had sold his plan to Roache on the assumption that the imperials were likely to take or break the city. In truth the invaders' vicious bark outperformed their mediocre bite. Were the gang lords to actually hold them off, to win a great victory, they might turn their triumphant rage against the fleeing Lazacorp. Or worse still, Lazarus might then sweet talk everything back to normal, and continue his machinations unhindered. No, Stinktown must be broken, there must be none Lazarus could rely on but his butler.

Namter glanced at Tullius, who nodded and flashed a blade.

Ronnie shut off the voxbox with a smirk. "Guessing we have a minute or two until the imperials start puttering in." He pointed his finger down at the street like a gun, and muttered *bang!*

"One quick question," Namter said, pulling something from his pocket. It was a pistol, custom-made. "Does this weapon look familiar?"

Ronnie squinted, then pointed to the engraving of a portly woman wrestling a slug-beast. "That's one of Britt's pistols ain't it? I've seen some of her captains flaunt them. She gift you one?"

"So it's easily recognizable," Namter said, ignoring the question. "Anyone who saw it would know where it came from?"

"I suppose so. I mean, I don't understand—there a reason you want to be fighting imperials with a Bloastbeast weapon?"

Namter chuckled and shook his head. "A relief, sir, a relief. You see, I had to make many plans in haste, and was not sure I got all the details right. You mess one thing up and your intentions can be lost, you understand?"

"Not quite—" Ronnie began, as Namter raised the pistol and shot him in the head.

In the corner of the room, the other raider tried to shout out something, but his shocked protestations were muffled by the hand of Brother Tullius, as he shoved a blade three times through the Rust Thorn's back.

Namter dropped the pistol, and with silent coordination rushed alongside his Brother out into the hallway. They turned leftward, confused shouts echoing from the Bloatbeast room behind them. In the direction towards which they dashed, round the bend, came the sounds of footsteps, much quicker than anticipated.

Swallowing a curse, Namter pulled open a window and jumped out, onto a rickety catwalk that might have been a fire escape, or just a way for a cheap slumlord to add extra living space. He slammed the window down just as Brother Tullius landed beside him. The two ducked low, as down the hall raiders rushed into the room. The first on the scene would be members of Britta's Bloatbeasts, Namter had assured they were the closest. Next rushed a group by the window, about seven strong. Namter risked a glance up to confirm that they were Rust Thorns.

He held his breath, as the Rust Thorns burst into the room, shouting angry questions. The risk here was that rational minds might prevail, that the Rust Thorns might give their hated enemy time to speak, to explain that they weren't the ones who kill Ronnie, to say that there must have been another party who had assassinated the lord and run—

Gunshots soothed Namter's fears. Shouts and screams and the sounds of death. A smile creeped over his face, perhaps this was what it was like being Roache, always playing off people's darkest natures, planning around their foibles and flaws and rarely being disappointed. There was some thrill in it.

With a nod, he and Tullius skulked down the creaking stairway, which shook as an imperial shell smashed into a tenement a few blocks away. Chaos spread quickly around them, at the speed of voxbox waves, no doubt. Bullets began to fly from window to window, room to room. Namter hurried quick to avoid getting caught amongst the crossfire. At the bottom, an autocar was waiting in the alley, Brother Avitus at its wheel.

"All goes well?" he asked, as he began to drive.

"The imperials will find no organized resistance here," Namter said from the passenger's seat, as the backstreets of Stinktown blurred by the window. "The core of the city will be open, the gang lords' fine manors will stare down the barrels of Principate tanks. They will not give those easily; they will spill their men's blood in the thousands to protect their holdings. It will give them little time to notice our escape."

"If The Flayed Prince wills it..." Avitus muttered.

"I will accept any judgement, if it should come." Namter nodded. "But I think our Master will find the trickery warranted. And what of your work?"

"Near all the slickdust is loaded," Avitus said, turning round a sharp corner, as an explosion tore through wood, metal, and flesh just a street down. "The Tribute is taking a little longer to pack, as can be expected, and we are waiting until we are near ready to leave before moving the last of the sangleum, as that may grab some attention."

"Wise, and what of the Veneficus?"

Avitus sighed. "I tried to catch the witch, but she was traveling with a group of Iron Strixes to reinforce some holdings in the center of the city."

"So it is," Namter said. Some disappointment was to be expected. He had hoped to catch Miga in the chaos and remove her as a threat, but not all schemes could be expected to play out.

He glanced through the rearview mirror, where he saw raiders dash in panicked retreat, a pair squabbling by some streetcorner with knives instead of words. Fires were beginning to burn, spreading from rotting rooftop to rooftop. Namter would not miss this miserable midden of a city. Soon he would be free of it, out beyond the fetid realms of man, with Tribute in tow. He would finally be heading back, back to where all this began. A return for he had ached for seven long years.

But first, there was still so much to do, many things left that could go awry. He must oversee the remaining tribute, load the sangleum, decamp what he could afford to, determine what could be left behind. He'd have to gather the Brotherhood, coordinate the furtive movement of the Lazacorp guards, make sure the caravans were well protected, and then, of course, pick up Lazarus Roache.

# CHAPTER 41

The stairs creaked as the four snuck up to the surface. The basement had been cold and filled with hanging slabs of dried meat, and as the Sylvaine crept around the counter, she could smell the remains of several dozen hastily eaten breakfasts, as well as a few corpses

"We're alone," she whispered. The space was dark and appeared to be the dining area of a raider equivalent of a deli. Outside the broken window the sun shone through yellowed billows of raging dust. There were already casualties, but by the odor their death had preceded the battle, internecine feuds that had wrought the neighborhood. The nearest corpse bore crimson tattoos around his lifeless eyes, and it wasn't much of a leap to connect that chaos to the accidental assassination two nights ago.

"Wait until the coast is clear, then we run," Belona said, watching from behind a table as scattered groups of raiders ran to and fro. The dust might obscure their movement some, but it hid the raiders just as well, and dulled Sylvaine's nose. They waited a few moments, the sound of artillery punctuating the distant muffled shouts and the roars of unseen machines of war. Sylvaine couldn't help but observe a pattern that the cities they've visited always seemed to end up as battle-scarred charnel fields.

"Now!" Marcel shouted, a bit too loud. They ran out the door, and as soon as they were halfway across the road, dust and dirt and loose wastepaper flying by, a squad of six appeared from down the street.

They dashed backed behind an autocar, as the raiders shouted.

"Who's that?" came the voice of one.

"We're just some... Rust Thorns!" Marcel shouted back.

"Aren't you supposed to be defending the eastern end?" came the raider's voice, as the squad approached.

"Why you hiding?" came another.

"We're just on our way—" Marcel began,

"They're going to hit us while we're distracted!" shouted a third. "Take down the Britta-Den!"

Before Marcel could protest, the raiders began firing, bullets shattering the autocar glass. Belona blindfired back, round the bumper.

Sylvaine glanced about and espied a break in the road a few metres out, dense pipework beneath. Without wasting time to think, she shoved her glove out and, æthersparks flying, lifted the mass of metal pipes up, then slammed them down into a wall of misshapen slag. Sylvaine panted. Chaotic a jumble as it was, she couldn't help but feel proud of the pure size of the makeshift barricade.

"Forward, forward!" Belona shouted, not wasting any time even to thank the woman as she rushed behind the metal and began to take shots.

"Oh, so you have an engineer!" came the leering shout of a raider. "Well, don't think that'll save you Rust Thorn scum! We'll cut your face and decorate our—"

Sylvaine never heard what they would decorate, as the sounds of roaring engines cut over the storms. The wall of a nearby shanty exploded into scrap and shards, as a dathkreis tumbled through wildly, motorguns firing blind, flank-blades covered in blood and oil. It skidded across the road, attempting a sudden turn, but lost out to its own inertia as it came crashing into the squad of raiders. Screams mixed with the crunch of metal against brickwork, the dathkreis smashing into a sturdier tenement.

Belona jumped up and immediately began putting bullets into the surviving raiders crawling from the smoking wreckage. From the side of the spherical dathkreis, now facing upwards, a soldier in a principate uniform stumbled out. He leaned on the remains of his own destruction and vomited.

"Move!" Kayip shouted, and they did not delay. From the hole the dathkreis had cut came several squads of Principate soldiers, firing erratically in their direction, as well as most other directions.

They rushed down the street, following Kayip. A mass of raiders appeared suddenly from the storm, eager to meet the Principate invaders. They hesitated a moment as they noticed the four, neither raider nor imperial. Sandwiched between the two forces, Kayip did not wait to become corpse meat, but sliced open a nearby door and rushed inwards, the other three following.

Inside they dashed recklessly from hallway, to stairs, to apartment, to hallway, no time to think, following what Sylvaine hoped was Kayip's memory, and not just desperate guesses. Doors, barricades, and even thin walls were of little concern, the monk sliced and kicked them down. It was clear from the furniture shoved into passageways and heavy chains lashed over apartment entryways, that the residents had been preparing for the grimmest of room-to-room combat. As Kayip hewed open one locked door, they heard a scream, and rushed past a mother of two clutching close her children. The monk smashed through a window, and they followed him down a rickety scaffolded stairway into a back alley. There he finally slowed, glancing back to see if they had been followed, before grabbing the map out of his pocket.

"Shit," Marcel said, panting. "Kids... I didn't know there'd be kids."

"Do raiders reproduce via spores?" Belona asked, scanning the darkened windows.

"No, I mean, I guess, I just thought..." Marcel shook his head. Sylvaine wanted to laugh at the man's naivety, but the truth was she hadn't considered it either. This might be a raider stronghold, but for every slaver and bandit that lived here, there had to be simple craftsmen, and cooks, and cleaners, and parents, and children. This whole thing was far messier than she would like to think of it, and she already considered it a mess-and-a-half.

They snuck out the alley onto a major thoroughfare. Buildings were covered heavy in dust, giving the colorful scraptown a monochromatic yellow-brown tint. Columns of smoke rose above the misshapen buildings, and the sound of gunfire rat-a-tatted from every direction.

As they scurried down the road, balancing haste and stealth, Sylvaine began to feel something in her glove. A strange pulse traveled from the tips of her finger. The hair on Sylvaine's neck, and back, and arms, and everywhere, began to stand on edge. Then suddenly, a motorbike flew through the dust, smashing sideways into the road behind them, unfortunate Principate biker on bottom. As the tempest slowed, Sylvaine spied an old woman in the middle of the road, gray curly hair squirming wildly in the wind, a massive misshapen ætherglove on her arm.

A crabbed-legged tank burst its way through some rubble, turning its cannon in the strange woman's direction. She cackled, and with a tossed spark, immolated the cabin of the war machine. Screams burst out from inside, as the metal behemoths tripped over its own warped legs. It was an impressive display of war-engineering, all the more unnerving because of the woman's unhinged laughter.

Kayip sucked in his breath, rage on his face that Sylvaine had never seen before. She wanted to ask if he knew the strange engineer, but it seemed too obvious a question.

Raiders cheered on and charged forward from behind the elderly engineer. She made to follow them before stopping suddenly. She turned, in their direction, squinting, bulky ætherglove raised.

"Was wondering if you were going to show up, you bald, cyclopean, taur-fucker."

Belona raised her rifle, but the engineer was quicker. A spark flashed. The imperial hastily tossed the melted gun, and reached for her pistol.

"No," Kayip said. He tossed his scattergun to Belona and gestured to a nearby building covered in sun-faded murals of naked mutant women half-painted-over with abstract eyes. "The path is in the basement, behind the false water heater. Do not bother hiding your path, just run, there is no ambiguity in directions."

"We're not leaving—" Marcel began.

"Roache is more important!" Kayip shouted, blade out. "This is for me."

Belona and Marcel nodded, rushing into the darkness of the abandoned structure. Kayip strode forward, towards the engineer, as raiders and imperials traded dust-obscured volleys behind her.

"This your end, Miga!" Kayip said.

"Ain't you the dramatic type," the engineer apparently named Miga replied. As a bullet whizzed past, she struck out her hand and collapsed a nearby water tower behind her, separating them from the fracas beyond. "I'm guessing you had a hand in Verus's death. Far as I see it that makes us even, lover for lover. More than even, since I didn't do the whole murdering thing, I'm just a contractor."

"This is not about petty revenge," Kayip said. "It is the Demiurge's justice!"

"Rusted pus, you're sounding just like those Unblind idiots." Miga ripped the hood off an autocar with a spark, and sent it hurtling towards Kayip, who cut the metal in two. "Truegods… Demiurge… Caught up with all this theological strix-piss. Can't you let a woman do her research in peace?"

Kayip roared and charged forward. Miga flung balls of molten iron at the man with an alacrity that belied her age. As the monk closed the distance, she grasped tight a girder from the collapse water tower, and extended it, launching herself metres away toward the other side of the street. As she landed, she tore the top of the metal, and reforged it into a flying blade, which Kayip parried.

Miga laughed again. "Oh, you're making me feel young again!" She sent out a volley of metal shards. Sylvaine focused and shot a bolt of æther, fusing the projectiles back into one clump of dross that bounced off the scrap-infused pavement.

"Who is she?" Sylvaine asked, catching up with the monk.

"A witch, an old enemy, a monster who helped Roache first invent that horrid slick—" Kayip blinked with surprise. "Sylvaine! You should be with the other two."

"Gear's-grit's Kayip, I'm not leaving you," Sylvaine said, pulling out her pistol. "Last time you went all revenge-fury, you almost got yourself killed."

"Ah!" Miga cried. "You're Roache's experiment. Fascinating to see in flesh, though I could have told him how it would end." With that she shoved her glove into the ground. Pipes burst up from the rubble, a wave ripping towards the two. Kayip lunged and grabbed Sylvaine, managing to just avoid the eruption.

"This is not your fight!" he said.

"If it's your fight, then it is mine," Sylvaine replied. "We've gone this far together, if you think it's important enough to stop our Roache-hunt for this woman, then I'll be here with you."

Sylvaine aimed her pistol, and Miga turned it quick to slag. As Sylvaine dropped the sizzling gun, Miga lifted up one of the legs of the once-tank and hurled it. Sylvaine managed to knock it to the ground with a spark, and then sent it back. The old woman dodged, laughing all the while.

"You made a friend!" she said. "I didn't know you monks were allowed to talk to women. Then again, you're running out of options, aren't you dear? Lots of corpses left behind."

Sylvaine thrust out her hand, aiming her spark at Miga's 'glove. Slag that, and the engineer would just be an unarmed centenarian. Miga snaped an opposing spark, and the air flashed in a dazzling display of æthermantics. The woman did not wait to gaze, but leapt forward and swung the previously smashed motorcycle at Sylvaine.

With a grunt, Sylvaine smashed the oncoming motorbike into the ground, but failed to stop the wreck's momentum. It rushed towards her, front light shattered, wheel fused haphazardly into the engine.

A swing and Kayip split the tumbling vehicle, a loose pipe taking a cut from his arm before as it passed. Then he turned round and sliced from the air a flying hunk of water tower, which Miga had tossed when they were distracted.

"This is an unneeded risk!" Kayip said.

"Safer than you fighting alone," Sylvaine replied, re-aiming her glove "You go left, I go right. She can't aim at both of us."

"No, this is not you—" Kayip stumbled over his words. "It is more important to— Roache, if he is not taken down then..." The man shook his head, then groaned. He suddenly grabbed Sylvaine and pulled her back. She ran with him, confused, into the darkness of the scrap workshop, behind the immodest murals, to a maze of rust and smashed containers.

"Where in Inferno you running to?" Miga shouted. "You can't tease a girl like that!"

Kayip knocked over a pile of rotting crates behind them, as he led Sylvaine down through the mess into the basement, where, behind a recently pushed and hollow water-heater casing, lay a straight-carved underway passage.

"What about Miga?" Sylvaine asked as they ran.

"I am a fool," Kayip said. "Eaten by anger and vengeance. If Miga dies, Roache continues. If Roache dies, Miga is nothing. What madness it would be to give up so much on the altar of revenge. And if I were to lose you while attempting such insanity..."

"Sorry for ruining your vengeance."

"No." Kayip smiled. "You remind me only that there are things beyond retribution, reasons yet still to live. Now, quickly, we may catch up with the other two yet."

They continued down in the musky, unlit passageway, as swiftly as they could without tripping over rubble and the roots of strange subterranean plants. Sylvaine mulled over the monk's world. *Reasons yet still to live...* If Kayip could believe it, could she one day? As Sylvaine clenched her ætherglove, she tried to imagine a life where she was as she had been, only without her dream left to distract her from her misery. Returning home with some excuse on her lips, putting her textbooks and equipment away into the attic, pursuing a life as an accountant or a teacher or a pitiful mechanic, all the while being nothing more than just a Ferral. Could she every convince herself to suffer such a life?

* * *

As swift as they were, they did not catch Marcel and Belona by the time they reached the basement of the power station. They snuck up the stairs and came across only one guard, already quite dead, by the imperial's hand if Sylvaine had to guess. The storm had whipped itself up into a real frenzy, sending slapping the tents and straps of the Lazacorp camp. At least those that remained, many were being packed up and loaded onto autotrucks in a frantic hurry. Lazarus's personal tent seemed to still be in place, it was easy enough to spot. No others were quite so large, or ornate, or purple. Sylvaine strained her ears trying to hear inside, for all they know Roache may have already flown the coop. But she could make nothing out over the roars of the storms.

"I will go through the front, you shall sneak through the workshop in the back," Kayip said, pointing to a massive metal structure that was probably the reason Lazarus's tent had not yet been disassembled.

"No, I'm not leaving you—" Sylvaine started.

"Not leaving," Kayip said calmly. "Just for a moment. He will likely run; we need to cover both exits. Though with luck, Marcel and Belona have already completed their task."

Sylvaine undid the chain-link fence with a snap of her glove. If Roache was indeed dead, her powers would have departed her. She hated that she felt relief. No, it was too late to dwell on what might be lost. She nodded, and skulked down the back of the tent, as Kayip snuck round the front.

She pressed her glove to the uneven scrap wall, pulsing out, and found a weak spot, which seemed to have already collapsed in and been hastily re-welded. With a careful finger, she sketched out an entrance for herself, then tip-toed inside.

The workshop, as it were, resembled something between a laboratory and an abattoir, an ill-kempt one at that. Bodies of desiccated mutants lay sprawled on rusted gurneys. Men and woman in twisted forms, faces of agony. It was a grim a reminder that what they were fighting for was bigger than them. For a moment she thought of Ysabel, and prayed despite her atheism that she had died before coming to a place like this.

There were notebooks left scattered, with the name *M. Veneficus* written on them. It hit her suddenly that the Miga they had fought was no doubt the same engineer who had left her notes in Narida Heights. Sylvaine wanted nothing more than to tear into those books, see if they held any insight on what was to happen to her. But, of course, there was no time, so she simply grabbed one and shove it into her jacket.

What was worrying is that she had not heard Kayip's roar of vengeance, nor the screams of Lazarus Roache, nor even any gunshots or other sounds of violence. As she snuck towards the heavy metal door that led into Lazarus's tent, she began to make out something. Muttering, grunts, the cocking of pistols and the clinking of metal, but no gunshot. There were people in the room, that much she could tell, but far more than she had expected. Had Lazarus surrounded himself with a squad of bodyguards? With great care she pushed open the door, trying not to release even a squeak.

On the other side was a strange and quite unexpected situation.

# CHAPTER 42

Marcel found himself in a baffling and quite shit situation. Lazarus Roache was in his tent, which was good, and had been caught surprised by their ambush, which was better. What Marcel had not predicted was the dozen mutants already holding up the tycoon, several of whom had now turned their scatterguns and pistols in his, Belona's, and now Kayip's directions.

"I was not expecting so many guests," Lazarus said in a bitter tone, holding a gash on his side. "My apologies, I should have brought a charcuterie board."

The man looked as Marcel remembered, no alteration in outfits during his waste-wandering. Same short-brimmed hat, same striped suit, same vicious eyes. How had Marcel not recognized his malevolence before? His mask of gentle avuncularity seemed so thin now, his cruel avarice clear in every twitch and glare, though the man had not changed at all. No, that wasn't entirely true, Lazarus looked far more tired than Marcel remembered. Older even, as if the stress of his exile had tacked on two decades to his face. Then there was the stress of have a rifle pointed to his chest, of which he currently had three.

Beside the tycoon stood several Lazacorp guards, one of which was holding a young mutant, knife against his throat. The mutant wore a leather vest decorated with bones and gemstones, open in the middle to reveal a great garish scar across his torso.

"Kill them, both of them! Now!" the scarred mutant shouted, as the guard pressed his blade closer, nicking his skin.

Corpses littered the floor, a few Lazacorp guards, a couple of laborers, and a single mutant. The mutants seemed to have had a pretty good ambush going until the shirtless one got taken hostage. He must have been their leader, as the other mutants hung on his knife-quieted mutterings. Marcel did not need to wonder if these mutants were somehow from Huile. Besides the fact that he recognized none of them and that their clothing was uniformly waste-style, each and every one was a Womb Mutant, of uniform features, symmetrical horns, identical lizard-slit eyes, evenly toned skin (ignoring the occasional pox-mark or scar, which was to be expected). These were mutants of the Wastes, and Marcel hadn't the faintest clue of why they were here.

"Listen," Marcel said, eyeing the bayonetted rifle aiming at his stomach. "I don't know who you are, and you don't know me, but we clearly all hate Lazarus Roache, so let's stop pointing guns each other and start—"

"I know who you are," the mutant leader spat, his captor loosening the knife grasp to let him speak. "You're another set of the murderous monk's flunkies. Eat taurshit, we'll never fight alongside you."

Kayip's blade was shaking in his hands, his face pale, his mouth moving but no sounds escaping. When Marcel and Belona had made their entrance, the mood had been one of panicked confusion. Just as they had started to explain that they weren't Lazacorp goons, the monk had rushed in, and that seemed to have transformed suspicion into outright hostility.

"What did you do?" Belona hissed.

"I did not expect..." Kayip mumbled, his blade tracing aimless lines on the floor. "Vapulus..."

"If anything happens," Belona said, "I'll put a round of buckshot into Roache's face. Came too far to give up on that."

Marcel glanced at the Lazacorp grunt who was pointing his pistol at Marcel's head, and hoped the woman was bluffing, though he knew she wasn't.

"You do that, the mutant dies," Roache said.

"I still fail to see why we should care," Belona said, aiming.

"No!" Kayip shouted, "we cannot allow that!"

"Fire you cowards!" the mutant leader screeched. His captor pushed the knife in slightly, silencing him with a drop of blood. The other mutants seemed quite uncertain, switching their aim with nervous twitches.

"Give us Bladescar," one of the mutants said, a woman with braided black hair and vivid green eyes. "We care not for Lazacorp thugs or… whoever you two are. Lay down your weapons and we'll take Roache and the monk."

"I'm not… finished," Kayip said weakly. "My oath, I gave you my oath."

"We're not giving you Kayip, we don't even…" Marcel shook his head. What in Inferno had happened between these mutants and the monk? Either way they weren't going to spend him up as a negotiation chip. But they were so close! Just a bullet away from ending this all. And a bullet away from being ended. The mutants were looking quite antsy, and Marcel wasn't confident he'd make it out alive if fingers started hitting triggers, to say nothing of Kayip. Outside the wind was rushing, the dust storms obscuring the shouting match from the ears of the untold thousands of raiders and Lazacorp goons that hustled around the camp. But they would not remain hidden forever.

"Let's just all be calm," he said, trying to follow his own advice even guns swayed. "We can take out Roache now, which is why we are all here, and then discuss… whatever else needs to be discussed somewhere else, somewhere safe."

"Stop hesitating," the mutant apparently named Bladescar hissed. "We have them both. Forget me! Avenge the name of Vapulus. Finish the tycoon and the kin-slayer!"

"My cherished chieftain, please shut up!" said the female mutant. "I promised your father—"

"Now this is all quite ridiculous!" Lazarus Roache interrupted. He reached down, a mutant following his movements with a rifle, and picked up a cup of tea. "Damnations, its cold," he said as he sipped. "It's clear you have gotten yourself in quite a situation Marcel. In over your head, with a bunch of brutes and barbarians you don't even understand."

"I understand enough," Marcel said, which was a bit of a lie. "I know what you've done, I know for Huile to be safe, you have to die."

Lazarus chuckled. "Ah, the self-assurance of youth. The world is just so simple, so black and white. Heroes and villains, eh Marcel? And you always playing the knight in shining armor. Well let me ask you, brave defender of the Resurgence, what do you know about the woman who's been traveling with you? Does the title Butcher of—"

"Tesakovgrad, yes, figured that out," Marcel said. "General Agrippus, my enemy at Huile, yatta yatta yatta, we've been through this."

"Right," Roache said, somewhat taken aback. He recovered quickly and turned to Belona. "And my dear general, has Marcel told you—"

"Yes, I know what's he's done," Belona said. "All on your orders. We agreed to finish you first."

"So, what, forgive and forget?" Lazarus Roache snarled. "So easy for you two to kiss and make up, but you drag your collective asses halfway across the Wastes to harass me?"

The slight twitch of movement caught Marcel's eyes. There in the back of the room, he noticed the movement of brown fur and the glint of metal. Sylvaine! The engineer was trying to sneak around while everyone was distracted, tiptoeing between Roache's half-unpacked dressers and stacks of overflowing travel bags. Marcel glanced around, but it seemed none had noticed the engineer's entrance. If there was anyone who could extract them from this situation, it was her, one snap of her ætherglove could turn a loaded rifle to slag. Of course, there was a lot more than one rifle, Sylvaine could just as well set off this powder keg. Yet Marcel could see no alternative, he had to trust her. Perhaps Roache had been stalling for time, hoping that some squad of guards might bumble in and save him. Now time was on their side, Marcel just had to make sure that no one tried anything crazy until Sylvaine was in posi—

A sudden shout, and before Marcel could turn his head, Belona had grabbed the black-haired mutant, and held her scattergun under her chin. *Stopstopstop* he desperately tried to mouth.

"This stupidity ends now," Belona said. "I don't give the Imperator's left asscheek as to what your petty feuds are, mutants. We are taking Roache's head and leaving. The time for discussion is over."

"Do you think I am afraid to die?" hissed the mutant woman. "I am of a line of ancient soldiers, do what you will! Vapulus will have its justice."

"Prisca!" Bladescar shouted to the best of his ability, a look of fury upon his face. "Let her go!"

"Belona," Kayip said with despair in his voice "Do not harm her! If I must give up my oath to make peace, then there can be no place—"

"Shut up, we're not negotiating," Belona said. "Bring Roache to us, and no one will die."

"No!" Kayip said, turning his sword in her direction now. "Release her now! I cannot allow anyone else to be harmed."

"Have you lost your damn head?" Belona shouted, holding her hostage close.

"Prisca!" Bladescar cried again, the ferocity in his voice cracking, desperation leaking out.

"Let's all just remain calm!" Marcel pleaded, glancing as Sylvaine snuck forward, centimetre by silent centimetre."

"It is myself who is the cause of consternation," Kayip pleaded. "Let them take me and Roache, and leave."

Lazarus Roache chuckled to himself. "You know what they'll do to him, right? An eye for an eye isn't the law of these lands, not that our monk friend has many to spare. A head for a finger, that's the justice of the mutants. And our dear friend Kayip here, why he took quite more than a few fingers. Tell them, great warmonk, of your valiant crusades!"

Kayip was silent a moment. "Marcel, Belona, please leave us," he finally whispered, letting his blade snake itself back into a bracelet. "It is the only way, this was never truly your fight."

"What are you talking about?" Marcel asked Roache. He wasn't too concerned about whatever old feuds these strange mutants were hashing out, but as long as they were busy chatting, they weren't shooting at Sylvaine.

"Perhaps our disfigured friend can better explain," Lazarus gestured to his hostage, the Lazacorp grunt lowering his blade slightly.

"Burn in Inferno, you ghul, you leech!" Bladescar spat at Roache, before turning to Kayip. "You too kin-slayer, join your rotting master! And you two, you blind oozeflies! You who would follow a murderer, do you even know who you're fighting for? What these men unleashed together?"

*Murderer? Unleashed together?* "Wait, what are you talking about?" Marcel repeated, with genuine curiosity this time. "Kayip's fighting to stop Roache. We're on the same side." He glanced at Kayip for confirmation, but the monk simply stared out, glaze eyed.

"Fighting to cover his crimes! To hide the fire and blood that he let loose! And... And let Prisca fucking go!" Bladescar swore and scrambled to get free, stopped only by the grip of another guard, and the return of the knife to his throat.

"Hmm, disappointing, I was hoping our little chieftain be a bit more... intelligible," Lazarus said, scratching his chin. It was disquieting how calm the man seemed, considering he was being held up and had already taken a nasty gash to the— actually the wound that the tycoon had been holding earlier seemed to have stopped bleeding, Marcel could not even make out the laceration, though the man's suit was badly torn. "And I must say I'm disappointed in you too, Mr. Talwar. You really are a substandard private investigator. I even warned you about the mad monk! Warnings I could make all too well, considering he is a very old colleague of mine. A partner, almost. Well perhaps that's overly flattering, a *contractor* then." Lazarus gave an exaggerated sigh.

Marcel tried with his eyes to grab Kayip's attention, to get the monk to refute the nonsense spewing out the tycoon mouth. This was all a good distraction, but it wasn't, couldn't be... true?

"My, my, if only you had listened," Lazarus tutted, "you would have saved yourself so much bother and pain. You could be back safe and happy in Huile, yet like the proverbial needlecat you have followed your curiosity to your own despair. Tell me, have you never asked yourself why a such a fervent devotee of the Demiurge might lack the ability to cast miracles? Does it not sound like a mystery an investigator should, well, investigate? No matter, I'll elucidate you. It is a punishment. A punishment for the many crimes for which our dear hieromonk has committed. Crimes whose victims now seek recompense in blood, victims who seem to have skuttled your little assassination attempt, or perhaps you there's? Crimes he committed in his willing service to—Sylvaine please! Adults are having a discussion."

The engineer squeaked, frozen mid-sneak as half a dozen guns suddenly turned in her direction.

"Yes, yes," Lazarus continued. "Is it such a surprise I noticed you? Not all humans are blind without your Ferral nose, there are senses stronger indeed. We're bonded, you and I, slickdust as the rope. What do you hope to accomplish? Kill me and return to the animal you were? Come now, Sylvaine, you are an engineer, you know all machines need a power source, and there is not engine greater than I. So let's say you end this foolish months-long temper tantrum, and fuel up." With that Lazarus Roache lifted a red baggie from his pocket.

"F...fuck you," Sylvaine muttered, staring at the bag, as did several of the Lazacorp guards.

"You can't even muster the hate of your comrades." Lazarus smiled. "And why should you? They're not your friends, you know, you're just a weapon to them, a rabid dog to be let loose on your enemies. I'm the only one who had ever believed in you Sylvaine, I helped you, I can still help you."

Sylvaine raised her shaking glove. "If I have to give it up... to be free of you... I'm prepared to..."

"See, even you don't believe yourself," Lazarus said, shaking his head. "I'll provide the confidence for both of us. Take off your glove."

Sylvaine's free hand suddenly reached for the back of her ætherglove, starting to push it off before she caught herself.

Lazarus's voice grew louder, more commanding. "Come on now. Give. Me. The glove."

Sylvaine shook, ætherglove stuck in a fist as her other fingers tugged. Slickdust commands clearly battling against her own will, her body indecisive in this civil war.

"Sylvaine!" Kayip shouted. The engineer blinked, frozen in motion, a look of despair written on her face.

Marcel held tight his pistol, mind racing. They really hadn't time for all this theatre, each moment that passed was another chance for someone else to barge through that door and—

"...The æther-oil tanker is finally filled, if your private furnishing are ready, we are prepared to leave," Lazarus' butler said as he barged in. Guns swiveled, and the butler blinked surprise with his lone eye. That was a new development, probably. The man was quite forgettable, but Marcel was somewhat confident that last time he saw him he had both eyes still. Otherwise he looked as he always had, probably, though his drab suit seemed more dust-covered and bloodstained than normal. The butler glanced around and tapped his pen on his clipboard.

"Hmm... My apologies I was not aware we were to host guests," he said, pen bouncing up and down with a nervous twitch. "Mr. Talwar, I am glad to see you are well. Miss Agrippus... General Agrippus? Apologies, I am not aware of your current title. And Bladescar, what a surprise, how is your father?"

"He's dead, as you shall be," the mutant chief scowled.

"My condolences. Ah, Ms. Pelletier has joined us as well. Though I'm afraid we are not currently hiring new engineers. And Kayip..." He broke his friendly façade to spit that name, tapping his pen with even more ferocity. Up and down and up and down it went. "Well," he said, up, down. "I see we have found ourselves in a complex situation." Up, down, up, down. "There are many competing interests here." Up, down, up down. "I believe I can suggest a solution that—"

A click, a tiny, curbed blade from the back of the butler's pen as it swung up. It hooked into the string of his eyepatch, nicking flesh, and with a single sudden swing Namter tore his eyepatch off.

"No!" Kayip shouted.

Then, all Inferno burst loose.

# CHAPTER 43

The world faded away to blurred nothing, as Sylvaine stared into that void, that nothingness that existed where Namter's eye was supposed to be. A caliginous expanse of impossible size, seeming to bend dimensions to fit an infinite roiling ætherspace, as black as ash, and scarlet as blood, and yet of no color and hue, shapeless and distinct, uncaring and full of furious malice, this void rolled over Sylvaine and threatened to—

Her eyes shut tight, her claws out, her fur on end. A primal thing inside her pulled her away, some reptilian neurons screeching out from the base of her brainstem, unable to comprehend the sight or understand her existential horror, but fully capable of recognizing a threat.

She jumped down, moving without thought. The thump of the floor knocked her conscious mind back into place. The world roared around her, gunshots cracking, people screaming and shouting, strange words in horrid tongue echoing about. There was a mass on the floor, maybe a body once, now just a pulsating crimson mash. A fire was burning between it and Namter, and when bullets flew in that direction they seemed to fizzle into smoke. Several in the room stood enraptured by the butler's glare, including Marcel and the Lazacorp guard who had been holding knife to Bladescar's throat. The mutant chief broke free, and began to strangle his captor, as the unenthralled mutants fought Lazacorp guards, more of whom streamed into the tent. Kayip lopped off the head of one of the intruders, and then dodged the blade of a mutant, kicking the assailant away.

Sylvaine scurried back, away from the crack of gunfire, on instincts as much as intention. Everything had collapsed in an instant. She had had a shot at Lazarus, a chance to take the man down. There had been no guns pointed at her, with a snap she could have sprayed molten metal into the tycoon's face or launched a lug nut at a deadly velocity. Instead she had snuck, waiting for... what? A perfect opportunity that would never show? Or was she waiting for the strength to face losing her powers for good? Well neither came. Instead had just gotten caught in Lazarus's chains, again, reminded of what a bound animal she was.

An alluring, acrid sent caught her attention. She turned to see Lazarus Roache crawling behind his desk, a bullet hole oozing in his chest. The man pulled himself, slowly and painfully, each breath a moan, towards a smashed vial of slickdust on the floor. He grabbed a pinchful and snorted it, microshards of class cutting his nose.

"Look away!" the man growled.

Sylvaine's head turned sharply away. In the center of the room a pool of gore was bubbling. The liquefied remains of man and mutant began to writhe, shadows flashing across its surface. The odor was unlike anything Sylvaine had smelled, artificial and biological, oil and feces, amniotic fluids and putrefied flesh, burning offal and stinging incense. Diminutive figures rose from the puddle, each the rough shape of infant, bulbous and squat. Their hands were claws of rusted metal. On their backs sat wings, frames of iron and burnt bone with a leather-something stretch across it, though the dried hair and pale skin tones did not look of taur origin. And for their own skin, the ætheric aberrations had none. Beating organs hung naked, open flesh dripping with every movement. The mockeries of infants blinked eyes of pupilless white.

With the screech the everted monstrosities were airborne. One flew at a horrified mutant, claws tearing through the poor man's skull like a spoon through pudding. Another dived towards a Lazacorp soldier, carving through his chest without slowing. It seemed they did not spare allies, ignoring only Namter and his cloaked companions, who had begun to appear in force, blackfire bursting from their hands as the butler shouted confused orders. Kayip rushed forward and cut one of the cloaked men in twain, before dodging the swipe of the flying aberrations. It flapped itself around for another strike, but Kayip lunged, cutting wing from torso, and sending the mock infant careening toward the ground, blood spurting. A drop flew near, landing on the side of Sylvaine's boot, where it sizzled like acid, and awoke her from her horrified daze. The tent had quickly become a warzone, the bullets and blackfire ripping apart the purple canvas, letting the dust storm rush in and making mockery any distinction between the camp and Lazarus's personal quarters.

*Lazarus!* The man had escaped her attention, because... shit, because he had told her to! That voice still made its residence deep in her mind, ignoring her desperate attempts to control her own will. She turned to find the tycoon gone. How had he moved in his condition? Only the drip of bloodstains on the floor hinted towards his rapid flight.

With a curse she scrambled out to the back workshop, bullets whistling, men shouting, wind screaming. Even in the chaos Roache's blood-scent was clear. She followed it out the hole she had carved, into the roiling storm. Past tents and 'trucks she rushed, struggling to keep the dust from her eyes and nose, the trail dashed apart by the wind. She pushed into a metal shack, half-filled with rifles and jars of dried beans. Her ears twitched as she snorted, the taste of earth and smoke in her mouth. With effort she could separate the cacophony outside into a hundred smaller noises. Raiders yelling, vehicles groaning, feet against dirt and concrete, gunshots, the roar of artillery, the blasts that came after, scraprats running in confused swarms beneath, skragger flocks squawking in the distance, a man nearby coughing and snorting, swearing quietly to himself—Roache!

Sylvaine tore open the side of the shack, claw and ætherglove in unison. She rushed through the flapping tarps, and into a large brick and iron structure, a refurbished ruin that was set up not unlike the workshop. Medical equipment and engineering supplies, corpses of mutants, flesh mutants, left pale on gurneys, their necks cut open, funnels laid beneath where cold blood had been drained into cracked glass flasks. In one corner lay a stack of body bags, in another a large hulking machine that Sylvaine did not recognize, all pumps and tubes and dripping crimson. At its far end was a metal basin, its top open, Roache bent over. The alluring scent of slickdust emanated from machine, mixing with Sylvaine's horrid realization on how the drug was made.

Lazarus Roache had once mentioned that his own blood was a crucial ingredient, but his was far from the only sacrifice made. How many had been killed in its production, how many lives had she tasted? Like those cannibalistic ferrals from pulps, she had consumed human blood. Even now, with the abhorrent knowledge, she still hungered for the slickdust, its scent pulling at her.

Sylvaine staggered with nausea, righting herself on a creaking support beam. Lazarus turned suddenly, hands full of slickdust, nose and mouth covered in red, like a ghul fresh from a feast. Yet his feature were not ghoulish, if anything he looked healthier than he had in the tent, skin more vibrant, hair golden. Where his gaping bullet hold had been was now just stained skin, his earlier wounds completely healed.

"Tracking your prey, Sylvaine?"

She raised her shaking glove.

"Put that down!" he demanded. Her glove shot down before she could react. With her left arm she grabbed her right and tried to pull it up.

"You've played engineer long enough to know how this works," Lazarus said, reaching into his coat pocket. "You're a machine, Sylvaine, and I am working the levers. But machines have their purpose, and you've outlived yours. Now, do as you're commanded, and stand still."

With that she caught a glint of gold in his hand. A pistol, gaudy and deadly, stained on the handle with slickdust. Sylvaine felt her limbs stiffen, as she struggled against the mental chains. Every centimetre of her body, skin, muscle, bone, seemed bound to the man's words. She heard him pull the hammer back, could visualize the cartridge, the primer igniting the gunpowder, the bullet flying from its casing, through the air at 350 metres per second, directly into her skull, turning her into another body on the floor. Sweat dripped through her fur, her breath faster and faster, fear streaming from her frontal cortex down into her brainstem, awakening that thing inside her that was more her than her. It was not her body that was bound, it was her mind alone. Her blood pumped, her instincts roared, her torso rocked, teeth barred, fur on end.

With a horrid howl, she lost herself, staggering about as the bullet went off, whizzing past her ear.

"I said stand fucking still!" Roache shouted, aiming again.

She barked and growled, roared and shrieked, sparks of æthericity escaping her clawtips, turning tables into slag and burning lines of ash into the bricks. Lazarus pulled the trigger a second time, but nothing happened. The machine behind him burst into a cascade of sparks.

"Broken!" he shouted, though about his pistol, the machine, or Sylvaine herself, she could not guess. She could not even think. Between

Roache's chains and the beast within her there was no space left for a conscious mind, no room for a person. She rocked back and forth, stumbling over bodies, and bursting open hidden pipes with uncontrolled surges of ætheric rage.

"Stay! Stay! Stay!" Roache shouted, fear in his voice as he ran from her, the true her, all claws and fur and wild fury. Part of her felt compelled to stay, an equal part felt hungry for blood, man blood, Lazarus blood, skin and bone and meat. Sylvaine hated both parts of her, hated the chains, hated the beast, hated the whole of what she remained. With tears, she fell to the floor, shuddering and shaking. Memories flashed, school, boys laughing, girls making cruel jokes. A trip to the zoo cut short, whispers and giggles, fingers pointed at the wrong side of the cage. Questions her father couldn't answer, cinegraphs that could, that showed her in the flashing of filmstrip what she was. Belona's mocking asides, Gearswit's corpse on the ground, the taste other peoples' blood, viscera gleaming on her claws.

Lazarus Roache was wrong, she was no machine. She was an animal.

Sylvaine lay on the concrete, motionless. Outside the winds still moaned, guns still cracked, and the rumble of war machines grew ever louder. The world passed on by her, careless and cruel. Sylvaine was not sure if she could stand. She did not try. She could not find a reason to try.

After some time, seconds or minutes she could not say, a figure ran into the structure.

"Sylvaine?" came a voice. Kayip's. The monk stared down on her. His body was covered in dust and blood, not his. His eye was wide. With concern? Fear? Or just adrenaline?

"Sylvaine?" he asked again, to the slumped mass on the ground. She almost managed to move her mouth, to say his name, but only made a soft moan that communicated little more than she was still living, technically. But he could see her, could see her pain, physical and more. He had saved her before, nursed her back from the edge of death and despair. When she had run ragged from Icaria, he had found her, when she had been knocked out by Felik, he had carried her, when she had lost herself in that garage in Stinktown, he had soothed her. Now he stared at the broken thing she was.

Suddenly there was a familiar shout. Roache's voice in the distance. Kayip looked in the direction the tycoon had ran. Then back at Sylvaine. Then, after a slow moment, he ran onwards, in pursuit, as Sylvaine lay behind.

So even the monk had left her. All his gentle words, the secrets shared between them, and he had left her. Of course he had, why should he not? He had devoted his life to hunting Roache, she was just a means to that end. The man's kindness had been the empty affection one would give to a pet. A bloodhound, who couldn't even keep herself together long enough to bite the bastard she had been trained to bite. All her agony, all her sorrow, it came from her trying to convince herself that she was something she was not. A person. Worthy of love, friendship, admiration, as much as any human. Stupidity. How could she have ever claimed to be an engineer? What engineer ignored all evidence that was shoved repeatedly in her face? It made no difference if she had died in Icaria, or here, or lived an empty life back in Taliers. She was just another lonely beast of the Wastes.

# CHAPTER 44

Gunsmoke, and bodies, and burning canvas. The firework blasts of tanks sending shockwaves through the swirling dust, the crackle of unseen rifles a discordant symphony. Men shouting, screaming, a naked, skinless demon-child screeching as it flew. Belona aimed, shot, shot again, a third time, now down at the maimed monstrosity, its flesh melting into hateful, steaming sangleum. Not waiting, she turned, and with scattergun transformed the head of some rushing raider into ground meat, before ducking behind the half-smashed remnant of Roache's armoire to reload. Belona was covered in dust, grime, blood, some of it hers, but she was alive, blessed Imperator she was alive!

Lazarus's tent had been torn to shreds by bullets, demonspawn, and the raging storm. Those shreds were now being stomped by rushing Lazacorp soldiers, robed freaks, panicking raiders, and meddlesome mutant savages. Belona blindfired around a corner. A shout of pain indicated she hit someone, it didn't much matter who at this point. There were no innocents here, no civilians to put chains on her bloodlust. Surrounded by enemies with a weapon in hand, this was why Belona had been birthed! Laughter escaped her lips, taken away by the wind.

"Belona!" Marcel shouted, frightened and relieved, as he stumbled down beside her. "Where's Kayip and Sylvaine? Where's Roache?"

Belona glanced round the armoire, a bullet spitting off splinters a half-meter above. The tycoon was nowhere to be seen, had escaped sometime in the chaos.

"Target lost," she said, hoping that one of the mutants might manage to get their axe in the bastard's skull, but suspecting they were too inept for even that simple brutality. Idiots, these waste-born mutants were proof of the necessity of civilization. A whole race outside the wisdom of the Principate, without the guiding hand of the Imperator. Humankind without humanity, living lives nasty, brutish, and short. It was no surprise they acted with little more forethought than troglyns, no surprise they ruined everything. She should have taken the shot at Roache while she could, damn the consequences, damn the monk's equivocating! Yet there was no time to waste on regrets now.

In the distance she could see bursts of black fire. Illuminated in its unnatural and paradoxical shadowy light she could see what looked to be Lazarus's butler. She aimed in his direction, but midways through her bullets' flight, a flash of dark flame arose with a strange screeching sizzle, and the cloaked man beyond it remained unharmed.

"Did you know of the butler's demoncraft?" she asked Marcel.

"No, he was nothing like this before," Marcel said. "He must have joined the cult recently."

Thinking back three years on Roache's mysterious escape from her clutches, Belona had to doubt Marcel assumptions, but such details did not much matter now. When she turned to fire another round, the man had vanished into the smoke and dust. Belona swore silently to herself. Accursed æthermancer or not, the butler was a pusillanimous wretch, fleeing a good battle.

"Let's move," she said. "Plenty of other soft targets."

Belona dashed forward to the smashed remnants of a raider warbuggy, driver crumpled some metres off. With a dust-mucked repeater-rifle she found slung to a dead passenger, she fired off in the direction of raider shouts, tossing the weapon when it predictably jammed. Best to conserve her own ammunition when possible, there was no telling how long she might be able skulk around, how much damage she could do, and she didn't want her spree cut short by an empty clip.

Marcel scrambled to her, like a panicked dog after its master. "Kayip must be after Roache. But what's our plan? Retreat, escape, find a vehicle or—shit!" A bullet whizzed past, a centimetre from taking off Marcel's ear.

*Retreat... Escape...* How craven. A battle was finally gifted to them, a chance to earn true honor, and the man was planning to run? To think at times Belona almost respected Marcel.

She glanced back toward the obscured smoking bulk that was Stinktown. Her machinations had been successful, the vile raider stronghold was in flames. From its direction rushed masses of blue, men running, bayonets out, firing in all directions. Between them the long-slumbering war machines of Holtag came groaning, weapons from her glorious past, no longer following her direct orders and yet grinding along to her will. Soon they would haphazardly destroy the remnants of the Lazacorp camp, wiping from the face of the Wastes two enemies of the Imperator's Order. A messy victory, but a victory nonetheless. Even if she were never honored for it, even her name should lie slandered, it would be one last glory for the name Agrippus.

"The plan is to leave Lazarus Roache and his raider scum with nothing," Belona said.

"Then what—?" Marcel began, but she did not wait. Belona dashed forward, taking out a surprised a raider as she climbed the slight slope of a dust-covered refuse pile or miniature hillock. Whether Marcel followed her or ran off on his own didn't much matter. He was a poor shot and did her as much harm as help. Of course he did follow, for whatever reason. Fear and indecision most likely.

She gazed out as best she could over the battlefield. In the distance, over the smoke, she could see a structure at the far end of camp, likely some sort of garage or vehicle-loading bay. If they could reach it, they could potentially do some damage to the retreating forces, but during time it would take to navigate the battlefield, the enemy would have ample opportunity to escape. No, best to stay put and use the chaos to strike trapped or disoriented targets, like how Vastium lions of old would hunt out the weakest deer of a herd.

"There!" Belona pointed towards a nearby tanker-truck, plodding through the detritus and blood-soaked mud. She grabbed a grenade from her bag.

"Cover me!" she said as she ran, not that she trusted the man to follow through. She dashed forward, around corpses and a fallen warwalker. Marcel struggled to catch up.

"Wait!" she heard him cry, followed by a misplaced gunshot, and grunts. It seemed the man got tangled up with some raider, but she couldn't slow herself for his behalf now. Her plan did not include living through the day, so if Marcel perished buying her some time, that was about as honorable a death a Resurgence traitor could strive for.

The tanker was massive and slow, the perfect target. Blocking it were a half-dozen raiders, shouting as they waved rifles and blades. The driver frantically tried to negotiate with the crowd, and was just starting to find some success pushing through by force. Belona pulled the pin from her grenade about a dozen metres away. The driver caught her in his gaze, but lacking a gun or time to use it, merely cried "no!" She ignored the coward and chucked the explosive. It flew in a beautiful arc, landing right on the metal back of that sangleum-engorged tick.

Belona jumped back to avoid the burst of force and heat, tumbling onto the ground. She leapt up, singed and exhilarated, ears ringing. A great pillar of smoke burst upwards, far above the battlefield. Chunks of burning metal fell like a midwinter's hail, a bent sheet with the burnt letters *LAZ* bouncing by her feet. The smell of burning æther-oil was pungent and glorious. The glow of the burning 'truck flickered heliacal reds and oranges, matching the dust-drained sun above. How she had missed this! Belona shouted praise to the Imperator, not in words, but sound alone, gleeful and triumph.

As the ringing in her ears faded, the sounds of battle returned. Amongst the normal shots and gunshots, came screams of pain. Curses and pleas, in raider slang and vulgar Bastillian patois. And another voice, in uncommon tongue, in the guttural, erudite vernacular of Kaimark.

Belona blinked a moment in surprise, and turned to see amongst the bodies, a man in imperial blue, a scout's uniform, screaming and writhing amongst the dirt. She rushed towards him, his chest perforated, his face twisted and burnt by scalding æther-oil.

"Imperator! Imperator help me!" he pleaded, pulling at his charred skin, which flaked off at his fingers' touch, blood splattering amongst the dust.

"Stop moving!" Belona ordered, searching for medical supplies she knew she didn't have.

The man turned to her, agony across his mutilated face, but recognition in his eyes.

"Agrippus?" he asked. "Traitor. Traitor—" He began to cough, to choke, hands grasping at his throat as his lungs filled with blood.

Belona froze at the horrid accusation, made suddenly real coming out the lips of a Principate soldier. Though she had been accused as much by Lechslov and that raider bastard, the terrible truth hit her with a force she had not expected. She stared at the man, sent by her secret plans, like so many others, to die again by her hand.

The soldier's mouth opened, but only agonized gasps escaped, his anger replaced by desperate terror. How far he had traveled from home, not with visions of glory, but confusion and ignorance. He knew not why he fought, why he was asked to sacrifice, why he was now lying on the floor, drowning in his own liquids. The man grasped at her, pleading, for help, for time, for a single breath of smoke-tainted air. But there was no aid she could offer, no succor, only minutes of a slow, inevitable death.

Belona pulled her pistol from her belt and ended the soldier's suffering. Not her soldier, no, it was not even her army, and yet the deaths were *hers* all the same. How similar his suffering had been to the thousands in Huile, the thousands she had abandoned to the terrible fate born from her mistakes. She holstered her pistol and placed the soldier's limp arms upon his chest.

Another shout jostled her from her grief. Marcel's voice, crying out her name. She scrambled in that direction, over the legs of the fallen warwalker, and spied him. Hand in hand with some bedraggled, bloodied raider, Marcel was trapped in awkward fumbling dance, the two trying to punch, or gouge, or choke the other, in erratic succession.

"Talwar!" she shouted, pistol raised, looking for a clean shot. The raider, taller by a quarter-metre, got his arm around Marcel's neck, and pulled him up. The man fought like a captured cat, flailing and kicking with no success. Belona squinted, had an even shot at the raider, could blast his smirk off his face, but if Marcel twitched or squirmed, his skull fragments would be bouncing alongside the raider's. Not a great loss from a tactical perspective, and he was, by all logic, a Resurgence traitor... A traitor...

Belona swore and tossed the pistol to the ground, before charging forward, knife out. She smashed into the two, launching Marcel free, taking the raider to the ground. He did not hesitate, but grabbed at her throat. She bit down on his hand, *filthy,* and began to stab and stab. Blood burst out in lines, decorating the man's tattoo's chest with abstract shapes of crimson. Again and again, she stabbed, a rhythmic squelching, until she felt someone pull her back. She spun around, and nearly stabbed again, until she saw it was Marcel.

"He's dead, I think," Marcel said.

Belona glanced down, then back. She spat dirt and blood.

"You're *my* Resurgence traitor, Talwar."

"What?" he said.

Belona shook her head, then went to retrieve her dropped pistol. She took a moment to orient herself, the cracks of rifle fire still abounded, the storm had not yet abated. There was no reason to die here, no reason to sacrifice while Roache still lived. No reason to let the bastard take more of her soldiers from her.

"We need to get moving," she said, pointing in the distance. "There may be still some 'trucks or other vehicles we can make a getaway in."

"So the plan is retreat?" Marcel said, with some weary relief.

She nodded, bitterly but resolute. Even the Lioness of Vastium had to know when to retreat.

# CHAPTER 45

Right outside the grotesque charnel hut that Sylvaine had been left in, abandoned by enemy and friend alike, an artillery shell went off. The ground shook, men screamed, Sylvaine's fur stood on end. The battle was inexorably approaching, the sounds of tank fire echoed, the shouts of raiders and soldiers grew more frantic. Despite Sylvaine's despair, her senses sharpened. She wished to remain lying on the floor, as a sack of despondent nothing. She had no desire left to live, but that thing inside her, her primitive instincts, they clung on to pointless life with gouging claws, shouting at her to *move,* to *run!*

With weakened will she tried to argue with them, tell her instincts it was pointless, that there was no life to flee back to. But this thoughtless mind ignored the logic of her self-pity, threatened to take her limbs, and move them as it would. If she would not stand and flee, this primal id would. So, if only to undercut it, if only to pretend she was in control, Sylvaine pushed herself up from the ground.

She stumbled away, in the direction that Kayip and Roache and fled because... Gear's-grits she had no idea anymore. It seemed a direction to move. Or maybe her instincts were pushing her there, vaguely aware that they had fled away from the oncoming imperial assault, towards something that could be imagined as safety. Sylvaine tried to pretend it was a conscious decision, but she had no idea who was leading her body now, who in Inferno she even was.

As she snuck outside she could see, between the flapping tarpaulins, Principate blues, a squad of scouts engaged with raiders, bullets traded, bayonets thrusted. Past her sprinted terrified Lazacorp workers, chasing after an autotruck already in acceleration, its cargo bed oversqueezed with battered workers who desperately pushed away the newcomers with brooms and rifle butts as the 'truck smashed through unoccupied and semi-occupied tents. Sylvaine could hear shouts from the building she had just left, raiders searching with rage for Roache, howling out for vengeance for their abandonment, only to shriek in glee as they discovered the forgotten cache of slickdust. Invectives followed soon after, and gunshots, which simply faded into the thousands of others.

Elsewhere raiders seemed entirely unsure of who the enemy was. Sylvaine skulked around the edge of a clearing in the camp, two mobs of raiders, one adorned with bulbous wigs and the others with jagged jewelry, arguing vociferously about whether they were still allies, or whether the battle had turned to the golden principle of 'every gang for themselves.' The debate did not last long, interrupted by the sudden appearance of an Imperial troop transport vehicle, which slammed through men and women before collapsing into a ditch. Principate soldiers rushed out, firing blindly in every direction. Two of them wore suits of autoarmor, clanking exoskeletons of iron, gears whirring, smoke bellowing from backborne exhaust pipes. One held a motorgun in its mechanically augmented arms, firing off a stream of lead. Sylvaine jumped down into the earth to avoid the spray, tasting dirt. The other soldier had more trouble, its rusted right arm sparking and immobile, the soldier forced to use a diminutive pistol gripped awkwardly in his metal gauntlet. The assault didn't last long. Hooded figures appeared from the dust clouds, black flames in their hands. Sylvaine did not wait to see what they would do.

She moved quick and silent through the mess of a battlefield. It wasn't difficult, she made no decisions, just letting her body move as it wanted to. She heard familiar voices. A glance down what constituted a thoroughfare in this tent labyrinth, and she spied the forms of Marcel and Belona. The two were firing off at a large squad of raiders, who themselves split between firing back, fighting imperials, and taking shots at a second squad of raiders. Sylvaine could not guess the politics of what was going on, only that it was true chaos. A raider rushed Belona. Marcel shot in his direction, a miss, but it distracted the man long enough for the imperial to put a scattergun round through his chest, before turning and taking out a sharpshooter who'd just missed Marcel's oblivious head by a centimeter.

The two seemed... perfect together. Moving and shouting and shooting as a bickering yet stable unit. In all their idealism, their hypocrisy, their mutual hate and jagged reconciliation, they somehow fit together. They fought with confidence in each other, as if each understood the other, in a way as odd as it was deep, in a way that no one had ever understood Sylvaine, would ever try to understand her.

Raiders continued their assault undeterred. Sylvaine raised her shaking glove to help, trying to find focus. Nothing came. Sparks fizzled on her fingertips; her mind lost inside itself. Engineering was the art of precision, of civilized study and personal perfection. Hacks without such discipline could only produce junk, and she was not even a fraud or novice. She was below that, a beast, and beasts built nothing. What could she hope to do here? Pretend again to be an engineer, a soldier, a human? Pretending that if she were gone, she would be missed?

Sylvaine scampered away, not daring to glance back. If she were to die today, better it be in some hole somewhere. What humiliation it would be for her disheveled body to be found for one last mockery.

As she neared... wherever it was her body was taking her, Sylvaine sensed a familiar energy. Somewhere, not far, was that strange engineer, Miga, bolts of æthericity flashing in the sky, a warwalker tiptoeing above the pandemonium brought suddenly low. If there was anyone who could understand Sylvaine it would be her. Perhaps if she went to the old woman, she could explain what had happened to her, discuss the details of slickdust, and its interactions with the Ferral form. But why would Miga waste her breath? The mad engineer would rather dissect her. Another lab experiment, another page of scribbled notes in a journal. Perhaps this fate was the best Sylvaine could hope for, but her body kept moving.

Finally she came to a rectangular structure of scrap and canvas, a sign in blocky paint declaring it "CARAVAN PORT C." She crept through its open doors. Metal walkways stood on metre-tall legs in rows. There was space between them for several hundred 'trucks, now only about two dozen or so remained, most in states of disrepair. One looked in good shape at the far end, its back filled with crates, and by the driver's door, Lazarus Roache. But the tycoon was not alone. In the nearer end, not far from Sylvaine, stood Kayip, sword out. In between the two, in near exact the middle of one of the concrete lanes, stood the mutant chief, Bladescar. On the mutant's back was an axe, and in his hand a pistol, which turned indecisively in the direction of both Lazarus Roache and Kayip.

"Please," the monk begged. "We fight for the same cause."

The pistol flicked back and forth. "Do not speak to me, murderer," Bladescar spat.

"I'm still surprised you let him live, way back when," Lazarus said, confidence flagging in his voice, as the pistol aimed in his direction. "Didn't he kill—"

"It was not my choice!" Bladescar shouted. Sylvaine hadn't a faintest clue as to what the men were talking about and could not muster the energy to theorize. She felt as if she were watching a theatrical performance, lost in a tale that wasn't hers. An audience member, no, less than one, an unnecessary set of eyeballs for a person that wasn't truly there.

"Please, together we can end this," Kayip said.

"We had almost ended it, until you showed up," Bladescar accused. "Clan Vapulus needs no aid, you and your kind have only brought desolation."

"I do not ask for forgiveness, only to do what I gave my oath to do. Let us destroy Roache, and all he has created, here and now."

"Oh yeah, trust the monk," Lazarus said. "See how that works out for you. The man supposedly been trying to kill me for seven years. Does it not strike you odd that I remain so very much alive? Perhaps you should—"

"Shut up!" Bladescar shouted, to both of them.

Silence for a moment. Wind whistled through holes in the tarps.

"I beg you," Kayip said, pain in his voice. "Let us put hate aside. It is what your father commanded; it is what he would have wanted." He paused. "I am sure it is what she would have wanted as well."

Bladescar bellowed with a sudden rage, turning his pistol decisively in Kayip's direction.

A click.

Just a click.

The afternoon sun shined a golden glow off the gilded, broken pistol.

Bladescar tossed the pistol to the ground and charged, axe in hand. Behind him Lazarus jumped into the 'truck, whose engines burst into life.

"No!" Kayip shouted. The monk tried to rush forward, but Bladescar swung his axe. Kayip dodged, and tried to dash again, but the mutant did not relent in his assault.

The 'truck turned with an inept haste, smashing its bumper on a near autocar, but not slowing. Sylvaine raised her glove to stop Roache but, again, nothing came to her. How could it, there was nothing left of her?

"No! No!" Kayip shouted, as Lazarus's autotruck sped out into the dust storm.

"Fight me, kin-slayer, you craven piece of skragger offal!" Bladescar spat, swinging his axe. Kayip blocked it with the side of his sword.

"We were close... He was there. We could have ended it."

"I was close," Bladescar said, with another swing. "Clan Vapulus had near our revenge. You alone soiled it. Now fight me!"

His next swipe cut Kayip's cheek. Yet it was obvious who the more skilled combatant was. The mutant fought with an imprecise fury, the monk moved with perfection, even as tears welled in his eye. Kayip made no attempt to strike back, merely blocking and dodging, and blocking and dodging.

"Please..." Kayip muttered. "After all we have sacrificed."

"It is too late! It is seven years too late. You cannot undo what has been done. If you are truly repentant, then let me slate my vengeance."

"I made an oath to your father—"

"He is dead!" Bladescar shouted. "The old, soiled blanket has finally been buried, his guts skragger food, his horns just another set of fucking rocks in the Wastes. Forget about your oaths. If you owe any oaths, then you owe them to Clan Vapulus, you owe it to me. And my command is simple. Die."

Kayip opened his mouth but said nothing. His arm went limp, his sword twirled around into a bracelet. He took a hesitant step forward, pointing to where Roache had been, before shaking his head. With a sigh, not even mournful, not even surprised, just defeated, he kneeled.

"I... I did try..." he began.

"Shut up," said Bladescar, as he lifted his axe.

"Stop!" someone shouted. The weapon burst red, axehead flying off and landing as slag. Sylvaine was surprised to find that it was her arm up, her voice echoing in the structure, herself suddenly very much a person, here and present and not willing to see her friend die.

Bladescar looked at her, Kayip looked at her.

With a growl Bladescar pulled a knife from his belt and charged in Sylvaine's direction.

"No!" Kayip said suddenly, pacifism forgotten as he rammed into the mutant, the two of them tumbling into the dirt.

"Knew your supplication was a trick," Bladescar hissed, as the monk pinned him to the ground.

"You can have me," Kayip said. "Not her."

"No, Kayip, fuck you," Sylvaine said, jumping down from the walkway. "He can't have either of us."

"What right do you have to negotiate the terms of my revenge?" Bladescar scowled.

"She is innocent," Kayip said.

"Your hands are covered in blood, monk, so much that it stains everyone you touch."

"Listen," Sylvaine said. "I don't know what Kayip did to you, but it doesn't matter, you can't kill him."

"Sylvaine," Kayip began with a heavy voice. "I have not told you all of my past, guilt has kept me from elucidating—"

"I don't care!" Sylvaine shouted. "I don't care what you did in the past, I know you now, and I won't let this revenge-crazed maniac take you!"

The pinned mutant chuckled bitterly. "You are one to lecture me, engineer. You who fled Icaria, abandoned your life, abandoned everything to hunt down Roache."

"How do you know—You know what, doesn't matter," Sylvaine said.

"I know what you all have sacrificed," Bladescar said, "turned a whole city ablaze. So Kayip, you once claimed that to atone for your sins you would offer your life to us. You have yet to prove this. Let me go, let me take your head, and do not dare ask me what I will chose to do afterwards. If not that, then kill me, I grant you no other choice."

"That's not... I have to... But..." Kayip could not get a thought out, glancing with a pitiful despair between Sylvaine and Bladescar.

"Bladescar!" A shout burst into the garage, followed by a woman, the black-haired mutant, Prisca, rifle in hand. Kayip disarmed Bladescar and released him, the mutant chief staggering to his feet, as Prisca aimed at the monk.

"Take the shot!" Bladescar shouted. Sylvaine had raised her glove, half a plaintive wave, half a threat.

"I do that, and the ferral will kill you," Prisca shouted.

"So what?" Bladescar spat. "Roache is gone, all our plans turned to ash. The monk's ruined our one chance. We're lost everything!"

"Lost everything?" Prisca shouted, her hair bedraggled, her coat bloodstained. Sylvaine could smell the salt of her tears. "Our clan is in retreat! They do not know where to head to. We still have not received message from camp, do not know if your children and ill have kept hidden. We need orders, Bladescar! We need our leader!"

"I..." Bladescar began, pointing at Kayip. "The monk."

"Our clan! Bladescar, our clan still lives, for the moment at least, don't you dare abandon us now!"

Bladescar grit his teeth and snorted out a curse. He stared hate at Sylvaine and Kayip, then with what seemed immense effort, shut his eyes tight. "I shall find you again monk, engineer," he muttered quietly, before dashing off in Prisca's direction. The woman gave a quick dismissive glance at the two, before following her chief and disappearing into the whirling dust beyond.

And then there was just them alone, with only the sounds of battle as company.

"Sylvaine—" Kayip began.

"You didn't want to leave me, Roache was getting away, if you survived you would have come back for me, you warned me not to stay, the mission was more important, if we fail there's a thousand years of darkness whatever, so on, what's one life, sacrifices, all that..." Sylvaine shook her head. "I mean, the excuse doesn't even matter. I came crawling here, following you. I was always going to." She leaned back on one of the walkways, glancing at the ground. "I guess I need to feel useful, feel valuable, like I'm someone I'm not, someone who belongs. You make me feel like that, so I couldn't let you get yourself killed. Selfish really."

"You always seek the darkest view of yourself," Kayip said. "Could it not be that you care for your friends, even when they fail you? That you have empathy?"

"Empathy's not part of the engineer's lexicon." Sylvaine tried to chuckle. "It's just inefficient moralizing, like what your Church specializes in."

"And yet you find it, while I have nothing but blood and dust to offer." Kayip sighed. "I abandoned you for nothing. I have done so for many others. Could I dare ask for forgiveness even if I had a trophy to offer?"

"We can still catch him," Sylvaine said, trying for an optimism that had long left her.

Kayip shook his head. He took off his mask and blinked his mutated eye. "Seven years I've hunted, to redeem this. Seven years. and all I've done is enrage those I sought absolution from."

"Redemption, absolution, all this immaterial cog grease, what's going to change? I've been seeking my own redemption my whole life. For being born with all this," Sylvaine gestured to herself. "Fantasizing about some future where everyone who's ever called me a beast, or said my engineering dreams were nonsense, would realize that their mistakes, would come to me, to tell me they're sorry, they were wrong. But they weren't wrong."

"Just because fools never admit their fault, does not mean they are right," Kayip said. "You know this."

Sylvaine grunted and leaned on a 'truck. "Maybe... Point is, searching for their approval has done me no good. Very much the opposite in fact. So you did some horrible stuff..."

"You are owed the truth, after all the pain my crimes have caused, all that I've asked of you."

"Will this truth get us out of here? Will it take down Roache? If not, it can wait. You're who you are now. I am who I am now. That's all any of us are." Sylvaine pet her glove with a sad softness. "And it seems like you've already paid a good price, I mean, you gave up on your past life. Whatever you were doing before, I imagine it must have better than all this. You've lived that sacrifice you ask."

"No." Kayip shook his head. "I had already lost it all, there was nothing left to sacrifice. I have asked others for things it was cheap for me to give. There is a cruelty there, one you should never forgive."

"And what if I decide to, anyways?" Sylvaine said.

Kayip was silent. He pulled out his Cracked Disk and studied it a quiet moment. Not finding whatever it was he was looking for, he lowered the relic and glanced up, at the loose tarp that hung above the port, the sun hidden somewhere in the dust above. Sylvaine followed his gaze.

"I'm not saying I am," she said. "Forgiving, I mean, the whole abandoning me thing. It was messed up; I could have died. Just that, you know, forgiving is my decision. If I wanted to, I could, move past... things... for you."

The far scrap wall of the port suddenly burst into fire and shrapnel, as an errant shell fell upon it. Embers flew off the burning canvas. Kayip watch them fall to the ground below.

"You chose life, Sylvaine, I've chosen death." The monk looked old suddenly, tired, and old. "Somehow, I thought death could bring back all that I've lost, all that I've destroyed. Some things even the Demiurge himself cannot restore."

"Life and death?" Sylvaine mused. "I suppose that's paradigm. So what do we do if we choose life?"

Kayip slid his mask back on. "We try and salvage what we can. Save who we can."

Sylvaine nodded. "Marcel, then. And Belona too, I guess."

# CHAPTER 46

It was the lack of recoil that finally clued Marcel that his pistol was dry. Aiming through the swirling dust, he slammed the trigger of his Frasco six-shooter a good eight or nine times before registering the lack of lead flying from his barrel. He quickly ducked down behind a slightly-on-fire tent to reload, as bullets whizzed and men screamed.

*Count your ammo.* He reminded himself. *Count your ammo.*

"Count your ammo!" Belona shouted. Or maybe that had always been her. It was hard to tell with the cacophony that surrounded him. "Move, Talwar, move!" she added unnecessarily.

The two of them had been retreating for the past five, or thirty, minutes, time was hard to hold onto. They moved slowly but continually in the direction of the edge of camp, where they might find an escape. And hopefully Kayip and Sylvaine as well, wherever they had disappeared to. Marcel couldn't find the seconds to wonder if Belona truly knew where they were going, all of his mind was set on the task of putting foot after foot.

A man appeared from the miasma of smoke and dust. His cowled face bloodied; his hands covered in black fire. One of those deranged cultists, like the butler, what's-his-face. Though he had disappeared in the pandemonium, his æther-mad friends were causing enough destruction with their Infernofire and demons to match that wrought by imperial artillery and dathkreis. Words escaped the cultist's mouth, in a foul tongue that cut through the wild screeches of the storm. He stared at Marcel, enflamed finger pointing, and made it to the fifth loathsome syllable before Belona put a round of buckshot into the cultist's chest.

"Target down, keep moving," she said, kicking over a collapsed canvas wall, and rushing forward. As much as he hated to admit it, Marcel was thankful that imperial was there. She clearly knew her way around a battlefield. Just about everyone else seemed lost or confused. The dust storm had begun to abate, but in its place came plumes of smoke that cut visibility down to a handful of metres. Every few seconds Belona would pause to fire at some raiders or cloaked figures. Never, Marcel noticed, at those wearing imperial blue, simply ducking down and moving past them. This amnesty was not mutual. Marcel wasn't sure if the imperials knew who they were shooting at, or thought the two of them looked raider-like, which, to be fair, they did.

As Belona was turning round a bend a Principate scout caught Marcel's gaze. The soldier raised his rifle at Marcel, as Marcel raised his pistol at the soldier. Marcel froze, time seemed to slow to a tepid crawl. The soldier's short-cut black hair reminded Marcel of a boy that he played pipeball with on the streets of Phenia as a child—*No!* This was war, he couldn't be distracted. This softness was what lost him his leg. It was Marcel or the soldier, and he had to make that decision in a quarter of a second.

He tried to pull his finger back but found his hand unfathomably heavy. The trigger seemed as if it were fused to the barrel through some unseen æthermantics. He realized, suddenly, that he wasn't going to fire, that he was going to let this damn Principate shoot him straight. How out of place he was in war, all the lies of his personas laid bare. Marcel the soldier, Marcel the war hero, Marcel the private investigator, Marcel the hardened vigilante, Marcel the man who couldn't shoot someone because they kind of sort of looked like a kid he had played with a total of three times in his childhood. How many soldiers, he wondered, had died in the exact same way he was about to?

"Talwar!" Belona shouted.

The Principate scout turned suddenly, in the direction of this new threat, aiming his rifle directly at Belona.

The gun went off.

The imperial fell.

Marcel stared, as the body crumbled. It hit with a deafening weight.

"Target down," Belona said, as the smoke from Marcel's pistol joined the dark clouds around.

Marcel stepped over and glanced at the remains of the scout's head. It was a mistake. He leaned over and wretched what little he had in his stomach onto the dirt.

"It was a clean shot," Belona said, with a grim tone.

Marcel wiped his mouth. He leaned back and stared at sun, veiled by the fumes of war. All of this suffering, over one man. All this destruction, all this death, because of one tycoon's desire for more than any man could ever need. History bent to a single individual's empty ego and petty greed. Perhaps it was ever such. The world could be a mad place.

"We need to keep moving," Belona said.

"I know." Marcel nodded, glancing around. "I'm just... It's all gone crazy. This tempest of man against man, where will it end? "

"Talwar..."

"All the bullets, the blasts, the fire..." he muttered, dazed. "The empty deaths. Demiurge, I think of Opus's Glory, those men and women there, stuck fighting, forever. Cycles and cycles, repeating the same violence... Belona, sometimes I wonder if this is all—"

Marcel fell to the ground hard. It took him several seconds to realize the sudden sensation in his left arm was a bullet wound. The shock of the fall had knocked the rest of him numb. *Idiot. Such an idiot. Philosophizing on the battlefield...*

"Talwar!" Belona was beside him suddenly.

"Leave me, go on..."

"Don't be a fool," Belona said, studying the wound. "It's superficial. We get you to a medic you might not even lose the arm."

*Lose the arm... another cog-limb to add the collection,* Marcel mused. But perhaps Belona was right. He had been told that that when dying, all sensations left, and one was at peace with the world. He felt no peace, but the pain in his arm was starting to roar fierce over his shocked numbness.

"Fuck!" he said, as Belona lifted him up.

"There's a structure nearby, a caravan loading area or garage, I think," she said. "Can you stand?"

Marcel found that he could, though every movement sent waves of pain. He gritted his teeth. "Good. I'm good."

Suddenly that accursed language returned, uttered by unseen cultists. Marcel glanced back into a wall of flickering smoke, from where he could see a few distant figures, united in an ear-scratching chorus. Belona fired into the black, and one voice disappeared in a sudden scream, but most kept chanting. Marcel squinted, there seemed to be something hidden inside the smoke, something large, and growing larger.

The horrid chanting affected all within earshot, Marcel saw several raiders and imperials scamper away in fright. Nearer was what Marcel had taken to be a raider corpse, but whose sudden panicked movement made him realize was actually just playing dead. The young raider gave up the act quick, desperately trying to pull himself forward. A claw burst through the smoke, metal and flesh, the size of a torso. It slammed down and pulled the terrified raider back. His screams became a sudden pained screech, the sounds of crunching melting and sloshing liquid downing out his terror.

Something started to move within the smoke. Large heavy footsteps that shook the ground. When it deigned to crawl from its smoke, the thing, demon, ætheric aberration, whatever, was nearly indescribable. Unfortunately only nearly. It was as large as a tank and a half more, mostly flesh, of a pallid color, bulbous, in only the vaguest approximation of a human, or beast's form. Around its skin, and skewered into it, were misshapen chucks of rusting machinery, pipes and beams and pumps and bone-grinding gears, all culminating on a large bulk on its back, that looked halfway between furnace and a church organ, smoke bellowing from its top in rhythm with discordant sounds that might have been music. On its side and belly hung bodies, human bodies, stitched to the aberration and perforated with medical tubes. The bodies seemed to still be living, groaning in pain as viscous black liquid coursed through them. Near the top of the monstrosity was a veined protrusion that might have been a head, an impression enhanced by the mask the creature wore, too small for the creature, of uncracked, unblemished porcelain, with an expression of total serenity.

Belona unloaded her scattergun at the thing. It reacted as if it had been brushed by a gentle gust of wind.

"Retreat," Belona said. She seemed to say a lot of unnecessary things.

The two ran back, as the demon-aberration-thing smashed its claw down. Pain burst through Marcel with each step, and he tried not to slow. Belona was always a few steps ahead, turning round at moments to fire off a few shots and let Marcel catch up. The aberration roared, not through any mouth of its own, but through the guttural groans of the dozens of bodies grafted onto it. Belona pushed Marcel suddenly, and he tumbled towards the ground as aberration slammed its protrusion of flesh that might have been a head.

Marcel struggled to his feet, nearly stumbling over a collapsed tent. A dozen metres away Belona was climbing around a thoroughly trash imperial scout buggy.

"Distract him!" she shouted.

Marcel aimed his pistol and fired four shots. The first squelched into amorphous flesh, the last tinked off the creature's mask. It turned his serpentine neck in Marcel direction.

"Troglyn piss," Marcel muttered, as the mass of rusting metal and fetid flesh started to accelerate in his direction. He glanced around frantically for any sign of cover, as the monstrosity rushed forward. As it was near upon him, he jumped into a drainage ditch, splashing into stagnant mud. His indecisiveness perhaps protected him, as the aberration did not notice his motion, smashing into the tents, and shacks, and damaged war machines beyond.

Suddenly there was a blast. Marcel pushed himself up to see a burst of meat and black liquid from the back of the best. He turned to see Belona hefting a mortar. She loaded another shell and fired again. The demon roared and turned, just in time to be take the shell directly in the head-growth. Its flesh burst apart like a fallen pan of meat casserole. Viscera sloughed off the monster's front, revealing a flattened, metal core, where a second face was hidden, mouth of twirling blades, eyes of obsidian glass.

The aberration let lose a screeching metal howl. Its long claws dug desperately into the fallen mass of flesh. It pulled out the mask, still undamaged, and shoved it awkwardly onto its new face, where it covered nothing.

Marcel glanced to Belona, waiting for a fourth shot, but none came. She abandoned the empty mortar and started to fire whatever she had left at the demon, rifle then pistol. It did not slow.

Without time to think, Marcel stumbled forward and grabbed what he could, a long tent pole, canvas shredded. He rushed to meet the charging aberration, pole bouncing. With a groan he jabbed his ersatz weapon into the ground, and aimed it at the oncoming wall of metal and flesh. As it came upon him, the end of the pole slammed into its metal face, forced upward into and behind the mask. The force of the aberration pushed the pole like a lever, snapping it in half, and sending flying the mask. Marcel too was sent flying, though luckily not at quite such a velocity, landing only a few metres away.

The aberration screeched and stumbled to a half, turning in the direction the mask had flown. It scrambled forward, long misshaped arm held in front of its face, as if overwhelmed by shame.

Belona rushed over and helped Marcel to his feet.

"I got him," Marcel said with disbelief.

"You bought us a minute at most Talwar, not slain a dragon."

A horn blared. Behind them an autotruck screeched to a half, Kayip in the driver's seat.

"In, in!" came Sylvaine's shout from the back.

Belona jumped up, then helped Marcel into covered bed of the 'truck. The autotruck accelerated forward with a lurch, almost launching Marcel back out, but Sylvaine grabbed his jacket, while Belona scrambled for the largest weapon she could find.

Behind, the aberration had found its mask. It turned round, searching through the smoke, idly swatting a suicidally brave raider into mush. Belona managed to get standing an motorgun turret and began launching a steady stream of lead at the demonic mass. This grabbed its attention, and maybe even annoyed it, but did not take the monstrosity down. Instead, it started to crawl towards them, matching their speed within seconds, bodies flying off its flank as the aberration clanked metal teeth.

Belona shouted nonsense words of delighted rage as she fired. Marcel was out of bullets, so he threw a chunk of scrap with his good arm. It did very little. Kayip swerved right and left, collapsed structures, flaming war machines, and of patches of artillery-churned earth flew past, the aberration not slowing.

"It's getting close!" Marcel shouted, looking around for anything else to throw.

Sylvaine pushed forward. She held up her glove, sparks fizzing off her fingertips, sending her hair whipping in waves.

The aberration roared, black fire and crimson smoke leaking from its grinding mouth. It leapt forward, claws out. A flash escaped Sylvaine's hand, as a bolt of æthericity met the creature's grotesque hand. The metal frame warped and fused, flesh sizzled, and the mass was forced back, over cracked and bent elbows, into the bulk of the creature. It tripped, suddenly, metal crunching, bodies flying free.

Marcel cheered with delirious laughter. Belona let her gun quiet, as Sylvaine collapsed with exhaustion.

The 'truck turned and accelerated. Suddenly the tents they zipped past were no longer replaced by more. The smoke cleared; the dust faded. Marcel glanced around and could see that they had burst clear of the camp and the battlefield proper.

"We did it!" Marcel cried, glancing in every direction, at the vast freeing openness beyond the burning camp. "We did it! We actually did it. Demiurge-be-damned, we di—" he paused, his stomach turning suddenly. "Lazarus Roache! Sylvaine, did you see what happened to Lazarus Roache?"

"Yes," she said, weakly.

"And you got him, right?" Marcel said, trying to keep desperation from his voice. "He's, he's, I mean, you got him, right?"

Sylvaine didn't respond. She might have shaken her head slightly, but that could have just been the motion of the 'truck.

"Roache lives," Kayip said, clear, from the front.

Marcel stumbled up towards the monk. The pain in his arm, buried by the waves of adrenaline, now dug itself up with a fury. He nearly tripped, grabbing onto a support beam.

"No," Marcel said. "He had a wound, and then went down, and then, I mean, he couldn't have gotten far."

"He is more resilient than he looks," Kayip said, gaze locked forward on the rough wasteland beyond.

"But, come on," Marcel said. "With the chaos of the battlefield, I mean, we just almost got smashed by a giant fleshy demon, aberration, *whatever* that was. There's no way some weak, pampered businessman like Roache got out alive!"

"We saw him," Sylvaine said, not quite angry, not quite frustrated. Tired more than anything else. "We saw him, Marcel. He got away."

"I—fuck!" a bump in the road sent a burst of agony from Marcel's arm. He slunk to his knees and held tight the bench. It wasn't possible, not after all they had sacrificed, not after all the kiloms they had trekked, the war they had started, the death and destruction and Demiurge-damn-everything!

"Hold still," Belona said, kneeling down beside him. "Sylvaine, find me a first aid kit, if you can, we can't afford an invalid."

The imperial tended to Marcel's arm, cleaning the wound with burning alcohol, as Kayip kept up his pace.

"Could be worse, Talwar, could be worse," Belona mumbled, as she pulled shudders of agony from the man.

"What happened?" Marcel said, replaying the maelstrom of the day's events in his mind. "We got to him, just a bullet away... and then those mutants." He stared at Kayip, who kept his eye straight out over the Wastes. Or was he trying to avoid Marcel's gaze?

"Is it true?" Marcel asked him.

"What?" Sylvaine answered, as she started to organize what supplies she could find from the crates and nooks of the truck.

"What they said about you, Kayip?" Marcel flinched as Belona worked. "That you were there, at the start of all this?"

"Yes," Kayip said simply.

"Shouldn't that be— you didn't think to mention that!" Marcel said. "This thing you told us about, today, this sleeping demon aberration whatever! You had a hand in it? You worked with Lazarus Roache?"

"It is more complicated..." the monk muttered.

"I mean, we worked with Roache too," Sylvaine said, checking the chamber of a rusted rifle.

"We didn't unleash a demon-god!" Marcel shouted. "We didn't get a mutant clan going on some crazy vendetta! We didn't murder... whoever in Inferno you murdered! We didn't do whatever else you haven't fucking told us!"

Kayip was silent a long moment. Marcel stared, the monk's face giving away nothing. All this time he had been suspicious of Belona, and yet the monk hid even more destructive secrets. Now everything was lost, gone, ashes in the Wastes' winds.

"You are right," is all Kayip said.

Marcel wanted to curse him out, but could think of no words to express his exasperated rage. Instead he bit his lip, as Belona splashed burning alcohol on his wound. Sylvaine for her part, splayed out what she had found. A few weapons, a few days rations in dried meat when split four ways, perhaps enough fuel, perhaps not enough water.

"It's not much," she admitted. "And there's not exactly any friendly æther-oil stations or corner shops out here."

Marcel shook his head and stared at the back of the 'truck. He could see still a swarm of men and vehicles rushing into the camp, the Principate army making its assault, the rear of the column not yet aware that the front had achieved victory. A flanking maneuver, much like what Agrippus had led, though with far less precision. A triumph achieved only because of the disordered recreancy of their foe. And yet that foe was not destroyed. Marcel could see a loose mass leaving in the other direction, like effluent from a factory pipe, autotrucks and motorbikes and taurs and horses. Lazacorp, their raider allies, and their less-friendly raider associates, temporarily putting any strife aside in their combined flight, out westward, the same direction Kayip was driving.

"They have nowhere to go," Marcel said.

"I wish that were true." Kayip shook his head. "There is still one place left for them. Where this all began. Where that horrid thing we half-awoke roils in its hypnagogia."

"But—ah!" Marcel bit his lip, tasting a hint of blood, as Belona pulled a splinter of metal that had found its way into his arm. "But they don't have enough, right? To awaken that thing?"

"I do not know," Kayip said. *Of course he didn't.* All his secrets, and the monk didn't know a damn useful thing.

"Then I have to get back. To Huile, to warn them," Marcel said. It's what he should have done in the first place. He kept convincing himself that he could stop Roache, that he could make everything right. How long he had kept Desct waiting, how much time he had wasted on this quixotic quest. He had almost realized his error back with Alba, but then the monk had dropped that demonic revelation... No, even then he had been looking desperately for a reason to keep playing hero. The city had needed him, and he abandoned it, finding any excuse he could. It all seemed so obvious now.

Belona stared at the devastation behind them. "How do you plan on doing that? Lechslov will be searching for us, and even if he wasn't, we look like raiders and I can promise you his raider policy will be 'shoot on sight.'"

"Then you three can go on," Marcel said, "just find me some motorbike and I'll take my chances—"

"Don't be idiotic" Sylvaine said, pointing to his arm. "You can't make it east on your own, and we... well we'd need a ton of luck and many days supplies to make it back ourselves. We don't have either."

"Then... then..." Marcel realized he didn't have a 'then.' Alba would head back without Marcel, to explain without evidence her findings. She'd leave him again, to try and fix what he had broken. With his absence,

Huile's fate would be left entirely to paranoid Resurgence officers, ears filled with Lambert's lies. That is, if the city wasn't already burning. His promises to Desct were now worthless dust. He had failed Huile worse than he ever thought possible.

"We've lost the battle, but the war must continue," Belona said, trying a bandage around his arm. "We will not conduct our duel yet, not while Roache lives."

"Then tell us our next move, *general!*" Marcel said, pulling away. "What's the grand plan? To starve out in the Inner Wastes? Are we going to try and smash through a raider army, try to take out Roache without either the element of surprise or even any guns worth a damn? Or are we to just turn ourselves in to his vengeful mutants, or your vengeful imperials, for that matter?"

"There is still someplace safe, deeper in the Wastes" Kayip said, voice heavy with a resolute despair. "For you three, at least. I have asked of you so much, too much. There is little I can offer you now, this is the only repayment I can give you. But it will be a refuge, from raiders, from the Principate, maybe even from what will come."

"Where are you talking about?" Belona asked.

"A citadel, an outpost beyond the arms of civilization. Where I was raised, where I lived, where my Order still resides." Kayip sighed, and his sigh bore years of sorrow. He stared out, at the emptiness beyond, the bald hilltops, the shapeless ruins, the torn landscape and the dirt and the dust and the blackened sand. He stared out at something Marcel couldn't see, something beyond the horizon, beyond the bounds of civilization, and beyond even the hand of barbarity. He did not smile, he did not frown, he simply nodded with a weary resolve.

"I shall bring you home."

# Epilogue

*Home.* Lazarus Roache had many of them over his natural lifetime, and after that as well. Some had been luxurious as any gilded manor of a forgotten age, some simple squalid rooms in petty waste-inns. Others were mobile, walls shaking and creaking, motor groaning, the staccato of churned up rocks banging against the floor, the smell of exhaust omnipresent.

Lazarus Roache sat in his new home, a Lazacorp autotruck trundling westward, surrounded by the remnants of his old, pitiful few as they were. A torn portrait (the unnammed nobleman now headless), a dusty silk blanket, the cone alone of an antique dictaphone (little more than expensive scrap), some porcelain dishes, a small oak stool (his favorite leather armchair laying kilometres away, smashed, burnt, buried), and a handful of gold and silver knickknacks of no real importance. It had taken Namter only a few seconds to log them all in his inventory sheet. The tycoon struggled to remain on his seat, mixing slickdust with water in his canteen as the 'truck juddered. Namter had not the ability to make his master tea due to the conditions of their travel, yet he felt no guilt for this negligence of duty.

"45,000 litres of refined æther-oil in that tanker..." Roache mumbled as he sipped, gray hair goldening slightly. "And they blew it up! What idiot blows up good æther-oil? This Lechslov doesn't know how to run a damned army, and he still rolled over those worthless gang lords. Unless it was

Bladescar or some other Vapulus who blew my tanker to Inferno. Or the monk, or Agrippus, or one of those other taur-brained scumsuckers…"

As Roache mumbled a list of possible enemies, incensed by each and every one's unjustified betrayal and unforgiveable stupidity, Namter double-checked the fastenings that kept what remains of Lazarus' estate from tumbling about.

"Refined! Refined! Even with the sangleum we have, what use is it be without the infrastructure to refine it? Without Huile, or Stinktown, our refining capabilities are—shit!"

It was an accurate assessment, though the expletive was in fact in response to a sudden bump which had sent Roache's canteen flying, slickdust-infused water splashing about onto the floor.

"Here you are, sir," Namter said, proffering another canteen and a vial of slickdust. The tycoon took them greedily, then mixed and drank.

"Namter, Namter, if I did not have you…"

Namter smiled genuinely, though perhaps not for the reason the tycoon might think. "I think our situation may not be quite as dire as you imagine. We have evacuated most Tribute successfully, as well as slickdust necessary to slack the thirst of raiders, at least until the Reification."

Roache walked over to the wall, almost tripping, and glanced out the small bullet hole that he used as a window. The 'truck they rode in was just one of dozens that looked the same, ostentation replaced by fearful anonymity. "They're furious, mad, murderous," he muttered. "Any one of them could get it in their head to try and drive a knife into me."

Namter put a hand on his master's shoulder, who jumped slightly at the touch.

"The raiders hate each other with more vitriol than they can summon towards us," Namter said. "We still hold the reins of power, there is no need to worry about something as petty as their 'opinions.' And my Brotherhood is more than capable of protecting you from any errant assailant, especially with your gift."

Lazarus gulped down the canteen, and gestured for another, which Namter provided. "And The Flayed Prince—"

"Is pleased with our perseverance," Namter closed his eyes, as if listening to a distant whisper. "Yes, I can hear him, even now. Louder and clearer as the day approaches. He…" Namter paused, hand moving as if tracing unseen patterns. "Yes, there is greatness awaiting. Our coming… 'down-payment' as it were, will provide him much strength. Strength not yet to take physical form, but more than capable of bestowing upon you a far greater gift. This," and he grasped gingerly his master's fading hair, "was but a trifle. Greater ambitions rouse in his ancient heart. An empire... yes! He desires an empire, built for his arrival."

"Seven more years?..." Lazarus began, fingers rubbing against each other with apprehension.

Namter forced a convincing chuckle and grabbed Roache's hand. "What is a delay of seven years to a God, what even a human lifetime? This task will demand time, dedication, and its rewards shall be commensurate. For The Flayed Prince needs a planner, an organizer, a schemer even, a *leader,* eventually, to rule in his stead as he gathers his power. And this position need not be an uncomfortable one, my master."

Lazarus Roache glanced around at the shaking scraps of his life, which resembled less and less the triumphs of the last seven years, but more the decades of itinerant poverty that proceeded them. His eyes flickered, Namter could see paranoia and greed fighting it out, the miserable truth versus an alluring lie. Namter knew which one would win in the end, Lazarus had trained him too well.

"You will be given all that you deserve," Namter said, now being honest.

Lazarus was silent a long moment, too long a moment. Then he turned suddenly to Namter and squeezed his hand tight.

"We will *earn* all that we deserve!"

Roache's tone was hopeful... and yet was something else as well, something Namter could not quite place. Even after a lifetime of service, there were still inflections in his voice that were illegible to Namter, glints in his eyes that refused explanation. The tycoon's widening smile bent deep wrinkles around his face that had not been seen in seven years. Namter could not help but wonder what secrets might still hide in those creases, what schemes were flocculating inside Roache's skull. But he hid such suspicions behind a congenial mask, a smile matching in its pristine artifice his master's.

* * *

After biding Roache a polite leave, Namter alighted from the back of the slow-moving truck, into the churned dust behind. Around him were the remnants of yesterday's battle, Lazacorp 'trucks and raider buggies, mog-lizards covered in baggage and taurs whipped forward by haggard herdsfolk. Lines of men and women and children stretched in both directions, some raiders, some slaves, all desperate and despondent, wandering westward, following the allure of slickdust, the promise of fuel and food, or simply pressed onward by blade and bayonets. Each one was a potential threat, filled with a hunger for vengeance or simply violent desperation. But each was also a potential Tribute, a sack of pumping blood waiting to be purified, to be sanctified, a worthless life given purpose in its final moments.

Namter turned from the shambolic migration and walked up a nearby hill. He pressed his obsidian-black leather shoes into matching earth, the scarred soil crunching like glass. The ground here had been untouched by man or beast since the fiery rebirth of this land. Pure. Each footprint as he ascended leaving its indelible mark.

At the hill's crest, Namter stopped to stare out over the Wastes, the Deep Wastes, the Inner Wastes, the True Wastes. He studied with reverence its immaculate desolation. The layers of life and history that plagued the Outer Wastes had been stripped from the land, leaving raw earth exposed to the scouring, vindictive winds that raged in every direction. Where there remained human marks on the naked stone and dirt, they were faded and abstracted, mounds where there used to be cities, blackened shapes that may have been factories, a fissure of boiling mud that could have once been an underrail station. Growths of tumorous metal burst out from the stone in odd angles, jagged shapes that that cast shadows like specters over the long empty plains. What plants persisted did so in mockery of life. A rooty growth nearby stretched itself in the shape of cogs and gears, and if Namter squinted, he could almost make out the hint of a face, warped in glorious agony.

Truly this was the Holy Land. A place touched by righteous rage, clearing away all that was rotten, leaving a fertile field for some distant future generation, one punished and purified and reunited with their divinities. Men and women as men and women should be. Perhaps they would be told by their Masters of their dark past, of the filth wearing human skin that desecrated the lands of the Truegods, of those few who sacrificed all to return the world to its rightful order. Or perhaps they would have no use for such sordid tales. Their minds unblemished, filled with love for their creators. Such thoughts always came to Namter when staring out at the devastating, empty beauty of the Inner Wastes. How grand it was to return!

He glanced back down at the misshaped mass of bodies and vehicles. Stinktown was finally united. What no gang lord could consolidate with their victories, what not even Lazarus Roache could unify with his scheming, had been brought together by defeat, by humiliation. An immense exodus, desperate and ragged. Few in the mass knew for sure where they were headed, but Namter knew. They were heading to their death, to where this all started, to a glorious, burning, paradise.

Namter had done it. Though it was not the great plenitude he had hoped to offer his Master, he was sure that between what slaves they had left and those raiders who could be tricked or overpowered, there would be sufficient Tribute for the Reification. The Principate invasion had been a blessing disguised as a catastrophe. Even the rash violence of Bladescar and the monk had simply pushed Lazarus into Namter's arms. Yet there still niggled some uncertainty. Namter had discovered much that was hidden, and even so he was not sure what else had been snuck away. What cards were not on the table, not even on the floor, but somewhere stashed away in Roache's stripped suit?

The task ahead of the Awakener would be difficult. Namter would have to keep the peace among the raiders and extract what he needed, all while keeping Lazarus on the proper path through guile and trickery. Yet despite the trials and tribulations, Namter felt the warmth of hope. Though much had been lost, he had kept his twin duties so far. Soon he would return to his Master, his true Master, as both a Watcher and Awakener. Soon, so very soon, all mistakes would be rectified, all wrongs righted, all injustices punished, all transgressions burned from petty, fetid flesh.

Below a figure waved in the evening sun. Brother Avitus, it seemed. The man shouted as he ran. Namter shook his head and strode down to meet him, he hadn't the time to waste on these idle musings.

"What is it Brother?"

"Awakener," Avitus said, glancing around, as if someone might sneak up on them in this vastness. "We found a prisoner. A mutant woman."

"Clan Vapulus?" Namter asked. It would be far from the first.

Avitus shook his head. "With them, Awakener, but not of them."

* * *

They kept the mutant woman in a small cave, away from the eyes of the raiders and Lazacorp, Brothers with rifles staring out into the bright. She was on the floor, tied, a sack over her head, but even with all this Namter could see she was not of Clan Vapulus. Uneven crimson painted her skin, bumps and growths grew with no symmetry, a flesh mutant for certain. In fact, the patterns of her mutations quite resembled those of their past slave-workers in Huile.

As if hearing his thoughts, Avitus nodded. "She was with a few of them, escaped workers seeking Lazacorp blood. They died, she survived. Though I heard one of them calling her 'Celina.'"

"Celina..." Namter repeated, as he tore the cloth off. Yes, he recognized the hateful glare the woman gave him, she had offered the same back when. Even amongst a crowd of unwashed, personless filth, he had noticed her animosity glaring out. During the violence in Huile, he had no doubt she had been in the front lines, had been first to smash pipe against skull.

"Eat taurshit, butler," Celina said, followed by a globe of spit.

Namter wiped the insult off his face. "Tell me," he demanded softly. "Tell me what you saw."

"Why would I tell you bastards anything?" she said with a smile. "Do you think I'm afraid of death?"

"No," Namter said. "Nor should you be. Death is kind, death is the end of suffering. What should scare you is what comes before death. That long space that exists between you and death's release. You will learn to fear that quite soon, and with that fear, will find reasons to speak, to release every thought both vital and superfluous. This will not save you, not at first, not until everything has been wrung from you."

Namter raised his hand up to his eyepatch and gripped tight the band.

"So yes, you *will* tell all that we ask you. You will tell us everything you saw, who planned what and how. You will tell us what happened to Verus, how our Enterprise came to ruin. And you *will* tell me *everything* you know about Lazarus Roache."

*There, in the grand center of my now nameless home, I sat on slag that might have been once a park bench. Before me stood the visage of a man I had first seen in black and white upon the cinegraph screen, standing before the marble halls of The InterRegno and declaring the birth of a new state. A man whose face I had seen age in the photographs upon newspaper pages, until he seemed to split into twain, for some a hero of wise eyes and chiseled chin, for others a monstrous figure, bent and bloodthirsty. All of these images came at once to me, as I stared at his statue, one I had seen so many times before, one which I had somehow never truly looked at, back when life was life, and death was death. Here I studied him, a man staring up with pride at a future he could not see, and beneath his finely carved boots were the following words in bronze:*

*IMPERATOR FRANZ DIEDREV*

*"FOR I HAVE BUILT YOU A NEW WORLD, ONE THAT WILL LAST UNTIL THE DAYS OF MAN HAVE FADED."*

*I turned round and stared at this new world, at the dust, and ruins, and endless nothing that surrounded me, and wondered if this man's words had been prideful boasting, or hidden threat.*

*—"Words of a Wastes Hermit" Author unknown.*

# Acknowledgements

There are too many people to thank, for help both big and small.

First off, I want to thank my mother Susan, my father Robert, and my sister Zoe, who have provided love and support, no matter how mad the venture. My uncle John for suggesting I write this nonsense down, and my grandmother Dolly for teaching my what it means to live a good life. My wife Bessy, for keeping me sane, and somehow staying sane herself.

I also want to thank my professors at Calarts, particulary Janet Sarbanes and my mentor Brian Evenson, who helped me rework my first novel into something worth reading. Also my fellow students at CalArts, as well as my instructors and peers at previous writing programs I've attended, UCLA Extension and UC Riverside.

 I owe a massive debt to my writing group, who have helped me edit both of these novels and many more stories. Thank you Aatif, Rachel, Dom, Alex, and Jon, my writing career would have crashed and burned long ago if not for you! Also want to thank the members of the 2021 Debut Writers Group, in particular fellow members of the Swordfights & Spaceflights substack newsletter. Thank you Casey Berger, AJ Super, Katherine Forrister, M.J. Kuhn, Gabrielle Ash, and so many more.

Thank you to my many friends who have supported me, Joe, James, Josh, Jamie, Collin, and Noah. Thank you Gary Goldman, Amanda Silver, and Rick Jaffa. And thank you Tiny Fox Press, for giving me this opportunity to share my crazy stories with the world.

 Also thank you to everyone I haven't yet thanked. There have been so many people in my life who have helped and supported me, and I'm grateful for you all.

# About the Author

Noah Lemelson is a novelist, short fiction writer, and educator based in Los Angeles. Writer and lover of Science Fiction, Fantasy, New Weird, and "Insert-Noun-Here"-Punk. He received his B.A in Biology from The University of Chicago, and his MFA in Creative Writing from CalArts. His favorite monkey is the White-faced capuchin. He should probably be writing right now.

You can learn more and read some pretty decent stories at Noahlemelson.com

# About the Publisher

Tiny Fox Press LLC
5020 Kingsley Road
North Port, FL 34287

www.tinyfoxpress.com